I0760506

Also by the author,

In fiction:
The Fibonacci Series
Modi Ind0rum (Part 1 of The Jardine Trilogy)
Abbac1 (Part 2 of The Jardine Trilogy)
Zeph1rum (Conclusion to The Jardine Trilogy)

In non-fiction:
The Karmic Geometry Series
Arcs
Lines

THE HUMMINGBIRD FEEDER

Karma Lei Angelo

For more information, please contact:
Hummingbird@karmaleiangelo.com
www.karmaleiangelo.com

Facebook, Twitter, Instagram: @KarmaLeiAngelo
Karma@karmaleiangelo.com

Book Cover:
Original hummingbird images and backgrounds were licensed through Adobe Stock photos and not taken by the author. Book cover design by the author.

ISBN: 978-1-946385-19-2, ebook version
ISBN: 978-1-946385-20-8, paperback version
ISBN: 978-1-946385-21-5, hardcover version

First Edition
Karmic Muse

DEDICATION

To Tony: thank you for believing in me.

ACKNOWLEDGEMENTS

A book of this undertaking would not be possible without a team of people who helped. And, while some authors put their acknowledgements at the end of their book, I prefer to put these people ahead, because this novel would not have been possible without them:

Angela Walker, for her incredible help and encouragement spreading the word about the Fibonacci Series. You've been amazing and I can't thank you enough.

Tony Giunta, City of Franklin Mayor, for his support, kindness, and allowing me to use his name in my novel.

Leigh Webb, City of Franklin Historian, for guiding me to some incredible city history used in the book. Many thanks also to the wonderful librarians at the Franklin Public Library.

Geoff Symon, for answering all my questions and for the invaluable advice I discovered in your FORENSICS FOR FICTION series.

Crystal O'Brien for her incredible help developing my website at the same time as this book and her invaluable advice throughout this process.

My Alpha readers: Damien Hunting, Jared Myers, Brandon Shane Merritt, Candee Sue, and Paul Brady. Your feedback has really helped me polish this story and I'm forever grateful.

Mark Russell for helping me double-check my formatting. Even the smallest things have a big impact. Thank you!

Twitter handler and winner of my raffle, Four Quills. Thank you for murdering Quillard "Quill" Shaw, the character you helped name and decide their fate.

THE HUMMINGBIRD FEEDER

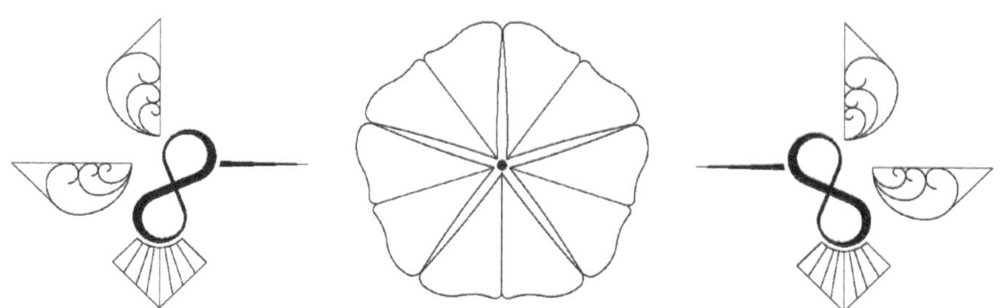

Friday, May 11, 2018

CHAPTER 1

AS THE freezer door creaked open and frigid air wrapped his ankles, Conrad dropped his flashlight. He heard it *kerclunk!* and rattle along the concrete floor in an echoing arc.

"Oh, God," he whispered to himself, something the typically stoic Deputy Director never did.

He quickly grabbed the flashlight from the floor and stared at the men, studying every intricate detail. They all stood at attention, each positioned in unique ceremonial and colorful fashion for their unexpected visitor. Such skyward-peering oddities he hoped to never see again.

Conrad heard a noise behind him, coming closer from the tunnel entrance. He stepped out of the freezer and shut the door.

"Sir?" One of his new forensic technicians, Peter Yates, stood at the entranceway. He held his arms out. "I brought the things you asked."

Conrad motioned. "Set it over there in the corner. Where's Sonnito?"

"She's documenting everything she's found so far, sir."

"How bad is it?"

Peter set the box down and ran a hand through his thick dark hair. "It's bad, sir. We've found several bone fragments and a few teeth. She's not sure how many bodies are buried up there, but she thinks it could be more than one or two...dozen."

"Shit!" The Deputy Director tugged his suit coat back into place and walked into the tunnel. "Mr. Yates, tell Sonnito to call in as many CSIs as she can."

"Yes, sir."

They walked through the tunnel and back up the ladder in the greenhouse. Once they were ground level, Conrad pulled out his phone and dialed Jack's number.

The call failed.

No bars.

Before he could try AJ's number, he was distracted by the lead forensic tech and then an officer. Each bore worse news. Each new fact laid out before him caused his heart to sink deeper into his belly.

He ran towards the halfway house. Flashing blue and red lights lit up the driveway and the front of the house. The Police Chief walked out of the home with another officer, then called Conrad up to the porch.

His brain continued to go numb.

Bad news.

Then more bad news.

He gripped the porch railing and sunk his head down. *How did I not see this coming?!* He pulled out his phone again, looked up AJ's number, then dialed.

"Come on, AJ. Pick up the damned phone."

A few rings later and he heard, "Hello?"

"Jardine, where are you?"

"We're getting in your car, sir."

"Jack's with you?"

"Yes, sir. He said you needed us back at the residence."

"Jardine, listen carefully to me. We found—"

Before he could warn his detective, he heard her scream

"JACK!"

He heard a series of muffles and thumps on the other line. His heart jumped back into his chest.

"Jardine?!"

What felt like several minutes passed by as the Police Chief and the other officers gathered around. Then he heard a familiar old voice getting closer. He heard a few more muffles through the speaker.

"Conrad?"

"Amanda! Where's AJ?!"

"Our little morning glory is here in the car with me. She's safe, as long as she keeps a level head and doesn't do anything rash."

"What have you done to Jack?!"

The woman on the other end laughed. "Unless you want him to die, Conrad, I suggest you get over here as soon as you can. Jack's had…an accident."

"What do you mean 'an accident'?!"

"He's bleeding out and I honestly don't know how much time he has left."

"What have you done?!"

"Tick tock, Deputy Director. I left the kid with a parting gift and told him where I'm taking our precious flower."

"Amanda!"

"Do hurry. Maybe Jack can do at least one courageous act before he dies. Goodbye, my White-Whiskered Hermit. Give Tony, my wonderful White-Necked Jacobin, my regards."

"AMANDA!"

The last thing he heard before the call went dead:

"Drive."

—¡—

Four days earlier…
Monday, May 7, 2018

Conrad scanned the drab cubicles. His frustration mounted as he walked down the aisles. None of his detectives were anywhere in sight, but he could not remember where they all were that morning. He quickly made his way back to his office and slammed the door. Reaching over the desk, he pressed the phone's call button.

A ring later and the receptionist answered. "Yes, Deputy Director?"

"Ellie, where's my staff? There's not a damned detective anywhere."

"Sir, Mr. Montgomery is on vacation all week. Ms. DeVry called in sick, again. Everyone else is at that training conference in Boston. You signed off on it two months ago."

"Shit. Is there *anyone* available? I need at least two detectives to go with me to Franklin. It's an urgent matter."

"The only detectives we have are the two new ones sitting in orientation right now. Would you like me to contact H.R. and send them up?"

"Yes. Immediately."

"On it, sir." She disconnected the call.

Conrad yanked his suit coat back down and pinched his fingers between his eyes, rubbing the inner socket area to relieve the mounting headache. He did not want to ask the two new recruits he hired—especially the woman—to join him on the drive to Franklin, but he had no choice.

He leaned against the desk and waited, closing his eyes to draw a memory deep from the past. What was it? Six years now since his detective and her partner had been murdered?

Or has it been eight years? I can't even remember now.

However long, it became a turning point in his career. Those events made him leave the F.B.I. and move halfway across the country to begin a new life at the state level. All he wanted to do was put the past behind him, forget all the deaths and mayhem.

But now, here she was, having applied for a position in the bureau. Human Resources remained skeptical of what the new recruit could do, but he volunteered to take her.

"You read her psych eval? She's damaged goods," his boss said. "You're better off with that new kid outta college."

"She's broken, but not unfixable," Conrad argued. "And she'll be my responsibility. She's got a drive in her eyes the kid lacks."

"Okay. But if anything happens and she quits, it's on you."

He recalled that conversation over and over as he waited for Ellie to bring the recruits up. He knew more about the broken woman than he would ever say. He knew he could trust her decisions, even if she never found out the truth about him and who he was. And he wanted to keep it that way.

She didn't need to know.

Not now.

Not if he could help it.

—¡—

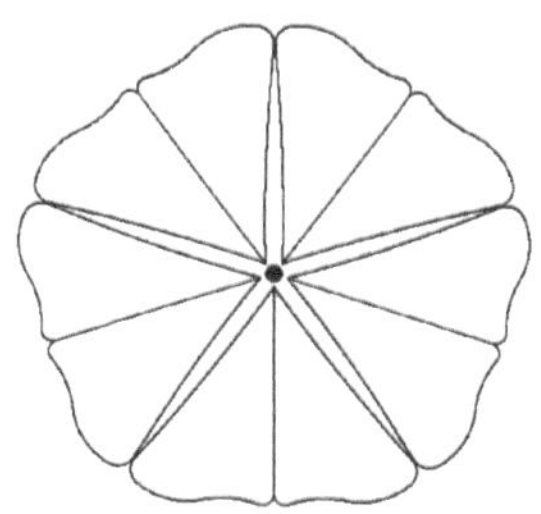

CHAPTER 2

NUMBING amounts of information poured from the pages of the three-ring binder as the Human Resources supervisor went over each in painstaking detail. Ameena Jardine drew figure eights across her notebook as she took the last sip of her coffee.

Staying awake proved a little challenging for the new employee. Her kids kept her out later than she wanted with baseball practice and last-minute project items needed. Anxiety from excitement and mounting nervousness did her in, though. Sleep-deprived, she hoped for a break soon to get more coffee.

Someone knocked on the door behind her. Ameena and the other new employees looked over their shoulders to see an older woman open the door.

"Becky," the woman addressed the Human Resources supervisor, "sorry to bother you."

Becky motioned for the secretary to come in. "Hi, Ellie. What can I do for you?"

"The Deputy Director needs to see Jack Kinston and Ameena Jardine in his office."

"Right now?"

Ellie nodded. "Yes, ma'am. It's pretty urgent. They'll be out the rest of the day."

Becky looked at the young man, then Ameena. "Kinston, Jardine, we'll reschedule for next week. You're dismissed. Keep the binders here."

Ameena grabbed her clipboard and pen, then joined her counterpart as they followed Ellie down the hallway towards the elevator. The receptionist pressed the button and waited.

Jack looked around, then cocked a manicured eyebrow at Ameena. Her stomach turned. She dealt with enough men like him at her last job.

Jack Kinston was lean, athletic, with a clean haircut parted neatly on the side and slicked back. His dark eyes matched his hair. The cocky grin he carried told Ameena all she needed to know about him: Jack would be better off as a Wall Street broker, not a forensic detective.

The initial force of gravity on her body made Ameena's stomach tighten. The ride up the elevator was in silence. Ellie occasionally smiled at the new recruits, but otherwise faced the exit.

You can do this. You can do this. Ameena repeated the phrase over and over, well after the elevator *ping!* released the occupants onto the third floor of the building.

Ellie led them down the corridor, past empty cubicles and drab offices. When they reached the corner office, the secretary stopped and knocked on the closed door. Ameena read the name: DEPUTY DIRECTOR CONRAD MCMILLAN.

From behind the wall: "Come in."

Ellie swung the door opened. "Sir, I brought the new recruits as requested."

"Thank you, Ellie," she heard.

"Yes, sir." The receptionist turned around and looked at Ameena. With a warm smile, she said, "Good luck. Welcome to the Investigative Services Bureau, Major Crimes Division!"

The detective-in-training looked inside the office to see the

Deputy Director, her new boss, sitting at his desk. The older man took off his reading glasses and stared at her with stolid eyes. His hair was a consistent mixture of salt-and-pepper black and silver-grey. His eyes were as dark as his skin; his face, as rigid as any seasoned poker player.

She gripped her clipboard harder and tried to pick at her cuticles.

"Jack Kinston and Ameena Jardine, correct?" Conrad finally said. "Set your things down at your new desks and join me down in the foyer in five. We're needed in the City of Franklin."

Jack smirked then walked out without a word.

The older man stood up and fidgeted with his computer mouse. She heard the familiar button clicks of frustration.

Say something, dammit! Don't just stand here like an idiot!

She straightened her back. "Um, sir?"

Without looking up from the screen, he said, "Yes, Jardine?"

"Sir, I'm ready right now. I didn't bring anything with me except my clipboard. And a notebook. And a pen."

"Okay." He continued to look at his computer monitor.

"And, um, sir?"

"Yes?"

"I have a request. I want to be called AJ here in the office."

He took his bifocals off and stared at her. "'AJ'?"

She nodded. Her muscles tightened as her new boss continued to study her. She would do anything to be able to read his mind.

"Shut the door and have a seat, Jardine."

She did as instructed and eased into the chair across from his mahogany desk. AJ could feel the blood slipping away from her cheeks.

Conrad crossed his arms.

She picked at her fingernails.

He continued to glare at her.

She continued to destroy the skin on her index finger.

"Why 'AJ'?"

"I-I'm sorry, sir. I didn't mean t—"

"Spit it out, detective. I don't have all morning."

She hesitated for a split second, then blurted out, "Because I'm trying to start over here with a new career and it's just easier if no one knows my past. I don't want *that* to get in the way, here, like it did my old job."

"Why?"

"I..." She looked down at her hands, clenched them, and wiped them on her pants. She felt disgusted with herself and a familiar lump kissed the inside of her throat. "...prefer not to say, sir."

Conrad leaned closer to her. "I know about your P.T.S.D., Ameena. I know what happened to your husband. And to you and the baby. I read everything in your file, including the psych eval."

She wiped her face and looked away, hoping he didn't see the emotion in her eyes. "I don't want to set a bad impression with you, sir. I'm just...trying to start over. That's why I want to go by AJ. Less questions that way."

"I know."

She looked at him. "I won't let my past be a problem. I promise, sir. I just ask for this chance to prove myself to you and this department."

Conrad stood up, still holding her eyes with his.

She stood quickly.

He tucked his glasses in an interior suit pocket and grabbed an old flip phone from his drawer. Without any words, he grabbed his gun and secured it in the holster, then walked around the other side of the desk to grab his briefcase. He stopped and looked at her.

AJ brought her shoulders back to attention and kept her head up, standing her ground. She thought she saw his lip form a gleam of approval on one side, but his ebony skin never betrayed emotion on his cheeks. The lines around his eyes never fluctuated.

Conrad opened the door and walked out.

AJ flanked one side and kept up the pace to the elevator. They waited in silence until a familiar *ping!* welcomed them inside. She stood closest to the corner inside the elevator while Conrad stood at attention in front of the shutting door.

He never looked at her.

The numbers slowly counted down to "1" and, before the door gave its exiting *ping!*, he finally said in a low voice, "Make me proud, Jardine."

As the door opened, she whispered back, "Yes, sir. I will."

The Deputy Director made a beeline to Ellie's desk.

The receptionist looked up at him as he placed his hand on the countertop. "Ellie, cancel all my meetings for this afternoon and reschedule to next Friday, at the latest."

"Yes, Mr. McMillan. Do you want me to contact tomorrow's two o'clock and see if they can reschedule as well?"

"Yes. In fact, reschedule everything this week. This new case takes front and center ahead of everything." He tapped the desk and walked off.

AJ stepped quickly to his heels and watched as Jack finally noticed and joined them. They walked out of the secured building to Conrad's government-issued vehicle.

He held up the keys for a familiar *beep beep!* of the Suburban's alarm.

Jack moved ahead of AJ and got in the front passenger's seat. He did not even bother to ask or look behind him.

She did not like Jack. Between his snide comments during the orientation and interrupting the Human Resources supervisor, his self-centricity annoyed her to no end. Her teenage son had better manners and attitude than this guy did. AJ climbed in the driver's side passenger seat behind her boss.

"So, what's this mission we're on, Conrad?" Jack asked.

AJ swallowed her disgust at the kid's gall.

Conrad took the onramp and punched the gas, heading north on Interstate 93. "'Sir.'"

"What?"

"When you are on the job, Mr. Kinston, you will address me as 'sir'. Or 'Deputy Director' or 'McMillan', do you understand?"

"Sure." Jack looked out the window.

"What we discuss here, in this vehicle or anywhere else, must be done with privacy and discretion. You do not discuss anything with anyone else except me."

"Sure, I guess."

AJ caught Conrad's dark eyes staring at her through the rearview mirror. She nodded. "Yes, sir."

"Good. Do either of you know Tony Giunta?"

"No." "No, sir."

"Mr. Giunta is the Mayor of Franklin. I've known him personally for a few years. He put in a call to my boss, specifically requesting me and my team. He requested we interview a person of interest—discreetly—to prevent a media frenzy from happening. This person of interest is a member of the Board, a prominent citizen of the town, and has many powerful friends around the States of New Hampshire and Vermont.

"I printed out a statement from Franklin PD and I want both of you to read it before we talk to the Chief. It explains everything I know to this point. Kinston, reach into the Manila folder from my briefcase. Grab your copy and pass the other to Jardine."

Jack did as instructed and passed a stapled piece of paper back to AJ. He skimmed the report and flipped it to the next page, then let out a long whistle. "Holy shit!"

"What's wrong?" AJ asked.

Jack rolled his eyes at her. "Do you have any idea who they're accusing in this?"

"No. Who?"

"Amanda Claremont."

—¡—

CHAPTER 3

- POLICE DEPARTMENT -
WITNESS STATEMENT FORM

Incident Type: Witness, discovered victim
Incident Location: 25 Coatlicue Road
Franklin, NH, southwest corner of property
at property line
Incident Time: 04:37 am
Incident Date: Monday, May 7, 2018
Respondent: Patrolman A. Kennedy

Full name: Daniel Leopald Norrington
Home Address: 25 Coatlicue Road
Franklin, NH
Business Address: Same as home
Phone Number: (***)***-****
Cell Number: (***)***-****
Email Address: ***************@*****.***

Race: Caucasian

Sex: Male
Date of Birth: **/**/****
Drivers License/ID: **********
Height: 06'01"
Weight: 185 lbs.
Hair: Gray
Eyes: Hazel

STATEMENT (PLEASE PRINT OR TYPE)

Around 2:45 this morning, my dogs started barking and woke the wife up. She then woke me up to go see what the problem was. Our Border Collie kept scratching at the door and demanded to be let out. Our shepherds just growled. I thought that was strange.

I let Sadie, our Border Collie, out thinking it was just a raccoon or possum or something else. She bolted out of sight and kept barking from a distance. Then the barking stopped and I got worried.

I called her name a few times and I didn't hear her.

I put my shoes on, grabbed a flashlight, and got my rifle. I went out to go find her. Before I made it a few yards from the house, she came running back to me. She seemed concerned and whimpered.

Then I saw the blood on her. I thought she'd been shot, but I didn't hear no gunshots. So then I thought she'd been stabbed or attacked by another animal. I rushed her back in the house and yelled for Debra, my wife.

We laid Sadie down on the floor and looked her over, but we couldn't find any wounds and didn't know where the blood came from.

Then my wife said, "Maybe Sadie found an animal bleeding out?"

I said, "That's possible. Maybe the coyotes got a deer or one of our sheep." Again, we've been having a wicked problem with coyotes this year and are worried about our sheep. We heard a pack of them nearby last week.

Debra got the shotgun and another flashlight. We let Sadie back out and she took off again in the same direction. This time we followed her across the front field, heading west to Claremont's place. We heard Sadie barking near the fence.

We installed some barbed wire between the properties for the cows and sheep. The barbed wire runs on our side of the stone wall, the main one that separates our properties.

Anyways, Sadie was angled towards the fence. She was looking at something. We saw something white whipping around and thought it was possums climbing all over each other.

We walked a little closer and it wasn't no possums. It was torn rags from what was left of clothing of some sort. When we shined the lights, that's when we saw him. He was splayed like Christ on the cross, like what it would've been during the crucifixion. My wife screamed.

Officer, you gotta understand something. She don't scream for shit. You know we own that slaughterhouse and have seen our fair share of death around here. So these things don't bother her. But this man, he'd tangled himself up in that barbed wire and scared the missus.

There was blood everywhere. His throat had been sliced from ear to ear. He had strange designs painted all on his face and across his chest. He looked like he stepped out a movie set or play or something ancient like that. He just had that cloth around his private area, ya know? Maybe he was pretending to be an Egyptian or something like that? It was just really odd.

And I honestly thought he was dead. He didn't move none. It wasn't bad enough to decapitate him, but it was still pretty horrendous. I had Debra hold the flashlight and call 9-1-1 while I tried to untangle the man.

That's when he groaned and opened his eyes. They

were lifeless, those eyes. It's the look you see in an animal hung up right before they know the life is gonna leave them. The look they give you when they know it's over. They've stopped fighting. They've accepted death and waited for the pain to go away. That was the same look in this man's eyes. That's something you never forget. Never, ever forget.

Well, he tried to say something. His mouth moved. Those dried split lips cracked but no sounds came out.

I asked him, "What happened? Can you talk?"

Of course, he couldn't say nothing. That's when I saw his finger, his right index finger to be exact, point over to the Claremont's property.

I asked him, "Did you come from over there?"

He didn't say nothing. His eyes couldn't even focus on me.

I asked him, "What happened to you?"

He wiggled his finger. Again, pointing in the direction of Claremont's house.

I asked him, "Did Amanda do something to you? Did one of the men from the halfway house hurt you? What happened to you?"

That's when the man dropped his finger and his head rolled back a little more. He never said nothing else. The fire department and ambulance arrived right after that and we let them do their thing. That's when you came over to talk to us.

My opinion? Amanda's sometimes an odd bird, but she's been supportive of farmers and the community around here for decades. I can't imagine she'd do anything to hurt someone. It just don't make any sense.

She'd only hurt someone if they came after her and hers and tried to hurt her first or tried to go after one of her employees. She keeps good company and we haven't had any problems in all the years we've known each other.

I just can't imagine she'd slice a man's neck from

ear to ear.

But honestly, I can't explain how he wound up in that barbed wire with his neck like that. I don't know why he kept pointing to her house over there.

And I most definitely can't imagine how Amanda would or could have anything to do with it.

—¡—

CHAPTER 4

AJ'S AUBURN hair was pulled back in a ponytail. She looked in the rearview mirror and made eye contact with Conrad. He stared at her hazel-blue eyes for a couple of seconds, then focused on the highway.

"Who's Amanda Claremont?" she asked.

Conrad heard Jack scoff. "Ameena—"

"—AJ. Call me AJ, not Ameena."

"Seriously? You wanna go by a guy's name?"

Before she could reply, Conrad interrupted, "Yes, she does. Now, answer the question, Mr. Kinston."

He could feel Jack glaring at him before turning to look at AJ. "Amanda Claremont is the owner of Claremont Farms and Nursery. She owns a large chunk of land in western Franklin. Even voted as having the sweetest corn in the whole state! She once ran for one of the Senate seats, but she didn't get it. Always does charity work and helps the community. Even has been trying to get one of the Franklin bridges revitalized, the one that burned up a long time ago. It's hard to imagine she, of all people, would've kidnapped or tried to kill someone."

"Jardine," Conrad added, "Ms. Claremont is a very successful businesswoman and entrepreneur. She's a humanitarian and hosts the annual Two Rivers Corn Maze and Haunted Happenings. She even owns a winery."

"*That's* her?! I took my son and his friends to that corn maze last year. Some of the employees there let them pick their own pumpkins. I've never had the impression it would be the scene of a crime."

Conrad nodded and continued to watch AJ's reaction. He could tell she had more questions. His other employee remained unfazed. "That's one reason why we've been called in. Mr. Giunta, the Mayor, needs a non-biased party to interview Ms. Claremont and see if there's any credibility to the witness's report. The witness himself doesn't believe Ms. Claremont would hurt anyone. No one wants to believe this could be an attempted murder."

"Why not head to the hospital and interview the victim?" Jack asked.

Conrad opened his mouth to answer, but AJ beat him to it. "If his throat was slashed deep enough, his vocal cords could've been damaged. Or, he could be in a coma from the blood loss. I doubt he's in any condition to be able to talk to us today."

"Jardine's correct. We let the doctors do their job so we can begin ours." He took the exit ramp off the highway and slowed the vehicle as they approached the traffic light.

"Sir," he heard from behind him, "where are we going right now?"

"The Franklin Police Department. We need to get more facts from the Chief and see what's developed since the victim was taken to the hospital."

"Why not go talk to Amanda? Why are we wasting our time with town cops?" Jack asked.

"If we approach Ms. Claremont right now, she could invoke her rights. She has powerful lawyers on her side and this could easily turn into a pissing match. We don't want that. And, because this may be a high-profile investigation—especially if she's involved—we need to proceed with extra caution."

"I can see that."

"Never rush to judge a suspect, a victim, or a body. Start from the outside. Look at the facts and evidence from that vantage point. Then, circle around closer and closer. That's when we have a better idea where the evidence is taking us. The victim, or body, is the last thing we consider in an investigation."

He glanced up in the rearview mirror and saw AJ staring back at him. She nodded slightly then looked at her clipboard and wrote something down.

Conrad knew she was easily twice the age of her counterpart but would undoubtedly make a better detective than him. Some people are better at certain professions than others. The Deputy Director could not see the young man lasting long in the bureau, but he hoped his intuition was wrong.

A few minutes later, Conrad parallel parked the suburban on Central Street in front of the Scott G. Dimond Police Facility. He looked across the street at the Winnipesaukee River, then over at the library. Bright forsythias exploded on the front lawn. Tulips and daffodils were sprinkled around the park area. Trees were preparing to launch full canopies of shade.

The three exited the vehicle and walked up the steps to the building. The mid-morning air felt fresh even though he felt a little out of breath.

Should've listened to Yas and gotten that treadmill she wanted. Need to get back in shape soon. He cleared his throat at the front door and cleared his mind of non-work distractions.

Once inside the facility, Conrad turned to his detectives. "Wait here. I'll come back and get you."

"Yes, sir," AJ said.

Jack gave a nod.

The Deputy Director checked in and walked down the corridor to Police Chief Galvan's office. He saw Doug reading something on his monitor. The old man leaned in to study the computer screen and tilted his head up, trying to read through the bottom lens of his bifocals. He silently mouthed words.

Conrad grinned, then gave a knock on the metal door frame.

The Chief looked over through the top lens of his glasses, then smiled from ear to ear. "Conrad! Good to see you again." He stood up slowly and extended his hand.

The Deputy Director returned a firm shake. "Good to see you, Doug. How's the family?"

The older gentleman motioned for Conrad to take a seat, then he plopped back down in his office chair. "Everyone's great. Clara just graduated college. Art degree. Chris is a Senior now. Can you believe that?"

Conrad chuckled slightly. "Jesus. They're that old now?"

"Hard to believe! How's your brood doing?"

"Aubreah's also a senior now, about to graduate next month. She's looking at pursuing a computer engineering degree. Duncan's in middle school."

"I remember when mine were that age. Make each day count, Conrad. They'll be gone before you know it. So will you."

"You mean both of us. I already see you struggling with those glasses."

Doug took off the bifocals and looked at them. "I hate these damned things." He then used the glasses to point at his friend. "Don't think I don't know about your pair."

Conrad tapped his coat pocket. "I keep them close to my heart." He cleared his throat. "Ready to talk shop?"

"Hit me."

"Senior staff's out today. I'm stuck with two new recruits. They're in the foyer."

"How new?"

"First day new."

"Oh. Sorry to hear that. Think they can handle this?"

"The woman can. My gut tells me that much. Not sure about the kid. Anything you need to tell me before I bring them back?"

The Chief exhaled and shook his head. "Damn, but this is a touchy one. I've known Amanda for decades now. How long have you known her?"

"Only a few years."

"There's no way she could be involved in this, Conrad."

"I want to believe that, too, but you know I have a job to do."

"Yep. That's why you're here. Tony knows you'll be fair and unbiased." Doug pointed behind himself. "Amanda's already in the back waiting."

"You mean she's here?"

"Yep. Came in as soon as she heard about the victim. Wants to help. Says she knows who the victim is."

"Anything I need to know that my staff don't?"

"Amanda's always been an odd character, Conrad. She's never been disrespectful to anyone. But she has this…tic about her today that I've never seen before."

"What's that?"

"She only made eye contact with my female staff. One of my guys brought that up. Could be nothing, could be everything."

"Hmm. Good to know. Anything else?"

"Not that I can think of right off hand." They both stood up and walked out the office.

"You're moving a little slower, you old fart."

"Not as slow as you."

—¡—

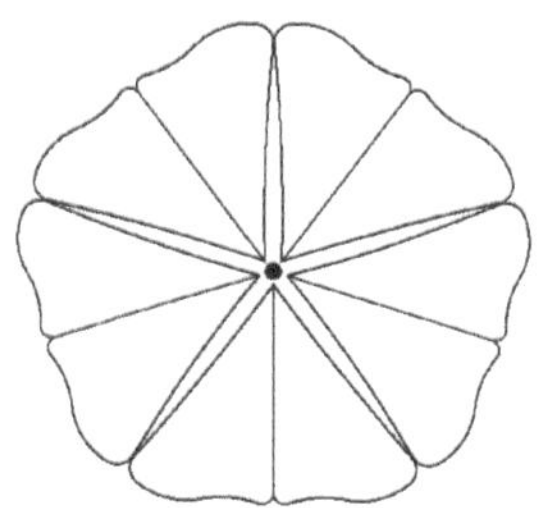

CHAPTER 5

NO ONE SAW the anxious look on AJ's face as she heard the buzz of the lock detach on the corridor door. She watched Conrad enter the hallway alone. With a sigh, she walked back to the front entrance. The new steel and glass facade starkly contrasted with the centuries-old red brick structure. She wondered what stories could be told inside the walls.

Before her imagination took over, she felt a nudge on her shoulder.

Jack crept into her personal space and whispered in a low voice, "What'd ya think of Conrad? He's a regular ball-buster, right?" His Boston accent came out.

AJ glared at the kid. "No. I don't think he is."

"Have you seen him crack a single smile yet?"

"No, he's just a hard person to read. I guess that's the nature of the business."

"Maybe he just plays hardball."

"You should really watch your tone with him. He deserves our respect."

Jack scoffed, something he did often. It made AJ grit her teeth.

"He gets the respect he gives. And he hasn't given me any yet."

She leaned away. "Wow…" She turned to walk off, but he touched her upper arm again.

"What? He thinks he owns the department and can boss us around. I heard one of the other girls—she's hot, too—talk about how he's restructuring the teams to make room for us. Sounds like a power play. You know, because he's overcompensating. Probably because he's…" Jack's voice trailed off.

"What? *Black*?"

Jack raised his hands up in defeat. "You said it, not me."

She felt her face go hot. "Race has nothing to do with this, Jack. It's about being a professional and doing a job. He's in charge and has *years* of experience that we don't. He earned that position."

"I think it's more than that." Jack leaned in again and whispered, "I bet he gets his thrills about bossing white people around."

She wanted to knock his perfectly straight teeth out. She crossed her arms and took a step back. "That was uncalled for. Race, sex, religion—none of that shit matters here."

"Who said anything about sex or religion?"

"Who's to say that's not the *next* thing you'll comment about? You'll probably say something about Muslims and Middle Easterns next."

"You said it again, not me."

AJ turned to walk off, but Jack touched her shoulder again. She jerked away.

"Hey?"

"What do you want, Jack?"

"Why're you so touchy?"

"Because you make me uncomfortable, that's why."

He smiled, apparently amused at her discomfort. "Ya know, one day I'll be your boss and you'll give me the same respect you give Conrad."

AJ scoffed. "If you survive that long. You're an arrogant ass and people like you don't last long in this field. Grow the fuck up and stay out of my personal space."

She walked over to the corridor door and stared through the panel window. Conrad and another man exited a room further down the hallway and walked her direction. She took a couple of steps back as the door opened.

"Kinston? Jardine? This way," Conrad said.

They exchanged pleasantries in the hallway. Police Chief Doug Galvan led the three past the interview room and into the adjacent watch room. Two computer monitors and a workstation faced a darkened window that overlooked the interview room. Other electronic equipment flashed red and monitored the sounds and sights of the room next door.

"I'll let you three talk a bit while I go check on Amanda," Galvan said.

AJ looked through the window down at the woman. Amanda was focused on her smartphone. She watched the woman's reaction as the Police Chief knocked on the door and entered. She intently studied the woman's reaction as they talked.

"Jardine!" Conrad yelled.

Startled, she spun around. "Yes, sir!"

AJ glanced at Jack. He leaned against the opposite wall and smirked.

"Jardine, are you okay?"

She nodded. "I'm sorry, sir. I was just watching the interaction between the Chief and Ms. Claremont. I wanted to study her mannerisms, watch her movements."

Conrad stepped closer and peered through the window with AJ. "What do you see? Start with the obvious."

She turned her focus back to the next room.

However, before she could respond, Jack interrupted. "She's in her early to mid-sixties. She's Caucasian. Blonde hair with a lot of greys. Thin for most women her age, probably fit. She's wearing an old yellow suit, like something my grandmother would wear. Has a bit of makeup on, probably to cover the wrinkles."

"What else, Kinston?"

He shrugged. "That's all I can tell. Other than what I know from reading about her career online and knowing who she is."

"Good." Her boss turned to her. "What do you notice, Jardine?"

"There's more to it than an old suit and her physical appearance. She's about business, but not high power. She's posed and professional. The suit is old, yes. But it's not yellow. It's a neutral beige. Could be from the 1980s or '90s. Maybe that's her favorite suit? The one she always wears? I can't tell."

"So, it's a cheap suit," Jack replied.

AJ shook her head. "No. I think she selected it on purpose."

"What makes you say that, Jardine?"

"Jack's right that she's wearing a little makeup. But not to cover the wrinkles. For someone who's made a living in the agricultural business, she's very pale and her facial features are soft. She doesn't have the hard ridges of sunbaked skin."

"That's because she can pay others to do the work for her," Jack said.

AJ nodded. "That could be true. But her makeup is neutral as well. Her eyeshadow is not colorful. In fact, the only color you can see on her is—"

"—the lipstick. It's red."

"Yes. But not just any red. It's a deep red and it matches the jewelry she's wearing. See her necklace and that bracelet? It's the same color red. Same as her shoes."

"So? She's coordinated. What does that mean for an investigation?"

"Mr. Kinston, it could mean nothing or everything," Conrad interjected.

"I don't think it's coincidence that her lipstick and bracelet match."

"That's so stupid," Jack said under his breath.

AJ ignored him and continued. "Some women like to coordinate. They'll match jewelry to clothing or scarves to shoes. Sometimes makeup to accessories. The rest of her outfit is neutral. I don't know anything about fabrics, but her suit fits her perfectly. I'd guess she had it tailored? The only pop of color coming out is that ruby red. I don't think it's insignificant. Even her hair is a light sandy blonde and her eyes look brown from here. Everything about her is neutral."

"Or dull, like this conversation," Jack muttered.

"Mr. Kinston, that will be enough."

"'What color was the horse?'" AJ quoted.

Her counterpart made a face at her. "What horse?"

"It's something I heard once."

"I don't get it."

"I think the story is something like this. Back in the 1800s in the Wild, Wild West, a gang of outlaws robbed a bank, killed the town sheriff, and rode off. The federal marshals showed up and began questioning witnesses and the town people. Each gave details and descriptions about what the men looked like, how tall they were, what they wore, what guns they used. They were even told what direction the gang went.

"One marshal was highly impressed. He said they could find the gang without a problem. But the second marshal said it would not be that easy. People can change what they look like and what they wear. They can toss the guns and get new ones. The robbers could even shave their beards and cut their hair, but there's one thing they probably would not change.

"The first marshal asked, 'And what's that?'

"The second marshal replied, 'What color were their horses?'

"That's what Conrad is referring to, Jack. I guess the modern equivalent would be, 'What about the shoes?' It seems like a ridiculous thing to pay attention to, but it's the little details that can make or break a case. You never know."

"What else do you notice, Jardine?" her boss asked.

"Her posture is straight, and she leans forward. She keeps her hands on the table. Sometimes she types something in her smartphone. Her smile is inviting, but there's something about her eyes that seems…off."

"Off how?"

"I'm not sure, sir. I can't tell from here."

"Anything else?" Conrad asked.

She shook her head.

The Deputy Director walked over to the door. "Let's see what she has to say."

They exited the observation room and walked down to the interview room. Conrad knocked twice, then entered. Jack followed.

AJ was the last to enter. She shut the door and when she turned around, Amanda was staring right at her. Jack and Conrad sat down across from the older woman. AJ continued to stand near the door.

"Amanda," Chief Galvan said, "These are Conrad's new recruits, Jack Kinston and Ameena Jardine."

Amanda ignored the Chief and continued to stare at her.

"Conrad, I'll let you all talk. Let me know if you need anything." Then, Galvan left.

"Jardine," Conrad said, "please have a seat at the end of the table."

"Yes, sir." She broke off eye contact with Amanda, grabbed a chair stacked in the corner, and sat down as instructed. Amanda continued to stare at her.

"Ms. Claremont, my detectives and I would like to talk to you about what happened last night and into this morning."

The woman finally broke her gaze and smiled at Conrad.

—¡—

CHAPTER 6

AH, CONRAD, I'm sure you know I've already told Doug quite a bit of what I know. And I'm sure we both know you're only doing your job.

The man that was found in the barbed wire? He was a young man I hired to help me around the nursery and in the fields. His name is Michael. He was with me for a couple of years, and he's –

Ms. Jardine, are you okay? You look like you've seen a ghost.

I'm fine. I promise. Please continue, Ms. Claremont.

I see you have manners. I like manners. And etiquette. It seems to be something lacking in so many people these days. Maybe it's their upbringing. Maybe not. I've seen it in the youth, but it's also trickled up into my generation.

I don't like rude people.

Anyway, the man the Norringtons found. His name is Michael. I think he's originally from Auburn, Massachusetts. I could be wrong. Honestly, the hired hands come and go all the time. I can't keep up anymore. I'm not as spry as I used to be.

Before you ask, I hire vagrants. Yes, vagrants. The homeless. The misfits. The ones who don't fit in anywhere else. The ones that the rest of the world forgot about or discarded like trash.

That's why they come and go, and come and go, and come and go.

Ms. Claremont, do you mind if I ask, why do you hire within this demographic?

I don't mind answering that at all, Conrad. Ever since the 1980s, when I came back and began building up my business, I wanted to give back to the community. After my husband Robert passed, I took off for a while and traveled the United States. Fell in love with the Southwest. But eventually, I felt the calling to come back here, to this town. I found a new purpose.

What was your new purpose?

To help others. And I figured out a way to do that. I decided to build a halfway house on my property. In exchange for their labor to help build my nursey and tend to my crops and orchards, I'd give them room, board, food. I'd take care of them if they took care of the land. It would be honest and good labor.

They could learn skills with farm equipment, stay clean from drugs and alcohol, and get the self-care they needed. I took care of their health needs and made sure they saw a dentist and a doctor. I showed them compassion when no one else did, but I also expected the work to be done. If they didn't put in their part of the bargain, they had to leave. If they <u>did</u> put in their fair share of the labor, they could stay for a couple of years before venturing out and doing whatever they want.

I've had dozens upon dozens of men and women come through my property over the last few decades. Primarily men. I learned to finally, and exclusively, just have men work for me in the fields.

Ah, I know what you're about to ask. 'What about the women?' Those miscreants who've tried to work for me were either whores or drug addicts. They'd rather spread their legs for a few dollars than spread seed in the fields. I learned I couldn't trust most of the girls in the fields or with the men.

I don't hate women. Quite the contrary. They are more resourceful and cunning than men. More deceptive and deviant.

More…calculating. My best employees are women. They help me—

What do you mean your best workers are women? That contradicts everything you just said.

Mr. Kinston, it's rude to interrupt a person talking. And I don't like rude people. If you do that again, we're done talking.

Yes, the laborers are all men now. I won't waste my time with women there. But I also need other workers. I need cashiers in the nursery, caretakers, women to clean and cook. I need accountants and designers. I can't hire the unskilled homeless to help maintain my business, but I can hire women for the more permanent positions. Society wants us to believe that men and women are created equal. But, no. They're not created equal.

Ms. Claremont, do you believe one sex is superior than the other, then? If that's too direct of a question, I apologize.

Of course, men are stronger than women, AJ. That's a stupid question.

Manners, Mr. Kinston.

Do you prefer to go by 'AJ' and not 'Ms. Jardine'?

Yes, ma'am. It's easier.

Interesting answer…AJ, then. To respond to your question, one sex is not superior to the other. Mr. Kinston is correct in saying that men are stronger than women. They are physically built different than the opposite sex. But that doesn't make the men superior. They are not created equal. They deserve equal rights—politically, religiously, and sexually. But they are not capable of doing the same things.

Women are better caretakers and nurturers. Men are better providers and laborers. Women can withstand unbearable pain. Men can endure hours of repetitive tasks. Women are more analytical and emotional. Men are more reserved and logical. It's a fair balance between the sexes.

Unfortunately, I think society believes that men and women can equally do the same job. And that's just not the case. They can't. And they don't. That's why the men come and go, and the women stay.

Do you think Michael was in the process of leaving?

He'd been with me nearly two years now. It's possible. I don't like them working for longer than two years.

Why, you may ask? A halfway house is exactly that. It's "halfway" between the life that was and the life that will be. I'm just the midpoint. I serve a purpose for them. They serve a purpose for me. We enrich each other's lives, then move on.

Michael's a hard worker. He spent the last month repairing the fences with the others. We're positioning the chickens across the primary fields now. We use them to—

Heh, chickens?

...I warned you, Mr. Kinston. No interruptions.

Conrad, we're done.

—¡—

CHAPTER 7

GOBSMACKED at Kinston's audacity, Conrad inhaled and clenched his jaw shut in a rare show of emotion.

Amanda stood up and straightened her suit jacket. She stared directly at Jack. "I warned you, Mr. Kinston. No interruptions." She looked at the Deputy Director. "Conrad, we're done."

Conrad stood up. His detectives followed suit. "Kinston, step outside. Now."

"But—"

"NOW, detective!" He glared at the kid and watched the man sulk as he left the room and slammed the door behind him.

"My apologies, Ms. Claremont, for Jack's behavior."

AJ reached her hand out. "Ms. Claremont, I'd like to offer my apology as well for my colleague's behavior. It was nice meeting you."

Amanda looked at AJ's extended hand and took it, clasping her hand over the other. She stared at his detective for a long time, fixated on the person in front of her.

Conrad studied the older woman's odd behavior. She appeared

lost in her thoughts for a split second before she stood straighter. She let go of AJ's hand, took a step back, then turned and left the room.

He walked to door and called Jack back in the office.

"What the hell was that about?" Jack asked.

Conrad ignored his question and looked at his other detective. "Jardine, please give us a minute."

She nodded and left, closing the door behind her. He glared at Jack and clinched his hands shut. He refused to let his subordinate see his emotion.

"Mr. Kinston, when we are interviewing anyone—whether a suspect, person of interest, or witness—abide by their wishes and be *extra* respectful. The slightest negative action you have can cause the largest negative reaction with the person on the opposite side of that table."

"I found chickens funny, tha—"

"There's nothing funny about what you did. If you do something stupid like that on this case again, I'll have the Chief ship you back to the office and you can finish up your orientation." Conrad opened the door and held the doorknob. "Get out. Have Jardine come in."

Jack tightened his jaw and Conrad watched his cheeks flush. Without another word, the detective-in-training walked out. A few seconds later, the other walked in. Conrad shut the door behind her.

"Yes, sir? Is everything okay?"

"No. What are your thoughts on Ms. Claremont?"

"It's obvious she doesn't like Jack." In a quieter voice, she mumbled, "I don't really blame her. I don't like him either."

"Jardine," he chided.

"Sorry, sir. She doesn't like Jack. I get the impression she knows and respects you."

He ignored the comment. "What do you think of her reaction to you?"

"Well, at first, I thought it was weird, but then I wondered if she's more comfortable around women. The more she talked, the more that made sense. Until her reaction when she held my hand."

"And what were your thoughts on that?"

"I don't know. Maybe I looked at her wrong. Maybe I intrigued her. Honestly, I don't have any benchmark to compare this to because I've never been in this situation."

"Do you feel that you can continue where this case may lead, no matter what path that might take?"

She nodded several times. "Yes, sir. I know I can do this job."

Conrad opened the door. He saw Jack leaning against the wall with one foot propped up, his arms crossed in a sulking manner. He walked down the hallway, detectives flanking, and knocked on Galvan's door frame. "Chief, Ms. Claremont left."

Doug leaned back in his chair and looked up. "She told me. Amanda's not keen on bad manners. You know that. It's one of her quirks. I'm assuming she didn't give you much?"

"No. She spoke a lot but didn't say much about the victim."

"Just like a politician, Conrad. She's a clever one, ya gotta give her that."

"Agreed. What can you tell us about the victim? Do you think he's in a position to be interviewed?"

The Chief shook his head. "Doubt it. He was extremely weak and passed out shortly after the Norringtons found him. He was rushed to Concord Hospital. Last I heard, he's in a coma."

"That's not good."

"Yeah. That's why, when Tony called me this morning, I knew we had a potential disaster here. We don't need rumors being spread or Amanda lawyering up. We need absolute discretion and an unbiased investigation."

"Understood." He reached his hand out. "Chief, always a pleasure. We'll check in on the victim and be back soon."

"Pleasure's always mine." Doug leaned in and added, "old fart."

With exchanges said, the trio left the building and walked down the steps to Conrad's vehicle.

"Where are we going?" Jack asked as they got in the car.

"What do you think our next step should be, detective?"

"Talk to the Norringtons?"

"Sir," AJ asked from the back seat, "If we can't talk to the victim, can we at least see him or talk to the doctors and get more information from them?"

Conrad checked his surroundings, then pulled out from the parking space. "That's exactly what we're going to do."

—¡—

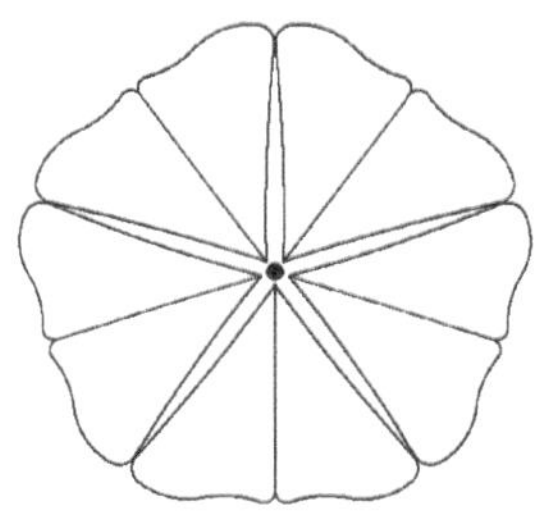

CHAPTER 8

ROUNDING the building corner from the parking garage, AJ abruptly stopped as the two men continued towards the hospital entrance. Her stomach tightened as she watched the automatic doors slide open and shut. She closed her eyes and tried to force the memories back down.

"What's wrong with her?" she heard Jack ask Conrad.

"Jardine? Everything okay?"

She nodded. "I'm fine. I…just don't like hospitals."

Conrad walked over to her and caught her gaze. In a low voice, he said, "I know this isn't easy, detective, but I need your full attention right now. When you start getting overwhelmed, take a deep breath in and exhale slowly. You will feel all kinds of emotions inside that building. No matter what happens, don't forget to breathe."

"Yes, sir," she whispered, nodding several times.

Jack walked over. "What's going on?"

"Nothing, Mr. Kinston." Conrad stood straighter and continued walking to the hospital entrance.

*Take a deep breath…*She swallowed her fear back down and

focused on her breathing. She felt a nudge on her shoulder. Jack was in her personal space again.

"You're not afraid of a hospital, are you?"

AJ wanted to punch the smirk right off his face. She ignored his comment and took another breath as they entered the building.

A few minutes later, they were on the fifth floor and walking to the I.C.U. wing. Conrad spoke with the staff at the desk.

They were escorted to a waiting area.

Jack took a chair closest to the television monitor, grabbed the remote, and flipped the station to a sports channel.

Conrad sat down at the opposite end of the room, his back to the corner.

AJ stood, preferring to ground her nervous energy that way. After several seconds, she walked back to the hallway and looked out the windows. Clouds puffed and skimmed just above the mountains in the distance. She rather liked having her back to the interior and her eyes focused as far away from the sterile environment as possible. Too many memories wanted to surface.

Finally, a nurse walked into the waiting area. "Mr. McMillan?"

"Yes, ma'am?"

"Doctor Wiseman will see you now. Please follow me."

The trio followed the nurse down the corridor and through a set of secured doors. AJ took another deep breath, pushing the nausea back down. She tried to tune out the echoing clips and clops of dress shoes dancing on the tile floors, but her mind's eye recalled a millisecond of a memory: her and her husband, Michael, taking their last walk together in San Antonio.

"Excuse me," her voice cracked. "Where is the bathroom?"

Everyone stopped and turned to look at her.

"We just passed it," the nurse said. "Head back down and take a right. It's the second door on the left."

Before Jack said anything, Conrad held a hand up and shook his head. He turned to AJ. "Jardine, take a few minutes. We'll wait."

"Yes, sir." She sprinted down the hallway.

"What's her problem?" she heard Jack ask.

The last thing within earshot AJ heard was Conrad's reply: "It's not your concern."

—¡—

With cold water splashed on her face and memories repressed again, AJ exited the bathroom and walked back to rejoin the group. She gave Conrad a silent nod. He, in turn, nodded to the nurse. They were led through the I.C.U. doors to the central nurse's station where Dr. Wiseman waited.

Conrad asked, "May we see the victim?"

Doctor Wiseman frowned. "We aren't allowing anyone but emergency contacts into the room to visit. You can see him from the glass if you like, but he's still very unstable."

The doctor led them around the station to the patient's room. The glass wall offered a solemn menagerie.

The man, in his late-twenties or early-thirties, was hooked up to several machines, each running in and out of his body. Monitors beeped and colors flashed. A milk-colored tube taped to his mouth forced air down his lungs. His diaphragm pushed up and slid down, mechanically and artificially. AJ studied the man's neck. Fresh stitches ran from ear to ear, closing whatever horrible gap was made. She could not see any paint on his neck or chest, not even in his dark hair. The only distinct color to the man was the ashen yellow his entire body took.

"Michael Smith, age 32," Doctor Wiseman said, still staring at his patient. "We ran some bloodwork and everything's clean. No drugs, narcotics. Nothing that would indicate this man has any serious health problems. His alcohol level was at .09, so he had been drinking last night. Ms. Claremont stated he used to be a heroin addict and drank on occasion. Since he's been clean, she said he donates blood regularly. That would explain the low hemoglobin and ferritin levels."

"What's ferritin?" Jack asked.

"Ferritin levels check for iron deficiency in the body. It could indicate if a person is anemic or has any underlying health conditions."

"Could these low counts have happened from last night and the blood loss?" AJ asked.

Doctor Wiseman shook his head. "These are lower than normal and indicative of long-term blood loss. That's why I believe he's a very frequent blood donor. That could explain the results I saw and the scarring at his elbows. He could also be donating platelets for extra money."

"Donating platelets?"

The doctor nodded. "Blood is removed, centrifuged to remove platelets, then returned back to the donor. People can donate once a week."

"Do you think those marks on his arms are because he's still a heroin addict?"

"No. As I stated, his lab work came back clean of all narcotics and drugs. Just the alcohol in his system."

"Did you save any of the clothing he wore? Or take pictures of the paint on his neck?" Conrad asked.

Doctor Wiseman shook his head. "Our primary job was to stabilize him. We washed him down and threw everything in the trash. You're welcome to gather the trash, but it will be contaminated and useless. Honestly? I believe he'd been at a party that went wrong. It's possible he was disoriented or drunk when he got tangled up in the barbed wire. It's also possible someone could've attacked him, but we just don't know."

"What other injuries did Mr. Smith have?"

"Other than the laceration across the neck and the scratches from the barbed wire? Nothing. He's as healthy as the next man his age."

AJ stared at the victim. "Why is his skin that color?"

"When the patient arrived here at the hospital, he began going into hypovolemic shock. We started a transfusion and worked to stop the bleeding. However, I believe we were too late. We've been trying to stabilize him, but I think his body is shutting down. We won't know for sure for at least twenty-four hours."

"It's possible he's dying, then?"

"Yes."

"It's also possible Michael will survive this, Ms. Jardine," a familiar voice said.

Everyone turned around to see Amanda standing behind them.

"What are *you* doing here?" Jack asked.

Amanda ignored the young man, then talked directly to AJ.

—¡—

CHAPTER 9

ARE YOU wondering how long I've been standing here, listening? Long enough. Why am I here, as Mr. Kinston rudely asked?

Stop! I don't want to hear another word from you. You would do well to leave the area while I have a conversation with Ms. Jardine and your boss.

Conrad, as I was about to say, after we were done at the police station, I went back to my nursery, checked in, then came here. Everything's fine at the farm. They don't need me there. This is where I need to be right now.

And I'm allowed to be in the room with Michael. I'm his emergency contact and the closest thing to a guardian or next of kin he has.

When my employees begin working for me—more specifically, the ones from the halfway house—I have them read and sign several legal documents. If they can't read, then I have a notary read the papers outloud. Everything's been checked out by my lawyers, so if you'd like to see copies of the contracts they sign, I can send them to you.

Each employee signs a confidentiality agreement and an emergency incident agreement. Because of the large farm equipment we use and manual labor we do, accidents can and sometimes happen. I can't have a transient thinking they can come here, conveniently hurt themselves, then sue me for everything I'm worth. I have to protect myself and my business. My gardens and farm are my life investments and I won't have anyone take that from me.

I also have Franklin PD run background checks and make sure no one has outstanding warrants or too much of a criminal history. I won't harbor the most wanted, but I will help those who seek harbor for a new life.

Therefore, each employee signs the proper forms. They agree to stay clean and sober. They agree to do the work. They agree that, if they don't have family to contact, they give me power of attorney in the event of something happening. More often than not, the men put my name down.

Michael was no exception to that rule. As I got to know him over these last two years, he told me he'd been in and out of foster homes all his life. He has no family that he knows of. He has no girlfriend, though he's grown fond of one of my employees.

Maria. She's been with me the longest out of all my permanent employees. Very loyal, almost to a fault. Runs a very efficient shift at the nursery.

Anyway, other than a fondness for Maria, Michael doesn't have anyone. He signed the Power of Attorney documents two years ago, just like all the others have. This is actually the first time I've ever had to use that particular form.

Oh, and yes, I make everyone sign and fill out Last Will and Testament documents. It's not to be morbid. No, quite the opposite. I want everyone to think and prepare for the future. Everyone needs to learn that actions have consequences and a person's life can change at the drop of a hat.

When the men have finally worked their two years, they take the documents with them. I let them. Except the confidentiality ones. They don't need those. But they get to keep their health care benefits for the rest of the year. They can keep their documentations. They earned it.

Oh, the benefits? Yes. Each transient, as an employee, is given health insurance. I pay for it. Because of the work we do, their health takes priority. They need to be strong, willing to do the work. I wouldn't send someone out to manage the crops or tend the animals otherwise.

Yes, I also make sure their vaccines are up to date. Flu shots are a must every year. Again, a person's health is everything.

But back to Michael. There've been accidents before, but nothing like this. Nothing requiring a hospital stay. This is new territory for me.

Look at him. He's peaceful, but is he really at peace? Is being hooked up to all those machines and monitors the way for him to spend his last moments, if he is, indeed, dying?

I'm not cruel. I won't pull the life support on him. I don't believe in a death like this. For me, I'd have a Do Not Resuscitate bracelet on.

I won't die like this.

But for him, he didn't want that. He wanted every effort given to him to live. And that's what I plan to honor. I should be in there with him. If he is dying, like what the doctor thinks, then Michael shouldn't be alone.

No one should die alone.

There should always be a witness.

If you don't mind, Conrad, Ms. Jardine, please excuse me.

—¡—

CHAPTER 10

MISSING no opportunity to end the conversation, Conrad watched Amanda walk to the sliding door. She grabbed some latex gloves and a mask from the nearby shelf and snapped them in place.

He watched her step into the room. She studied the instruments and readings, then sat down in the chair next to the man. She spoke to Michael, but Conrad could not make out what she said. The beeps sped up on the heart monitor, then slowed back down to their normal rate.

"Sir," AJ whispered, "do you think he knows she's there?"

"Anything's possible, Jardine."

"What do you think of what she said? About there always being a witness?"

He continued to watch the scene through the glass. He noticed the man's foot twitch a couple of times. "It's an odd statement, but we were warned that's part of her personality. What are your thoughts?"

"Mine, sir? She's nurturing. A caretaker."

"Is she? Or does she appear to be that when, in actuality, she isn't?"

"I don't know, sir. I think it's possible it could be either. The evil that humans do to each other doesn't appear to be without limits."

Conrad looked down at AJ.

She'll make a fine detective, if I have anything to say about it.

—¡—

Tuesday, May 8, 2018

"Deputy Director?"

"Yes, Ellie?"

"Chief Galvan is on the other line for you, sir."

"Patch it through."

"Yes, sir."

Conrad stared at his phone, waiting for the light to flash. He tapped his fingers on his desk. The button lit up.

"Morning, Doug. How can I help you?"

"Conrad, I got a call from Amanda first thing this morning."

"Oh, how'd that go?"

"Well, she was pleasant enough, as usual. I asked her if she had any updates on Mr. Smith and she said he was still not doing good. She'd go up to the hospital later today and check on him. She said the reason she called me was because your detectives made quite an impression on her."

"Interesting."

"She had a few choice words for the—and I quote here—'boy so green behind his ears his nuts haven't descended properly.'"

Conrad let out an unusual guffaw. "The kid definitely needs some stark humility in his life. I agree, his ego must weigh heavily on his shoulders."

Doug chuckled. "She went on for a couple of minutes about how she doesn't like him. Gave me quite the earful. When I could finally get a word in, I asked her about that woman detective twice Kinston's age. Conrad?"

The seriousness in the Chief's voice instinctively made Conrad straighten in his chair. "Go on."

"Amanda's taken an interest in the woman. She said that was why she called me this morning. She wants to talk to—Jardine, is it?"

"Jardine, yes. AJ."

"Amanda had nothing but nice things to say about AJ. She was professional, offered an apology she didn't need to, kept eye contact, and conducted herself quite well. Amanda said she'd entertain more questions and help out with any investigations into the Smith case only if AJ was there. Otherwise, she threatened to sic the lawyers on you."

"Hmm." He tapped his fingers on the mahogany desk. "How do you feel about all this? I know the Mayor wants us to have jurisdiction and the last thing I want is a pissing contest between our offices and Tony's."

"Conrad, that's the last thing that'd happen. I don't blame Amanda for wanting to talk to a professional detective, but remember what I told you yesterday?"

"She prefers women over men?"

"Yes. I think that if—and mind you, it's a big 'if'—Amanda had anything sinister to do with the Smith case, approaching her with someone she likes is the best thing we can do."

"Doug, do you believe she's capable of hurting a man?"

There was a pause before the Chief finally answered. "After nearly thirty years in law enforcement, the shit I've seen has stopped surprising me. We're a cruel lot. And anyone—male or female—is capable of anything these days."

"That's the damned truth."

"Amanda doesn't favor certain men in her life, but I doubt she'd hurt anyone. She's done too much for our town and this community, especially the farmers in the region."

"I'll keep that in mind."

"And Conrad?"

"Yeah, Doug?"

"If she *is* capable of slicing a man's neck from ear to ear, I wouldn't put it past her to be capable of much worse."

"Understood. We'll head up that way shortly."

"Good enough. Talk later."

Conrad hung up and sat in silence. He ran his hand across the smooth desk surface, an automatic motion he did when he was deep in thought.

It seemed he needed to put more trust in AJ than he wanted so soon into her new career. She handled herself well enough at the hospital, but he knew her P.T.S.D. would surface again. He knew he'd need to push her out of her comfort zone. But he didn't know if she could handle it.

He pressed the call button and buzzed the new detective's desk.

No answer.

He called the front desk.

"Yes, sir?" Ellie asked.

"Please find AJ and send her in."

"Sir, she hasn't made it in yet."

"Excuse me? Where's my detective?"

—¡—

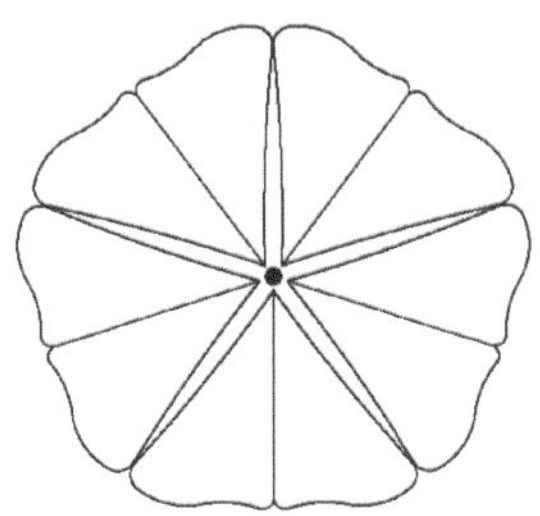

CHAPTER 11

"AMEENA, *habibti*!" her mother, Jamilla, yelled from the other side of the bedroom door.

Ameena's eyes cracked open and, half asleep, mumbled, "Momma, what's wrong?"

Her mother pounded on the door. "Sweetheart, you're *late* for work! Get *up*!"

"Oh, shit!" Ameena tried repeatedly to kick the tangled covers off before stumbling to the door and unlocking it. Her mother, dressed and ready for the day, stood on the other side. "Momma, what time is it?!?"

"It's nearly eight o'clock."

"Oh, my gawd! Shit!" Ameena ran back inside her room and swam through the sheets, searching for her phone. "Shit!"

"Ameena!" Jamilla's voice rang firm with authority and the younger woman stopped. "Are you *okay*?" Her heavy Middle Eastern accent emphasized the words with a mother's concern.

Ameena felt a hard surface on the mattress and grabbed the device. She started looking up the Investigative Services Bureau main phone number. "Sorry, Momma. I'm fine. Had another nightmare last night and was awake for several hours. Guess I fell back asleep." She dialed the office number.

"Do you want to talk about it, habibti?"

Ameena shook her head. "I need to get ready for work." Before her mother could say anything else, she heard Ellie's voice on the other end. "Ellie, this is AJ."

"Good morning, AJ!"

"Ellie, I'm *so* sorry, but I'm running late. Can you please let the Deputy Director know I'll be there in less than thirty minutes?"

"Of course! See you soon. Drive safe!"

Ameena hung up the phone and saw her mom still standing there.

"'AJ'? You want a *man's* name?" Her mom gave her a condescending look.

"It's not a man's name. And we talked about that. It's just—" She choked back the unexpected emotion.

"Stop." Jamilla walked over and touched her daughter's face. Her caring and deep brown eyes held Ameena's gaze. "You know whatever you decide, your father and I will always support you. We are very proud of you. Go into your boss's office with your chin up and explain what happened."

"But—"

"*Lah*! No arguments!" She gave Ameena a kiss on the forehead. "I made you a breakfast sandwich. You can eat it in the car on the way to work. Go get ready." She started walking out of the bedroom and added, "Don't worry about Jenna and Eoghan. I'll get both kids from school this afternoon."

With little time to think, Ameena rushed through her morning ritual, grabbed her makeup bag, and sped down the highway to the office.

She was pissed at herself for having nightmares again. *Don't think about that right now, dammit! What did Conrad tell you? 'Breathe'. Inhale...exhale...*

She tried to calm herself during the twenty-one-minute drive to Concord, but her voice cracked when she checked in at the front desk.

The receptionist said, "Mr. McMillan was looking for you earlier. He wants to see you in his office immediately."

AJ felt her hands turn clammy as the blood drained from them. All she could do was nod and rush to the elevator, wait while it slowly ascended, then rush to Conrad's office down the hall.

Then she waited again.

His door was shut. She gripped her clipboard harder and pressed her fingertips into the sharp edge of the metal clamp, hoping the inflicted pain would distract her anxiety.

She heard the Deputy Director yell at someone on the other side of the door. Minutes tick-tocked by. Finally, the door opened. A red-faced Jack Kinston stepped out.

He glanced down at her and mumbled, "You're next."

She stared at Jack as he walked over to his cubicle.

"Jardine."

The firm sound of her name snapped her attention back to her boss. She looked at him through the door. His arms rested on his desk, fingers interlaced. No smile, no emotion—the perfect poker face again.

"In my office, Jardine."

"Yes, sir."

"Shut the door."

"Yes, sir."

She closed the door and stood near it, clutching her clipboard in front of her.

"Have a seat." The monotonous voice heightened her anxiety, something already at a feverous pitch.

"Yes, sir."

"Now."

As she took a few steps closer, anxiety and fear of losing her job on the second day of work caused her knees to buckle. She fell forward. Instinctively, her hands lunged for the chair in front of her, causing her clipboard to projectile from her grasp and land dead center on Conrad's mahogany desk—metal end first. The spiral notebook, loose papers, and two pens exploded in separate directions. The clipboard slid and nearly knocked over the boss's coffee mug.

AJ tried to recover herself. "I'm so sorry, sir!"

"Stop!" Conrad's command mirrored her mother's not even an hour before. "Sit down."

"I'm so sorry, sir. I didn't get good sleep and I must've accidentally turned off the alarm on my phone, but my mom woke me up and I rushed into the office as soon as I could. It won't happen again, I promise!"

His eyes softened. Slightly. "Detective, relax. And don't make promises you can't keep. It will happen again. We both know it." He reached for the scattered papers.

Her hands shook as she grabbed one pen off the floor and the other from the corner of the desk. As Conrad stacked the papers, AJ picked up her clipboard.

That was when she saw the permanent scratch on his otherwise pristine desk.

"Oh, fuck me running sideways..."

She looked at Conrad as he glanced at the mark. His eyebrows dropped.

AJ swallowed her defeated emotion back, though it did not stop her voice from cracking. "Sir, this morning is so screwed up. I'll understand if you want me to turn in my resignation. The last thing I want to do is disappoint you and I feel that's where I am right now. And it's only the second damned day on the job. And, sir, I can't apologize enough for your desk or running late or—"

"Detective Jardine, put your things on the desk, sit down, and hold your hands up."

"Sir?"

He let out a sigh. "Stop calling me *sir* right now. Hold up your hands. Clench your fists as hard as you can. Hold it for a count of five. Then open your hands all the way for a count of five." She did as instructed. "Do it again...and again...and one more time...now, look at your hands."

She still held her hands in front of her. Her fingers no longer trembled.

"Jardine, I expect you to come to work on time. Period. I

imagine there are reasons you overslept this morning, but I can overlook those. I can overlook many things the first week of employment. What I can't overlook is the lack of professionalism one of my detectives would have towards a person of interest or victim."

"Sir, I haven't done anyt— "

"Dammit, Jardine, let me finish."

"Y-yes, sir."

"*You* have demonstrated professionalism with Ms. Claremont, and she's requested to speak to you again. She put in a complaint about Mr. Kinston and I've taken the appropriate action with him. Claremont has agreed to talk to us, primarily with you, at her place of business today."

"Her business and not the police station?"

Conrad nodded. "Claremont Farms and Nursery. Ball's in her court, Jardine. Kinston will shadow me the rest of the week. We'll talk to her employees while you're with Ms. Claremont. Don't lead the conversation to Mr. Smith. Let her lead and do most of the talking. See where things go."

"Yes, sir."

"Listen carefully to her. Your chitchat and casual conversations are vital to our investigation. Document everything she says, no matter how small the detail. And, if she wants to spend time with you, do it."

"Yes, sir."

He stood up and she followed, grabbing her clipboard from the desk. She stared at the permanent mark she created.

"Jardine?"

"I'm sorry, sir, for ruining your desk."

"We'll deal with that later. There are more pressing things right now."

—¡—

Conrad drove through downtown Franklin and turned on to Route 3A. The ground sloped down and opened wide to reveal the river valley.

She leaned over from the backseat to get a better look. She could see most of the Claremont Farms and Nursery, a large establishment that spanned over fifty acres. She could make out the cornfield and what looked like a winery closer to the river.

They passed by the Ag-Equip, a place regional farmers purchased or leased their farm equipment, then slowed to turn into Amanda's place. AJ could see several greenhouses and a large red building.

Conrad parked the suburban at the end of the aisle near some picnic tables and all three got out. AJ noticed the front portion of Amanda's property was asphalted and, just after the corner greenhouse, porous pavers covered the open field.

They zigzagged around a couple of corners and she took in the detail of the buildings. All four greenhouses were identical in shape and precisely laid out. She was fascinated by the flowers and plants on display in and around the greenhouses. The trio walked down a row of potted fruit trees.

The nursery's main building, what appeared to be a converted barn, was the focal point and tallest structure on the property. It welcomed visitors within its dark cherry-red walls. The front doors were propped open with planters full of petunias. A dozen or so patrons were scattered everywhere, engaged with some of the staff while others browsed columns of seed packets. Thick wooden planks opened up the interior. Hooks, iron skillets, and antique farm equipment hung from the rafters and every wall.

Jack scrunched his nose. "What the hell is that smell?"

AJ got a whiff of the odor where he stood. "Chicken manure. Makes good fertilizer."

"Ugh! It's disgusting!"

"Kinston, mind your tongue," Conrad said.

While they waited, AJ looked around the shop and studied all the garden ornaments. She touched one of the wind chimes. It sung with deep soothing tones like those found from a peaceful monastery. Then she walked over to the decorative water dispensers. She glanced back to see Conrad talking to one of the staff.

Jack stood with his arms crossed and hands tucked inward. He appeared afraid to touch anything.

A spark of light caught AJ's eyes and she turned to see the sun reflecting off some glass in the corner of the building. She walked closer and gasped at the stained glass ornaments and hummingbird feeders hanging on display. There were dozens of them.

"They're so beautiful," she whispered.

"Aren't they?"

AJ turned to see Amanda Claremont standing behind her. She was dressed in tan overalls and a white shirt. She had little makeup on but still wore the deep red lipstick. AJ caught a glimpse of the matching bracelet and smiled.

"These feeders are gorgeous, Ms. Claremont."

"Amanda. Please, call me Amanda." She stepped closer to AJ and whispered, "Between you and me, your colleague can still call me Ms. Claremont."

"Ma'am, I'm sorry he was so rude to you yesterday."

"Don't worry about it. He's the only one responsible for his own actions, not you." Before AJ could reply, Amanda continued, "Which hummingbird feeder do you like the most?"

AJ glanced back at the shimmering displays. "I don't know. They're all equally amazing. I haven't had one since—since a few years ago." She tried to stop the memory.

"I saw that same look on your face yesterday when I said 'Michael'. They're connected, aren't they? Those memories together somehow?"

"I apologize, Miss—I mean, Amanda. My husband died several years ago when we lived in San Antonio and it's still a very raw memory for me."

Amanda touched her on the shoulder. "There's no need to apologize for remembering something. If I had to guess, I'd say you haven't had a hummingbird feeder at your home since that time?"

"Yes, I hadn't thought about it, really. But seeing these feeders makes me miss a part of my old life. I miss gardening, too."

"Then let's make it part of your new life again."

—¡—

CHAPTER 12

OH! BEFORE I forget, let me show you something that I think is special. I want you to see some of the feeders we keep filled up around the nursery.

You can see, here, the generic and boring ones offered for cheap. Some customers don't care to spend the extra money on the blown glass ornaments and spiraling designs we have. They prefer to just buy these boring feeders, and then they come back a week later and don't understand why they aren't attracting the hummers. Not only that, the bottleneck is so small, you can't get a good scrubber in there to keep them clean. It's important to keep your feeders clean.

Or, customers come back and ask me why their plastic little feeder broke. I tell them it's because plastic breaks over time. You can't expect plastic to survive the sun and elements over the years. The feeders become brittle and give up altogether. Then where are your birdies?

These, here on the second and third shelves, offer customers different designs. I know for a fact some of these work and some of these don't, but customers like to experiment and learn on their own. My repeat customers—those willing to spend some extra money on trial and error—have a tendency to buy these. They think the elongated designs or the colorful glass will attract the birds and prevent them from fighting over the nectar.

It doesn't work that way, no matter how many times I try to explain that to them. But, still, they keep coming back, keep asking for refunds and experimenting with new designs.

These, the ones hanging around the windows, are my personal favorites. They range in price from inexpensive to outrageous, but these are our success stories. Do you see the one thing they have in common? No?

It's the color. It's always about the color.

Hummers look for that bold, apple red or rich maroon with the pop of yellow. That's what attracts them. That's what brings them.

That, and just the right amount of nectar. Not too sweet, not too sour. It has to be chemical perfection. One part sugar, four parts boiled or purified water. Absolutely no food coloring. That's the best thing to feed hummingbirds. You remember that part, right?

I'm sorry. Of course, you do. I guess my mouth is on automatic at the moment. It's a common question I'm asked. People want to know when the hummers will come back, what to feed them, how often to change the nectar, what flowers to plant.

They sometimes call me the Hummingbird Charmer because I know so much about many of the species. Did you know North America is only home to about two dozen out of three hundred species? The rest of them live in South America or the surrounding islands.

There aren't any hummingbirds anywhere else in the world. That's why there's no mythology or history associated with them anywhere else around the globe. But here? Native cultures are rich with the stories they tell.

I could go on for days about these tiny little birds. They're a passion of mine.

As are flowers. In fact, did you know that hummingbirds are attracted to morning glories? When I saw you yesterday,

I immediately thought of morning glories. Your aura, your presence—it just reminded me of delicate vines climbing their way to the top. I hope that doesn't offend you or seem too strange to you, but there's so much to say about morning glories and hummingbirds.

Oh my, I definitely get off topic quickly. Sometimes I can ramble on without realizing it. Especially when the topic is something I'm very passionate about.

Do you see this feeder hanging here? The one with the spiraling handblown glass flowers? The birds like this one a lot. I picked up this feeder in the southwest—Arizona to be exact. I think it was back in 1989 or 1991. I can't remember which year it was when I got it, but it was close to the early years of my farming business.

I've been running my nursery and farm for—what has it been? Over three decades now. After they found my husband's body back in the early eighties, I boarded up the house and moved out of state for a bit. Tried to make a life somewhere else, but that didn't work out. I'll tell you about that another time.

After a lot of soul searching and a few failures, I came back here and started new. Decided I wanted to be my own boss and run my own business. I still had plenty of money left over from Robert's life insurance and savings, so I started expanding my business.

Do you see that field in the back over there? Where those pyramids stand? That's where the corn maze goes every year. All of that land was owned by Old Man Bates. He had a house behind the nursery here, where the crops go.

He was retiring the same year I came back, so I bought his land from him. I think he moved to Florida right after that. Never saw or heard from him again.

Anyway, I had his house demolished—it wasn't worth the cost of repairs—and cleaned up the land here acre by acre. Bought some large equipment, flattened the land, removed the rock. Turned it into efficiently engineered farmland. I lease each sectioned acre off to farmers and allow them to grow their crops here.

Every year, we rotate the crops on each acre so that nutrients are put back in after certain crops take them out. Did you know if you plant soybeans the year after you plant corn it helps add the nutrients back in the ground for the corn?

Oh my, there I go again. Rambling off on a tangent.

Yes…bought Old Man Bates's land and expanded my original property out. I let Norringtons Meat Market next door bring some of their cattle over here to graze on the grass and feed them the extra crop we have left over at the end of each growing season. I don't like anything going to waste and I believe in giving back to nature.

Everything has a balance and a purpose.

It took about a decade to build the farm up to what it is today. We have a solid formula on what works best, how to rotate animals in and out of locations, and what to plant, when to plant it, things like that.

I actually named this road. Back in the mid-1990s, I invested a lot of money in the repair of this road and my neighbors' driveways. Since it's a short road, there was little resistance from anyone on changing the name. Used to be named Bates Creek Road, but Old Man Bates made a lot of enemies back then.

I proposed renaming it Coatlicue Road. Everyone mispronounces the name. They say 'coat-le-cue', almost like 'barbecue'. I'm fine with that, though. It's really pronounced 'quat-lee-quay'. Named it after the Aztec goddess. She's a mother of gods and mortals. She's a mother of all things, including nature.

Yes, I named the road. Have spent the last several decades helping the farmers in the area. I've achieved everything I dreamed I would, and my business plateaued at the top of the success mountain for the last few years. I couldn't ask for a more prosperous establishment.

Excuse me briefly, AJ. I need to help a customer eyeing the blood meal. Too much of that product and it'll kill the vegetation. Can't have that happen on my watch.

—¡—

CHAPTER 13

FROM THE other end of the building, Conrad and Jack introduced themselves to another of Amanda's employees. They followed her outside.

"What was your name again?" Conrad asked the young woman as she finished transplanting a fruit tree into another container.

"Kaylee Jenkins. K-A-Y-L-E-E. There's two Es in the name."

Conrad watched Jack write the name down. Then he asked, "And how long have you worked here, Ms. Jenkins?"

"Um, ten months, I think. I was hired last summer."

"How's the work been here?"

"Oh, it's been great! Amanda takes good care of us. Always wants to make sure we're happy on the job. She definitely keeps us busy all year."

"All year?" Jack asked. "How do you stay busy in a business like this during the wintertime?"

"Oh, that's pretty easy. After Halloween, and before the ground freezes, we start cleaning up the land and clearing the dead vegetation. Amanda wants everything prepped and ready for the next year. We also set up the greenhouses, move what we can indoors, and hold classes for gardeners during the white months. It's definitely not as busy as the green months, but we still have our fair share of customers."

"Ms. Jenkins, do you know an employee by the name of Michael Smith?" Conrad asked.

Kaylee leaned her head to the side and thought for a second. "We have a couple of Michaels here, but I don't know who you're talking about."

"Did you hear about the incident yesterday? About the man found tangled in the barbed wire?"

"Oh, yeah. Everyone's talked about that."

"The gentleman found was Michael Smith."

"I wouldn't call Michael Smith a gentleman." Conrad and Jack turned around to see another employee standing behind them.

The woman's dark eyes held Conrad's. She appeared slightly younger than AJ, but the crow's feet in her brow and the heavy lines around her eyes told him she worked hard for years. Her dark brown hair was pulled back in a low ponytail. Her eyes were almost the same color as Amanda's, and almost as devoid of emotion.

Jack spoke up. "And you are?"

"Maria."

"You must be the one Amanda mentioned, Ms. — ?"

"E-L-L-A-N-O-G-E-K. It's pronounced Ay-AHN-o-jek. It's Spanish."

"Ellanogek?" Conrad asked.

She nodded.

"Ms. Ellanogek, what makes you say he wasn't a gentleman?"

"Michael is an asshole. He assaulted one of our girls last year."

"Who was assaulted?"

"The girl doesn't work here anymore. She left after the incident."

"Can you tell me what happened, Ms. Ellanogek?"

"Michael came here almost two years ago to get clean. But his behavior never really changed. He found a new addiction."

"And that was?" Jack rolled his hand, gesturing for her to continue.

She turned to glare at the young detective. "You must be Jack. We were warned about you."

"Warned? About what?"

"Mr. McMillan," she repositioned her body to face Conrad, "Michael tried to rape one of our girls. I found him on top of her. Then told Amanda what happened."

"What did Ms. Claremont do?"

"She took care of it." Maria paused, her jaw clenched shut as she continued to stare at Conrad. Her eyes remained vacant; her tone, solemn. Maria's gaze focused on someone behind him. He turned to see AJ walking up.

"Hi, I'm AJ." The detective extending her hand to the employee. She was a few inches shorter than Maria.

The woman ignored the hand and glared back at Conrad. "Anything else you want to know, Amanda's the one to ask. The girls don't know anything."

"Thank you, Ms. Ellanogek."

"Hmm." Maria walked off without saying anything else, staring the entire time at AJ.

After she disappeared, AJ looked at Conrad. "Sir, did I say something wrong?"

He shook his head. "Doubtful, Jardine. Did you find out anything from Ms. Claremont?"

As AJ relayed everything she could remember, Conrad studied his surroundings. He noted all the employees as they waited on customers or stayed busy straightening and stacking displays.

He watched Jack walk over to a turnstile and study the columns of seed packets. Occasionally, the young detective would study the backside of the girls walking by.

"Sir, you should've seen the look in her eyes as she talked about the hummingbird feeders. She had—what's the best way to describe it? Passion, maybe? She had emotion in her words."

Jack piped up. "Probably because you brought up your dead husband and she's interested in finding out more. It's something you both have in common."

"What did you just say?"

"Jardine," Conrad interrupted, "Kinston has a solid observation. Perhaps she takes interest in you because of your past."

AJ opened her mouth, but before she could respond, a familiar voice spoke from behind. "Commonality is not a bad thing when getting to know someone. Wouldn't you agree, Conrad?"

Jack smirked. "Like attracts like. That explains you two."

Amanda stood straighter, even though she was still a head shorter than Jack. Her eyes never left the young man as she addressed his boss. "Conrad, unless you want me to permanently ban you and your detectives, please leave. Now. You can come back another time."

Jack dropped his arms. "But I didn't do—"

"Mr. Kinston, you heard Ms. Claremont. It's time to leave."

"But—"

"Mr. Kinston! Go wait in the car. Jardine, you as well."

"Yes, sir." AJ put her hand on Jack's arm. "Jack, let's go." The kid recoiled from her touch and stormed away. With a sheepish look, she told Amanda, "Sorry, ma'am."

When both rookies were well into the parking lot, Conrad turned to Amanda. Her stare was vacant and hollow, in much the same manner as Maria's minutes before.

"Amanda, I'm sorry. I offer my apology to you. Again."

The older woman dusted her hands off and crossed her arms in front of her chest. She leaned in and whispered, "When we see a diseased flower on a bush, we pluck it, so the rest will flourish. Your branch could use some pruning, Conrad, to let the *real* flower bloom."

She left before he could respond.

Furious, he crossed the parking lot and stood by the car. He took a couple of deep breaths and then got in.

"I didn't do anything wrong," Jack said.

"Mr. Kinston, when you address me, you say 'sir'."

"But I didn't do anyth—"

"Detective, shut up."

Conrad backed out of the parking spot and took a right onto the road. He tapped his fingers on the steering wheel.

"Sir?" AJ's voice was soft behind him. "Where are we going now?"

"To the hospital. We need to check on the status of Mr. Smith."

"Yes, sir." The quiet response was the last thing said in the car until they got to Concord Hospital.

—¡—

Conrad pushed the unlocked door and walked down the corridor. He heard the footsteps of his detectives behind him but did not bother to look at them. His sights were on the hospital staff in front of him.

As he approached the nurse's station, a buzzer sounded off. "Code Blue in Room 347. Repeat, Code Blue, Room 347."

The trio stopped as several nurses ran to a room down the hallway.

"Sir, isn't that—" AJ tried to ask.

"—Michael's room?" Jack finished.

Conrad walked in the direction of the victim's room. Several minutes went by before most of the nurses slowly came out. Two remained inside: one disconnected and turned off the surrounding machine; the other began removing the tubes from Smith's arm and chest.

"Excuse me?" Conrad knocked on the metal door frame.

"You can't be in here, sir." A nurse held one hand up to block the path while drawing the curtains with the other.

Conrad pulled out his badge from his pocket and introduced himself. "Can you tell me what's happening to Mr. Smith? We came here to get a statement."

Both nurses looked at each other and then at him. "Sir, he just passed away."

—¡—

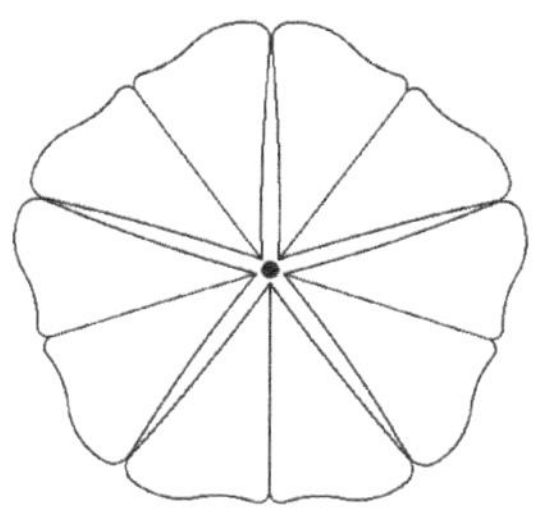

CHAPTER 14

"DON'T YOU think it's a bit 'coincidental'"—Jack made air quotes as he whispered—"that Smith died right as we got up there?"

"Jack, I don't know," AJ replied. "How could Amanda do anything from her nursery?"

Her coworker sat himself on the edge of her desk and leaned against the cubical wall. "I think the old hag offed him." He made a slicing motion to his neck and then laughed. "Pun intended in this case."

AJ felt the anger rush back into her face. "Do you think the death of someone is a joke?"

"How else will we deal with it on a daily basis? Death is part of this job. We can't take it seriously all the time or it'll kill us, too."

"Try to show some damned respect. We just watched a man die right in front of us!"

Jack shrugged and stared at her. She could see the contempt in his eyes. "What's wrong? Can't handle a dead body, Ameena?"

She jumped out of her seat, then yelled, "GET OUT of my

cubicle!"

He slid off the desk, smirk still in place, and walked down the aisle to his cubicle. "If you can't handle a dead body, AJ, how do you expect to do this job?"

Her phone buzzed. "Jardine?"

"Yes, sir?"

"My office." An immediate *click!* followed.

AJ walked around the corner to her boss's office and saw him motion to the door with his eyes. She pursed her lips, walked in, and shut the door, then sat down across the desk and waited.

"Everything okay?" Conrad finally asked.

"Jack's an asshole. I can't stand working with him."

"And?"

"He's rude. He's-he's selfish and thinks he knows everything."

"And?"

"And...I don't like working with him. He gets on my nerves and it's only the second damned day!" Her arms flared up around her.

"Is that it?"

She looked down at the new, very visible, scratch on his desk. She slumped back in the seat and nodded. "Yeah. I just think it might be a good idea if I work with someone closer to my age."

"That's not possible, Jardine. I'm short-staffed this week and I need you two to work together."

She rolled her eyes. "Just this week?"

"Don't know. Could be longer."

She glanced down at her hand and picked at one of the cuticles again. "Just what I need."

"Jardine, sometimes you'll be partnered with people you work well with. Sometimes you won't. But that shouldn't bring down the quality of *your* work or prevent *you* from doing your job in the first place."

"I understand that. It's just—his personality and mine are not cohesive. We're like oil and vinegar. Like bleach and ammonia. Like—"

"Jardine. You have years of experience working in a team

environment. Kinston doesn't. So teach him."

She scoffed. "How? He thinks he's God's shiny new gift to this department. How do I work with a personality like that, sir?"

"Play into his ego."

"What?"

"Ask him for his opinion. Think like he does. What will make him easier to work with?"

"A muzzle," she muttered under her breath.

"Jardine, don't let his attitude—or that of anyone else's—bring you down to their level. I expect better from you."

"Yes, sir." She tore more skin off her finger.

"Where do you think we should go from here?" Conrad asked.

"With Jack or the case?"

"You tell me."

"Are you playing into *my* ego now?"

He gave her a solemn look and leaned his head to one side like a disapproving father.

She sighed and thought about the right response. "I think Smith's death complicates things, to say the least."

"Agreed. What else?"

"Until we talk to the coroner, I think the best approach is to find out more about Amanda. She mentioned a few things that sparked my interest."

"Like what?"

"She said she renamed the road she lives on. It's Native American."

"Anything else?"

"Yeah. I think I should look into how her husband died. If that's really why she's willing to talk to me, then maybe that's how I can get her to talk. Find out about her past and maybe that provides answers in the present?"

"Good. Call around and see what you can uncover."

"Yes, sir. Is that all?"

"For now." He turned his attention back to his computer monitor, looking at it from above his bifocals.

She stood up and looked down at his desk. Guilt crept in again.

"Sir, I can fix that scratch."

"AJ?" His voice was tender and, when he looked at her, she saw a slight twinkle in his eye. "Get out of my office."

—¡—

The overhead fluorescent lights went out. Startled, she looked at the time.

"Oh, shit!"

She jumped up, causing pain to rip through the right side of her abdomen. She had not moved in hours from her chair and she regretted getting lost in her work. As her fingers from one hand massaged the tight muscles, she grabbed her phone from underneath the piles of papers with the other. She dialed her mom's phone number and listened for the rings.

"Hello, habibti," Jamilla answered.

"Momma, I'm so sorry! I forgot to get Eoghan from school. I've been doing some research and lost track of time. I'm leaving the office now."

"*Shway shway!* Slow down, Ameena. First, I told you this morning, I would get my grandbabies. Second, he's here. He rode the bus home."

"He did?"

"Yes, sweetheart. The sports were canceled this afternoon. So, he came home."

She sat back down in her desk, slightly relieved. Her right side still throbbed.

"Habibti, are you still there?"

"Yes, Momma, I'm just staring at the mess on my desk."

"Oh, okay. Are you coming home soon?"

"Yeah, I'll be there in a bit. I need to go through the stuff I printed and then I'll be home."

"Okay. Just be careful."

"I will, Momma."

"I love you."

"Love you, too." She hung up the phone before her mother

could say anything else, then stared at all the papers on her desk. She started sorting them into piles.

One of the documents caught her attention again:

TRANSCRIPT OF WITNESS INTERVIEW
(Clean Verbatim)

After another read through, she marked up the document and walked it over to Conrad's office. The light was off. She tried the knob.

Locked. Of course, you idiot, why wouldn't it be? She slid the document under his door. *We'll see what he thinks.*

AJ left for the night, hoping she made the right analysis.

—¡—

CHAPTER 15

THOUGHT you'd find this interesting. See the areas I underlined. ~AJ

TRANSCRIPT OF WITNESS INTERVIEW (Clean Verbatim)

INTERVIEWER: The day is Saturday, April 13, 1985. The time is 9:05 am. This is Sargent David Brady of the Franklin Police Department. This interview is being recorded in Interview Room 2 of FPD's main building. Please state your full name and address into the microphone.

AMANDA CLAREMONT: My name is Amanda Marie Claremont. I live at 21 Bates Creek Road in the City of Franklin. New Hampshire. I don't know why I'm saying the state. You know that already.

S.B.: That's okay, Mrs. Claremont. It's okay to be nervous.

A.C.: I'm sorry. I've never done this before. I'm still taking everything in.

S.B: It's okay. Can you please tell me your relationship to Robert Daniel Claremont?

A.C.: He's my husband...was...I guess he was my husband.

S.B.: How long were you two married?

A.C.: We've been married around thirteen years.

S.B.: And can you tell us the last time you saw Mr. Claremont, your husband?

A.C.: I told you all this months ago.

S.B.: I understand, Mrs. Claremont. But we have to repeat everything for the record.

A.C.: Okay...

S.B.: Mrs. Claremont?

A.C.: Yes, sir?

S.B.: When was the last time you saw your husband?

A.C.: It was on a Sunday morning, last year.

S.B.: And what was the date, specifically?

A.C.: <u>Sunday, May 6, 1984</u>...[inaudible]

S.B.: What was that?

A.C.: The last time I saw Robert.

S.B. Sunday, May 6th was the last time you saw your

husband?

A.C. Yes.

S.B.: Okay. Okay. What can you tell me about that day?

A.C.: It started out like most mornings. I woke up before he did and made him breakfast. He always asks for breakfast the same way. On Sundays, he always wants three pancakes, butter in between each. Two strips of bacon, never touching. Syrup bottle to the right of his plate. Coffee to the left. Always coffee to the left.

S.B.: How can you remember that after all these months?

A.C.: Because Robert is extremely specific in what he wants. Everything in the house has to be a certain order. He gets very unhappy if things aren't the way he wants. And breakfast on Sundays are always specific. Every breakfast is specific. When he works, he always wants three scrambled eggs with two pieces of toast. Never touching. Newspaper to the right. Coffee on the left.

S.B.: Okay. Okay. Can you tell me what happened after breakfast?

A.C.: He told me he'd been working on a big project. He'd been staying late at night all week. I didn't question it. I just made sure to have his dinner ready and waiting in the microwave. I know Robert well enough after so many years of marriage that when he worked late on project deadlines, he'd be under a lot of stress. And he liked to go walking on Sunday mornings, alone mind you, and clear his head.

S.B.: And you didn't think anything of it?

A.C.: Of course not! He walked out the door, went down the driveway. Sometimes he walks all the way to work and will stay overnight. It's not unusual for him to be gone all day. Or even the next day.

S.B.: And what did you do when he didn't come back that afternoon?

A.C.: I worked in my garden. The Thaw had passed, and we needed to get the vegetables in the ground soon. Then, I just waited. Like I always do.

S.B.: And what did you do after you worked in the garden?

A.C.: I came in the house, took a shower, and then started dinner.

S.B.: Do you remember what time that was?

A.C.: Of course not. That was almost a year ago. I just remember it was in the afternoon and the sun was starting to set. It wasn't late, but it was after two or three. I remember that.

S.B.: Okay. Okay. Fair enough. So, the last time you saw him was that afternoon.

A.C.: ...Did you not hear what I just said? [inaudible]

S.B.: I'm sorry, can you repeat that.

A.C.: I said you're an asshole! You're telling me that the body you just found is my husband's and questioning me like I'm a suspect and responsible! Do you think I murdered my own husband and spent months

<u>contacting you and waiting for any updates?</u>

S.B.: Mrs. Claremont, please sit back down. That's not what I'm implying.

A.C.: That IS what you're implying! [talking over S.B.]

S.B.: Mrs. Claremont, I apologize. I know this isn't easy for you, but we're trying to understand your husband's last moments and determine if there's been foul play or if this was a natural death.

A.C.: <u>What is natural about finding a body—my husband—in a ravine off the side of the road a few miles from our home?</u>

S.B.: I understand.

A.C.: No! No, you don't!

S.B.: Do you remember seeing anyone else on the road with him?

A.C.: Cars come and go all the time down our road. Even farm equipment. Did I see anyone else? No. How could I? I was working on the garden most of the day and came inside in the afternoon to shower. Robert hates coming home to a dirty house.

S.B.: Okay. Okay. So, you didn't see anyone on the road?

A.C.: No.

S.B.: No other walkers or runners?

A.C.: No.

S.B.: And you didn't see any strange cars driving slow?

A.C.: [inaudible]

S.B.: For the record, Mrs. Claremont shook her head no. And what did you do that evening?

A.C.: Roberts hates coming home to a dirty house, so I immediately took a shower. Then I scrubbed the bathroom and mopped the floors. I always start his dinner around 5:00 or 5:30 pm. He's always home by 6:00 pm during the weekdays and most weekends. Unless he's working late. Then it could be closer to midnight.

S.B.: Okay. Okay. So, it gets late. His dinner is getting cold. He's not home yet. Then what did you do?

A.C.: When it got dark, I assumed he kept walking to town or maybe stopped at the package store and called his secretary to pick him up. [inaudible]

S.B.: His secretary?

A.C.: Yes, sir.

S.B.: Do you know the secretary's name?

A.C.: No, sir. He had quite a few working for him at the firm over the years. They would always come and go.

S.B.: So, you think it's possible his secretary picked him up?

A.C.: Yes, sir.

S.B.: And that Robert would've stayed overnight at

the firm?

A.C.: It's not unusual. He keeps an extra suit in his office. And a spare toothbrush. He likes good hygiene. Sometimes he will work through the weekends to finish up a Monday deadline. I've just learned not to question him.

S.B.: Okay. Okay. So, he probably went to work that evening. Would he have spent the night at the office or maybe a hotel?

A.C.: I'm not sure. He's done both before, but he really hates to spend money. If I were to guess, he probably spent the night at the office.

S.B.: So, he spent the night at the office?

A.C.: Maybe.

S.B.: Why didn't you call the office the next day, on Monday, to find out if he was there?

A.C.: I DID call his office! I called to see if he'd come in that morning, but they said he hadn't made it in yet. I think they said he could be running late. I didn't think anything of it.

S.B.: And why's that?

A.C.: Robert doesn't like it when I call him at the office. He doesn't like to be bothered. Especially if he has a deadline. The last thing I wanted to do was ruin his routine. He'd be furious with me.

S.B.: Okay. Okay. So, the office hadn't heard from him either?

A.C.: [inaudible]

S.B.: For the record, can you respond louder, please?

A.C.: No. The office hadn't heard from him either.

S.B.: And what did you do Monday, while you thought Robert would be at work?

A.C.: I did more gardening.

S.B.: More gardening?

A.C.: Sargent Brady, you and Officer Matthews came to visit me that Tuesday, and I told you the same thing. You've seen my gardens. You know for a fact how big they are and how much time it takes to prep a garden by yourself! Why are you accusing me of not doing what I told you I was doing? Do you think I did something to my husband?

S.B.: Mrs. Claremont, you're right. I do remember seeing your gardens and your house. Let me state for the record that on Tuesday, May 8th, myself and Patrolman Matthews were at the Claremont residence interviewing Mrs. Claremont. We can confirm her statement.

A.C.: Thank you.

S.B. Tell me about Monday night. What happened?

A.C.: I had a full day in the garden again. Got most of the rows raked, weeds pulled. Started sowing some seeds. I was exhausted at the end of the day but assumed Robert would be home later that evening. Again, I didn't want to call him at the office. He wouldn't like that. And when he wasn't home for dinner, I assumed it was another late night. I left his dinner in the microwave and a note on the table telling him I was going to bed early. I fell asleep very quickly after my head hit the pillow.

S.B.: Did you wake up in the middle of the night? Did Robert come home that night?

A.C.: I'm a light sleeper and would've heard him come in the house. But he didn't.

S.B.: And what did you do the following morning, that Tuesday?

A.C.: When I woke up that morning, I saw the note still on the table and his dinner still in the microwave. That's highly unusual for him. That's when I realized something might be wrong. That's when I called you and you came over to take my statement.

S.B.: Okay. Okay. Did you receive any phone calls or visitors while Robert was gone?

A.C.: [inaudible]

S.B.: No?

A.C.: No. Robert and I didn't have many friends or colleagues come to the house. Robert didn't like other people in our home.

S.B.: Don't you find that odd?

A.C.: Robert is—was—a private person.

S.B.: Did you receive any phone calls while Robert was gone?

A.C.: In the last ten months? Of course.

S.B.: Okay. Okay. Is there anyone you can think of that might try to harm Mr. Claremont? Do you know of anyone who would want to murder your husband?

A.C.: Robert didn't talk about work much and he rarely went anywhere. He liked to be at home after work. If he had any enemies, it might be someone from work, but I honestly don't know.

S.B.: Okay. Okay. And is there anything you can tell me about the last several months? What you've done? If you've heard anything?

A.C.: You have all the records. You've seen how many times I've called and hoped for some word of my husband.

S.B.: Yes, ma'am. We have. We just need to verify everything again. Go over it one more time.

A.C.: I followed your instructions and six months after Robert went missing with no trace, with no news, I filed for a death certificate, but the town clerk told me the county refused to honor it without actual evidence of a crime committed or death.

S.B.: Did you talk to any of his family or friends?

A.C.: Robert had no family. He was an only child and both his parents died in a car crash last summer. That was up on the Kang in Lincoln. No one attended their funerals. It was such a shame Robert missed it. That's when I really knew he was gone. I felt it.

S.B.: You felt what?

A.C.: Robert would've been to his parents' funerals. I don't doubt that. And when he never showed, my heart told me something had happened to him.

S.B.: And did he have any other family or friends

show up to the funerals?

A.C.: He didn't have any other family that I know. I think he said they all passed. His mom was an only child and his father had only one brother who died from a bicycle accident. That's all I know.

S.B.: Okay. Okay. Now, I know my next question might sound a little personal, and I do apologize in advance. But this is something we need to ask. Amanda, was Robert ever abusive towards you? Did he ever harm or hurt you?

A.C.: My husband is strict. He can be demanding. He can appear to be cruel at times. But he is my husband and I support him in every way. He works—worked? I don't even know if I should use present tense or past tense right now!

S.B.: Mrs. Claremont, please take your time.

A.C.: My husband worked long hours at his firm. He was under constant pressure and stress and all kinds of negative things. He never wanted me to work, so I stayed at home. Yes, he expected me to be the caretaker, but I wanted to do that. I wanted to take care of everything for him because I knew he deserved it. I kept up with the gardens, I cleaned the house, I cooked for him. I did everything for him so that when he came home, his dinner was waiting and he'd be happy. I liked it better when he was happy. If you don't mind, I need to leave. I need to talk to the funeral director now.

S.B.: Sure, Mrs. Claremont. This was just an informal conversation. That's all. And, Mrs. Claremont, on behalf of the police department here, we're sorry for your loss.

A.C.: Thank you.

S.B.: Thank you for coming in. If you think of anything else that can help us find who did this to your husband, here's my business card. Don't hesitate to contact me.

A.C.: Thank you, Sargent Brady.

S.B.: For the record, Mrs. Claremont has left the room. This concludes the interview.

END TRANSCRIPT

—¡—

Wednesday, May 9, 2018

CHAPTER 16

HE HANDED the witness statement back to AJ and watched her pass it to Jack. As the kid flipped through the report, Conrad studied her. She appeared calmer, more confident than the previous day.

I'm still trusting my gut on this one. She's showing more initiative than I imagined.

"Okay," Jack finally said, giving the papers back to AJ, "she likes to garden. What about it?"

"It's not just the gardening. Did you see the other stuff I underlined?"

"Her husband was a hard ass. So?"

"Jack, have you ever taken any criminal psychology classes?"

Before he could answer, Conrad redirected the subject. "Jardine, start from the first page and explain what you see."

"Sir, it starts off like any interview, but did you notice the date? Her husband disappeared on the same day Michael Smith was found. Exactly thirty-four years ago."

"Could just be a coincidence," Jack said.

"Possibly, but she keeps repeating some of the same things

over and over. She talks about Robert being very specific about certain things and talks about her gardens all the time."

"Maybe she's lonely after her husband died."

"Jardine, did you find out how Mr. Claremont died?" Conrad asked.

"Not yet, sir. Just that his body was found in the ravine after the Thaw started."

"What else can you tell us?"

"Honestly, sir? I think Amanda could be an abuse victim and Robert was violent towards her."

Jack scoffed. "You got all that from an interview?"

AJ nodded. "Amanda repeatedly said she always did what he told her. She never wanted to displease him. That's what an abuse victim says."

"How do you know that?" Jack asked.

Conrad watched her reaction to the question. He already knew the answer.

She hesitated and blinked her eyes for a split second longer than normal. "I've seen it firsthand."

He saw Jack about to respond but cut in first. "What else can you tell me about the statement?"

"It's possible Robert was obsessive-compulsive. Amanda almost sounded…programmed."

"Programmed?"

She nodded. "It's a survival mechanism for some abuse victims. They're physically, emotionally, and-or sexually assaulted and broken mentally. They fear their abuser and can't escape from them. They're trained or programmed to respond a certain way."

Jack scoffed again. "That's absurd. Just leave. It's easy."

Conrad stood up and yanked his jacket down. He walked around the desk, then opened his office door. "Mr. Kinston, let's talk outside. Jardine, wait here."

The Deputy Director glanced at AJ and saw confusion on her face. He returned his gaze to the younger detective. The two men walked down the hallway to the print room area, well out of earshot. He crossed his arms over his chest.

"Mr. Kinston, do you have any experience with domestic violence?"

"No, why?"

"When we deal with domestic violence victims—or relatives of someone who's been murdered—it requires a certain amount of tact, discretion, and understanding. It requires compassion. And the best way to provide that is to keep quiet and listen to what they say. There are always hidden meanings behind their words. Do you understand, detective?"

"Yeah, I guess."

"When we are trying to solve a case or pursue leads, it's also important to brainstorm and problem solve. You have to keep an open mind. About everything. Don't make assumptions on what you know or think you know. It could get you hurt. Or even killed. Understand?"

"Yeah, I got it. Mouth shut, brain open." Jack raised a closed hand to his head and then popped his fingers open.

Conrad walked out of the print room as his subordinate followed. Halfway between the print room and his office, he stopped. "And Mr. Kinston?"

"Yeah?"

"Jardine's history is none of your damned business. Don't ask her any personal questions."

They walked back into the office and took their seats again. Conrad straightened his posture in his chair. "Jardine, please continue."

She looked at Jack then back at her boss, concern on her face. "Uhm, I don't remember where I was, sir."

"Domestic violence victims can't leave their abuser."

"Oh. Yeah. I think it's possible Robert was violent towards her and she was so brainwashed she couldn't see it. She kept saying he was 'specific'. He may have been obsessive-compulsive. Insistent on order. Controlling. Manipulated everything in her life. She had to keep everything clean, including herself. She was cut off from the outside world. Her only comfort or connection or even joy, for that matter, was gardening. And that could be why she turned it into a successful business.

"Also, Robert had no family, no connection with anyone else except her. Sometimes children who grow up with no family have tendencies to be loners or don't fully develop healthy bonds with others. Yesterday, she mentioned that after Robert died, she boarded up the house and left for a while. That was probably her first taste of freedom."

"It's possible. Anything else?"

"Maybe. I've noticed something about her facial expressions. They almost appear rigid, devoid of emotion, from time to time. Certain topics will generate an emotional response, but that's it. It's hard to pinpoint."

"Could that be because she's a businesswoman?" Jack asked.

"Could be."

Conrad nodded, then looked at Jack. "Mr. Kinston, what are your observations?"

"I don't know. She doesn't look capable of hurting anyone, much less a man half her age and twice her size. As far as the statement, I didn't see a victim. She's a widow grieving for her husband whose body was found months after he disappeared. Wouldn't anyone else react that way?"

"People respond to grief in different ways. Any other observations you want to share about the last two days?"

"That Maria chick seems creepy," Jack replied. "Did you see her glaring at all of us? It's almost like she wanted to stab us in the back with her eyes."

"Maybe just you," AJ muttered under her breath.

Conrad stood up before he heard any more bantering. "If neither of you have anything else, let's head back to the farm and finish our interviews. Today will be busy."

—¡—

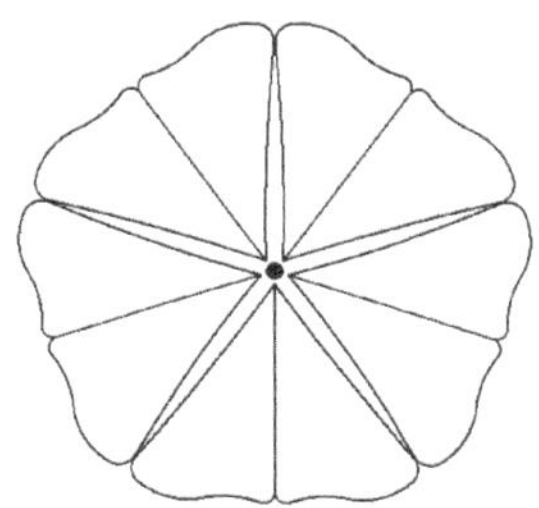

CHAPTER 17

EVER SINCE she could remember, AJ loved gardens. The colors. Smells. Feel of dirt on her hands. She could not help but smile as she stuck her fingers in one of the flowerpots and felt the damp, spongy soil.

"I see what you mean."

Amanda smiled back at the detective. "Good. Till up the soil a bit. You can use a small cultivator, nothing fancy. They make hand-held ones. The key is to make sure the soil can drain properly. Lilies need proper watering, but they don't do good with any standing water."

"And you think that's why I didn't have any luck last year with them?"

"Possibly. It's hard to tell the first year or so. Gardening requires patience and dedication. Sometimes you have to listen to the plants telling you what works and what doesn't."

AJ wiped her hands on the towel Amanda gave her. "Do you think my idea on the sunflowers will be okay?"

"I don't see why not. The stalks are more fragile than people think. The weight of a sunflower can sometimes cause them to droop like decaying candy canes with heads so big they arch like watching vultures. Just make sure they get full sun."

She handed the towel back. "They will. It's in the open part of our land, so plenty of sun."

"Let me show you a little area I'm working on. I think you'll really appreciate this one."

The detective followed Amanda around and behind the red nursery barn. On the back wall of the building were two benches. Framed lattices scaled the building's exterior on each side of the sitting area. Underneath, small gardens sported dark soils and green seedlings.

"Morning glories!" AJ smiled at Amanda. "I recognize those little heart-shaped leaves!"

"Thought you'd appreciate them." Amanda eased down on one bench and leaned against the building. She looked out at her property, then closed her eyes.

AJ sat on the other bench and scanned the horizon. To the left were the cornfields and stone pyramid structures. In front of her were the fenced off croplands. She could hear the chickens nearby. A cow mooed in the distance. Birds chattered and chirped all around her. The sun felt warm on her face and radiated off the siding; it was a glorious feeling. The energy of the plants around her made her want to go home and prepare her own flower beds.

"Why'd you stop growing morning glories?" Amanda finally asked.

AJ looked at her hands and the torn cuticles. "I wanted to leave the past in Texas, I guess."

"You can't run away from your past. No matter how far you travel or how far forward you keep going, it's always there in your wake. It will always catch up, always find you. And one day, you'll need to face it."

The detective leaned her head against the building. "You're right. Everything reminds me of my husband. I've just tried my best to leave it all behind. Out of sight, out of mind."

"And how has that worked for you?"

"Heh. It hasn't."

"Then maybe it's time to change that." Amanda stood up and dusted her overalls. "I'll be right back."

AJ watched the older woman walk off. She looked around again and could see a few men in the distance carrying large rocks and repairing the property stone walls. A couple of other men walked the edge of the barbed wire around the property, testing and repairing sections as needed.

Sound began to emanate from within the main building. Flute music. Subtle Native American flute music, enough to relax her mind as she let the warmth of the sun seep through her clothes.

Several minutes later, Amanda walked back.

"These are for you, my dear." The older woman handed her a large paper bag.

"Ms. Claremont, thank you! But I can't accept any gifts. It could be seen as a conflict of interest." AJ tried to give the bag back to Amanda, but the woman shook her head.

"Then give them to your family. Think of it as a pre-paid purchase for a starting gardener. Go ahead. Look inside."

AJ peered into the bag. Dozens of seed packages and a box were inside. She pulled each item out. Morning glories, foxgloves, columbine, petunia, and sunflowers—these were just a few of the variety given. She pulled out the box and opened it. A ring attached to thick string lay inside. She wrapped a finger around the ring and pulled the object out.

"It's beautiful!"

An ornate hummingbird feeder swayed back and forth on the string. The spiraling ruby red glass sparkled in the sun. Small glass flowers necked out of the bottom. Little metal perches branched out for tiny feet.

"This is one of my favorite feeders," Amanda said.

"I don't know what to say." AJ smiled. "Thank you, but I really shouldn't—"

"Nonsense. Think of it as a gift from one mother to yours. It's a starter kit for hummingbirds."

"My mom will love this. She may try to keep it on a shelf instead of putting it to use."

Amanda chuckled. "It's meant to serve a purpose. She can always come back to get more." Before AJ could counter with her argument, she continued, "Does your mom like to garden like you do?"

"Not as much. She loves to cook and host family gatherings. And dote on her grandkids."

"Very maternal, I take it?"

AJ nodded. "Sometimes a little over-protective and overbearing, but that's just how she is. Always very supportive of us, though."

"That's good. Are you close to her?"

AJ thought about the question. She wanted to keep Amanda talking, to open up more to her. If the compromise was her own personal information, she was fine with that.

"Yes. We're pretty close. I'm the only girl."

"The oldest?"

"Yeah, how did you know?"

"You carry it with you."

"I don't understand."

Amanda walked over to the other bench and sat down. "You carry an independence and authority when you walk. It makes sense that you're the oldest child."

"You can tell that from my steps?"

"Heh. Not just that. You aren't afraid to take control or do what's right. You want to set a good example for others."

"I guess that's true."

"I like that. It makes me wonder if my child would've turned out the same way, like us. Doing what we think is right." Amanda stared at the detective. "Ya know, you're about her same age."

AJ scrunched her eyebrows and studied the woman. "You have a daughter?"

Amanda leaned back against the siding and closed her eyes to the sun. "Careful the questions you ask, detective. You may not expect the answers."

—¡—

CHAPTER 18

"LEAVE the door unlocked."

That's what my great grandmother, my Gramma, used to tell me. I lived with her a short time while I was pregnant.

Yes, I was pregnant at one point. It was back in the early seventies. I'd been married to Robert only a short time, but we separated during my first trimester. I was really young—sixteen, to be exact—and I didn't know what I was doing at that age. I thought I finally understood love.

Things didn't work out, so I left for a little bit. I didn't know where else to go. No one wanted a pregnant teenager in their home, but Gramma didn't mind. So, I went to stay with her. She cared for me and taught me how to get back on my feet.

But the thing she used to tell me: "Leave the door unlocked." She always left the front door unlocked, hoping one day her Ernest would come home. He was actually lost at sea and never really came back, but she never lost hope.

Audrey—that's her name—was born in the late 1800s. She met my great grandfather, Ernest, on a farm. They immediately fell in love. The way she spoke of him, I've never seen anything like it.

It was a raw and unbridled love I wish I'd known. Never had it with Robert or anyone else, for that matter.

Audrey was ninety-three when she died. She only ever had one child, a girl, my grandmother, Victoria. Audrey was pregnant when Ernest's ship, the *Osminog*, was lost at sea.

Victoria was born in 1900. I don't know much about her. I know that she died in childbirth with her last daughter, Helen, back in 1934. Victoria had a few kids, but I don't know what happened to the rest of them. I wasn't really close with that side of the family.

Helen, my mom—well, to be honest, my mother. "Mom" is not the proper word I would use here.

Helen was not quite right in the head. I don't know if that was from the difficult childbirth, or if the doctors did something to her, or if she was just naturally born that way. But she never was right in the head.

My mother was always very impressionable. Very gullible. Her parents were always looking after her, trying to keep her out of trouble. But she was different. Had a fleeting mind of her own that didn't match anyone else's.

I was born in 1956. Helen had me at the age of twenty-two. Back then, that was considered old to have a first child, but she didn't care. She never told anyone who the father was. Imagine growing up, not knowing your father, as the bastard child of the family. It did not make me a popular person.

But Helen didn't care. She was always on a different plane of thinking. The family didn't like her much. They thought her interest in astrology and ancient mysteries of the world was devil work. They didn't like it when she asked what their moon or rising sign was, or things like that.

She thought she could heal people with her hands. She thought she could just hover her palm over a sore and they would heal faster. She scared away many people, and as a result, she was shunned. I think that just added to her mental instability.

When I was younger, she talked of dying. She welcomed death. Why would someone with so much to live for be so willing to die? It didn't make sense to me at the time. It excited her, though.

She thought she would exist in a different reality. Maybe she does now, I don't know.

She was so focused on herself, she didn't pay attention to me. I basically grew up taking care of her, not the other way around. And she wasn't surprised when I approached her at the age of 16 and told her I was about to get married.

Helen was actually happy for me. It was not the response I wanted from her. I wanted her to be angry, protective of me, anything but happy. I honestly don't know if she realized I would not be there to help her anymore. I don't know if that's what drove her to jump off that bridge.

From the look on your face, I take it you were not expecting to hear something so morbid? It's fine.

I guess Helen didn't—in her own way—take it well that I was getting married and leaving her. Then again, I don't know if she really understood what was happening.

She didn't seem depressed. She didn't seem upset. She was just constantly happy.

It happened a few months after Robert and I were married. It's one of those things that stays with you the rest of your life. She telephoned me that morning and told me she wanted to have breakfast at a local diner, here in downtown Franklin.

I told her I would meet her there and we chatted like everything was fine. She wanted to know how the marriage was going, normal things like that.

I'll never forget her smile. She seemed to glow sitting there across the table from me, enjoying her coffee and cigarette. Her makeup was perfect, her hair pinned back in stylish curl. She wore a beautiful white dress. I can still envision her face right now. When she smiled, her teeth were neatly framed by ruby red lipstick. She focused the conversation on me and didn't say much about herself.

We left the diner, hand-in-hand, and walked down the sidewalk away from the activity there. She was so happy, oblivious to some of the things that I told her were wrong in my marriage. To this day, I don't think she was concerned. Or maybe she couldn't remember. Or maybe she didn't even hear me, I don't know.

She wanted to walk down one of the trails here in town that meandered along the Winnipesaukee River. So, we walked together down the dirt path. The trees kept most of the way hidden, but I do remember the path inclined a bit. Our shoes were getting muddy and the bottom of her dress was soaked in mud. But she didn't care.

We approached an old train track, and she proceeded to walk across. I followed. It was an old mill bridge the railroads used, overlooking the Winnie. We held out our arms and balanced ourselves across the iron beams until we were halfway above the water.

She started telling me stories about the angels and birdies who were visiting her each day. She described each in incredible detail, talking about the vibrancy and color they held. She described their wings, some translucent and some dull. At first, I thought this was just another one of her stories she made up in her head. But the visions were so elaborate and the look in her eyes was so intense, I started to believe they were real.

"Angels and birdies?" I finally asked her.

She nodded, continuing to smile. "Yes, darling. They've asked me to join them. Each day they're more insistent. They're practically begging me now!"

"Helen,"—I didn't call her 'Mother', I called her by her first name—"What angels and birdies? Is this just your mind creating another one of your imaginative stories?"

"No, my sweet child. These are not just stories. These are legends, myths that are actually true. You'll see, just wait, my darling flower. One day, you'll see."

She held her arms out again and spun around like she was dancing. Perhaps the music she waltzed to were the winds on leaves and the chorus was nothing more than the birds around us. But she laughed and laughed and looked me in the eyes one more time.

"I'll see you again one day, my little bird."

And without warning, she fell backward.

I remember seeing the sheer fabric of her dress floating in front of her against the pull of gravity. I remember the mess of her hair trying to escape her head and how her feet came up above her body.

It was the very first time I ever saw that much blood. What didn't coat the dry rocks, swirled and feathered into nothingness with the turbulent flow. Helen, there, spread like a fallen angel, surrounded in crimson tide. She died looking at the heavens with a smile on her face.

I'd never seen my mother so happy. I've never had her treat me as a daughter as much as she did that day.

Honestly, it was one of the most beautiful things I saw, her blood on the stones, disappearing downstream in the Winnipesaukee River.

I know that sounds awful, to talk about how beautiful her unexpected and very tragic death was. But do you want to know what I found most profound? Why I thought it was the most beautiful thing?

Because no one dictated how she lived. She controlled her own life.

So isn't it fitting she controlled her death, too?

—¡—

CHAPTER 19

ANOTHER dead end with another employee.

Conrad and Jack questioned every laborer in the cornfield. Each gave the same response: they did not know how Michael Smith wound up tangled in barbed wire with his throat slit.

"Maybe it was an accident?" "I think it was that Maria chick. She don't like us no bit." "Bet he slipped on the rocks trying to climb the wall and sliced his neck himself." "Not sure what he was doing around here again. Thought he'd left." Each man offered a different plausible explanation.

"How many more employees do we have left?" Jack asked, brushing the dirt off his pants leg. Conrad noted the frown and frustration. Patience was not the young detective's virtue.

The Deputy Director made a beeline for the fence, ignoring Jack's question. He stepped on the other side to the grass path along the parking area then stopped on the gravel to wait for the young man.

From behind, he heard the tractors start back up, continuing on their cultivating path. The apple orchard and winery to his right were not as busy, probably due to the early season. He looked over to his left to see a few dozen cars parked around the greenhouses and nursery. Overall, Amanda's business was quite impressive. He had never seen such a large establishment in central New Hampshire.

Jack finally caught up with him. "Where are we going now? Are we leaving yet?"

"No, Kinston. We're not done."

They walked towards the main building, across the flat grass field, no doubt used for a few hundred parked cars. Tall masonry walls stood like building blocks to their left. Each contained a variety of mulch, stone, and dirt. Trucks lined up in front of their selected block and men loaded up trailers and beds with necessary material. Next door, the barn doors were thrown open and agricultural equipment came and went.

He wondered how Amanda could afford so much gravel and porous pavers, much less the amount of equipment used. Being an astute business owner was one thing. But this tract of land? It was an efficient marvel of ingenuity. He pulled out his bifocals, put them on, then pulled out his notepad and a pen. He flipped to the last page and started writing.

"What are you doing?" Jack asked.

"Writing down a thought."

"Why don't you just voice record it or type it up in your Notes app?"

"I use a flip phone." He continued to write down his thoughts.

Jack laughed. "Seriously? You don't use a smartphone? Not even a voice recorder?"

"No. I find those invasive and unreliable. Writing my thoughts on a piece of paper allows me to think clearer and see the bigger picture."

"But it takes longer. What if you lose your notepad?"

"I don't."

"You could always back up the data in a cloud service."

Conrad finished his thoughts, stuck everything back inside his suit pocket, and then answered his detective. "Mr. Kinston, I prefer to keep my thoughts to myself until I have more evidence and data for any case I work on. That's why I write everything down. Everything digital is traceable and hackable. Sensitive—or, worse yet, speculative—information has no business in a cloud service or on a server."

"Isn't that old school mentality, though? What if a building burns down and you lose all your notepads?"

"It's better to permanently lose information than to have it be abused or used against someone. Knowledge is power. And power is a very dangerous thing in the wrong hands."

They continued their walk past the rows of potted trees and over to the nursery area. Both men entered the nearest domed greenhouse.

Both ends of the structure were open with a large fan hanging on one end pushing fresh air into the space. Thick semi-opaque polymer arched across the skeletal aluminum frame. Rows of hanging pots lined each side of the center walkway. Vines crept down, begging to touch a passerby. Landscaping fabric carpeted the floor, and cinder blocks—used as table legs with long sheets of plywood and recycled doors on top—held the weed cloth down. Each make-shift table was filled with planters. Flowers exploded everywhere in streaks of vibrant color.

Conrad could feel the humidity and dampness lingering on the one end of the greenhouse. The collar of his dress shirt stuck to the back of his neck. He got a whiff of damp mulch and fertilizer followed by the strong aroma of primrose and lilac. He saw Jack reach up and cover his nose. Evidently, gardening did not sit well with the young detective.

An employee pulled a water hose behind, giving a final tug on the hose, then checked the end attachment. She adjusted the nozzle until it released a fine mist. Satisfied, she began methodically watering the flowers up and down the table. She held the nozzle and released the mist slowly over each row from front to back. At the end of the row, she released the nozzle and began the same routine again.

Conrad walked over to the young woman. After introductions,

he asked her name.

"Emily Vanderbilt."

"How long have you worked here, Ms. Vanderbilt?"

"Um, about two months now, I guess?" She continued her focus on the plants, misting them from front to back.

"You 'guess'?" Jack asked.

She looked around her then nodded and returned her focus to her work. "Haven't been here that long." She gave a new row of flowers a misting from front to back.

"Ms. Vanderbilt, did you know a Michael Smith?"

She shook her head. Another mist, front to back.

"Do you know of any men who work here?"

"No. We don't work with any of them. We're not allowed to talk to them much either."

"Why not?" Jack got the question in before Conrad.

"Mr. Kinston, please let me ask the questions." The Deputy Director watched the employee do another swipe front to back. "Ms. Vanderbilt, may I ask why?"

She stopped and looked up at him. Her eyes were distant with sadness and the line across her mouth tightened. She looked over beyond his shoulder and her expression changed. Her eyes widened slightly.

"I can't talk right now." She turned her body back to the flowers. Another pass with the water hose. Front to back.

Conrad turned around to see what spooked the woman.

—¡—

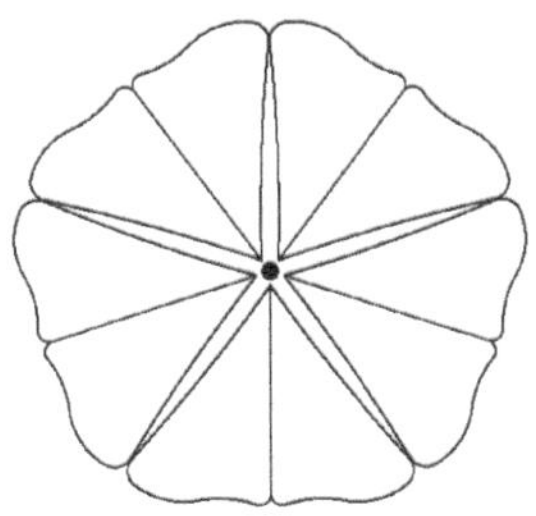

CHAPTER 20

UNSURE of what to say, she stared blankly at Amanda, waiting for the woman to continue. She could not imagine how a tragedy like that—watching your own mother commit suicide—could affect someone's life. She did not want to even think about it. Instead, she leaned her head back against the building's siding and stared blankly at the field in front of her.

Amanda finally broke the tension. "Tell me more about your mother, AJ. What's your family life like?"

"My mom is passionate. She commands the house and everyone listens to her. I'd say she is definitely the matriarch of the family."

"And you're fine with that?"

"Of course. Everyone knows their place and has a role to play in the house. My kids are happy. I'm happy."

"And what about your father?"

"My step-dad works for the school. He used to be a coach when he was younger. After his knees started hurting, he decided to teach science at the middle school."

"And what about your real father?"

"I," AJ hesitated, "I don't have a relationship with him."

"And why's that?"

"I'd prefer not to say right now, if you don't mind." AJ looked at Amanda. She expected to see pity or empathy in the woman's face, but her expression remained emotionless. "It's very personal for me and difficult to talk about."

"I understand all too well. Sometimes it's not what you say that has the biggest impact. Sometimes it's what you *don't* say."

Amanda stood up. She grabbed the walkie-talkie from her hip and flipped it on. "Abby, I'm behind the nursery. Can you come here, please?"

A pop of static came out of the speaker and then a cheerful voice replied. "Sure thing!"

Another pop of static clicked the device off. Amanda clipped it back to her pocket. She tucked a few strands of hair behind her ears. She then checked her hands and rubbed them together. "Hands can tell you stories of the quality of life you live. Did you know that?"

"No, ma'am." AJ looked down at her hands and the torn cuticles.

"Your hands show the rough life you've lived, detective. They show the secrets you don't want to tell. The tics of time."

Before AJ could reply, a young blonde in her early twenties walked out of the nursery doors and smiled when she saw the two women.

"AJ, this is Abby. She's been with me—how many years has it been, flower?"

"Oh," Abby said, "I think about four years now." She looked at the detective and smiled. Carefree strands of hair surrounding apple-shaped cheeks made the young woman appear almost fairy-like.

"Have a seat and tell AJ your story. I'm going to check on our other guests. I'll be back soon."

Abby smiled as her boss walked off. She sat down on the bench and turned to the detective. "What would you like to know?"

"Actually, I'm not sure. Amanda and I were talking about our parents."

"Oh, gotcha! Well then, she probably wants me to tell you about my dad and how I wound up here."

"Possibly." AJ gave a weak smile back to the girl. The topic was anything <u>but</u> what she wanted.

"Mom—um, Amanda, found me by a trash bin at a truck stop near Dallas a few years ago. I was homeless at the time and strung out on ice."

"Ice? As in crystal meth?"

"Yeah." She pointed to herself. "Former addict. Poor man's cocaine. That was my go-to drug. I'd been tweaking for five days straight. The only thing I remember from that day was looking up and seeing a vampire with a bloody mouth reach down to grab me."

"A vampire with a bloody mouth?"

Abby nodded. "That's what it looked like to me. Amanda always wears the same red lipstick. I was strung out and thought she was going to eat me." She chuckled. "Nothing could be further from the truth. Anyways, Amanda said she picked me up and put me in her car. Next thing I know, I woke up in a motel. I think we were somewhere in Tennessee at that point. Started going through withdrawals. I wanted to leave *so bad*. Would've done anything to get rid of the pain. There's nothing like the withdrawal. It's one of the *worst* feelings in the world."

"You didn't think she was kidnapping you?"

"Oh, lord no! I ran away from home at the age of fifteen. Had been on the street for a few years by then. A pimp found me and, ya know, I did what I needed to do to survive. Daddy G. said he'd take good care of me as long as I brought him that money. And he did. Until he didn't. Anyways, Amanda saw something in this little whore hiding behind a trash bin at some random truck stop. She got me sober, brought me here. She became the mom I always needed."

"Why did you run away from home, if I may ask?"

Abby looked out at the field and pulled her hair back in a bun. "My older sister ran away when I was twelve. Had this idea I'd pushed her away. I know, now, that wasn't the case. She left to get away from our father and the horrible things he did to her. And when she was gone, he turned his attention to me. He did to me everything he did to her. And worse." She wiped a tear away.

"I'm so sorry, Abby. Amanda just—"

She held a hand up. "It's fine. I promise. Whatever Mom asks for, we do it. She wanted you to know. And, for whatever reason that is, it's between you two." Abby smiled weakly and stood up. "Was there anything else I can tell you?"

AJ shook her head. She gave a quiet response. "No."

"That's in the past and I couldn't ask for a better life right now. I found my calling and gardening brings me the peace of mind I never thought I would have again. Guess you could say it's my new addiction."

"It is addicting," Amanda added as she walked back to the pair. "Thank you, flower. You can go back to the greenhouse now."

"Yes, Mom." The older woman squeezed Abby's shoulder as she walked off.

Amanda sat back down on the bench across from AJ.

"Amanda, may I ask why she called you 'Mom'?"

"All my girls call me that. They don't have to. They just want to. I rescued all of them in one capacity or the other. Off the streets or from a partner, parent, or pimp. I can see the good in each of them. I know how to help them and give them the salvation they always wanted."

"She said you found her in Texas, and she woke up in Tennessee somewhere. Were you on vacation?"

Amanda nodded and then shook her head. "More like a business vacation. Sometimes I attend gardening conventions or agricultural shows. In this business, it's important to stay current with the latest scientific information on improving crops, especially when it comes to environmental concerns."

"Do the men also call you 'Mom'?"

Amanda ignored the question. "Do you know why I asked Abby to talk to you?"

"To show me that my childhood wasn't as bad as hers?"

"To some degree, yes. But why else, do you think?"

"To show me that family is not what you're born into, but what you make, together, with the right people."

"Yes. Now dig a little deeper." Amanda's eyes softened.

AJ recognized a longing.

"You said you were pregnant once, but never said anything more. Something happened to your baby, didn't it? That's why you rescue others?"

A smile crept up one side of Amanda's mouth. "You are quite perceptive. I grow more than gardens, AJ. Everything I do is for all the precious flowers."

—¡—

CHAPTER 21

THE CHILDREN. Children, no matter the age or birth parent, are much the same as gardens. Our bellies heave in snowy Winter before we birth them in Spring. We watch them grow and blossom in Summer. We see them off to adulthood and college in Autumn. We watch them marry in Samhain and begin the new ritual on their own.

Children are the sacred flowers we nurture, water, and feed. They are the crops we reap and the future we plant. We sow long hours in their seedling phase and prepare for the "so long" when they germinate.

Women—Mothers like us, AJ—take our history and turn it into the best thing we can provide for our inheritors. We learn to grow our own gardens, mend our own paths, and weed out the shit in our lives.

When you said your husband had died, I did more research on you. I couldn't find a "Michael Jardine", but I did find a "Michael and Ameena Hawthorne" on the news sites. It took some digging to find the details, but your mother had given a statement to one of the newspapers and I started with that article.

Do you think that's strange?

No? Good.

What I discovered fascinated me to no end. You failed to mention he was murdered. You didn't tell me you were also gunned down and your baby hit, that you gave birth on the same day your husband died.

I know your baby lived. I can assume you wound up in New Hampshire because your parents live here? Why else would you leave your hometown and move thousands of miles away to the Land of Ancient Forest? Unless, perhaps, you've tried to outrun the pain and memory of it.

That never works, does it?

I don't pretend to understand what you went through that day, but I can tell you what it's like to lose a child. I can tell you what happened to me and why, I think, I'm drawn to you, like you're another one of my flowers.

But you don't need rescuing.

Women like you and me never do.

Yes, I lost my child.

When I was a few months pregnant, I left Robert. I had no place to go except my great grandmother's house. Audrey, my Gramma, welcomed me like she did Helen years before that.

A few months. That's all I managed to stay, until she passed away. I was so close to Gramma. If I've ever truly loved someone or felt loved, it was with her. She taught me to find my inner strength and be independent. She showed me what undying love was. If I could turn back the clock to any time in my life, it would be that brief moment where the generations met. It would be that little sliver of bliss I've tried to recreate ever since.

It's interesting because no one wanted anything to do with her. The rest of the family stopped talking to her. They couldn't get over her undying love for her husband—mind you, he passed decades prior. Everyone thought she was looney, thought she was senile.

Oh, my dear, she was anything except that. She listened to her spirit, much like all the women did on that side of the family.

Generation after generation, a few select girls were not meant to follow the masses.

I stayed with her until her sudden passing. I came home from work that day and found her scattering a trunk full of memorabilia across her bedroom floor. I thought she'd lost her mind, but she was just searching for one item, one specific picture.

It took us a couple of hours before I found the photo. She clutched it to her heart, climbed into bed, and later fell asleep holding it. It was a photo of her husband, Ernest, taken before he was taken.

When I found her, she looked so peaceful.

Death is sometimes like that. It can happen like a brilliant blaze of glory or it can pass like solemn, relaxing music.

No matter how it happens, Death changes you. For good or bad, you bear witness and Death changes you. The world is suddenly dulled. The wind has suddenly stilled the leaves because it's been knocked out of you. The calm in the eye of the storm quietens the world around you and the rain stops. It waits. Death is the pause before Life picks up again.

Death has the ultimate control over time as everything around you slows down to an idling murmur. Elapsing ticks and tocks cease.

Death allows you to take a breath from the running, to stop and look at the space around you. It allows you to re-evaluate your priorities.

Death changes you in ways you don't think possible.

But that pause didn't last long for me. Shortly after Gramma's funeral, Robert showed up to the house. He was furious I still wanted to leave him and have our baby, that I didn't need him anymore. We argued and his anger rose. He had a short fuse, that man.

He hit me across the stomach as hard as he could, and the force knocked me to the ground. I passed out. I think I passed out. I just don't remember anything else.

When I woke up, I was in the hospital and my stomach was deflated. Robert told me I'd given birth to a son and that the baby was stillborn. Because of the damage of the blow and the complications of the birth, he said doctors had removed my reproductive organs.

Back then, you didn't need the written permission of the woman. The husband could make all the decisions for you. Isn't that something? The doctor gave Robert authority to decide what could or could not be done to my body. Isn't that something indeed? Men controlling your body and having a say-so of what happens to your womb or eggs? They think they know what's best for you, but could they be any more wrong?

I'm sorry. I digressed.

Shortly after I was out of the hospital, Robert forced me to sell my Gramma's house. Back then, women didn't have many choices and I wasn't strong enough or independent enough to survive without him. So I thought.

He forced me to move back to New Hampshire with him. His house was near downtown Franklin at the time. A little two-story Victorian built in the mid-1800s with decorative trim around the porch and each of the windows.

I tried to make the best of my situation. As long as I fixed up the house and did everything the way he wanted and when he wanted, life was…manageable. But, oh!, did I think of my Gramma those years! Did I yearn for that freedom from the shackles of marriage!

Life with Robert was manageable sometimes, but there was always something that set his anger off.

I remember one day I spent most of my time scraping the paint off the porch and sanding the boards down. He didn't believe in wasting electricity, so it was all by hand. I did the best I could with the coarse grit paper. Back and forth. Back and forth. On my hands and knees, scraping back and forth.

I was so lost in the repetitive motions, I didn't notice the sun was in my face. My arms were burned. They blistered the next morning. Of course, Robert was disgusted.

I saw his car pull up and realized only then that it was incredibly late. He slammed the car door and just glared at me. I don't know what pissed him off more: me covered in dust and paint, the fact the neighbors could see me, or that I didn't have his dinner ready for him. Either way, he wasn't pleased, and I knew what he'd do to me later that night.

I quickly stood up and dusted myself off, apologizing to him. "I'm so sorry, sir! I forgot what time it was. I'll go clean up now!"

He didn't say a word while we stood outside. He merely opened the front door and studied me as I walked past.

I quickly went upstairs and discarded my clothes in the laundry bin. Robert sat on the bed waiting for me. He'd taken his belt off and held the leather in his hands. The buckle dangled off the bed.

I walked out of the bathroom, bared to him. He stood and before I could react, he'd swung the belt. The buckle smacked me across my stomach. I lifted my hands up to prevent him from hitting me again, but it was useless. All it did was force metal and leather to delicate bone.

The force of the next few blows made me crumble to the ground and the bruises across my thighs and legs took several days to disappear. He tried to—

Looks like we'll need to continue this story another day, my dear. I do hate these interruptions.

I rather enjoy my time with you.

—¡—

CHAPTER 22

HE STUDIED the blank expression in Maria's eyes as the woman stared at Emily. Experience told him she kept something secret, something Maria did not want the detectives to find out.

"Ms. Ellanogek, may we help you with something?"

"No," she finally said. "Emily, the plants in the southeast greenhouse need you."

Without hesitation—or glancing at either Conrad or Jack—the young woman nodded and pulled the water hose behind her. She exited the greenhouse.

"The reason the girls don't work with the men is because of their nature, Mr. McMillan."

"If you don't mind, could you elaborate, please?"

"I do mind. And no, I'm not the one to tell you why. Amanda will tell you." Maria grabbed her walkie-talkie from her hip and spoke into it. "David?"

After a few seconds of static, a man responded. "Yeah, boss?"

"Let the men know they can take their lunch now."

"Isn't it a little early for them?"

"The girls are still watering. They won't be done for another hour or so."

"Yes, ma'am. Half-hour or hour?"

"Hour's fine. We're ahead of schedule today."

"Will do."

Maria rehooked the walkie-talkie back to her belt. "Follow me, gentlemen."

When they exited the greenhouse, Conrad squinted from the bombardment of light. He turned and stared at the building. The light was diffused and ambient inside, something he overlooked.

Maria led them through the main building where the back doors mirrored the front and invited patrons outside to see the fields. When they exited the rear of the building, Conrad saw AJ and Amanda sitting on the benches.

"Amanda," Maria said, "they were asking Emily about the men."

The older woman gave Jack a cocky grin, then looked at his boss. "Conrad, have a seat, please. Are you enjoying your time here?"

AJ stood up. "Sir, you can have my seat. I'd like to stand and stretch for a bit."

"Thank you, Jardine." Conrad sat down and turned his body to face Amanda. "Yes, ma'am. You have a very impressive facility here."

She smiled and then looked up at her employee. "Maria, please take AJ's bag and show these two detectives around for a few minutes. Answer any of their questions. I'd like to have a chat with this gentleman."

After they were alone, Amanda said, "We all have our parts to play, don't we, Conrad?"

"Yes, ma'am, we do."

"Let me be blunt and cut to the chase. What would you like to know about the men? Do you want to know why I segregate them so fiercely? Were my answers at the hospital not sufficient? Do you think I'm old fashioned—a prude, in that aspect?"

Conrad shook his head. "Amanda, no. Not at all. You know

I have a job to do here. That's why Tony asked me to help out."

"Tony's one of the good birds, just like you."

"I try to be." He cleared his throat. "You mentioned the men are better suited for the harder labor in the fields."

"Yes. But there's another reason."

"May I ask?"

"Quill."

"Quill?" She nodded. "I apologize, I don't understand."

Amanda smiled. "Quillard Shaw. He used to work for me about eight or nine years ago."

Conrad pulled out his notepad and wrote the name down. "Eight or nine years?"

She chuckled. "Ever diligent in your duties, Conrad. Yes, Quillard Shaw. He used to go by Quill. He was one of the vagrants I found in the Boston area. I was down there one weekend for a seminar on gardening. As I was leaving the convention center, I saw a man digging in the dumpster nearby. I proceeded to strike up a conversation with him and offered him to come back with me."

"If you don't mind me saying, Amanda, that's bold of you to do."

"You know I'm a bold woman. I've a keen perception of people, most of the time. Just like I know Jack won't make it much longer as a detective and AJ will. She's a strong woman with a good head on her shoulders. You'll do good to water her passion and watch how tall she'll grow."

"I don't doubt that at all. She has a tough spirit."

Amanda leaned in and rested her elbows on her knees. She turned her head slightly to the left, never taking her eyes off him. "You have a very good poker face, my friend, but I can see that tiny flicker in your eyes. I know you. And I know you know more than you say, about her. Something you know that she doesn't. I find that interesting."

She leaned back, and before he could reply, Amanda continued, "*You* need to vet your employees, know all their secrets, quirks, and fears. I don't. I go by my instinct. That's what I did with

Quill. He had good shoulders and thin legs. I knew I could mold muscle on him and he'd make a fine worker. And he was for a few months. Until I saw him take notice of one of my girls, Angela."

"Do you have a last name for Angela?"

"I don't remember it anymore. She disappeared after the incident with Quill. He'd grown a little too comfortable in his position in the greenhouses and when he took to Angela, he became a little too pushy with her. I saw him—on more than one occasion, mind you—leave his duties to talk to her while she worked.

"One day, they were planting marigolds and he commented how he wanted to plant his seed in her. I overheard the conversation and reprimanded him. Told him there would be no such thing on my property without my consent, or the girl's. He didn't care. He stormed off and told me he'd fuck whoever he pleased, whenever he wanted. And that I couldn't stop him."

"Did you report the harassment to the police?"

"No. It was nothing more than his jaw jabbering, which he did a lot when he was angry. An emotional mouth is a vile thing to have. But I did report his disappearance."

"He disappeared?"

She nodded. "Angela was only a senior in high school at the time. She took up a job, here, to save money for college. I told her I'd match her savings to help her out. She was a remarkable girl. One day in July, she didn't show up for work. It wasn't like her. I called her house and spoke to her parents. They were frantic, hadn't seen her since the night before. Said they saw a strange man around the house and didn't know if she'd been kidnapped.

"My instinct told me Quill was involved. I went to find him, but he'd disappeared. I never saw Angela or him after that, the evening before they went missing. Her parents never found her. Never gave up hope either. I gave them money for a reward and offered to help them however I could. I don't know if you could call it guilt, but I felt partially responsible for her disappearance. All my girls are flowers to me, Conrad. I care and nurture them. I watch them grow and blossom into women. And when a flower is plucked from me, I lose a little of myself."

"And that's why you separate the sexes now?"

She nodded. "That's why segregation makes my business prosper. It's an old-fashioned mentality, but it works for me. I treat them all the same, the women and men. But each has their role to play."

—¡—

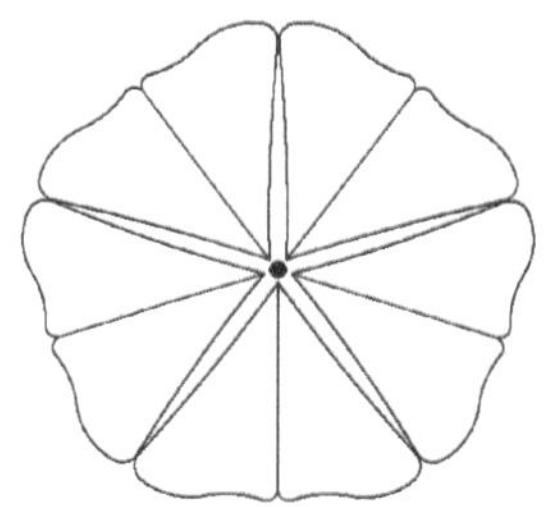

CHAPTER 23

ONCE THEY were in the vehicle heading back to Concord, AJ told Jack and Conrad about the conversation with Amanda. She included as much of the pertinent information as she could, except the part about her past.

"That's disgusting!" Jack said. "She thought blood was pretty after her mom killed herself?!"

"It's not that, Jack. It had a profound impact on her life. Think about it. She lost her great-grandmother, her mother, and her baby—all in a span of a few months. That'll take its toll on anyone, let alone a teenager. Maybe the color red is a coping mechanism for her."

"Are you defending that woman's insanity? If you are, then you're just as crazy as she is."

"Mr. Kinston, watch the tone," Conrad said. AJ saw her boss glance in her direction through the rearview mirror.

She could feel her cheeks warming. "I'm not defending her. I understand loss, that's all. I can relate to her on some level."

"Sounds like you can relate to her on more than one," Jack muttered.

AJ tried to ignore the young man's insult. "People handle grief and loss differently. She found something she could focus on to help her get through difficult times. Whether it was blood or not, she still carries the color red with her to remind herself of her past. Red, for her, is personal power. She's painted her success with it and wears it in her lipstick. How many countries in the world do the same thing with their flags?"

"If you say so. Are you gonna do the same?"

"What do you mean?"

"Paint your lips blood red like Snow White?"

"You mean wear my success like Amanda? Tell me, Jack, what bothers you more? The fact that Amanda has everything you never will? Or the fact that she's a woman of authority?"

"Jardine, enough." Conrad glared at her through the rearview mirror.

Her cheeks still felt hot. She sat back in the passenger seat and looked out the window as Conrad took the exit off the interstate. The more she was around Jack, the more she wanted to be around Amanda or anyone else the opposite of the young brat.

A few minutes later Conrad parked on the street in front of the Office of the Chief Medical Examiner Building near downtown. Down the elevator and a low-lit corridor, they arrived at the office of one of the medical examiners. The locked door stated the name: CASSANDRA OWEN, ADME.

Before he knocked, Conrad turned to AJ and Jack. "Ms. Owen is the Assistant Deputy Medical Examiner. Treat her with respect, regardless of her quirks, understand?"

Jack nodded.

"Yes, sir," AJ said quietly.

The Deputy Director gave a firm knock on the window and a short, stocky woman in her early to mid-thirties ran over to open the door. She pressed her hip into the door and held it open, keeping her hands high and away to keep the bodily fluids from getting on her guests.

"Deputy Director! Good to see you, sir! Come in, please!"

Conrad grabbed the door and the short woman walked over to

the garbage disposal. With her back to her guests, she continued to chatter away about the body on the slab as she removed her personal protection equipment. Her voice was sweet, almost child-like, and a stark contrast to the masculine silhouette her short haircut gave.

Cassandra turned back around. "There! All clean now." She looked at her guests then held her hand out to AJ. "I'm Cassie."

The detective smiled back at her and gave her a firm handshake. "AJ."

"Jack Kinston," the young man replied.

Cassie grabbed his hand for the introduction. "Well don't you have a limp noodle of a handshake!"

AJ covered her smile. She liked this woman's matter-of-factness.

"Ms. Owen, do you have the reports available for us?"

"Yes, sir," she said. The medical examiner grabbed a new pair of latex gloves. "The body's in the storage. I'll go get him."

"Wait, what?" Jack asked, standing a little straighter. "You're going to bring the body out here?"

Cassie stared at him blankly. "You've never seen a corpse, have you?"

"Well—"

"Trash can's over there in the corner. I have an ice pack in the freezer." Without another word, she snapped on her gloves, opened the storage door, and retrieved the body.

AJ ignored the blood draining from Jack's face and prepared mentally for the scene. She had seen plenty of crime scene photos and had been around death before, but she was not expecting to see a dead body her first week on the job.

She looked over at Conrad. He remained as unphased and stoic as ever. Jack, on the other hand, turned a new shade of ill.

Cassie wheeled the gurney over and began unzipping the bag.

AJ was so focused on the zipper and Cassie's hands, she failed to see Jack run to the trash can until she heard the contents of his lunch spew into the bag.

Cassie stopped, looked at AJ, then rolled her eyes. "Take a

deep breath, Jack."

Instead of listening to the medical examiner, he threw up some more, then wiped his chin and mouth with his hands.

"Mr. Kinston," Conrad said, "please excuse yourself. Go clean up in the restroom and wait outside until Jardine and I are done."

Without another word, Jack bolted for the door and walked out of eyesight down the hallway.

Cassie looked at Conrad. "Twenty bucks says he doesn't last more than two months."

"And I was going to give him three." AJ saw the twinkle in her boss's eye.

"Anyways, shall we continue?" The medical examiner grabbed the zipper and continued all the way around the body, then peeled the material back.

AJ expected to see a horribly disfigured body with wounds everywhere, but what she saw was a well-toned, muscular man greyish in color. Cuts littered his arms and upper torso. She expected the neck wound to be a gaping hole from ear to ear, but it was a clean slice, stitched back together.

"Let's start with the prelim tox panel. It was clean of all drugs except the ones the hospital administered. Elevated alcohol level, but not worrying. Overall, he was extremely healthy. No poisons, no weird stuff. Cause of death was exsanguination. He just lost too much blood before the doctors could get to him."

"What can you tell me about the wound?" Conrad asked.

"It's a very clean slice. I'm actually a bit impressed! I wouldn't be surprised if a surgical knife was used to make the laceration to his neck. Now, all these other wounds on his arms are just serrated scratches. They're consistent with the barbed wire he was found in."

AJ stared at the man's inner arms. "What about those marks near his elbows? Are those track marks, like from a drug addict?"

"That's what I thought at first, but they're just a little too big for that. And they're more recent."

"He donated blood regularly. Sir, isn't that what the doctor said?"

Conrad nodded.

"I'd almost agree with that," Cassie said, "but that's a shit ton of blood donated over the last few years. I don't know any hospital or blood bank who'd take a guy or gal more than every eight weeks, but this guy gave blood every month, I'd guess.

"Now, there is some bruising starting to surface. Let me show you." She grabbed a handheld light and held it closer to the man's ankles. "See those marks there around his ankles? There's similar banding around his wrists. It's possible he was restrained, but that could just be speculation."

AJ took a step closer to examine the markings. "Wow, this is very fascinating. I didn't know bruises could show up after death."

Conrad's phone started to ring. He fished it out of his suit pocket and stared at it. "Excuse me. I need to take this. Jardine, when you're done, come outside. We'll be waiting." With a flip of the phone, he opened the door and left.

Cassie smiled at AJ.

"To answer your questions, post-mortem bruising is very common. So, you aren't getting a little queasy at the sight of a D.B.?"

AJ shook her head and looked at Cassie. "Not at all."

"Not like Jackie Boy there?"

"You mean Jack Ass? Nope."

Cassie reared her head back and snorted. "He looks like an ass. He's emitting some serious cocky vibes and energy there."

AJ rolled her eyes. "Oh, you have no idea."

Cassie snapped her gloves off and grabbed the reports. She handed them to AJ and winked. "You got some spunk to ya. I think I like you."

With equal bravado, the detective replied, "I think I like you, too. May you not have another jack ass walk through your doors any time soon."

AJ left the medical examiner smiling and joined her boss.

—¡—

Ameena pulled up at the house and grabbed the large bag from the passenger seat. As she walked up the hill to the front door, it flew open and two large, young mutts came running out. They nearly rammed the mother of two.

"Abbott! Costello! Get down! These aren't for you."

Her mother, Jamilla, stood at the door while the dogs ran off and chased each other. "Habibti, you're home! How was your day? Are you okay? Why are you home so soon, sweetheart?"

"Yeah, my boss said I could come home a little early since I stayed so late the other night. We finished the day sooner than he expected." She handed her mother the Claremont Farms bag. "This is for you, Momma."

As Jamilla pulled out each item from the bag, her excitement grew. Her voice fluctuated more. "Who gave you these? Look at these flowers! Habibti, I can't accept this, it's too expensive!"

"Momma, we can hang the hummingbird feeder outside the office window, over by the lilac bushes."

"Are you sure? What if it breaks?"

"It's fine! I promise! These are meant to be used. Amanda, the owner of the nursery, said all the flowers she gave us attract butterflies and hummingbirds. That's what you've wanted to do, right? Plant more flowers?"

"Of course. Shukran! Tell her thank you for me!"

"I will Momma. I'm gonna lay down for a bit before dinner. My stomach is hurting again."

Jamilla continued to jabber in Arabic while Ameena walked into her room and dumped her backpack on the dresser. She flopped down on the bed and stared at the ceiling. A few minutes later, her phone rang. She picked it up and saw a call with a 603 area code.

"Hello?"

"AJ?"

"Speaking."

"It's Amanda."

—¡—

CHAPTER 24

READY TO continue our conversation? I hope you don't mind. I truly did not appreciate the interruption we had.

I don't mind at all.

Where was I?

You were talking about your husband.

Oh! That's right...Robert.

Robert gave me a good beating on that day. He gave me quite a few over the years, but I held my tongue. I still loved him in the capacity I understood at that age and time.

By the way, it feels refreshing to talk to you. Almost like a church confession, only there aren't enough Hail Mary's to save me. I don't need saving, just your ear, my flower.

I call all my girls flowers. Each remind me of a separate blossom. Every girl who's worked for me is as unique as the species I grow. And in a way, I cultivate my girls, plant them with ideas and thought. They stay with me as long as they want, unlike the two-year limit I restrict with the men. I let the girls stay longer until they're prepared to scatter seed in their own gardens.

All my girls are flowers. I told Conrad about a girl named Angela. She was a marigold. So bright and robust. She had a vivacious personality. Everyone liked her.

Emily is a petunia. She has this streak about her where her anger can rise up, but it's frivolous and she soon forgets why she was mad in the first place.

Kaylee is a bright sunflower. She reminds me of Angela in many ways. She's inquisitive and devoted, bright and equally robust. If her personality could ever be bottled and sold, she'd be the next espresso.

Maria, now she's a foxglove. Foxgloves attract hummingbirds, and as sweet as their nectar is, they're also poisonous if humans consume them. Maria is like that: sweet or toxic, her emotions can go strong either way. Her words either harm or nurture. She tries to find balance in moderation, but that is not always easy for her. Yet she's a gorgeous specimen of resilience and strength.

Yes, each of my girls is a flower. I see so much of them in you. That makes you my flower also. You're a morning glory, Ameena Jardine, as rich a blue as those eyes that stare back at me.

I apologize. I digressed again. I didn't call to talk about flowers. I wanted to finish telling you my story about Robert.

He would beat me for the most trivial reasons. At first, I had such fear from him and the pain of the beatings. I never wanted to piss him off or upset him. Sometimes, though, no matter what I did—or didn't do, for that matter—he'd still get pissed at me. I think he needed a release of some sort. And, if he couldn't get his release from fucking me 'til I bled, he'd make me bleed a different way.

And you know what's odd? When I'd spit the blood from my mouth into the sink, I'd watch it swirl in the water as I washed it down the drain. When I'd get up from the toilet and flush, I'd stare at the spinning amounts of red as it pinkened the bowl before disappearing down the throated pipe. I'd stare at the swirling patterns in the water and my thoughts would immediately go back to that bridge and seeing Helen looking up at the heavens. My thoughts would drift back to the first time I saw the blood and how beautiful it appeared to me.

I got used to the sight of my own blood. I grew to love the smell of iron and the beauty of the color as it trickled down sores. I marveled at the spongy softness a forming scab would make and how sticky coagulating blood could be. Sometimes, when Robert would be away on weekend business trips, I'd pick at the deeper scabs and watch the blood dribble down my arms and legs. I'd study it, appreciate the texture as it hardened.

And you know what, AJ? Sometimes I'd take a finger and draw designs on my body. I'd pretend I was a Viking or Native American or some aboriginal member of a long-lost other-worldly tribe, and it was my duty and sense of responsibility to decorate myself in blood. I was a warrior. I was on a spiritual journey to find my calling and independence. It finally became a necessity to paint myself for war.

When Robert wanted steak or some other meat dish, I'd yearn to smell the wet slab of animal parts and grip it so tight in my hands, the red liquid would ooze between my fingers and trickle down my hands.

To some, it seems disgusting and disturbing. But to hold the essence of another being in my hands was a power I held that he did not. I was the one with the power, not him. I was in charge, not him.

And I continued to crave that sight because it was the only control I had against that excuse for a human being. The sight of blood became my salvation and drug.

Most people wondered if I still hated Robert, after all the things he did. But the answer to that is no. I forgave him. Such a freeing thought, forgiveness.

People still ask me, "Amanda, how can you forgive the man who lied to you, who abused and beat you? How can you possibly forgive the person who got rid of your baby, who took the chances of motherhood away from you?"

To which I always answer, "He taught me so much about the life I have now. How could I ever hate the man who made me the woman I am today?"

He disappeared thirty-four years ago this month. Just went for a walk and disappeared. I filed a missing person's report, gave my statement, did everything a dutiful wife should do. I checked in with the police week after week.

Nothing.

But you already knew that, didn't you?

I bet you didn't know that a few months after he went missing, I was cleaning out his office and going through all the paperwork he had in there. Most of the stuff I found was boring. Tax returns, legal documents for work that I boxed up. Just a bunch of trivial things in all kinds of drawers and on all kinds of shelves.

Then I found the key to his safe. He'd taped it to the bottom of a hidden compartment in the back of his desk. I scrambled to the safe and thrust the key in, excited to see what I'd find. I hoped it was additional money or something I could use.

What did I find instead? Not money, not jewels, not even my Gramma's ring or ruby necklace.

More documents. I found the titles to a few cars, a checkbook of a bank account he kept hidden from me—so much stuff about a secret life he led that I knew nothing about!

All those late nights he spent at work?

Lies, AJ! All lies and deceit.

But do you know the thing that shocked me the most, more than the double life he led? The thing that knocked me out as hard as the punch to my pregnant gut?

I found a birth certificate. Dated 1973. It had my name, Amanda Marie Claremont on it as the mother. Robert Daniel Claremont was listed as the father.

The baby's name was left blank. But the sex?

A girl.

Robert told me over and over that the baby—a boy—died, but the bastard lied about it! I gave birth to a living girl and I never knew about it until more than a decade later. Do you have any idea what that's like? To spend years and years believing a lie because the truth is much less believable?

That day I found the birth certificate, I sat on the floor screaming and crying. I scratched and clawed my legs raw, raking them over and over and over with my nails until the blood appeared. I stared at my legs and scratched them some more. I wanted to peel my skin off and get to my arteries and veins. I scratched away until my palms were maroon.

Then I stared at the blood until my mind calmed. That calmness and joy came back as I pushed the hatred away. I pushed the negativity to the back of my mind and locked it in a safe just as he locked that birth certificate away. I swore I'd not turn out like him, that one day I'd find my daughter and make it up to her.

I pushed the hate away. I forgave him, especially after they found his body during the Thaw the next year. I forgave him after the police said animals had eaten away his insides. I forgave him after the medical examiner said he probably died of a heart attack or natural causes or knocked himself unconscious after taking a spill and never could make it back up the embankment.

But I'd be lying if I said I thought he didn't deserve such an awful death.

Karma comes for all assholes eventually.

—¡—

CHAPTER 25

'TIS BEST to weigh the enemy more mighty than he seems.
Act 2, Scene 3, Henry V ~ William Shakespeare

Conrad read the saying again before he flipped the desk calendar page over to the next day's quote. He tapped his pen against the notepad in front of him, then studied the news article on the laptop.

Search continues for missing FHS student, vagrant worker

Police expanded their search today for missing Franklin High School student Angela Briggs, age 17, to include the Merrimack River area south of Franklin. She was last seen leaving Claremont Farms and Nursery after her shift ended on the evening of Friday, July 16, 2010. Amanda Claremont, owner of the nursery and Angela's boss, stated, "This is not like her at all. She wouldn't just disappear."

Angela was last seen talking with one of her co-workers, Quillard Shaw, age 25, who has also gone missing. "Quill has worked with me for a few months now," Claremont said. "He's been a good employee. He took a liking to Angela and I did have a talk with him about that, but he's never exhibited any kind of odd behavior. I'd never put my girls in harm's way. Period." Claremont added that she's offered a hefty reward for information on the whereabouts of Shaw and the safe return of Ms. Briggs. Anyone who can help with the case or volunteer to search are asked to call the town police department.

"Baby?" Conrad looked up to see his wife, Yasmin, standing in the doorway, her arms crossed in front of her. "Did you not hear me call your name?"

He quickly stood up and closed the laptop screen. "I'm sorry, dear. Just reviewing my notes. Was lost in thoughts again."

"Mmm hm." Her voice sounded annoyed, but her brown eyes gave away the playfulness. "Go find your thoughts and bring them to the dinner table. Your steak's getting cold."

He watched her turn around and walk out. His work could wait for tomorrow, but his stomach could not. He walked into the dining room and saw his son, Duncan, and his daughter, Aubreah, with their heads tucked down as they played on their phones.

Yasmin walked back in from the kitchen carrying a side dish of broccoli and cheese. "Get off those damned phones. I'm not gonna say it again!"

"Yes, Mom," came a unified response.

As everyone sat down and helped themselves, Conrad asked his kids, "Did you both finish your homework?"

Duncan nodded as he stuffed his mouth with a biscuit.

"I just have a little bit of Calculus left and need to practice the clarinet some more," Aubreah replied.

"Good. Pass me the rolls, please."

"Aubreah, tell your dad about the mail you received."

The girl put her fork down and looked at her dad. "I've been accepted into the Air Force Academy."

He stopped chewing and swallowed the rest of his food whole. Aubreah glanced at her mother then back at him. The longer he studied his daughter the more she morphed into the little girl who used to have pigtails and play with dolls. He blinked quickly a couple of times to see his teenage daughter staring at him.

"Baby," Yasmin said, "what do you think? She wants to follow in her Daddy's footsteps."

The table went silent with the exception of Duncan stuffing his mouth with another biscuit.

"I think," Conrad carefully worded his thoughts, "this is something we should sleep on and talk about over the weekend."

"Dear, Aubreah wants to make you proud. She wants to keep the family tradition going after you and your father and his father before that."

"I *am* proud, but—"

"So, let her go and spread her wings. What's wrong with her taking flight from the nest?"

"Dad, I can wait until after college." Aubreah's eyes held hurt she would never admit.

"I know, sweetheart. I'm just…not prepared for this conversation tonight."

"I don't mean to disappoint you, sir."

Conrad shook his head. "No, no. It's not that, sweetheart. Ultimately, Aubreah, it's your life and your decision. Your mom and I can't make that for you. Right now, my head's swimming in a case and I'm not in the right frame of mind to talk about this."

"What has you so distracted from your kids that you don't want to talk about their future?" Yasmin asked. She set her napkin down and put one hand on her hip.

"A cold case about a missing high school student here in

Franklin. It's possibly related to the case I'm working."

"Kids at school have a song about a ghost girl who went missing years ago," Duncan said between bites.

"What ghost girl, Bubs?"

"It goes something like this:

"Ms. Briggs? Ms. Briggs!
She's gone with the twigs
Down the river to bank.
The quills and bills
Poked her heart for thrills
Down, down her body sank."

"Yeah, there's always been rumors at the high school about that," Aubreah said. "Wasn't her name Angie or Angela?"

Conrad nodded. "Yes. Angela Briggs."

"There's another verse my friends know. It's like a spooky Halloween thing that goes around at the haunted corn maze every year. Some urban legend." She looked up and thought about the lyrics, mouthing invisible words before she recited the verse:

"The farm! The farm!
She's gone to the farm
To murder the men in the maze.
She set a big fire
To the barn and inspired
The flowers to grow in a blaze."

"Sweetheart, that's morbid!" Yasmin said.

"Yeah, but that's what the kids say. They said her phone was found in the river near Penacook with footsteps leading away from the riverbank. Kids think she's making her way back home and will set fire to the property one day."

'To murder the men in the maze.' I wonder how much truth is in that.

—¡—

Conrad crawled into bed and stared at the ceiling. A little more research after dinner was out of the question. Yasmin saw to that. He knew she did not like his attention divided when he was home, though she also knew that was sometimes an impossibility.

"What are you thinking of, baby?" she asked as she stepped out of the bathroom. She rubbed lotion across her neck and arms. Her face was covered in a mask and her curly, black hair was tied behind her head. She stopped and stared at him. "Are you still thinking about that missing girl?"

"Yes and no." He turned and propped himself on his elbow. "I can't help but to think of Angela Briggs' parents. That could be *our* daughter missing."

Yasmin went back into the bathroom and washed the beauty product off her face. Conrad did not understand why his wife thought she needed those products. Her brown skin was always flawless and perfect in his eyes, but he also knew not to question her. He might rule the bureau, but she ruled the nest.

"But it's not our Aubreah and it never will be. You know I hate when you bring work home."

"I know, baby. I'm sorry."

Yasmin walked back out of the bathroom. Her hair was down and she slipped her bathrobe off. Her skin was near perfection. She crawled in the bed next to him.

"Have you told her yet?" she asked.

"Who? Aubreah?"

"No. *Her*."

Conrad shook his head as he stretched his arm out for his wife. "I don't think it's a good idea."

"Tsk-tsk. This is going to bite you in the ass, baby. You need to tell your new detective you knew her husband."

—¡—

Thursday, May 10, 2018

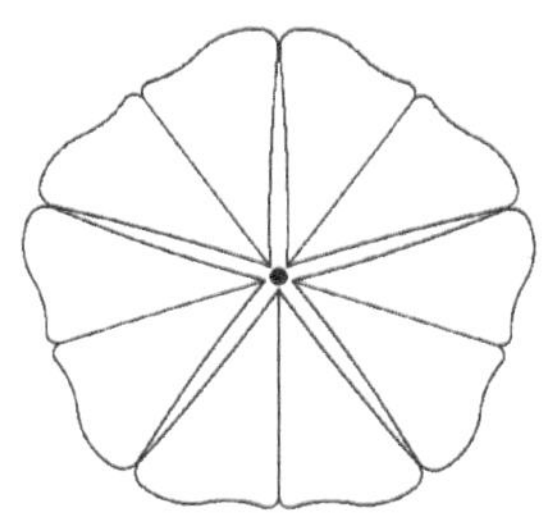

CHAPTER 26

SHE FIDGETED in the office chair while Conrad stared at her. AJ repeated as much as she could remember from the phone call. After several seconds of uncomfortable silence, she finally spoke.

"Sir, did I do anything wrong?"

"No, Jardine. Just thinking."

"Oh. Is that what that looks like?"

He narrowed his eyes slightly.

"Sorry, sir." She cleared her throat and waited.

And waited.

"Sir? Is there something you want to say to me?" she finally asked in a quiet tone.

He put his hands down on the desk and glanced at the scratch. "Jardine, there is a lot I'd like to say, but now's not the time or place for it. One day, perhaps."

She opened her mouth to reply, but someone knocked on the door and opened it.

"Sorry, I'm late," Jack said, walking in. "There was a traffic accident on the interstate."

"It happens. Jardine, please relay to Jack what you just told me."

AJ repeated everything she told Conrad. She studied Jack's facial expressions and saw his cocky smirk creep up one side of his mouth. The more she told him, the more of a sneer washed across his face.

"Shit, AJ, all the looneys are attracted to you, huh?"

She shifted her body in her chair and positioned herself more to face him. "What the hell is that supposed to mean?"

He shrugged. "Amanda's crazier than I thought. I mean, who finds blood attractive?"

"Who finds football interesting?" She mimicked his shrug. "People have different tastes. Granted, hers is a bit out there, but I can see where she's coming from."

Jack crossed his arms and leaned back in his chair. "Oh, do tell."

AJ swallowed her anger in a controlled sigh. She wanted to beat the smirk off his face. "Jack, when a person is being abused or traumatized, sometimes they disconnect their minds from their bodies. They take their minds somewhere else as a safeguard. They can focus on a specific ceiling tile or see patterns in wallpaper or textures. Children can develop nervous tics that last them into adulthood.

"Amanda's first traumatic event happened when her mother killed herself in front of her. A few months later, her great-grandmother died unexpectedly, and Amanda found the body. And then, as if that's not enough, her husband traumatizes her and she spends *years* believing her baby died. Between that and the pregnancy hormones, possible post-partum depression, and then being thrown into menopause after a forced hysterectomy—it's enough to shape a person's brain much differently than yours or mine...Trauma changes a person."

"You sound like you know a lot about that yourself, AJ."

"I do. I've witnessed a murder...and, anyone who saw what I did, they know...it changes you." She looked down at her fingers and started to pick the cuticles.

"And are *you* as screwed up in the head as *she* is?"

AJ pointed a finger at her colleague. "Fuck you, asshole!"

Conrad slammed his hand down on his desk. "Kinston! Jardine! Enough." He stood up and grabbed his coat. "I don't want to hear any more talk like this. You're a team. Act like it."

"Sorry, sir," AJ muttered.

"Sure, boss," Jack said.

"Let's wrap up our interviews today. We also need to stop by the police chief's office and investigate a couple of cold cases. It'll be a busy day. For all of us."

—¡—

The clouds crept through the sky occasionally allowing the sun to peek through and heat AJ's face. She noticed the shades of lime green and watermelon painted across the treetops and knew the trees were ready to explode in summer greenery.

They walked between the greenhouses up to the red nursery building with its inviting doors spread wide. Each girl they passed smiled and greeted them, then returned to their tasks. Perhaps the warmth and intoxication of springtime infected everyone.

When they stepped into the darker interior, AJ's eyes took a few seconds to adjust to the scene. All antique agricultural equipment was stripped from their hangers and the walls lay barren, except the new décor going up. Dangling stained glass flowers hung randomly in the windows.

Amanda stood inside the building space, looking up. A couple of men stood on ladders, hanging large paintings of hummingbirds. A few were already positioned on the walls and they hung neatly positioned and evenly spread, standing at attention for visitors.

AJ stared at the paintings. Each bird was positioned in a different flight pattern or sat perched on a limb. Each had distinct and vivid markings from a different unique species. Each had an accompanying and distinctly different flower. The paintings brought life to the canvas.

"Ah! Conrad," the older woman said when she saw them, "welcome back. We're doing a little redecorating today. What do you think of my hummingbirds?"

"Very impressive."

"Thank you." Amanda looked at AJ. "And how are you all enjoying this weather today?"

"Can't wait to go biking soon with my buddies," Jack answered.

"I'm looking forward to doing some yard work soon. Hopefully, Bug Season doesn't last long this year," AJ said. "By the way, my mom loved the gifts. Thank you again!"

"My pleasure, AJ."

"Ms. Claremont, if you don't mind, Jack and I would like to finish interviewing your employees today."

Amanda flicked her wrist. "Absolutely. Go. I'll take care of AJ for you."

The older woman gave the detective a wink and they watched Conrad and Jack walk out of the building. Amanda turned her head back up and smiled at the work the men did. "So, tell me the truth. What do you think of the paintings?"

AJ smiled. "They're gorgeous. There's a lot of detail and color. Acrylic?"

Amanda nodded. "Yes. I made some of the colors myself from the flowers we have."

"You painted these?!"

Amanda smiled again and gently looked at AJ. "Yes. It's one of my secret talents. I can't wait to tell you about the rest."

—¡—

CHAPTER 27

"ALL SECRETS beg to be told."

Gramma used to say that. She said secrets are seeds buried deep in people's minds. We're all hiding the deepest parts of ourselves we don't want others to know. Stuff so dark we'd be judged by it, no matter how long ago it happened. But no matter how far down or how much you abuse the soil or how long you can go without watering the Earth, secrets can—and do—push through. They yearn to be exposed. They're weeds. And weeds always find ways.

Each of these paintings I'm hanging tell a story, a secret. In fact, everything that grows here on my property begs to be told. The skeletons in the closet—or in my case, the garden dirt—won't remain there. My painted birds on the walls won't remain silent. They want to sing and chirp as their migration has come to an end. They've come back to their breeding grounds and are ready for new life.

I'll tell you about each of these birdies tomorrow, sound fair? I have to wait just a little longer, get them all hung up. There are dozens of paintings I've done over the years. Each is a vibrant story. Each is named. I'll tell you only about the important ones, the significant hummers.

More tomorrow, I promise, my dear. Let's take a walk, for now. I want to show you the corn maze and finish telling you about some of the things Robert did.

I don't remember every beating, every slap, nor each smack and bruise. How could I? It happened so often. It's like being stuck in day-to-day traffic. You must sit through it and then go about your daily job. It becomes mundane, just a part of a life you don't care for. The same roadway, the same vehicle, the same sounds—you don't remember the daily and mundane, do you? No. All the days blend together. Each day is the same, one after another. After another. After another.

It's only when you come across an accident or weather phenomenon or something profound—only then do you recall the day or what you wore or the color of the clouds in the evening sky. Maybe you see a sun pillar for the first time and you're in awe at the towering light reaching for Heaven. Or maybe you see the sky unleashing its fury ahead of you only to be overtaken by a snow squall or hailstorm.

It's those moments that stand out. Only those.

And it's the same thing with Robert. The profound moments are as bright as today's weather. Waking up in the hospital to what he had the doctors do to me, that was significant. Losing the baby, that was significant. Forcing me to sell my Gramma's house. That, too, was very significant.

Yes. There were many things I could forgive Robert for. Bones and wounds heal. Memories fade. But the one thing I couldn't forgive him for was forcing me to sell Gramma's house. That was the one thing that was mine, that I thought he could never take from me. I thought I could keep it, that it would be my safe house, my haven for me and the baby.

I was so wrong, my flower.

I keep telling myself that it was only a house.

But it was more than just planks and cinder blocks. It was more than just a home pre-ordered from a Sears catalog—if you can believe that. It was built from scratch by Gramma's own father. My great-great granddad. William—something or another.

He was a good man, supposedly, but he held a grudge against Audrey. William could never forgive her for killing his wife in childbirth. He was tough and brutal with her, but she learned from him what she didn't want in a man. That's why he hated Ernest so much. At least that's one of the stories she told me.

Audrey and Ernest. Ernest and Audrey. They had the perfect love story you only see in the movies.

William built the home for himself more so than for Audrey. He'd hoped to lure a fresh young wife with the prospect. And it worked. Twice, actually.

The first wife managed to stay married to him for around five years, but she could never give him any more children. He wanted a son more than anything. I guess he was tired of dealing with a little girl.

Tell me something. What is it with men demanding they want sons over daughters? Wouldn't anyone just want to have a healthy baby? Do men not understand that <u>they</u> are the ones determining the sex of a child? It's <u>their</u> seed that determines whether or not they have a boy or a girl? Why prefer one sex over the other? Do they worry the girl is not good enough, not strong enough? That a <u>boy</u> will solve their ills? Is it because of their namesake and passing on their silly nomenclature? Is that the legacy they wish to leave?

I'm sorry. I digressed again. Certain topics do that.

William's first marriage didn't last long, especially after he started abusing her. I can't remember her name. I just remember being told that Gramma didn't miss her that much. We never could find any pictures of her, so I don't even know what she looked like.

The second wife, her name was Jean. Gramma always had nice things to say about her. Jean loved Audrey more than she loved William. That's what made their marriage last so long. At least, that's my opinion. Jean stayed for the sake of the little girl.

Jean made William happy, though it wasn't always

reciprocated. She tolerated him. And his mess. But she doted on my great-grandmother. She's the one who taught Audrey what to look for in a real man. And she adored Ernest, too.

They lived in that house on Hazel Street for several years. Though they tried, they never had more children. Cancer finally took William around the turn of the century.

Jean had her own money and never needed to remarry. So, she didn't. She was strong-headed and independent. A little flighty, but never needed a man to feel secure. She taught Audrey to be the same.

That's in our DNA. We women are independent and driven. Yes, Robert abused me, but I let him do those things to me. Don't think of me as a victim. Ever! Because I'm not. Sometimes you have to slush through shit to get what you want. Sometimes you have to get your hands dirty in blood meal and manure to bear the best gardens.

I have respect for Jean for taking care of my Gramma. Audrey passed that knowledge to Victoria, my grandmother. And Victoria would've done the same thing for my mom, Helen, had she not died in childbirth. But it's in our DNA and Helen was also the same, though she was more independent and freer than the women before her.

We all had memories of growing up in that house on Hazel Street, and that house is also engrained in our DNA. That house has made the women grow and sculpted us to who we are today.

I kept telling myself that it's only a house, but that house was my Gramma's sanctuary, her haven, her fond memories. Each board repaired, each shingle replaced, every garden that grew—that was generations of life and spirit and soul.

We had our traditional Christmases there and Gramma decorated the tree with angels, bells, and cherubs. The floors would creak as we walked through. The front portion was heated by a gas heater tucked in the corner of the living room with the yellow-orange flames that rose and fell and flickered and leapt while the cat slept on top.

The kitchen was heated by a wood stove near the oven and

when the wood stove was replaced, a gas heater provided warmth and another cat benefited from the arrangement. The Mexican tiles above the kitchen sink told stores of exotic vacations, hand-selected souvenirs, and little girls curious about the senorita carrying cool water and the pot boiling over an open fire. The cabinets smelled of Ernest's cologne that Audrey would spritz in there from time to time.

The house held joy and protection and Gramma refused to sell it because she was so attached to it. It was hers and Ernest's. She had to wait for him, never admitting he was dead.

"Leave the door unlocked, beloved. Leave the door unlocked!" his last letter read.

And she did.

For decades, even after the demographics started changing, even after the murder in her alleyway, even after each neighbor was long buried and gone, she kept the door unlocked. She kept vigil. She never, ever gave up hope that Ernest would one day come back.

And, over the years, the house lost its luster and sagged. The weeds overtook the flower beds. But it was still home with the best memories I've ever had. The euphoria inside was the closest thing to magic I've ever felt. And I helped her fix it up, even while pregnant and working. I helped her return the house to the glory she remembered. We put a lot of blood, sweat, and tears into that wooden anchor where all her memories were harbored. We finished a few of the projects she'd started years before.

And then she passed away one evening. She just went to sleep and never woke up.

I'd like to think the noise I heard—the noise of the front door opening and shutting, and then the footsteps—was her Ernest coming home decades after his ship was taken at sea. I'd like to think they're finally together, and the house is as new and bright as the day it was built. I'd like to believe that the new owners have taken care of the tiles and the molding and the decorative trim. I'd like to think that Audrey is proud and happy for me, even though a part of my soul died the day I signed that deed over.

So many generations of family memories, gone because of inked scribbles on paper. And so, I kept telling myself it was only a house. I kept telling myself I had to let go.

But I never forgave Robert for forcing me to sell that home. And I told myself one day I'd make him pay.

—¡—

CHAPTER 28

NEARLY every employee answered Conrad's questions the same: Amanda Claremont was a respected and fair boss, worked hard, and everyone loved her.

Conrad looked at his notepad and compared it to the list of employees Jack acquired from the manager. They only had a couple of workers left to talk to, including one they needed to re-interview: Emily Vanderbilt.

Jack blocked the sun with one hand and looked all around the field. "I don't recognize that guy over there." He pointed in the distance to a tanned man shoveling dirt into a separator.

Conrad squinted. "Let's talk to him, then find Ms. Vanderbilt."

Careful to step over the rows and not disturb the raised beds, both men trekked over to the field worker.

After they introduced themselves, the man said, "Yeah, I know who you are. Everyone's been talking about it."

The man, possibly in his early thirties, stabbed the ground with the shovel, stepped on the top edge, and pushed it into the dirt with his weight. Conrad noted the new steel-toed boots. His jeans did not have many stains or holes in them. His long-sleeve neon shirt reflected the sun off. His face was shiny. He smelled of sunscreen.

"And your name?" Jack asked.

"Mark Graves." He lifted the shovel full of dirt and dumped it into a wooden-framed sifter. Tiny stones bounced in the wire mesh while dirt fell into the wheelbarrow underneath.

"Mr. Graves, did you know Michael Smith?" Conrad asked.

"Nope." He did not look up from the next shovel of dirt he dumped in the sifter.

"Can you tell me what you've heard about him or possibly anything you've learned about Mr. Smith?"

Another shovel of dirt went into the sifter. "He was a bit of an ass, according to the guys."

Mark jammed the shovel in the dirt and wiped his brow. He shook the rock-filled sifter and carried it to the vehicle nearby, dumping the stones in the bed of the truck. He finally looked at the two men.

"I got here about six weeks ago. Detoxed for the first few, then I've been in the field ever since. I was told to keep my head down, work hard, and I'll be rewarded with a better life. I don't know anything about anyone here other than the chitchat at the house."

Conrad watched him walk back to the wheelbarrow and place the sifter on the ground. Mark reached into a nearby bag, scooped up some fertilizer, and sprinkled it in the area he just dug. He then dumped the dirt from the wheelbarrow on top of the fertilizer.

Jack sniffed and scrunched his nose. "What the hell is in that?"

"It's blood meal. Good for the soils in small quantities."

Conrad looked at the bag. "'Claremont Blood Meal'? Where do you get the material to make it?"

After repositioning the sifter on the wheelbarrow, Mark went back to his task. "Amanda gets it from the Norrington's Meat Farm next door. See that path over there?" He pointed to a dirt and gravel trail on the other side of the barbed wire fence. "It leads straight to Norrington's. The other guys said she's got an arrangement with them. They give her the blood and meat scraps from the animals, and she lets their cows and chickens graze in the fields here. She rotates the animals in and out of the sections we have. Some sorta system you'd have to ask her about."

"Wait, that stuff is leftover animal parts?" Jack asked. Conrad watched the detective's face go solemn.

Mark nodded. "We make our own bone meal, blood meal, and all kinds of fertilizer. What we don't use, we sell to the public or give to our neighbors and local farmers."

"Do you know if Mr. Smith was also involved in the process of making these materials?" Conrad asked.

Mark shook his head. "Nah. Most of us from the halfway house aren't involved in that. We maintain the corn, fields, and vineyards. The women look after the nursery and greenhouses. Sometimes Amanda or Maria will shuffle us around to learn other tasks. Very rarely are the men and women put together to work on something."

"Mr. Graves, do you mind me asking about your living conditions at the halfway house?"

"Not at all. It's great. Anyone detoxing is kept under supervision. We're fed good. We sleep on the most comfortable beds I've ever been on. Amanda takes us shopping as we need stuff. We have housekeepers that come in and clean during the week so we can rest on the weekends."

"Sounds like you have it made, then," Jack said.

Mark chuckled. "Don't get me wrong. It's a lot of back-breaking work, but we're taken care of here. I can see why everyone really likes Amanda." He finished the last shovel of dirt and stabbed the ground with his shovel again. "If you don't mind, I need to finish this row before I can take a break."

"Thank you, Mr. Graves." Conrad watched the man dump the sifter full of gravel in the truck bed.

"Can we go find Emily now?" Jack asked. "I'd like to get away from this stench."

"This stench provides food on your table, Mr. Kinston."

"Think I'll stick to my frozen dinners, then," Jack mumbled.

They walked towards the red main building. Conrad surveyed

the fields again. Cows grazed in one fenced section; each looked well-fed and healthy. Another man stopped the tractor in a nearby section; the Deputy Director heard chickens coming from the large enclosure pulled behind. The worker used a hydraulic system and lowered the mobile coop down to the ground. The birds, probably a few dozen, began pecking the ground everywhere. Another chicken coop was lined parallel to that one, with another worker repeating the same steps as the first.

A couple of men in front of the Deputy Director pushed rotating gates and moved from one field section to another. They held the gate open for Conrad and Jack to walk through before swiveling the gates closed and locking them into place.

He looked up at the vertical column in the middle. The wooden structure was covered in carvings that appeared Native American. The large turnstile creaked as the gates locked behind them.

"Hey, Joe! We need to grease this one," one man yelled to another one across the field.

Conrad stopped. "Mr. Morgan? Am I remembering the name correctly?"

The worker dusted his hands off and extended his right. Smiling, he said, "Mr. McMillan, good to see you again. Yes, sir, that's correct. Please, call me Richie." He looked at Jack. "Good to see you, too, sir."

"Richie, I wanted to ask you about these gates. I just noticed the carvings on this one. What origin are those, do you know offhand?"

He squinted as he looked up, then shrugged. "Not too sure. Some sort of Native American thing. In fact, all the turnstiles are decorated."

"Fascinating."

"What I *do* know is that Amanda is huge on recycling materials. She likes it when we go online and find people giving away stuff like furniture we can use or pavers or stuff like that."

"These look like electric poles," Jack said.

"Yep, all of them," he pointed to each section corner, "are

recycled power poles. The gates are constructed from old chain link fences. We even uninstall and remove old barbed wire from people who need it gone, just so we can use it here. Wherever Amanda can reuse or repurpose, she does."

"But she spares no expense on the farm equipment?"

"That's different. She talks about investments versus expenses. Farm equipment, housing for her workers – those are investments. 'Good sleep makes good workers and good workers make good crops,' she says. She treats us better than most employers I know. As long as we stay away from the girls and do our daily tasks, she treats us like kings.

"And the farm equipment? I think she's got some sorta deal worked out with the tractor place next door. She owns that land and lets them rent it in return for the use of their tractors and excavators."

"Richie, do you know of any gentlemen who are unsatisfied here?" Conrad asked. "Maybe someone's not happy with her rules?"

"Oh, yeah, all the time. But those men never last long. That's one thing Amanda doesn't tolerate. You don't do the work, you're out immediately. No second chances."

"And what happens to those men?"

"Amanda invites them into her house for a meeting, gives them some cash and paperwork, then drives them – or has Maria take them, I think – to the bus stop somewhere. We don't ever see them again."

"Do any of the men ever contact you through social media?"

Richie chuckled. "We don't use social media here. We aren't even allowed cell phones."

Jack scoffed. "You're kidding me? Who doesn't have a smartphone or gaming system these days?"

"We don't. It's for our protection. Amanda doesn't want us to associate with the people of our past and fall back into the same destructive routines we were in. I mean, think about it. Do you know how easy it is to get ahold of heroin or pot in this area? You can find anything you want on social media."

"And you're fine with this rule?" Conrad asked.

"Of course! We don't need cell phones because we can place calls anytime we need from the house or nursery."

"And what about the use of computers or tablets? Does Ms. Claremont restrict those?"

"Eh, to some degree. Social media sites are blocked, so we don't log onto those. There's no temptation if there's no access. We do have access to certain recycling sites. That allows us to find the stuff we need for the property. But we have all kinds of movies we can watch and books to read. Amanda encourages us to read."

"Ugh, I hate reading," Jack said. "It's so boring."

"Thank you, Mr. Morgan," Conrad interjected. He held out his hand and gave the worker a firm shake.

"Yes, sir," the man replied with a smile. "We owe a lot to Amanda for turning our lives around." Richie walked off to check the next gate.

The two detectives continued their walk to the nursery.

"You think the guys really are that happy here?" Jack asked.

"To each their own, Kinston. It's possible, but I don't rule anything out nor jump to conclusions about investigations. Cases aren't always what they appear to be. Neither are people."

—¡—

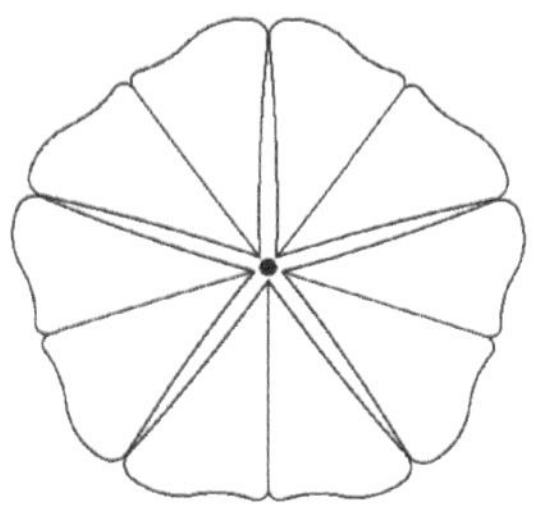

CHAPTER 29

AMANDA led AJ through the asphalt parking lot and onto the porous pavers. They walked past potted shrubs and young fruit trees. The older woman talked about her great-grandmother's house and more of her family history.

The detective looked towards the field and saw Conrad and Jack in the distance talking to a man near a truck. She continued to listen to Amanda's story as they walked past a small decorated koi pond and the barn where the farm equipment was kept.

"But I never forgave Robert for forcing me to sell that home. And I told myself one day I'd make him pay."

AJ stopped. "Pay? How?"

Amanda also stopped. She smiled. "I wouldn't allow him the pleasure of thinking he could hurt me ever again. I played a mental game with him, AJ. He thought he was breaking me with every hit, with every contact made to skin. But do you know what he was doing instead? He was toughening me up, making me stronger. I pushed my emotion away and build a fortress around my heart. Never again would he hurt me. That's how I made him pay."

"And you had nothing to do with his disappearance?"

Amanda stared at her with solemn eyes. "That's a bold question, flower."

AJ took a step back. "Ms. Claremont, I didn't mean—"

"Relax, dear. I sometimes forget you're only a detective doing her job and I'm another person of interest. You've read the police statements I gave years ago?"

"Yes, ma'am. I picked up on the abuse from some of the things you said. The way he wanted his eggs. How the table had to be set. How 'particular' he wanted things."

"Clever, clever girl." Amanda chuckled, then sighed. "Yes, the signs were there, but few people ever picked up on that. I never said anything bad about Robert to the police or to anyone. I didn't want to taint the Claremont name."

"But if he was that abusive, why not go back to your maiden name after his body was found?"

"Partly to honor his memory. After all, he did make me who I am today. Come, I want to show you the corn maze."

They walked by cinder block walls holding soil, mulch, and other fill material. One front-end loader backed out of the enclosure and dumped its load into the bed of a customer's truck. The customer waved at Amanda, as did the worker driving the loader.

The older woman led AJ down a corridor of bushes at the entrance of the corn maze. A large stone and concrete pyramid stood in front of them. The octagonal structure had steps leading up each side to a covered gazebo around three meters in elevation.

"Want to see the view from this one or the one in the center of the maze, closer to the river?" Amanda asked.

"I'd love to see the one closest to the river."

"Follow me."

They walked around the stone structure. AJ noted how precise the granite stone was cut. Sunlight glittered off the surfaces of each step. Shadows danced across the carvings. They walked down the original worn path, avoiding the rows of leftover corn stalks.

"This looks so different than in the Fall."

"You've been here before?" Amanda asked, stepping around a mud puddle.

"Yes, last year with my son, Eoghan, and some of his friends. I chaperoned that night. My daughter didn't want to come." AJ looked down and saw drowned worms in the muddle water.

"And why's that?"

"Well, for one, she's too young. She'll be six this year. And two, she said she had a dream of a skeleton man with owl feathers. She told me—and I'll never forget this—that the skeleton man instructed her not to come to the maze. It was just meant for the boys. The skeleton man also told her to start collecting all the feathers she finds. They're gifts from the gods, she said."

Amanda smiled again. "'Gifts from the gods'?"

AJ nodded. "Yeah. Jenna has a vivid imagination sometimes. She's been drawn to birds ever since that dream and started collecting their feathers."

"She's a precious gift from the gods herself, wouldn't you say?"

"She is. She definitely is." AJ paused and Amanda must have sensed the change in her tone.

"You're thinking of the day she was born, aren't you?"

"Not a day goes by that I don't. Unfortunately." She quickly changed the subject. "Do you have the same path every year for the corn maze?"

"Oh, no," Amanda chuckled. "Too many drones and too many aerial images from online maps. No, I like to change it up every year."

The woman stopped at a dead end and studied her surroundings. AJ saw another pyramid in front of them several meters ahead. It stood identical to the first.

"If you don't mind getting your shoes a little dirty, we can save some time and cut through some of the corn patches."

"I don't mind at all."

"Good. The ground's softer off the beaten path and you may have to push the stalks down a bit." She stepped between some of the dead plants and pushed them aside for AJ. "Tell me a little about your kids, if that's not too bold of me to ask. Then I'll tell you about the cornfields and give you some history of the place."

"It's not too bold. My son is the oldest. He was born about two years after Michael and I got married. I didn't gain much weight with him. Had a pretty easy pregnancy. Did everything the doctor told me to. I ate right, exercised, kept my blood sugar in check. Towards the end of the pregnancy, the doctor said he was ready to come out. He was born healthy as can be. Really, I had no complaints or complications."

"But not so much with your daughter?"

AJ shook her head.

They stopped in front of the second pyramid. Amanda walked around to the right and positioned herself in front of the steps. "We'll cross over more corn here until we line up the pyramid on the left with the one on the right. Then we'll be back on the path again."

They continued walking through some of the soft dirt. Several of the broken stalks fell over effortlessly as they were pushed aside. AJ felt the sun's warmth on her face and inhaled the air. There was a cool touch reaching out from the shadows and a warmth from above tugging on her collar.

"Tell me about your other pregnancy, flower."

"It started out similar to Eoghan's, but I gained a lot of weight with Jenna. I was always craving cheese. Couldn't stand the smell of some meats. The hormones weren't too bad…the birth was definitely more complicated. Honestly, I don't remember it… just-just that it was a C-section. And the C-section got infected and it took months to heal after that. What else can I say?"

AJ realized her voice cracked and her tone sounded sharp. She knew Amanda noticed the same thing because the older woman said, "We don't have to talk about it today. How about we save that conversation for tomorrow?"

"Why tomorrow?"

Amanda shrugged. "Because today is not a good day for those memories." She picked up her pace through more of the corn patches until they both finally emerged in a long pathway directly between the two pyramids Amanda had pointed out. "We go left to that one. It's the closest to the Merrimack."

The rest of the walk was done in silence until they reached the third pyramid. It was identical to the others, with the exception of some of the carvings. They both climbed the steps up to the gazebo. Amanda positioned her arms on the railing and looked out towards the river.

The Merrimack was barely visible from their vantage point, but AJ could faintly hear the rapids further down. The land behind the corn maze sloped gently downward and a dense tree line protected the rocky shore from prying eyes.

She scanned the horizon and looked around her. The apple grove blocked her view of the vineyard, but she could see the winery and picnic tables. The fields to the south were being worked by more than half a dozen men and she could make out a few buildings on the other side.

"What's that over there?"

"That's the halfway house where the men live. My house is up that hill on the left. It's hidden by the trees."

AJ continued to scan the horizon. She saw part of the top floor and rooftop of Amanda's house. She looked around again. All the buildings were beige, except the main nursery. Even the gazebo above her was a natural wood color; the granite rock, a darkened grey. Neutral. Everything was neutral.

"Is that another greenhouse over by your home?"

"Yes. It's a special greenhouse."

"Why's that?"

A wry grin crept up one side of Amanda's mouth.

—¡—

CHAPTER 30

MY, MY, MY, detective. You do ask a lot of questions. Are you curious for the sake of your job? Or are you naturally curious about everything around you?

Doesn't matter, really. Curiosity is a good thing, unless you're at the wrong place at the wrong time. Have you ever been at the wrong place at—

My apologies, flower. Of course, you have. I don't mean to bring <u>that</u> up again. Not today. We'll get to your story tomorrow when I tell you about my hummingbirds.

Myself, I've been at the wrong place at the wrong time. That was before I expanded this property and started my business.

After Robert disappeared, I knew he wasn't coming back. I knew he was dead. There are some things I just don't question, no matter how many times the local authorities did.

"How do you know he's dead?" they would ask.

"Because this is not like him at all," I'd reply.

"Did you kill him? Is that how you know?"

"Do you think I'm a fool or capable of murder? He went for his walk and just disappeared. Does that sound like I killed him?"

"No, ma'am." They would apologize, but their apologies fell on deaf ears. I didn't want their condolences or pathetic remarks. I wanted them to find my husband, find Robert and bring him home.

After six months of the same dance with words, I tried repeatedly to file for a death certificate.

"I'm sorry," the coroner told me, "we can't issue a death certificate without a body. There needs to be proof he died or some legal document that declares he's dead."

"That's not fair!" I yelled. "I need to sell my house because I can't afford the mortgage! And the life insurance policy he had is useless without the death certificate! I can't pay my bills!"

Can you believe that, AJ? There was a time I was nearly destitute and couldn't pay the bills Robert had accrued. We were deeper in debt than I ever knew. He had taken out a large loan and purchased a second house in Massachusetts. I discovered this when I started opening all his mail.

He never allowed me to open a single envelope we received. I thought it was because he had so many projects and legal venues he worked. No. It was another way to keep control of me and keep his secret life hidden from me. There was debt and no matter how much I worked, I got further and further behind. It was never-ending stress. It almost made me miss the beatings.

And then, after the Thaw came, the police showed up to my house one afternoon.

"Mrs. Claremont," Officer Brady said. His voice was so quiet and respectful. He was always respectful. "Mrs. Claremont, I'm sorry to be the one to tell you this, but we found a body down a steep ravine. It matches your husband's description. We need you to come identify it."

My whole body shook, and I slumped down on the floor. "I told you! I told you! Why didn't you believe me? I knew he was dead!"

Officer Brady lifted me up and helped me to the couch. He took the blanket and wrapped me in it.

His partner—I think that was Officer Matthews, but I can't

remember if that's the name—just stood by and said nothing. What could he say? What do you say to a wife who just finds out her husband has died?

You know. I see the emotion developing in your eyes. Your eyes always give you away. Yes. We both have experienced many of the same life events and tragedies.

We may not live parallel lives, but ours do fall in tandem. I'm just a few years ahead of what you can and will accomplish.

After the police calmed me, they took me down to the morgue and wheeled the gurney over. One wheel flapped and squealed off its axel. The room was colder than I expected. The body was draped in a sheet with the feet exposed. Back then, they still used toe tags. It was beige with a maroon string around it. Of all the things to remember, I remember that blood-red string on Robert's decaying toe. The body was almost unrecognizable. But the clothes—what was left—were the same. The hair color was the same. I just knew it was him.

I had him cremated and had a service held for him. Do you know how many people showed up?

No one.

Even in death, he wasn't missed. No one cared. Is that a bad thing? Should I feel bad? Because I didn't back then.

After that, there was no issue settling the estate or the debt or the life insurance. Such a silly thing, a small certified piece of paper, to have such a profound effect on a person. And I did what I needed to do.

I traveled.

I put everything into savings, boarded up my little house you see there, stuck my valuables in a safety deposit box. I went to New York City first to try my luck in the Big Apple. I was there for a short moment, but when my spirit was heavy of the accelerated pace, I left.

I went back home, very briefly.

Yet, Something tugged on my soul and told me to leave again. "Go west," that Something said.

"Where do I go?"

"You'll know when you get there."

I drove west through mountains and plains, pine trees and prairies. I drove all the way across the country to Colorado and then to Arizona. I wanted to see the southwest and the painted deserts and the Grand Canyon. I wanted to walk the art shops in Albuquerque and climb the mountains in Taos. I visited Roswell and laughed at the alien conspiracies. I drove further west and then north to Flagstaff and saw the Hoover Dam. Have you seen the Grand Canyon? I don't know why they call it "Grand". It's not.

It's majestic. It's humiliating splendor. The color of the hazy air against the barren rock is beauty you've only dreamed about. The enormity humbles you to your knees as you struggle to realize how insignificant you truly are in this world.

I saw everything I wanted to see at that moment in my life and then I drove back east, through Tucson, through El Paso and down to Big Bend. I saw so much soul-humbling wonder around me that I cried. And then I went deep into west Texas and stared at the night sky like it was the first time I'd ever seen the stars and the galaxy's rim.

I was lost in deep contemplation, unsure of what my future held. I was so lost. I begged the universe for a sign.

And then the next morning, as I sat on the patio, they came. The hummingbirds showed up one at a time to the feeders. They dove and spun, spiraled and zoomed. Dozens! And not just Ruby Reds! Costa's and Black-Chinned. Allen's and Anna's. I'd never seen anything like it. The morning sun would hit their feathers and the iridescence blinded me with color. I didn't need LSD or drugs to hallucinate visions of warriors dancing and fighting a choreographed scene. I only needed my hummingbirds.

They chirped and hummed. They dove and hovered in figured eights, in eternal fashion.

Oh, the hums! I still remember the hums to this day! It's the most glorious sound I've ever heard, flower. It was more peaceful than rain tap dancing across tree canopies. It was more peaceful than the lulling lush of waves licking the shores or pounding the rocks.

I traveled and experienced so many wonderful and horrible things on my road trip. As soon as I came back, I ripped the boards off the front door, went straight up to my bedroom, and I curled under the blanket to keep warm that winter. I hibernated, mulled over each vision I remembered. I dreamt and longed for those hummingbirds again. Desired them on so many levels.

And it was some point during that winter, I finally had my answer. My life's legacy danced in figure eights. My mind's eye slowed the beating of wings and I watched feathers go down and back, then swoop up and forward. Over and over and over again.

These scenes played out for an infinite amount of time. The hums drowned all noise and sound. The bold dark eyes ate at my spirit. My world turned on its end, flipped up and forward, back and down.

And I knew the hummingbirds were my answer, my glorious irredescent salvation.

Because these birdies, too, have made me who I am today.

—¡—

CHAPTER 31

EMILY WAS in the same greenhouse, repeating the same process of watering the plants: water on, mist from front to back, water off. A total of three times for each row.

But she was not alone this time.

Maria and another coworker stacked a few cinder blocks in one corner, then placed an old wooden door on top. They brought in fresh seedlings standing at attention in repurposed egg cartons. The girls placed them on the makeshift tables.

Conrad approached the young woman. "Ms. Vanderbilt, we have a few more questions to ask you, if you don't mind."

"I'm, uh, a little busy right now," she replied, not looking up from her plants.

"We won't be long, I promise."

Emily did not say anything.

"What are you watering?" Jack asked.

"Perennials," she murmured.

Jack leaned in closer. He appeared to make a failed attempt to charm her. "I saw that from the sign outside. What kind of plants are these?"

"This is St. John's Wort. Those are bellflowers next to them. We have some asters and bleeding hearts on the other side."

"Ms. Vanderbilt, can you remind us how long you've been working here?" Conrad asked.

"About two months, I guess."

"Emily," Maria said, "when you finish here, we need you to make a run to the hardware store and pick up those supplies. The list's in the office."

Emily yanked the water hose further down the walk aisle. "Sure. I can finish watering this area and then leave, if that's okay?"

"Come see me in the main building when you're done here." Maria nodded slightly to Conrad without saying a word. The two men watched her walk out with the other employee.

Jack crossed his arms and shook his head. "Why does she always look at me like she wants to kill me?"

"She probably sees you as a nuisance." Conrad turned his attention back to Emily. "Ms. Vanderbilt, are you able to talk to us, freely, right now?"

She made another pass with the water hose and then stopped. In a low voice, she whispered, "I can't talk here. There are too many people watching. Meet me at the diner in Tilton. I— " She paused and looked around, then finally made eye contact. "Just meet me there. Thirty minutes."

Without another word, she grabbed the water hose and yanked it behind her, walking out of the greenhouse.

"What do you think that's all about?"

"Our cue to leave. Any idea where Jardine is?"

"Meh. Probably exchanging widow stories with— "

"Kinston, enough." Conrad pulled out his flip phone.No bars. He frowned.

"What's wrong?" Jack asked.

"Do you have phone service?"

Jack pulled out his smartphone and looked at it. He shook his head. "No bars either. Think it's the greenhouses and buildings interfering?"

"Could be the location more in the river valley. Seems I can get service in random places."

"Same here. At least we get service in the parking lot."

"Let's go find someone with a walkie-talkie to relay a message to Jardine. Then head to the diner."

—¡—

Conrad pulled into the packed parking lot of the diner and drove around behind the building to find a spot for his SUV. They got out of the vehicle and were walking towards the front entrance when Emily ran up to them. Red splotches covered the apples of her cheeks as she quickly checked her surroundings. Her eyes were lit with paranoia.

"Can we change locations? I didn't realize the diner would be this busy." She quickly glanced around again. "The Chinese place next door is safer."

"Ms. Vanderbilt, are you in any danger right now?"

She shook her head and swallowed. "Can we just meet at the Chinese place? Please?"

Conrad nodded and watched the girl run back to the Claremont Farms company van. They followed her to the second location in the adjacent shopping center.

Emily quickly parked and joined the men as they walked into the restaurant. Only a few patrons sat in a couple of nearby booths. As the three sat down and ordered their food, Emily nervously kept watch of her surroundings.

"What's the matter? You seem freaked out," Jack said.

"I asked if I could take lunch first and then make the supply run in the van. They shouldn't miss me for at least an hour or so. It's just—honestly, I don't know where to start."

"Try at the beginning, Ms. Vanderbilt. Take your time."

She nodded her head several times. With a big gulp from her drink, she said, "I've been working at Claremont's for about two months now. They hired me in March to start planting and prepping for Spring. They hired a few girls actually."

"And how has the work been?"

"It's been great. It's a lot of work, but I love what I do." Her foot tapped rapidly under the table.

"Then why're you so spooked?" Jack asked.

She swallowed hard and turned her glass of soda on the table. "Amanda has a few extra bedrooms upstairs in her house and she lets a few of us live with her. Maria shares the bedroom with Amanda and—"

"Wait," Jack interrupted. "Amanda and Maria are sleeping together? That explains a lot!" He started laughing.

Emily sat back and crossed her arms in defense. "They share the same bed, but they aren't having a relationship or anything like that. Amanda's not a lesbian, if that's what you're implying."

"Mr. Kinston, no more comments." Conrad gave Jack a chiding stare. "Please go on, Ms. Vanderbilt."

"Me, Kaylee, and a few younger girls have the other two bedrooms. Not *all* of us live there, just a few. We all pitch in to help out and we haven't had an issue in a long time. We just have to abide by the rules, that's all."

"What rules are those?"

"One, we aren't allowed in Amanda's office. Two, we are never, ever allowed in the basement. And, three, we don't ever go visit the men at the halfway house. That's it. Three rules. That's all she asks of us."

"Doesn't seem too bad to me," Jack said.

Emily nodded. "It's not really. Kaylee's curious and wants to sneak down there, but the other girls told her not to or Amanda will kick her out of the house. Amanda—she doesn't allow second chances when it comes to the rules."

"Ms. Vanderbilt, why are you scared? Are you afraid of the girls in the house?"

"Are you afraid of Amanda or Maria?" Jack asked.

The young woman looked around again. "Look, I don't know what's going on. I just know things haven't felt right since the morning Michael was found." She flung her arms outward. "I didn't know him. I don't know anything about him. But Maria and Amanda have been acting strange ever since. We've heard them arguing a *lot* in the bedroom. And then—"

She stopped to look around just as the waiter walked up. After Conrad sent the man away, she continued. "This morning Amanda left the house earlier than normal. When the rest of us were ready to leave, Maria pulled me aside and told me to wait. Once we were alone, she told me Amanda had a special job for me.

"Maria took me into Amanda's office. First time ever seeing it, and, honestly? I didn't feel right stepping into that room. I'd never seen a room like that before. But Maria said it was okay. She said this was what Amanda wanted." Emily looked around again.

"What happened next?"

"Maria walked over to a cabinet and pulled out something wrapped in a cloth. She said Amanda wanted her to give it to me, and that I'd know what to do with it." Emily reached behind her, raised her arm up to lift something from her back, then placed the object on her lap, staring at it. "Honestly, I don't know what to do with this and after Michael died and you started asking all these questions, I knew I couldn't keep this a secret. I..."

She shook her head. Conrad could see the mental struggle she carried in her mind. "Ms. Vanderbilt?"

"Yes, sir?" Her grey eyes were stained pink as she tried to hide the emotion. "I don't want to believe this. But I think someone in the house killed Michael."

She carefully picked up the cloth and positioned it on the table in front of her. Then, she slowly pushed it over to Conrad.

He looked at the wash-worn towel and the faded green fibers. He took his unused chopsticks and lifted one edge of the fabric, then the other fold, peeling it back to expose the contents. He stared at the black object in front of him as Jack leaned in to examine it.

"Oh, shit!"

"This can't be good."

—¡—

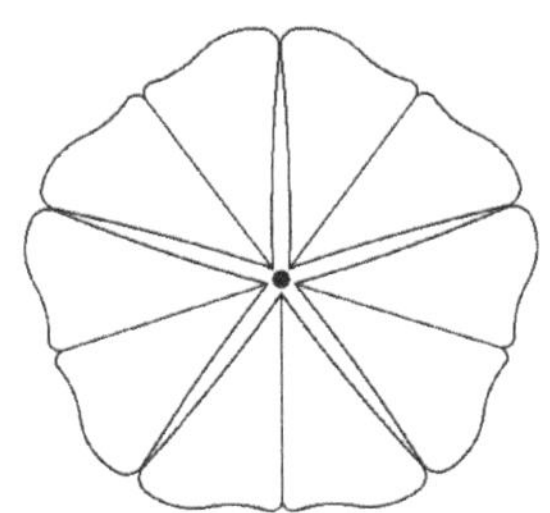

CHAPTER 32

"YES, VANESSA?" Amanda replied into her walkie-talkie.

"That director's looking for his female detective, the one you're with."

"AJ? She's right here with me. We're in the cornfield under platform number one."

"Okay." A few seconds passed. "He said to let AJ know he and Jack are leaving for a little bit. They need to head down to the police station."

"Do they need me to join them?" AJ asked Amanda.

The older woman repeated the question in the speaker and waited a short moment.

"No. They said they'd be right back. That she's fine."

"Okay, thank you, Vanessa." Amanda hung the radio back on her trouser pocket. She pulled out a tube of lipstick from the other pocket. It was a rich cherry red. After applying it to her lips, she stuck the container back in her pocket. "Would you like to walk down to the river? It's not that far from here."

AJ nodded. "Sure."

The two women left the gazebo and carefully made their

way along an obscure trail, then down the embankment to the water's edge. The gravel quickly turned into large, tumbled rocks. She could see smooth, rounded stones blanketing some of the riverbed, but the water elevation was higher than normal from recent rain events. Rapids roared in the distance, almost drowning out other sounds.

Amanda eased herself down and sat on a large boulder. AJ took a seat on a nearby boulder and inhaled the cooler air. She wanted to bring her children here in the summer, once the water had receded, and watch them balance across rocks as they pretend to pirate and pillage an imaginary village. The thought made her smile.

"I sure will miss this," the older woman said under her breath.

AJ saw Amanda frown and noticed her eyes turn a nearly-invisible hue of pink. The natural light made her skin look weathered and her expression appeared worn. Faint blotches of sun damage dotted her forehead.

"What makes you say that?"

"None of us get out of here alive, flower. We aren't immortal. We aren't immune to aging. And time is never, ever on our side."

They sat in silence for several more minutes until the boulder became an uncomfortable reminder of old scars and nerve damage. AJ shifted her weight to one side and tried to ease the back pain. Finally, she found a slightly better position, then broke the silence.

"Amanda, may I ask you something? And I hope this does not appear too forward or rude of me."

"Be my guest, dear."

"Why are you telling me all these private and personal things about yourself? You just met me a few days ago. How do you know you can trust me with this information?"

Amanda repositioned her own body and crossed her legs in front of her. She stared at the detective long enough for a flock of geese to fly by the vacant section of tree canopy where the river divided the forest. The older woman gave an equally impressive poker face as Conrad.

"All my life I've been able to study and watch people, get a sense of who they are in the first few seconds they enter the space around me. Very rarely have I been wrong about someone. From the moment you walked into that interview room, I knew we were connected somehow. I can't explain it. I just knew I could trust you."

"How do I know I can trust you? If that's not too bold to ask."

The smile lines deepened on the sides of Amanda's lips. "You don't. But you're thinking too hard about your surroundings and analyzing too much to let your gut instinct take over. You're always second-guessing yourself. It's one of your flaws."

AJ looked down at her fingers. "Yeah, I have a lot of those."

Amanda tsked. "No, no, no. You don't have as many as you perceive. But your past holds you back from what you're capable of achieving. It weighs you down. *You* are your biggest enemy right now. You just need to get out of your own head sometimes."

"And you were able to see all that after I walked into the interview room?"

"The more we talk, the more I pick up on. I know you're keeping secrets buried deep away. But remember, all secrets beg to grow and push through the dirt. Nothing ever stays hidden, not even those ugly feelings you have about your husband or children."

"Excuse me?"

"You heard me. Ugly little feelings you're ashamed of."

AJ felt anger rush to her cheeks. "I don't have any negative feelings about my family. And if I did, I don't think it's any of your business."

Amanda pointed at her. "That right there. That says it all."

AJ stood up a little too quickly and she gasped. Her stomach rebelled against her, punching her with a sharp pain in her lower abdomen. She cursed her body and the jabbing pain. With one hand on her right pelvis, she slowly stretched to release the muscles. She knew she would need to see a therapist, soon, to release more adhesions.

"Your emotions betray you just like your body, flower."

AJ shook her head. "Please don't call me flower. I'm not some pretty little thing in your garden."

Amanda carefully stood up and faced the detective. "You did it again."

"Did *what* again?"

She took a step closer to AJ. "Everyone puts on a mask when they go to work or when they meet someone for the first time. In fact, we all wear masks, to some degree. Some people become engrained with their mask and never learn who they are because they've learned to be who the mask is. Some people can quickly take off the mask because they don't care what others see or think.

"But you? You're stuck between. Your mask is broken. And every time someone tries to get a glimpse of who the real Ameena Jardine or Ameena Hawthorne is, you push them away and cover the shattered pieces with trembling hands. Isn't that the real reason you go by 'AJ'? Afraid of letting others in to know the true Ameena, the real spirit and essence of who you are? I don't ask these questions to hurt you or drudge up your past and beat you with it. I don't point out your flaws to shame you and have you cower at my feet. No. Quite the opposite."

"Then why ask these kinds of questions? Why make assumptions about me?"

"Because I want you to heal. You can't be the best detective or mother, yet. You want to spread your wings and wrap them protectively around the people you love, and you want to soar as high as you can in your own nurturing field of study. But you're shackled with the weight of your past. You haven't healed from the fuckery you faced. And you haven't yet faced the fuckery."

"I—" AJ shut her mouth. Her chest tightened with the grip of Amanda's words. What would she say to the woman who just read her like an open book?

Amanda was right. She always seemed to be right.

"Are you ready to head back to the nursery?" The detective nodded. "Good. I still have so much more to tell you before this over."

—¡—

CHAPTER 33

WE'LL BE back to the nursery soon. I know the girls are wrapping up some final tasks today and preparing for tomorrow. This weekend we expect an onslaught of customers, eager like little bees, to plant, seed, and grow during the Green Season. This time of year is always the busiest.

Tomorrow we have the shops closed as we finalize everything before the weekend.

Tomorrow will be an exciting day.

This time of year is my favorite. Autumn is another. I love how the Earth is blanketed with a duvet of leaves. Then Winter throws on the white comforter during its hibernation, allowing fetal growth between the frost heaves. Mud Season—or the Thaw, depending on who you ask—is nothing more than the land shedding its dirty placenta and using the nutrients from it to birth the first signs of Spring.

Each flower opens itself like a young woman having sex for the first time. The carpal is exposed like an eager clitoris begging to be touched by pollinators. In and out, in and out, the eager little suitors penetrate and excite the stamen. And every year, the flowers gush their anthers and open their labial petals for more. Life grows and, in full bloom of Summer, is impregnated again with next year's seed.

Sounds graphic and violent to many, but Summer is full of fornication and the "dirty deed" happening in front of everyone's eyes. And yet, no one cares beyond their own climatic life. Most are oblivious to the sex and joy of reproduction around them. The only thing they understand is how much they enjoy Summer.

I see you look a little uncomfortable. All this talk about sex and fucking is not for everyone.

How about we change the subject?

I never did tell you about this corn maze, did I?

Where you see the front fields and all the way back to the corn maze and river—I bought all that land from Old Man Bates. He left me the old ag equipment and I slowly leveled the area over the years. Back then I only had a few men helping me out, and it took months to get part of the land planted and growing crops. We started with a handful of acres in the front and then worked our way each year to back here.

Every season, when we till the dirt, we always find more boulders and gravel. You've studied geology, so you must be aware of some of New England's history and how frost heaves push the glacial rock up to the surface.

The stones, here, were deposited in the region from bedrock that was uplifted and scattered by the glaciers tens of thousands of years ago when this area was covered in ice. The stones laid buried deep, deep under layers of soil for hundreds and hundreds of years. That is, until we colonized this area in recent centuries. That's when the Newcomers—eager to stay warm in their little shingle-sided homes—stripped the land bare of trees.

They farmed.

They stripped more trees.

And as they did that, the Earth retaliated. She said, "I won't let you rape my land anymore. I'll wake my guardians and send them to ruin your naked fields."

The Earth shook her guardians awake, and the ground

rumbled. The rocks lifted, coming up, up, up through the soil. The guardians broke metal plows and tried to break backs of the pilgrim invaders.

But the two-legged animals were determined to shave the land bare. They took the stones and made walls, giving boundaries to what they claimed was theirs and continuing to rake and scrape the Earth with brown scars. These animals hoped to work the land for years to come.

But the Earth had other plans and the guardians kept coming. The stones kept rising, year after year, decade after decade. The smaller guardians were easily plucked for walls, so the Earth sent larger ones. But the larger ones required ox and horse and several strong men. Finally, the Earth wakened the bedrock and sent the rains to wash the soils away.

Slowly, the two-legged workers realized the ground did not want them. The plants also listened; they grew later and later and left earlier and earlier. There were no more trees to cut down to keep these invaders warm. And when the Earth sent her coldest winters to bite the settlers, they knew they were defeated.

Finally, the newer generations listened to the whispers on the winds, guided by where the Earth said to go. They said, "We should move west. There's more opportunity to the west."

Their parents shouted, "No! You must stay here! Who will take care of us if you go?"

"You can come with us. But this land doesn't want us anymore."

Off they went, wagon after wagon, of immigrants and pioneers. South and west, the droves left, away from this ancient Appalachian place.

The Earth rejoiced and the stones stood watch over their land until decades and decades of farms were finally reclaimed by the forests. And the trees, they celebrate their victory every Autumn with explosions of color waving in the wind.

But the Earth didn't drive everyone away. She whispered to a few, the ones who took care of her and listened, "Stay."

"How can we? When the others have left? How will we survive these winters?"

"Have patience, my caretakers. I'll take care of you, but you? You give back and keep the balance."

So, the Earth sent turkey and bear, geese and squirrel. She gave a select few of those two-legged animals the means to survive the winters: food to eat, bone for tools, fur for warmth. She had them collect the twigs and dead branches for fire and her trees stayed healthy.

From time to time she still sends her guardians to remind the people there is always a price to pay and she will decide who gets to farm, who gets to have the successful crop each year.

And every year, the farmers in this area give back to the land. We celebrate the Earth and give her the nutrients she desires. She still sends us the occasional large stone to pull from our fields, but it's only a reminder of her power and promise. We thank her for the annual gifts she sends and add them to our own walls, fortifying our property.

That may sound highly superstitious to you, but for us, the farmers here, we listen. We pay attention to the signs. We are more in tune to what the plants, the trees, the very dirt under our shoes, wants. And this—the listening and studying and learning—has helped make me a success.

That's why I was able to expand my business and purchase that winery over to the west. I was able to add more fields for farmers to lease. I was able to provide apple orchards and share the fruits of my labor with the locals.

And I was able to add this corn maze. It was a fun experiment at the time that turned into a prosperous endeavor. We're able to teach the children about conservation. We're able to educate the parents and show them the importance of self-sustenance, of giving back and taking care of the land. Heh, and we're even able to scare a few teenagers while we're at it.

This maze has become a pride and joy for the town and for me. The first couple of years, we had wooden platforms erected, but each year we had to replace them. It was costly and a waste. I do hate waste, don't you?

Finally, one Thaw, we had more stones than usual heave

themselves up in the cornfield. I stared at the ground, littered with these little lumps of granite and quartz. And that's when I heard the whispers Earth was telling me. I heard her answer to my problem.

"Build the platforms out of stone," the ground murmured. "Build me monuments."

And that's what I did. I had the men dig up the rocks and stack them in neat piles. Then I researched ideas, settling on specific stone pyramid designs. I heard the leaves rustle, "Yes! Build that!"

The ground rumbled in agreement. "Build us pyramids like we had in Central America. Boulder by boulder, build!"

It took two full years to gather all the rocks and cement to create the six platforms you see now. Each stand tall, just as they did for the Aztecs. Each is carved and dedicated to the past civilizations who knew how to farm and knew what the Earth wanted.

Each year, I create a unique design, always sure to incorporate my platforms. Sometimes, I repeat the pattern, but I like to change it up every year or two. Keeps it fresh and keeps customers coming back for a different experience.

Every year, before Memorial Day, my men will clear the maze field and clean the pyramids. We hold an annual fireworks celebration for all the farmers around here and I treat them to a feast and barbeque.

Then we take the leftovers, create the bone meal, grind up the meat and salads, and pour it all over the fields. We till the mixture in and give back to the Earth because that's what she demands.

We always give back.

But now, she's demanding a <u>different</u> sacrifice than the celebratory discards. She's tired of that.

"I want something different this year," I heard her say in April. "You know what I desire."

"Yes, Mother Earth," I replied. "I do."

"Don't fail me, Amanda, don't fail me."

"I won't. I would never fail you. I love you too much."

And that's why tomorrow the shops will be closed as we make

final preparations.

Tomorrow I give her what she wants.

—¡—

CHAPTER 34

INSPECTING the knife placed in front of him, Conrad used a chopstick to turn the towel around and view it from all angles. He reached into his right pocket and tossed his keys to Jack, then pulled his glasses out.

"Kinston, go in the rear compartment and grab an evidence bag. They're on the left, by the HazMat suit."

Jack nodded and, surprisingly, did not rebuke the command with an improper comment.

Conrad put his glasses on and continued to study the knife. The thick wooden handle branched out several inches and offered a solid grasp for the wielder. The ends of the grips were wrapped with leather. The butt of the knife had a carving burned into it: a hummingbird. The blade itself looked rough like the back of an alligator, but the black surface reflected the light from the restaurant lamps. The knife's blade arched in the same direction as the handle and came to a fang-like point. The edge was, undoubtedly, sharp.

"Obsidian," Emily said. "That's what Maria told me. Part of a pair of ceremony knives Amanda brought back from Mexico a long time ago."

"Obsidian? Volcanic glass?" Conrad looked above the rim of his glasses to see Emily nod several times. "Where's the other knife?"

She shrugged. "I don't know. I've never seen this before."

Jack walked back to the table with the evidence bag and the keys.

"Hold the bag open." Conrad took his chopsticks and covered the knife back up.

Jack held the bag open at the table's edge while the chopstick slid the object and towel inside.

Sealing the bag and signing it, Jack stared at the contents as he sat back in the booth. "Think this is the murder weapon? Think this is what killed Smith?"

Conrad pulled out his small notepad and pen. The last page was almost completely full and he would need a new one soon. "We can't jump to conclusions, Kinston. Ms. Vanderbilt, you said you were in Amanda's residence when Maria gave you the knife?"

She nodded. "Yes, sir. In her office."

"Did you see anything else out of the ordinary?"

"Just what looked like a lot of artifacts, like Mayan or Incan or something. Amanda has a passion for Native American cultures and always talks about her travels to the southwest and Mexico. There's all kinds of crazy things in that house."

"Who do you think killed Michael Smith?" Jack asked.

Emily shook her head. "I don't know if he was murdered. I can't tell you if anyone—including Amanda or Maria—did anything wrong. I don't even know if that knife is a weapon or not. It just feels…too coincidental, the timing of it all."

"Ms. Vanderbilt, what can you tell us about Ms. Claremont's office?" Conrad asked. "Who has access to it?"

"Just Amanda and Maria. No one else is ever allowed in there. She keeps the door locked. And the basement door, too. It's always locked."

"Have you heard the other girls tell stories or say anything about the basement?"

"No, sir."

"Have you noticed any strange smells coming from either location?"

She shook her head.

"Are there any other places on the Claremont Farm or Amanda's property you are not allowed?"

Emily's eyes went bright. "Yes! Almost forgot. No one's ever allowed in her greenhouse, the one by her house."

Jack scoffed. "Why the hell does she have a greenhouse by her home when she has four at the nursery?"

"It's her personal garden and sanctuary, she says. She's always in there. Sometimes for hours. And she keeps that door locked. Always."

"You've never been inside?"

"No. Neither have any of the others. There was a girl—can't remember her name anymore—she peeked in there and told us it didn't have any plants in it. She was gone the next day."

"Gone?" Conrad asked.

"Yes. Her stuff was packed, and I watched Maria drive off with her. Never heard from or saw her after that."

"Does Maria always drive the ex-employees off the property?"

Emily nodded. "Most of the time. I've heard the police have escorted a man off once." She looked at her watch then scrambled out of the booth. "Crap! I have to go. I'll be late getting back."

The detectives scooted out of their booth.

"Ms. Vanderbilt, thank you for meeting with us. If you need anything, please contact me." Conrad handed her a business card. She stuck the item in her pocket and walked away without making eye contact with anyone. After they paid and made their way back to the car, Conrad sat in the driver's seat and examined the evidence bag.

"So, what now? Do we arrest Amanda?"

"No. We don't."

"Why not? She's gotta be guilty."

"What makes you say that?"

"Just look at the crazy things she told AJ, about the blood, about her past. It's all adding up."

Conrad shook his head. "No, Kinston, it's not. Never jump to conclusions or allow a perceived notion and prejudice of a person convince you someone's guilty. We follow evidence and fact, not the truth we may think we know."

"Well, truth is, the woman's crazy, just absolutely insane."

"Peculiarities and eccentricities may make one crazy, but insane, it does not. Again, we don't jump to conclusions."

"So, what do we do next?"

Conrad put the evidence bag in the back seat and started the car. "Now, we get more facts."

—¡—

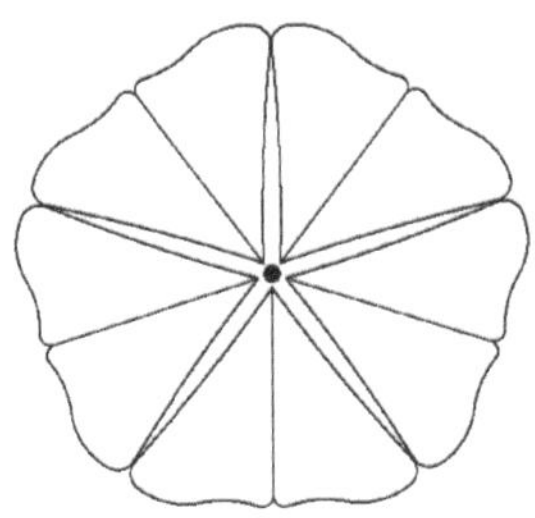

CHAPTER 35

LISTENING carefully to the way Amanda worded her sentences, AJ's hair stood up on the back of her neck.

"What do you mean by that? You'll give the Earth what she wants?"

Amanda chuckled. "It means tomorrow we fertilize the fields and the corn maze. Nothing prospers without some blood, sweat, and tears."

They walked back up the meandering trail and stood at the tree line, examining the corn maze. AJ thought she saw Amanda's lip quiver, but any faint emotion quickly disappeared. The woman's face went rigid as the stone structure in front of her.

"What would you like to see next, my dear?"

AJ glanced around and her eyes rested on the stone platform in front of them.

"Good choice," Amanda said.

"What do you mean?"

"You want to know why. Why the homage to Central America and cultures long extinct."

"But, how—"

She chuckled again. "Flower, you're as predictable as the direction a sunflower will face on a cloudless day."

AJ pressed the ball of her foot into the soft ground. "That doesn't make me a good detective, does it? If I'm that predictable?"

"I already know you'll be a great detective, once you get out of that head of yours. My advice? Don't ever hesitate in your actions or decisions. It could get you seriously hurt or killed."

"That almost sounds threatening."

Amanda shook her head. "The same principle applies out here. You have to trust those you work with and work with those you trust. You have to trust the soil to tell you what it needs. The crops here, they mean life. They mean families are fed and livestock can reproduce. You can't hesitate about getting the ground ready or delay planting the corn because you want to think about it and you doubt the time's ready. No. Your action—or inaction, depending on the course you're taking—has a ripple effect on everything around you."

"Everything's connected."

"Yes. Everything's woven together. Everything on this farm is connected in one way or another."

"Even these pyramids you created?"

"Especially these. I hold nothing but absolute respect for the Aztec and Mayan cultures. If there ever is anything in this world that makes me feel pure and exhilarated, it's them and the way they lived."

"Didn't they sacrifice people on altars though?"

Amanda dismissed the question with a flick of her wrist. "That's a small part of it. Did you know they were able to get six to seven harvests of corn every year? Did you know they believed in thirteen heavens and nine hells? They also thought the earth was flat."

AJ rolled her eyes. "Oh, gawd. Please tell me you don't believe that."

"No. Not at all. I know some of their beliefs were not true, but I still honor them on my farm. They were one of the most advanced civilization in Mesoamerica. Everything they did—

from stone carvings to the sacrifices to their market days and economic structure—were amazing feats at the time.

"I've added carvings everywhere that represent the culture. Eagles, coyotes, armadillos—everything I could think of. I've traveled many times down through Mexico to see the original temples and pyramids for myself. I even try to go down to the Southwest at least once a year and immerse myself in the history there."

"I've never been to Mexico, but I've driven through the Southwest before. I'd love to visit the art shops in Albuquerque again one day."

"Ah, so you've been? What did you think of the Southwest?"

"Honestly?" AJ paused to reflect. "There are things I liked and didn't like about it."

"Tell me what you didn't like first."

"It's a barren wasteland. It's too hot. It's too…brown. The ground, the sky—it's all brown all the time."

"Oh, flower, it's so much more than that! It's vast open spaces and wide horizons not hidden by trees or hills. It's exposure and nakedness that leaves you feeling vulnerable. It's a delicate balance between everything and nothing."

"It's also flatness with nothing for miles and miles. What if the car breaks down and you're a hundred miles from the nearest gas station? It's scary to think of that, especially with young children. Not to mention all the stories of human trafficking, kidnapping, murders."

Amanda pointed to her head. "That's the *fear* talking. That's an irrational emotion convincing you to never go out on your own and explore the world. That's how people never pop their little bubble and see the bigger one waiting for them. Fear consumes and holds you back."

"Eh, I guess that's true."

"Put the fear aside. Put aside the fact you don't like the desert and the flatness. Now, close your eyes. Focus on the beauty you see around you. What do you remember? What's the first thing that pops into your head?"

AJ closed her eyes and thought back. "Michael." She opened her eyes. "I'm sorry, I don't want to do this."

Amanda held her hands. "Get out of your hiding zone and remember. Just a little. Tell me about the memory with your husband."

AJ closed her eyes again. "Michael and I drove down Interstate 10. We were somewhere west of San Angelo and the wind started picking up around us. It started turning the ground a hazy brown."

"Go beyond the brown. What else do you see?" Amanda whispered.

"We saw something to the left of the road. It's large and moving towards us."

"What was it?"

"A tornado. A large dust devil. The sky was a hot blue and the ground was a beige brown. But the dust devil swirled closer and closer. We'd never seen anything like it before!"

"What happened next?"

"He punched the gas and we sped up. We were going miles and miles above the speed limit. The dust devil was getting closer and closer to the edge of the road. We saw tumbleweeds flying by us, but Michael sped up. He said he *knew* he could outrun it. I gripped my seat belt and started panicking."

"And?"

"The wind shook the car and the dust devil crossed an old barbed-wire fence on the right-of-way. We could feel the car vibrating sideways. We skated past it by a second or two and watched in the rearview as it crossed the road behind us and kept going on its merry way. Michael laughed. I saw the confidence in his eyes as he reached over and grabbed my knee." AJ opened her eyes. "It was a good memory."

"Indeed. Tell me something else."

"I remember the mountains in Taos with all its pueblo buildings. The clouds tried to hide the trees and some of the city. I remember rocks painted red. Art shops everywhere. Silver and turquoise against smooth dark skin. The cultures and museums."

"See, it's not all bad memories or fear, is it?"

AJ looked down at her hands and shook her head. "No, it's not all bad."

"What else do you remember?"

"I remember the drive back. We swung down from the interstate and stopped in Fort Davis. We went to the McDonald Observatory that night. We—" She stopped and shook her head. "We had a good vacation. That was a good vacation..." Her words trailed off.

"You saw more stars than you ever thought possible. You thought the night would pass too quickly, and in the morning, while eating breakfast, you remember the dozens of hummingbirds fighting over the feeders outside, just under the balcony of the visitor's center."

"H-how did you know?"

Amanda stepped closer and held the detective's gaze. The older woman smiled.

—¡—

CHAPTER 36

LITTLE flower, because I've been there. I probably sat on the exact same concrete bench in that circular gathering place, looking at the same exact sky you did. I've looked through the same telescopes, stood on the same stepladders. I've browsed the same gift store and their infinite cosmic gifts.

And, I sat on the same patio as you, watching the feeders, delighted by the dazzling display and aerial performance you once saw. I've witnessed the inferno of humming, chirping, the buzzing around me. The birds zipped and zagged, crissed and crossed, danced in figure eights, vying for that nectar.

And while I've had the occasional handful of birds come check out my shop here in Franklin, I've never seen that many hummers in my life! I've never seen the fuchsias or violets or bright orange necks as I did then!

I sat for hours just observing them. I didn't want to move. I didn't want to disturb their reality and existence. I held my bladder until pain made me get up, slowly, as to not disturb them.

But you know what? They didn't seem to mind. They kept at their business. Occasionally one would come check out my clothing or buzz by, tilt their head one way then the other, and zoom back to their feeding frenzy.

It was one of those trips and that scene—for me, anyway—that really drove my passion and obsession over hummingbirds. I had to know more about them. I needed to learn what attracted them, how to bring them to my farm. I wanted to paint them and own jewelry shaped like them. I wanted to recreate their colors and draw them to me like the Star of Bethlehem brought the wise men.

I wanted the best digital camera and lenses I could find. I wanted to capture them—freeze them—for all eternity. I've taken thousands of photos capturing every angle so I could study muscle and movement. I wasn't after the money shot. I was after the detail of feathers and eyelashes.

I wanted flowers that would attract my little saviors.

Foxgloves and morning glories. Honeysuckles. Columbine, petunias, lupines, daylilies. Impatiens, cleomes. So many! And it was another sign I was on the right path, that this—my garden, my farm, my land, my work—was my calling.

To be honest, there'd always been the attraction to hummingbirds since before I could remember. My mother loved them. She was obsessed with anything that had wings. She decorated the house in pastels and painted Spring with beautiful gardens.

She had angels hanging on every wall and faceted crystals in every window. Prisms of light danced across frozen cherub faces, tickling them with emotion. She grew a surreal garden of light inside and an unnaturally bright garden of flowers outside. She was surrounded by brightness and boldness at every turn.

I once asked her, "Helen, how do you make your garden grow?"

She replied, "With blood and sweat and tear. With love and laughter. With smiles and kind words spoken to each plant."

She talked to her plants. She told them secrets and they grew taller. She claimed they spoke back to her. She had conversations with the ground under her feet. She would even lay down in the fields and talk to the dandelions.

All the while, people would ask me, "What's wrong with your mother? Why does she talk to herself? What do the voices say?"

"How would I know? She never tells me."

"But you lived with her before. You should know there's something wrong with her," her neighbors would say. "This is unholy and she's not well."

"Is there something wrong and unholy?" I'd ask them. "Or is everything with her, in truth, righteous and well, but we're too blind to see and too dumb to hear?"

They would get offended and walk back to their side of the stone walls, going back to their own business. They'd stare at us through their windows, suspicious of anything we'd do. But that was the norm back then.

I did try to ask Helen about her gardens from time to time. How could her flowers be so much taller and larger than everyone else's? How could she attract so many songbirds?

"Good soil makes the garden grow," she said.

"What makes the soil good, Helen?"

She would smile. "In the darkness grows the light. You have to bleed and weep and sweat to make the soils rich."

"But, how do you do that?"

She always smiled at me and her eyes shone with pride. "The Earth, she tells me what she wants. One day, she'll tell you, too."

—¡—

CHAPTER 37

"WHERE are we going now?" Jack asked.

Conrad concentrated on the road in front of him as the traffic crawled through downtown Franklin. "We need to pick up Jardine and then head back to the office. First, I need to stop by my house."

"Do you live far from here?"

"Not too far. Up Route 3A."

"Wait. You live here in Franklin?"

"Yes." Conrad focused on the road. He did not care for all the questioning.

"So, you know Amanda pretty well, then?"

"She's as important of a figure here as Mayor Giunta. Many residents know her." He turned right onto Route 3A and punched the gas. He quickly exceeded the speed limit.

"And that's why you were asked to take this case? A little political favor?"

"Mr. Kinston, your questions are inappropriate."

"That's not a denial."

"Enough, detective."

"You're doing this as a favor, aren't you?"

"Detective, what did I say?"

"Sounds like some shady practices, if you ask me."

Conrad slammed on the brakes and jerked the wheel over. Jack's hands flew in different directions as he braced himself for the sudden deceleration and stop. The car spat gravel and dirt in the shoulder. He forced the vehicle into 'Park' and glared at the young detective next to him.

He bore his eyes into Jack and wanted to rip the kid from the seat. Dialing back his anger, he counted to ten—twice—before saying anything.

The young man sat rigid, too stunned to say anything.

"Mr. Kinston," Conrad's words were steady and slow, "you are less than one week on the job and less than one day from getting fired. I suggest you practice silent contemplation and reflection before you open your mouth again."

"But—"

"Dammit, SHUT UP!"

Jack flinched and sat further back.

"I'm going to be brutally honest. You don't have what it takes to make it in this career. And if you don't learn your damned place on my team, you can kiss this field goodbye. Not only in New England, but from the entire Eastern seaboard all the way to Texas. I'll ruin you with permanent marks on your record for being an arrogant, cocky, disrespectful, ignorant asshole and no one will ever hire you again.

"If you want to redeem yourself and keep what little dignity and chance at being a detective you have left, then shut up and sit there in *absolute* silence until we get back to the office. Nod your head if you understand those simple instructions."

Jack obliged and quickly nodded his head.

"Not one single word to me. Or Jardine. And don't ever question her history or background again."

Conrad sat back and jerked his suit in place. He gripped the steering wheel and counted to ten—twice again—before slamming the car back into 'Drive' and peeling out from the shoulder.

—¡—

"Baby, who's that in your car?"

Conrad kissed his wife and walked down the hallway. "Jack Kinston."

"Oh, you mean the kid you called 'Jack Ass' the other night?"

"One and the same."

Yasmin stood in the doorway of his office and dried her hands with the kitchen cloth.

Conrad sat down and swiveled in his office chair. He tried opening the bottom desk drawer, but the wood stuck before giving way. "Shit. Why is this damned thing always sticking?"

"The weather's warming up and it's humid outside."

He dug through the drawer looking for something obviously not there. "Fuck," he said, slamming it shut.

He stood up and saw her glaring at him. She crossed her arms and arched an eyebrow at him. "Conrad Marcellus McMillan, what is wrong with you?"

He stopped and watched her. He wanted to remain angry at the desk, angry at Jack, and angry for not finding a new notepad, but the way his wife leaned against the doorframe and pushed her hip out made him forget. He could not stay mad, especially around her.

"I'm sorry, baby. I need a new notepad and thought I could come home and quickly grab one. Jack Ass—as you so eloquently put it—pissed me off a few minutes ago." He walked over and wrapped a loving arm around her waist. He gently kissed her on the forehead. "I shouldn't've snapped."

"No. You promised you'd never come home angry. Hang that at the curbside or in the ditch, but never bring it in here."

He nodded. "You're right."

She pulled back and grinned slyly at him. "I'm *always* right. And by the way, your notepads are stacked behind the desk on the bottom bookshelf. You haven't kept them in the desk in a long time."

Conrad snapped his fingers then retrieved a new notepad. He quickly stuck it in his front suit pocket as he walked back by Yasmin. With two quick kisses on the lips, he smiled at his love.

"When will you be home?" she asked.

"It might be a late night tonight. I have a feeling this case is about to blow up."

"TV dinner in the microwave, then?"

He nodded. "You know how to warm my heart. And my food." He winked.

She tried to swipe at him with the rag. "Get your ass outta here before I forget how much I love you."

—¡—

They pulled back up to the nursery and Conrad parked under one of the shady areas.

"Wait here," he told Jack.

Kinston said nothing and never made eye contact.

Conrad did not care. He walked towards the large red building and went inside.

Paintings of hummingbirds were still being hung above the windows and along the rafters. Feeders were displayed outside every pane of glass. The shelves were emptied and the girls were removing the items to clean the spaces. The cashier and checkout area were spotless, and a bench was placed in front.

Most of the men were gone, probably back in the fields or repairing stone walls. The women took inventory and cleaned, getting ready for the big sale on Saturday, so he assumed.

Why else would there be so much activity?

—¡—

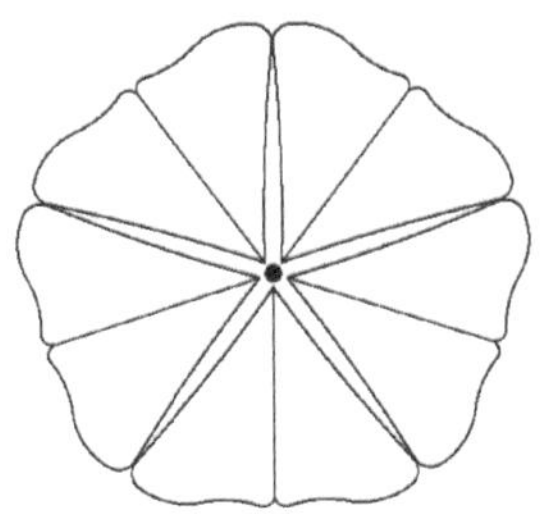

CHAPTER 38

RAKING her hands through the cool and damp soil, Amanda grabbed a handful and stood back up. She rubbed both hands together and then inhaled the scent. AJ did the same.

"Close your eyes. What do you smell?"

Hands stained a rich color, the detective inhaled. "I smell…a little bit of fertilizer, maybe?"

"Inhale again. Can you smell the phosphorous?"

She took in the scent again, careful not to get any particles in her nose. "It's almost garlic-like."

"Yes! What else can you smell?"

"Earthworms. The dampness."

"And?"

She took in the aroma one more time. "Metal. Almost like iron."

"Bingo!" Amanda chuckled again. "You have a good nose for this."

"I used to play in the dirt as a kid. Would always help my parents in the garden."

"What's your favorite garden smell?"

AJ looked up in thought and smiled. "I love the smell of cucumbers and radishes. I could smell the radishes as I picked weeds, feel the roughness of the leaves against my skin."

"Mine are the pumpkins. I love watching the bees pollinate the flowers. By the way, do you know never to plant watermelon next to pumpkin?"

"No, why's that?"

"Plants are living creatures and communicate all the time. The viney ones tend to be a little more selfish. Pumpkins don't like to share the bees and pollinators with the melons, and vice versa. They sabotage each other. I once planted both side by side. I had this beautiful melon which looked like a watermelon on the outside but was nothing more than a pumpkin on the inside. When I cut it open, I was so disappointed. But that's the Earth saying, 'I told you not to plant them together.'"

"I've never heard of that!"

Amanda nodded. "And you can have a pumpkin on the outside with watermelon seeds on the inside. It's funny how nature does that sometimes. What's meant to happen, does."

AJ wiped her hands on her jeans. Her fingers were still stained, but she did not care. She looked around again at the cornfield and then the front fields with the posts standing tall. Everything Amanda Claremont had accomplished over the years amazed her.

The detective shook her head. "I honestly don't know how you did all this."

"How I did what?"

"Learned all the little details about gardening and farming. Seems like a lot to me."

"Not at all. How do *you* know so much about geomorphology and engineering?"

"How did you know about that?"

"Eh. Conrad told me a little bit. You've told me the rest."

"But I haven't said much."

"You don't have to talk to communicate, flower."

Amanda stepped over a few more corn stalks and outside of

the cornfield. Both women stood on a gravel road that ran parallel and between the cornfield and the front crop fields. They started walking towards the nursery.

"The key to good gardens is listening to the plants. They tell you everything. If they start turning yellow, you might not have the right nutrients in the soils. What do you like to grow, for vegetables?"

"Um, I love zucchini, peas, tomatoes, swiss chard—actually all kinds of vegetables except one. Eggplant. My mom loves eggplant though." AJ shuddered.

"Heh, everyone has their Achilles' heel. The plants you listed—many of them—love acidic soil. Peas, beets to some degree, turnips, especially radishes—they all like a good iron content in the soil. It helps with chlorophyll."

"Chlorophyll…I'm trying to remember what that's for."

Amanda kicked a loose rock from the path. "Chlorophyll is vital for plants to harness the sun's energy."

"Oh, that's right! It helps plants and trees convert carbon dioxide to oxygen."

"Correct. Rhododendrons, camellias, gardenias—these are plants that also love an iron-rich soil. The darker the leaves, typically the more they love or have iron. But not too much. You don't want to burn the plants or have soil so acidic nothing grows."

"That makes sense. That might explain why my peas didn't do good one year."

"Well, peas are a little more delicate than you think. They don't need the hot, direct sun like corn or tomatoes. You can plant them in the shadow of corn or on the eastern slope of a hill. That might help them."

"I think I'll try that this year."

Amanda nodded. "Good. And what do your kids enjoy? Do they garden, like you?"

"Eoghan, not so much. He's busy being a teenager who loves sports. Jenna, though, she loves green beans." AJ smiled at the thought.

"Tell me about that, the green beans."

"Jenna had a slow start and the school district thought it would be best to hold her back a year. She doesn't mind. She needed help with her speech. What she might lack in development, she makes up for in patience. She can stay focused on a task for hours and hours."

"Let me guess, she likes to watch the seedlings push through the dirt."

AJ laughed. "Yeah. She once brought some turtle beans home from a school project. She told me she wanted to plant them the following year, so she put them in a little paper envelope and set them aside. The next year, we dedicated two rows to her turtle beans and she carefully packed the rows up, then pushed each seed in the ground and covered them up.

"They did great, believe it or not. And when it was time to pick them, she didn't want to. She wanted to wait until they dried up so she could harvest the beans. We waited until late August and she picked every single pod off the dying plants. Then, she sat in the kitchen one afternoon and pulled every little bean from its pod. We saved some to replant, but we took about two cups of beans and boiled them in a soup. She loved it. She ate the entire pot."

"I love how your face lights up talking about her."

"I love my children." AJ looked down at the gravel. The pronounced ruts had seen many tractor passes. The afternoon sun made the aggregate glimmer in the light as they walked past. "I really want to bring my kids here this year for the maze. I'd love to show them around."

"There won't be a maze this year, my flower."

"Why's that? I thought you did this every year."

"Ah, but the corn won't grow. The ground is asking for something else this year."

"How do you know?"

Amanda smiled, then looked up at the sky.

—¡—

CHAPTER 39

EARTH, Mother Nature, Gaia, Coatlicue—however you want to call Her—She says things. She sends her guardians from the deep and provides me stone to build. She sends me bees and bugs to pollinate, birds to pluck the nasty insects from my plants, and strong men to work my fields. She tells me who's worthy enough to be here, who's not. She communicates in ways most normal people don't understand or appreciate.

She's taught me about poisons and medicine, labor and rest. She'll take her vengeance out when needed or blanket us with protection. We just have to listen to what she says.

And, since my gardens were my only escape from Robert's temper, I learned to listen to her early on. I grounded myself in her healing energy, tiptoeing barefoot in late Spring. I felt her essence ignite my body.

Over the years, I heard her more and more. She guided me in making my farm as prosperous as it is now.

"Don't plant the corn this year," she says to me sometimes. "Plant soybeans. The corn took too much from me. Soy wants to give back this year."

Or sometimes she will say, "Bring the animals. Let the chickens take care of the ticks this year since Winter wasn't cold enough." Or "The cows will birth many calves this year. Give them your grounds to nourish their bodies."

There are so many things she says.

She told me to work with Norringtons' Meat Farm. She whispered her plans in the winds and I could smell that fresh manure, see the cows lift their tails and plop it in my fields. I know others think I'm crazy for enjoying the smell of fresh shit, but it's not bullshit I smell. It's nutrients, it's fertilizer, it's the growing cycle that spins round and round each year.

Birth, placenta, eat, grow, nourish, shit, sustain, impregnate, swell.

Repeat endless times.

Then decline, degenerate, die, decay.

And back to birth.

It's a cycle that goes round and round. A perpetual wheel like our days and nights, a year, a spiraling galaxy. Circles and spirals and spheres. That's the essence to everything around us, an infinite loop, skating across time in infinite figure eights.

I could dive down that philosophical black hole but let me come back to the Give-Take of Life, the balance that's called for.

Even in death and decay, the animals help the plants grow so the future animals can eat. The Norringtons, they help provide me with the organics I need.

Take blood meal, for example. It's a byproduct, very important to corn. It adds nitrogen back and can make the soil more acidic. If you're ever having problems growing your tomatoes, squash, cucumbers, or cabbage, add some blood meal to the soil. Not too much though. You don't want to over-fertilize.

But the blood meal is exactly what it says it is. It's a meal for plants made from blood. The Norringtons have no lack of that when they slaughter their beef or silence their sheep or specialties of the year. They save the vats of liquid gold and I sweep in, processing it down to the blood meal I need for my crops.

We also make bone meal from the animal parts we get. It adds phosphorus and calcium back to the soil. Doesn't burn your plants.

And the whole process, the Give-Take, it doesn't stop there. I'll send my men over sometimes to help the Norringtons separate the skins, hooves, and horns. We can make glues, toothbrushes, gelatins—you name it. We tan the hides and make gardening accessories with it. We utilize the entrails in everything from sausage link casings to marshmallows. The livers, tripes, and tongues are full of nutrients and we cook meals with those on occasion.

Everything gets recycled back. Nothing goes to waste.

Nothing ever goes to waste.

—¡—

CHAPTER 40

VINEY PERENNIALS hung low from the ceiling joists. Each looping tendril stretched out towards the windows hoping to see sun before the day's end.

Conrad stood in the middle of the main building and studied the elaborate paintings. Each hummingbird's throat and forehead were vibrantly colored. Each bird was in a different pose: one sat on branches with its neck periscoping for a better view, another flew upside down and backward. One stared straight at the admirer, following the patron with its beak and eyes. Yet another appeared ready to defend its nectar.

He noted the different flowers, branches, and backgrounds for each bird. Then he saw some wording near the bottom of each painting. Conrad stepped forward to study the word of one of the canvases: ABRAN. Before he could check another painting, Amanda and AJ walked in from the back.

"Nothing ever goes to waste," Amanda said, ending some conversation the two women had. "Ah, Conrad, good to see you again."

"Ms. Claremont, the same."

Amanda turned to AJ. "Do you mind giving us a moment, please?"

"Not at all." She glanced over at Conrad.

"Jardine, please go wait in the car. Kinston's already there."

"Yes, sir." With a nod to both individuals, the detective walked out of the building.

Amanda looked at the other girls left in the shop and nodded. Each stepped out and shut both the front and back doors. Conrad watched the silent exchange between all of them. He wondered if the employees knew what he had in his possession.

The old gardener sat down on the bench that faced the paintings. She patted the seat next to her. "Conrad, have a seat with me here, please."

Obliging, he straightened his coat and sat down. He crossed one leg over the other as he looked up at the drawings. "The paintings are quite impressive, Amanda."

She smiled as she kept staring at the artwork. "Glad you've finally dropped the formalities, Conrad. You'll be glad to know the Cumbersons came in yesterday after you left. They purchased a couple of pear trees and some rhodies."

"And how are they doing?"

"Really well. They said you and your family unit are doing equally as good. They respect you and keep an eye on your place for you."

He raised an eyebrow. "Oh? Glad to see your neighborly spies are checking up on us."

"Tsk-tsk. Shame on you, my sweet White-Whiskered Hermit."

"That was a bit of a tease, Amanda, I promise. Jordan and Genève are good neighbors. We help them out when we can."

"I know. You're one of the good ones, old bird."

"Thank you." He cleared his throat and added, "I'm assuming you know what I have in the car, then?"

She nodded. "Tomorrow will be a busy day for all of us."

"What's your angle this time, Amanda?"

She chuckled. "There is no angle. My bones ache. My head never stops hurting anymore. My time in this business is done.

I'll be shutting down my farm and nursery soon. That's it."

Conrad turned to study her. He noticed the extra strands of silver pushing from her scalp. Her skin looked worn and aged around the bright red lipstick she wore. He reached out and held her hand.

"Do the others know?"

"Only one," she whispered. "She'll keep her mouth shut, though she doesn't like it. I knew this time would one day come, but it's sooner than I expected. I truly hoped to have a few more prosperous years to give back to the community. Seems Mother Nature has other plans. 'You're done now, Mandy. One last hoorah.' That's all she's giving me, Conrad. One last spectacular firework's display."

"Better to burst like bombs than disappear like fading embers."

She nodded, clutched his hand a little tighter, then let go. Her face quickly went rigid and the dark rings accented the devoid emotion. She stood up, then escorted him to the door.

"Send your family my regards, Conrad. Tell Yasmin, I have a final package being sent to her tomorrow. The best heritage seeds we have, all for her vegetable garden. Tell her to use them wisely and they'll last for years."

"You make it sound like you're saying good-bye, Amanda. Anything else I need to know about?"

"Nothing you won't find out soon enough. I intend to have a long conversation with your little flower. Maybe even have a few cutting remarks for that young vulture."

"Jack?" He stood at the door and looked down at Amanda. She still hid her emotions.

"Mmhm. He rubs me the wrong way. He's not built for this job, you know that?"

"I do. That's why he's shadowing me, not interrogating you."

"Is that what Morning Glory's doing? Hadn't noticed."

"'Morning Glory'? I thought you called Aubreah that."

She nodded. "I do. Your daughter's a gorgeous Moonflower. AJ's more of a delicate Heavenly Blue."

"She's been through a lot, but she's not as delicate as you may believe."

"She just needs that push out of her comfort zone. I'll be sure to give her a motherly nudge from under that stone she's hiding." Amanda extended her hand out for a firm shake.

"Ms. Claremont, it was good chatting with you." He gave a respectful and slight bow.

"You have a job to do, Conrad. I expect you to do it. Just remember, tomorrow's promised to the chosen few. But the day after that, to none."

—¡—

The car ride back to the office was done in silence as Conrad's mind filtered through Amanda's cryptic words. Jack's eyes never left the passenger window and AJ appeared busy in the back seat doing stuff on her phone. When they arrived back at the office, Conrad had his detectives take care of some of their new employee paperwork before reconvening half an hour later. It was an excuse for him to gather his thoughts.

He shut his office door and walked around to his chair, then stood and looked out the window. The view of the Merrimack River, the same body of water that ran miles and miles upstream alongside the Claremont Farms, was something he enjoyed staring at when his mind felt unsettled.

Three days ago, the investigation was just into a possible assault or attempted murder against her employee, Michael Smith.

Two days ago, it turned to murder or wrongful death.

Yesterday, two missing and former employees, Quillard Shaw and Angela Briggs, were added to the investigation, though he did not know the full connection yet.

Today, a possible murder weapon was delivered to him. And, he learned she would be closing her business this year.

Something's not adding up.

"Amanda, what have you done?" he whispered to himself.

—¡—

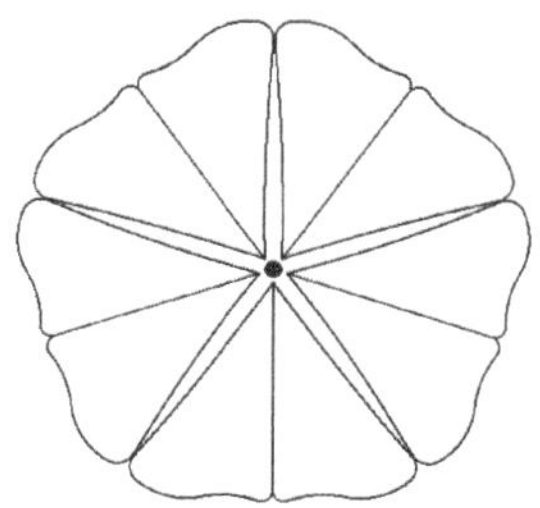

CHAPTER 41

EVERY CUBICLE stood in silent vigil as the three made their way back to their desks. AJ heard Jack swear under his breath. She heard Conrad's door shut from the corner of the building. The distant hum of the fluorescent lights and HVAC system were muffled by her computer firing to life.

She was halfway through reading her stack of new employee paperwork when her boss buzzed for her to meet him by the elevators.

"Bring Kinston."

"Yes, sir."

She walked to the adjacent row where Jack's cubicle was. Her coworker had his feet kicked up on the desk. He played on his phone while the paperwork sat blank beside his computer.

"Conrad wants to see us by the elevator."

Without looking at her, Jack waited several seconds before he finally made an effort to get out of his chair. She walked off, not caring if he followed.

A couple of minutes later, the Deputy Director led them down the corridor to the other side of the building. The brightness and white interior starkly contrasted the dark and drab cubicles on the other end. Large glass windows allowed passers-by to see technicians working in the labs, though the lights were turned off and most employees were gone for the day.

Conrad knocked on one window and a young technician sat up. As they rounded the corner, the forensic specialist opened the door.

"Evening, sir!" the man said.

"Mr. Yates, I'd like you to meet my two new detectives."

The young man extended his hand out and smiled at both the detectives. "Peter."

"Jack."

"AJ." She noticed how his dark eyes matched his hair and his smile was as warm as his voice.

"Mr. Yates, have you had time to test the blade?"

"Not yet, sir. I just opened the evidence bag and was about to start."

"That's fine. We'll watch."

"Yes, sir."

Peter quickly walked around the table and grabbed a new pair of latex gloves and mask. He pulled out a package from the drawer and ripped it open, removing a large cotton swab and an eyedropper of fluid. He grabbed another small container of distilled water and added a couple of drops to the swab tip.

With circular motions, he rubbed the swab across both sides of the knife blade. The tip turned a dull color. He set the stick aside on a sterile surface and grabbed the eyedropper. Holding it vertically in front of him, he broke the ampules within and carefully swirled the container. He picked up the swab in one hand, and with the other, let the chemicals drip onto the tip. The cotton immediately turned green.

Holding the swab up to show Conrad, Peter said, "Positive for blood, sir."

"Is that human blood?" Jack asked.

"Not sure. We determine that by the next test."

Peter grabbed a kit from another drawer. AJ made out the

abbreviation "OBTI". He set it on the table, opened it, and removed an ampule and a package with an applicator. He took another cotton swab and wet the tip with distilled water again. The forensic technician repeated the same circular motions across both sides of the knife blade. He unscrewed the kit and swirled the swab inside the liquid for several seconds. When he was satisfied, he sat the swab down. With the lid back on the kit vial, he shook the contents and set it aside while he opened a test strip. Then, he grabbed the vial, broke another ampule in the lid, and put three drops of the mixture on the test strip.

"Reminds me of a pregnancy test," AJ said.

Peter chuckled. "Similar process but this is less messy." Then he looked at Conrad. "Not like I would know…sir…" He chuckled.

AJ smiled. The technician's laugh was contagious.

He looked at the test strip again and nodded. "Positive for human blood, sir." He tilted it over and showed the others. Two lines appeared in the center, one lighter than the other.

"Do we know who's blood it is?" Jack asked.

"They have to send that out for a DNA match," AJ replied.

"There could also be multiple donors on the blade," Peter said.

"What makes you say that, Mr. Yates?"

Peter turned an overhead lamp on and shined the knife under it. "See how shiny the surface is here, including the handle down here?" He pointed his pinky finger to the hilt. "All of this reflective area is dried blood. Some areas are shinier or darker than others. That could be layers of older blood, but it's hard to tell without running more tests."

"All victims?" Jack asked.

AJ shook her head. "We can't make that assumption. It could be Amanda's blood or one of her employees."

"How long will the DNA test take, Mr. Yates?"

"There's a little bit of a backlog, sir. It could be a couple of weeks at the earliest."

"Go ahead and send it off for testing." Conrad looked at his watch and then his subordinates. "Call it a day. We'll pick up tomorrow. I have some paperwork to catch up on."

The Deputy Director walked out, followed by Jack. AJ watched both men through the other side of the glass as they disappeared down the corridor.

She turned her focus back to the knife and watched Peter place it back in the evidence bag. Her mind was so fixated on the detail and shape of the weapon that she did not hear the technician's question at first.

"Earth to AJ!"

"Oh, sorry. I was just thinking about that knife."

"I was asking if you've been on the job long?"

"Me? Since Monday." She looked around the lab. Everything was in pristine and immaculate condition. "What about yourself?"

He looked up at the ceiling and swayed his head a couple of times. He looked half her age when he did that. "Oh, about six months, I guess? Time flies when you're having fun."

"How do you like it so far?"

"Pretty good, I'd say." He sealed, signed, and dated the bag. "What about you?"

"I like it. It's not what I expected for my first week."

"I know how that goes. They throw you off the cliff with no mercy. Either sink and drown or swim like the fishes!" His stomach grumbled. "Mmm, fish…" He chuckled again.

"You like fish?"

"I like all kinds of food. My mom's Chinese and my dad's Mexican. Sushi or tacos. Sometimes both. Ever had cactus salad with goat cheese? It's *so* good!"

"I've never tried that. My mom's Lebanese, so we have tons of Middle Eastern food all the time."

"Oh, man! I love stuffed grape leaves! I'll mow your lawn, clean your house—whatever you want for the recipe to that."

AJ smiled. He reminded her so much of her own brothers. After several minutes of conversation about various ethnic foods, she finally made her way back to her desk. The light was still on in Conrad's office, though she knew Jack had left promptly after the meeting in the forensics lab.

She sat down and looked at her computer. Something about

the knife bothered her, but she couldn't place her finger on it. She opened up a browser and typed 'obsidian knife', then hit 'Search'. After half a dozen scrolls of the mouse, she stopped at one image. A tightness developed in her chest.

"Oh, shit..."

Her abdomen resisted when she jumped up. "Easy, easy, easy," she told herself. Holding her side, she walked over to Conrad's office and banged on his door.

"Come in," she heard from the other side. She swung the door open. "Everything okay, Jardine?"

"Sir, I think the knife's part of a ceremony. I think someone was trying to sacrifice Michael Smith!"

"Have a seat and tell me what's going on."

"There was something about that knife that looked ancient to me, so when I got back to my desk, I did a search for obsidian knives. I came across a website about Mayan cultures and sacrificial sites and they used knives just like the one Amanda has! Didn't you say it was part of a set she got in Mexico?"

"Yes."

"What if everything—the corn maze, the carvings in the crop fields, the color red, the talk of blood—just everything is Amanda and her employees replicating what the Mayans or Aztecs did in the past?"

Conrad took his glasses off and leaned on the desk. "Go on. I'm listening."

"Smith was found in something similar to a loincloth. His ankles and wrists had bruising around them, more so on his ankles. I reread the autopsy report, that's how I know. What if Amanda and-or one of her employees have been sacrificing people and spreading their blood through the crops? She goes on and on about Coatlicue, the Aztec culture, blood meal, bone meal, how important blood is. Sir, what if she's about to do a big sacrifice tomorrow before the crops are planted?"

Conrad leaned back and remained silent for several moments. He tapped his fingers on the desk in thought. "Everything you said is plausible. Do you think there's enough here for a search warrant?"

"Sir, I don't know. I'm still new to all of this."

"Think, detective. Is there enough probable cause here? Do you think Ms. Claremont, or one of the women living in her residence, is capable of murder?"

"What if I give you the wrong answer?"

"There is no wrong answer, AJ. Is your answer a logical conclusion based on an educated hypothesis? Do you have enough evidence that warrants a search of the residence?"

She thought for a moment, then nodded. "Yes, sir."

—¡—

CHAPTER 42

AFFIDAVIT IN SUPPORT OF SEARCH WARRANT

I, Conrad M. McMillan, being duly sworn, depose and say:

I have been employed by the New Hampshire Department of Safety, Division of State Police, Investigative Services Bureau, Major Crimes Unit for six years and nine months. I have been the Deputy Director for the Investigative Services Bureau for four years and three months. I am authorized to investigate criminal offenses, interview witnesses, and process crime scenes.

This affidavit is respectfully submitted in support of an application for a warrant to search the following premises and vehicles pursuant to RSA 630:1-a, I (b)(2) found in NEW HAMPSHIRE TITLE LXII CRIMINAL CODE and that it involves the disappearance and death of witnesses:

(1) STRUCTURE #1: Franklin, New Hampshire, a

multi-family residence located on the property of Claremont Farms and Nursery at 21 Coatlicue Road. The residence has white painted wood siding, black trim around all windows and doors, and a red front door located in the front center of the home. The home is a Colonial-style dwelling with two windows to the left of the front door and two windows to the right. It is a two-story structure with a high-pitched roof and an attached garage to the right of the front door. Stone pavers lead from the driveway up to the front door. The search will include the interior of the home from the basement to the attic, the garage, and all interior spaces, including the immediate vicinity around the dwelling. Tax records indicate Ms. Amanda Claremont was deeded the property on June 15, 1985, and has lived at her residence since September 1974. Prior to the property deeded to her name, said property ownership belonged to Ms. Claremont's husband, Robert D. Claremont, now deceased.

(2) STRUCTURE #2: Located west of Structure #1, a large greenhouse with frosted glass windows and aluminum trim. The building is an arched structure with a metal door on each end. The rear metal door is welded shut. The front metal door has two deadbolts.

(3) AUTOMOBILE #1: A vehicle with New Hampshire registration, number [REDACTED] and Vehicle Identification Number [REDACTED]. The vehicle is described as a 2001 Ford Crown Victoria, white, four-door sedan, and is registered to Amanda Marie Claremont, 21 Coatlicue Road, City of Franklin, New Hampshire. Ms. Claremont is the sole owner and primary user of said vehicle.

As discussed below, there is probable cause to believe that a search of the aforementioned premises may result in the collection of evidence relevant to an ongoing criminal investigation into the death of Mr. Michael Smith in violation of RSA 630:1-a, I (b)(2) found in NEW HAMPSHIRE TITLE LXII CRIMINAL CODE.

OVERVIEW

The Investigative Services Bureau, Major Crimes Unit (hereinafter "ISBMCU") investigation into the death of Michael Smith has led to the identification of Ms. Amanda Marie Claremont, owner and founder of Claremont Farms and Nursery of Franklin, New Hampshire, as a person necessitating further investigation for several reasons:

(1) Mr. Michael Smith, prior to his death, when asked who harmed him, pointed towards the Claremont household. During the medical examination of the body, a precise incision across Mr. Smith's throat and neck was consistent with a surgical blade and deliberately inflicted wound.

(2) An employee of Ms. Claremont's provided myself and Detective-in-training Jack Kinston with an obsidian-made knife, claiming that it could have allegedly been used in a crime.

(3) The obsidian-made knife has a surgical edge and is capable of inflicting the wound on Mr. Smith's neck and throat.

(4) When Forensic Technician Peter Yates tested the knife for the presence of blood, preliminary tests came back positive for human blood. The knife has been sent for further testing and developing of a DNA profile of the blood found.

(5) Fingerprints were extracted from the blade and those were compared to the fingerprints on file for Ms. Claremont. The fingerprints came back as a positive match to Ms. Claremont.

(6) There is also a possible connection between Mr. Smith's death and the disappearance of Quillard "Quill" Shaw, a 25-year old male who is sought in connection with the possible kidnapping and disappearance of 17-year old high school student Angela Briggs on July 16, 2010.

Based on this evidence and an oral account by Ms. Claremont's employee, there is probable connection to the death of Mr. Smith.

I hereby incorporate this affidavit by reference herein. See Exhibit A.

FACTUAL BACKGROUND

Over the course of the past few days, myself and Detectives-in-training Jack Kinston and Ameena Jardine conducted interviews with all the Claremont Farms and Nursery staff and field workers. Ms. Jardine conducted extensive interviews with Ms. Claremont directly, while myself and Mr. Kinston interviewed the employees.

During the interviews with the employees, Ms. Emily Vanderbilt came forward on Thursday, May 10, 2018, with information regarding the obsidian-made knife. Ms. Vanderbilt stated that another employee and roommate of Ms. Claremont's, Ms. Maria Ellanogek, gave Ms. Vanderbilt the knife as allegedly instructed by Ms. Claremont. Ms. Vanderbilt said the obsidian-made knife was part of a pair and that the other knife was allegedly at the residence of Ms. Claremont. Ms. Vanderbilt also believes that Ms. Claremont could have some knowledge of the crime against Mr. Smith.

With respect to the greenhouse, we have a written statement from an anonymous person with claims that the greenhouse is frequented by Ms. Claremont at odd hours of the day and night. The letter also states that Ms. Claremont could be keeping the other obsidian-made knife in the greenhouse and that it could allegedly have been used in other crimes. See Exhibit B.

With respect to the vehicle, it is constantly parked in front of the residence and may have pertinent evidence critical to this investigation.

CONCLUSION

Based on the foregoing, I submit that there is probable cause to believe that a search of the Subject Premises may result in the collection of evidence relevant to the investigation of murder or murders and kidnapping in violation of RSA 630:1-a, I (b) (2); RSA 633:1, I (c) and (d) found in NEW HAMPSHIRE TITLE LXII CRIMINAL CODE. Specifically, there is probable cause to believe that a search of the Subject Premises as described in the attachment to this Affidavit, may reveal other relevant documents, writings, photographs, computer records, and weapons in said crimes.

Because this affidavit is part of an ongoing investigation that would be jeopardized by premature disclosure of information, I further request that this Affidavit, the accompanying Order, and other related documents be filed under seal until further order of the Court.

The statements contained in this Affidavit are based in part on information provided by reliable witnesses, observations by Detectives-in-training Ameena Jardine and Jack Kinston, and my experience and background as a senior detective and Deputy Director for the Major Crimes Unit. I have not included each and every fact known to me concerning this investigation. I have set forth only the facts I believe are necessary to establish the solid foundation for the search warrant.

____

Conrad M. McMillan
Deputy Director
Major Crimes Unit
Investigative Services Bureau
Division of State Police
NH State Department of Safety

Sworn to before me this _____ day of ______, 2018.

____

Honorable District Judge
Franklin District Court
Merrimack County, New Hampshire

Friday, May 11, 2018

CHAPTER 43

LOOKING down at the blinking red light on his office phone, Conrad quickly pressed the speaker button.

"Morning, Doug."

"Conrad?"

"What can I do for you, Chief?"

"I don't know how, but Amanda found out you have a search warrant for her property."

"Shit!" He tapped his fingers against his desk and stared at the new scar across the surface.

"She stopped by with one of her lawyers."

His fingers abruptly stopped and his palm went flat. "Say that again?"

"She stopped by with one of her lawyers. She won't contest the warrant. Said she'll keep the sharks at bay…under a few conditions."

"I'm listening."

"First, one of her lawyers shadows you while you serve the warrant and do your searches. And second, your female detective, AJ, has to keep her company all day today."

"That's it?"

"Eh, more or less. She has one lawyer waiting at her house and two on standby if her demands aren't met. She said you can do what you need, but if she's interrupted at the nursery, there'll be consequences."

"What kind of consequences?"

"Remember that lawsuit she filed years ago against that Fortune 500 company? The one about contaminants in the river?"

"Yeah. It dragged on for three or four years."

"Yep. She was aggressive. And won. She'll do the same thing here if need be."

"This is going to get messy, isn't it, Doug?"

There was a long pause on the other end. "Yeah. It could."

—¡—

Conrad pulled out of the I.S.B.'s parking lot and took the access road to the interstate. Jack still appeared to sulk some, though he did make eye contact with everyone and appeared more polite. He glanced in the rearview mirror. AJ had her head deep in paperwork, reading the affidavit and its attached exhibits. She took the highlighter and marked up certain areas. She was methodical and analytical, something he liked about her. An image of Aubreah brushed his mind and he returned his gaze to the road.

One day she'll know. Now's not the time.

Behind his SUV, the crime scene investigation bus followed. He could see Peter Yates, the newer forensic tech in the passenger seat while Pat Sonnito, the senior and lead for this assignment, drove. Her white hair sharply contrasted Peter's.

As they took the interstate exit, AJ looked up and caught his occasional glance. Her eyebrows were tight with thought and a question.

"Yes, Jardine?"

"Sir, are we going to have enough time to search the entire house today?"

"Kinston and I will be doing the search. Ms. Claremont has requested you stay with her."

He heard Jack chuckle. "Guess you get to babysit while the men do the work."

Conrad saw AJ's eyes grow big and her mouth open to rebut. Before she could, he said, "Kinston, that's enough."

"Sir, I know she likes talking to me, but wouldn't I be better off at the house, helping you two?"

"No. She specifically requested you and that's where you need to be. If Amanda has committed murder or knows anything at all about Michael Smith's death or the disappearance of any other employees, then you are needed to listen and talk to her."

"Do you want me to ask her directly if she did it?"

"Absolutely not. Do anything to piss her off, the lawyers step in. She's more powerful than you can imagine."

"You make it sound like she's a crime boss," Jack said.

"Her lawyers have drudged up all kinds of secrets on all kinds of high-ranking officials, including a few in the state's capital. I wouldn't doubt it if she has private investigators or nosy neighbors in her pocket."

They meandered down Central Street, past the large monumental wheel in Trestle View Park and scenic downtown Franklin. As the car sat at a traffic light near the dam and bridge, Conrad watched AJ put all the papers back in a folder and fasten it to her clipboard. She tucked everything into a backpack.

Several minutes later, the car rolled past the nursery and farm, then took a left into the residential driveway. Large maple trees guided the vehicle slowly up the graded pavement. They crossed a gravel intersection perpendicular to the driveway and near the road. Conrad looked in both directions; one end shouldered the front fields, the other went to the Norringtons' meat farm. He continued the meandering climb. The area opened up to a small pond on the left. Ducks splashed around as they took off.

Adjacent to the pond was the halfway house. A large residential home and a converted barn attached with a closed walkway sat back slightly from the drive lane. A large parking area for multiple vehicles or farm equipment was neatly framed with landscaped and manicured plants.

"Are we also processing the halfway house?"

"No, Mr. Kinston," Conrad replied as the car dipped off the asphalt and onto dirt. "Only what's ahead."

The narrowing path snaked steeper up an incline. The tree canopy thickened above them before opening back up to reveal Amanda Claremont's home. It was a colonial-style building with several landscaping gardens peppered around it. The grass was freshly mowed. Amanda's car and one other sat in front of the garage door. Steps led from the ground level edge of the driveway up to the first-floor front door. He could see the greenhouse set further back.

The crime scene bus parked behind him and everyone in both vehicles got out. Conrad led the group to the front door, but it opened before he could knock.

—¡—

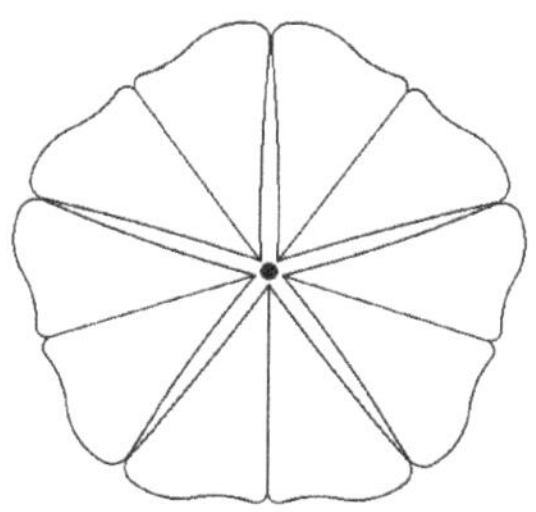

CHAPTER 44

"MR. MCMILLAN, we've been waiting for you." AJ peered around her boss to see an older, plump man in a dark suit standing in the entry. He quickly shut the door behind him and blocked it from the investigators.

"My apologies, have we met before?" Conrad asked.

"Not officially. I'm Maurice Juniper, one of Ms. Claremont's attorneys. She's inside the residence right now."

Conrad handed the attorney the search warrant then folded his hands in front of his suit. Maurice did not bother to read it.

"There's another condition besides the one Police Chief Galvan gave you this morning, Mr. McMillan."

"I'm listening."

"Ms. Claremont must be allowed to stay with you while you search the basement."

"That's illegal," Jack said. "She can't be in the same space with us."

The lawyer ignored the young detective and stood taller, though it did not help his short stature. "There are delicate items of utmost value in the basement that require my client to be present and monitor, Mr. McMillan. I will also be present to ensure nothing happens to any of her equipment or property. If even ONE—" he quickly shot a finger up in the air "—item is broken, ruined, or ceases to be functional, your department will be held accountable and immediately sued to the full extent of my firm. Are we clear?"

Conrad looked behind him to the forensic technicians, then to Jack and her. She could see him thinking about his options and what to do. He looked back at the technicians.

"Mrs. Sonnito, Mr. Yates, please wait in the bus until we call for you. Send any officers in to find me when they show up."

He turned around and took a step up closer to the lawyer. "Mr. Juniper, we accept this condition. Please lead the way."

"Very well, follow me."

Instead of opening the front door for all to enter, he walked around everyone and down the steps to the driveway.

Jack spoke in a low voice. "How can you let her get away with this?"

In an equally low voice, Conrad replied, "Sometimes it's better to fold a hand than bet against the odds, Mr. Kinston. We'll be fine."

Maurice pulled a garage door opener from his pocket. With dramatic flair, he pointed it to the door and the motor came to life. The door crawled open and, once it stopped, he continued to walk inside.

The garage itself had a large oil tank, hot water heater, and furnace—typical New England maintenance equipment. Shelves of planters, gardening equipment, and boxes lined one wall while cabinets, tools, and stacks of wood lined another. There was barely enough room to fit one car, much less two.

AJ watched the lawyer smile as he stopped in front of the basement door. Another hand quickly came up with two fingers extended. His eyes went back and forth between the trio. "We have TWO sets of doors to walk through. We cannot open the second until the first is closed. There's enough room for two people at a time. You will go in one at a time with me as your escort." He turned his body to Conrad. "Mr. McMillan, you're first."

Maurice opened the door and the pair walked in. He closed the door behind the new detectives. They looked at each other and shrugged, waiting for entrance. A few minutes later, Maurice came for Jack and repeated the process.

She waited alone in the garage and looked around again.

Looks so much like Dad's garage. Maybe cleaner.

A few minutes after that, it was her turn.

She stepped inside a meshed cage as the lawyer closed the first door. He pressed the garage door opener again and she heard the garage close. He took a couple of steps around her, brushing his gut against hers as he twisted himself around to the second door. His overwhelming cologne invaded her nostrils, making her eyes water.

Maurice lifted the latch and pushed the door open, letting himself and AJ inside the basement. They took a few steps down to a lowered floor.

"Holy…shit…" she said under her breath.

Three walls were lined with cages, from floor to ceiling, each sticking out about the width of her arms-spread and twice as wide. Tile lined the floors and exterior basement walls inside each enclosure. Potted trees and plants adorned interior spaces of the cages. Screen doors were fastened shut on most of them. A couple of screened side panels were pulled from between three cages, opening up the interior space to make a larger enclosure.

Lattices ran like rafters across the ceiling. Flowered plants hung from baskets across the way. Vines and ivies wove in and out where they could. The air felt humid and tropical. The temperature was warmer than expected and she could feel her blouse starting to stick to her back. The smell was a mix of summer on a hot southern morning. Sometimes she could hear fluttering and buzzing and a gentle hum from the lights. Mostly the space was silent.

Two very long and narrow tables ran parallel to each other in the center of the basement area. The middle aisle was equidistant in width to the aisles between the tables and cages. Under each table were dozens of aquariums and stacks of Tupperware. Various pieces of equipment and supplies stood at attention on the countertops.

She turned around to see the caged entrance where she stepped into the basement. The fourth basement wall housed a small kitchenette on one side: a deep sink, dishwasher, and portable stove waited for a user. On the other side of the entrance rested a short bookshelf with dozens of books and several stuffed hummingbirds on display. A shawl hung above the birds. She studied it closely.

"Hummingbird feathers," came a familiar voice from inside one of the cages.

AJ looked over her shoulder to see Amanda step out with a bucket and sponge. She wore a white blouse matched with cream trousers.

Neutral as always.

"Hummingbird feathers," the woman said again. "That is a cloak I'm making with hummingbird feathers."

"What is this place?" Jack asked. "And what's that dank smell?"

"That smell, Mr. Kinston, is the smell of nature and of you leaving to wait outside."

Jack shot a protesting look over to Conrad, but the Deputy Director shook his head.

"Not today, Kinston. If Ms. Claremont has asked you to wait outside, please do so."

"But I haven't e—"

Conrad stepped closer to Jack and glared at him. "Mr. Kinston, wait outside or you can walk back to the office and put in your resignation."

"Maurice, see this kid back to the driveway, please," Amanda said. "And wait for the rest of the team by the front door."

"Yes, ma'am," the lawyer said. "Follow me please."

Jack scoffed and pushed AJ aside as he walked by, making no effort to hide his anger or disgust. No one said another word until the first door was shut again and the basement was minus two people.

"Amanda, may I ask what this place is?" AJ wanted an answer to Jack's original question.

"You may. This is my aviary. I'm not just the bird and garden whisperer. I'm the hummingbird feeder."

—¡—

CHAPTER 45

TELL ME something, both of you. Have you ever seen anything like this, in all your years of working on the job or off? Do you understand how special this place is and why I won't allow anyone down here?

I can't begin to tell you how many years it took to perfect the engineering marvel you see. Allow me, if you may, to walk you around so that you can see and understand what I've created. I doubt anything in this room will help you find the evidence you're looking for, but you're still welcome to look. You have a job to do. And do, you must.

AJ, you were looking at my cloak when I stepped out of the cage. How about we start there and work our way around the room?

Do be careful! Don't touch anything without asking permission first. There are many things in here with feather and wing, but I also have many things with legs and fangs. I wouldn't want to see you harmed from carelessness.

The cloak over here on this wall. I'm making it myself, each year I'm able to add a couple of inches to it. When I'm done, it will touch the floor and I'll adorn my back with evanescent splendor.

The Aztec priests wore cloaks like this. They'd adorn themselves with the cloaks and it was said it gave them special powers to mediate between the living and the dead souls. Isn't it fascinating to think the link between the gods and us shines in a cloak of eight thousand birds?

Yes. It would take eight thousand birds to make one cloak, but I'd never kill any of my hummers. And I won't need eight thousand birds to create this masterpiece. Instead, I use the feathers from cadavers given to me or ones who've died here in my sanctuary. Sometimes, I take donations from other aviaries around the world.

But I never kill any of my birds. It's highly illegal. One of the best things our country ever did was establish that Migratory Bird Treaty Act back in 1918. And, because I wanted to raise and care for these birds, I became a licensed rehabber—my certificate is on the wall over here. I did everything legally and lawfully, even secured all my federal and state permits. You're welcome to check.

Killing the birds would also be sacrilegious on more levels than the Aztecs had heavens and hells. Thirteen and nine, respectively, if you're curious.

The hummingbirds on display around the cloak were donations given to me from other official aviaries and zoos. Same with some of the books. During my travels, I've also collected as many books as I could find on the history, etymology, characteristics, and mythology of these creatures. This is a personal library I refuse to part with. You're both more than welcome to check everything out.

The cages you see along the walls hold my hummers. If you walk around, you'll see basement windows letting in extra light through each of the frosted windowpanes. Never direct sun. Too much heat and it'll kill my precious babies. So, the frosted glass panes keep the heat—and, yes, the many snooping, prying eyes—out.

Each enclosure houses one or two hummers. No more. Especially with the more aggressive breeds.

I see that look, Conrad. You don't believe these tiny little, delicate-looking things could be savage? Oh, quite the contrary. They're vicious warriors, the lot of them. Hummingbirds are not only the smallest birds, they're the most aggressive. Very territorial and protective of what's theirs. Don't let the cuteness fool you.

They will kill.

I don't typically house any Ruby-Throated. They're found naturally around here and every mid-Spring through early Autumn they bless the lands with their presence. They're also the predominate little flier found along the East Coast, so again, there's no reason to have them in here, unless I'm asked to rehab them.

Very rarely does New England get Calliopes or Rufouses. They're considered vagrants, those two. On occasion, I've been lucky to see one, but the sightings are sparse, many times years apart.

As you walk around, you'll see Allen's, Costa's, Green-Breasted Mango, Anna's, Xantus's—basically only the species that are found in the United States. There are a few dozen that are found in North and Central America, but only less than two dozen in the United States.

Can you believe that? Over <u>three hundred</u> species of hummingbirds and none found—natively, of course—in Africa or the Old World. And only twenty-three bless America and Canada.

I grow their local flora for my precious fauna. I've brought succulents and all kinds of flowers they enjoy. That's why you see the hanging pots. Some of the vines snake their ways into the cages while others remain outside. I'll let them out on occasion to enjoy the flowers in the middle of my basement.

Mostly, I have several small tubular feeders set up. I bought a bulk amount and switch them out every day or every other day. The used feeders are then hand-washed, steamed on the stove, and dried in the dishwasher.

I'm over precautious, if you're wondering. The slightest bacterial infection can kill them.

I don't want that.

I've never wanted that.

Each cage is adorned with bushes and flowers. I use an artificial light-tracking system to grow them. You can see the array of individual bulbs. Like the sun, the light bulbs graduate in intensity, east to west, and fade off at night. I had an engineer fabricate the mechanisms and programming behind the lighting, even adjusting the intensity to match the seasonal angle of the sun. I'd like to think that my artificial world here is the reason my plants and birds survive as well as they do.

Ah! AJ, I see you eyeing these little aquariums and trays. Allow me to bring one up to countertop.

Hummingbirds are not only nectarivorous, they're also insectivorous. This little aquarium holds fruit flies. See them buzzing around in there? I let them out closer to June when I see nests have been constructed. Some of these other containers hold gnats and other insects that provide my birds with the proteins they need to survive. On occasion, I'll leave banana peels out for the gnats to consume, hence the lingering smell you may have noticed. Hummingbirds are also known to snack on ash and dirt, so I make sure to supply a little of that as well.

There are a few Tupperware containers that house crickets and grasshoppers. Oh, the hummers don't eat them.

Those are for the spiders.

Yes, spiders. I keep a few in some of the other aquariums, primarily the orb weavers and funnel-web spiders. If they don't produce the webbing I need, I milk them for it. Not an easy process, but I need their sticky string. I'll place the webbing around some of the plants and cages so the females can grab it for their nests.

If you notice, the windows are covered in cobwebs. Those are from the basement and house spiders that stuck around, hoping to catch the occasion rogue fruit fly. I leave them there. I found they don't go after my birds and the birds will use what they want. It's a mutual arrangement they have.

Why the spider webs? The material is stretchy and allows their little nests to expand as the babies grow. Babies can double in size in the first few days alone. The little hens will use plant fibers and surround them with the spider silk, then adorn the outside with lichen or moss, which, by the way, I bring in from outside or grow in another aquarium.

If you look in this cage here, up to the left corner, my Xantus has made her nest. I leave plant debris down—even have one of my girls bring in some dog and cat hairs—so they have something to build their nests with.

It really is a marvel of ingenuity.

Raising new hatchlings in captivity is the most challenging part. Many don't make it past the first month of life. My success rate is between seventy and seventy-five percent. Better than some hummingbird aviaries I'm aware of.

But listen to me. I'm rambling on about my little darlings here. And you both have a job to do. Please, do look around.

And ask me any questions.

—¡—

CHAPTER 46

HE HEARD birds rapidly chirp from the corner of the room as he looked around the space. Amanda continued talking.

Conrad walked around the tables and inspected each aquarium and container, carefully listening to the details provided. He looked at the small kitchenette area.

"...Please, do look around," the older woman said. "And ask me any questions."

"Do you ever release any of these birds in the wild?" AJ asked.

"Only the rehabbed Ruby-Throated. Never the others. Most probably wouldn't survive."

"Why not? I thought they'd do good up here."

"As vicious as these little creatures can be, they're equally delicate. Their life balances on as thin of a line as the spider silk used for their nests."

"I've never imagined hummers as *vicious*."

Amanda chuckled. "Hummingbirds have an extremely high metabolism. They expend the most amount of energy of any other bird species in the world. They need to feed—constantly!

A food source means life or death for them and, once they find a good reliable one, they will defend it. I've seen males attack each other and females defend their little feeders from the males. They can also stab each other with their beaks, killing their enemy."

Conrad walked around each cage and examined the sides and contents. Nothing appeared out of the ordinary. Nothing he could readily see.

"Conrad, do you have any questions?"

"No, ma'am. May I have a word with my detective?"

She nodded. "Come out the garage door and Maurice will be waiting for you by the front door to let you in."

Conrad watched as Amanda let herself out. He turned around to see AJ smiling at one of the cages. She appeared delighted to watch the birds dart back and forth.

"Jardine?"

"Yes, sir?"

"What are your thoughts?"

"She's a hummingbird specialist."

"And?"

She let out a sigh. "I don't know. I'm looking around at the engineering of this place and it's dumbfounding, the detail involved. There are drains at the base of each cage, misters for the plants, temperature-controlled weather—it's almost like an experimental laboratory, but with birds."

"Do you see *anything* here that would suggest the reason we have a search warrant?"

AJ walked around the tables again, then studied the ceiling. She finally shook her head. "No, sir. The only thing remotely ceremonial—if even that's the word for it—is that cloak on the wall." She walked over it to study it, then knelt down to read the titles of the books. "Every book here is specific to hummingbirds. There are a couple of ones about mythology. Nothing stands out, though."

"Very well. Let's document what we need and take notes."

Conrad walked over to one of the open cages—the same one Amanda came out of—and studied the interior. The sides of the cage were built with removable screen panels that could lengthen or shorten enclosures together. The door was also screened and most were fastened shut to keep the hummingbirds from leaving. Trees, shrubs, vines, and all manner of flowers decorated and filled the interior space of the cage.

Grouted tile created intricate designs on the back wall. A drain outlet sat neatly in the center of the floor. The cages could easily be kept clean.

Each additional space offered a similar layout, the only difference being the vegetation from time to time and the species of bird.

Nothing looked out of place or out of the ordinary.

Minutes and multiple photographs later, Conrad looked around again. "Almost done?"

"Yeah," AJ said, shining a flashlight under the tables. "Don't see anything anywhere."

"Me either."

She stood up and dusted her jeans. "What happens now, sir?"

"Now, we split up. Jack and I will work on the home and greenhouse. You keep Amanda company."

"That's all she wanted?"

"Yes," he said, as he unlatched the enclosure door and stepped in with AJ.

They were nearly pressed against each other as she looked up at him.

"Sir?"

He could see the worry in her eyes. He had seen that same look in Aubreah's eyes many times: a longing to not disappoint the man she admires. "Yes?"

"She's starting to ask more personal questions."

"I know."

"Is this a good idea? Me alone with her?"

He sighed. "Between you and me, AJ, I've known Amanda for several years now. She's invited me and my family to dinner on more than one occasion. I've never known her to hurt anyone."

"But I don't know her. And you don't know me."

Ameena, if you only knew the truth.

Conrad gently placed his hands on her shoulders. He opened his mouth, wanting to tell her he had worked with her husband, Michael, and knew why he had been killed, but the words would not come out.

"Sir? Is something wrong?"

Instead: "You're right. You don't know Amanda. And, truth be told, I may not know her like what I think. For all I know, she could have bodies buried on a property this large. But, for whatever reason, she's chosen *you* to talk to. For the sake of us processing this area so we can find what we need, do what she asks. Your job is as vital as finding a potential murder weapon. Answer her questions. Do your job by keeping her occupied so we can do our job searching the premises. Understand?"

"Yes, sir."

"If I didn't think you were capable, I would never leave you alone with her."

They stepped out into the garage and he re-latched the basement door shut. As he and AJ walked out, he saw the forensic technicians waiting in the van.

Pat made eye contact and Conrad shook his head. The senior tech gave a simple nod in understanding.

They walked up the steps to the front door where Jack, Maurice, and Amanda waited.

"Mr. McMillan, are you satisfied with seeing the basement?" Maurice asked, his pompous belly jutted out as he spoke.

"Yes, Mr. Juniper."

"Conrad? Any questions for me before I take AJ to the nursery?"

He looked at Amanda and studied the expression on her face. Her skin looked extra-rigid and worn underneath the makeup she wore. The red lipstick accentuated the lines around her mouth. For a split second, she appeared to be hiding something, but as quick as the notion came, it was gone.

"No, ma'am."

"I'll take my leave now, gentlemen. Maurice? See to their needs."

"Yes, Ms. Claremont." Maurice opened the front door and walked in. Jack followed.

Amanda faced AJ. "Shall we go for a walk to the nursery?"

Appearing unsure of how to answer, AJ glanced at her boss for approval. He nodded once. "Sure. I don't mind a good walk."

As they started down the driveway, Amanda turned to make eye contact one final time. It was a primal stare, like someone ready to fight to the death for what they wanted.

He wondered if that was the same look a hummingbird gave another, protecting what it cherished most, ready to kill if needed.

—¡—

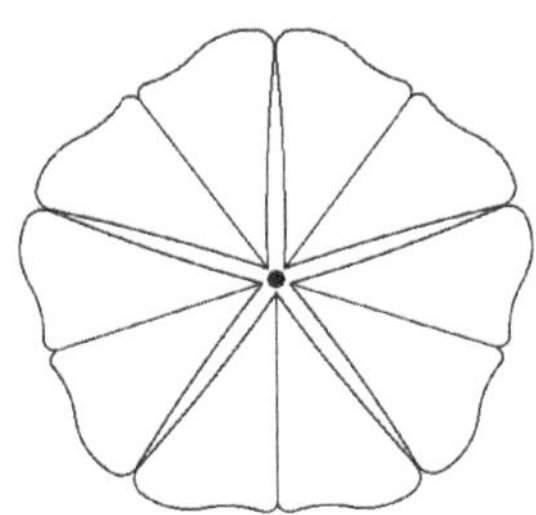

CHAPTER 47

EARTHWORMS, drowned in shallow puddles along the edge of the driveway, laid bright and pale white against the mud. They almost looked as if someone sprinkled the ground with spaghetti. The cold scene contradicted the activity and joy chirping from the treetops around them.

Both Amanda and AJ walked down the incline, side by side, as they made their way towards the gravel trail which would take them to the nursery on the other side of the property.

To their right, the halfway house became visible. As they approached, AJ noticed all the curtains were drawn and the front door slightly opened.

"The men have the day off today. You won't see them," Amanda said.

"I thought you're preparing for a big sale tomorrow?"

"I am. But they sowed the fields yesterday, staying extra late to get everything done. We all had a midnight feast and I told them they could sleep in."

"It's almost noon."

"Wouldn't you sleep like the dead if you worked double-shifts in the fields for days?"

"Touché." AJ smiled.

They walked past the pond.

"Did you find any of my men attractive, while you were here this week?"

AJ's smile vanished. "Why would you ask that?"

Amanda glanced at her, then back at the gravel. "Defensive, are we? It's an honest question."

"And I honestly don't want to answer it."

"It's okay if you prefer women."

"I'm not lesbian either."

"Never said you were. I said it was okay *if* you were."

"Can we change the subject? This is making me uncomfortable."

"Are you uncomfortable because I asked if you liked women? Or uncomfortable because I asked if you liked any men after your husband was murdered?"

AJ stopped. Before she could reply, a patrol car pulled into the driveway. The older officer rolled the window down and stopped.

"Ms. Claremont, good to see you."

"You, too, Officer Matthews."

"I'm truly sorry I have to be here."

"It's fine, I promise. The others are at the house waiting for you. Do your job, and I'll always be proud, no matter what happens."

"Yes, ma'am." The officer continued up the incline and disappeared through the trees.

Amanda kept walking. AJ was forced to pick up her pace to catch up. A moment later, they were at the gravel intersection.

"This is the trail the Norringtons use to bring their animals over to my property and feed them. It's also a nice worn path to the nursery. Typically, I'd use a golf cart or tractor to drive back and forth, but today...today, I wanted to walk the trail to the heart of my business." She looked up at the sky, then continued down the path. "Doesn't this feel amazing?"

"The weather is nice, yes."

"What a dull response, flower. Are you upset from my question a few minutes ago?"

AJ shrugged. "I don't know. It made me uncomfortable."

"You can't hide in comfort *and* do this job, detective. You can't hide in comfort and truly *live*."

"You make it sound easy."

"No. I call it how I see it. You let your past shackle you in place."

"No, I don't."

"Then answer the question. Do you find any of my men attractive? They're young. Muscular. Solid workers, most of them. Many of my girls find them attractive on one level or another. Do you?"

AJ shook her head. "I don't. I'm not interested in anyone right now."

"And why not?"

She clenched her jaw. "I'm just not interested in dating." As they walked by the fields, she quickly changed the subject. "Did you say you carved the poles in the field, the ones around the gates?"

"Ah. Yes, the tall poles you see act as a fixed point for the gates to rotate open and shut. Much like a revolving door. Each pole is decorated like a totem, paying tribute to many native peoples."

"You must really love the cultures."

"I do! We've misunderstood them and lost touch with what they can teach us. Some people are drawn to Celtic and Viking cultures, others to African and Eastern. Myself? I'm drawn to Mesoamerican civilizations. There's so much I could teach you. But, what do *you* like, flower?"

"I'm drawn to Middle Eastern and Celtic music. I love the Viking mythology and Lebanese food. I'd love to learn more about the Scots since my dad's parents were Scottish."

They rounded the corner of the fields and walked towards the back of the main building. Maria and another employee stood by the back entrance, waiting.

As AJ and her companion walked through, the girls shut and locked the doors behind them. The rest of Amanda's employees chattered inside until the closing doors echoed within.

AJ looked at the open space in front of her. Everything was gone. The middle of the barn lay bare except for a table and two chairs.

The skin on the back of AJ's neck crawled into her scalp when she saw Maria staring at her. The detective surveyed her surroundings. The presence of the women, the uniformity of their work outfits—all felt ritualistic or cult-like. AJ did not like it.

"My flowers," Amanda addressed them, "I want to thank you for all the work you've done and for all the time you've been employed with me, especially the last two months. Take the van and enjoy the rest of the afternoon. We've prepared a feast at the halfway house."

Amanda hugged each of the young women and the chatter picked up again. AJ chided herself for her own reaction.

Dammit, Ameena, it's fine. You'll be safe, just like the rest of this week.

"Do you want me to stay, Amanda?" Maria asked.

"No, it's fine. Take the girls to the halfway house, enjoy the rest of the afternoon, as we discussed."

Maria nodded, then the girls left. The front doors shut and the sound bounced across the walls of the empty space.

Amanda walked around and looked up at the paintings above her. She made a single pass around before she turned her attention to the detective again. She stood across the table from AJ and stared.

"Do you know why I wanted you to keep me company today? Do you know why I want to be alone with you?"

"Are you going to hurt me?"

Amanda's laughter echoed through the barn. "Hurt the most precious flower in my garden? What on earth gave you that idea?"

"The search warrant."

Amanda walked away. She went behind the cash register. "Would you like something to drink? Water? Soda?"

"Not right now, thank you."

AJ heard a static noise in hidden speakers around her, then Native American flute music serenaded the space. Smiling, the older woman came back and sat down. She motioned at the chair across from her.

"Please, have a seat, Ameena." Her voice was firm as she took a sip from the soda can. Her lipstick left a print on the top.

AJ slid into the chair and waited.

"Do you know why I picked you? Why you're here, babysitting an eccentric old businesswoman? While the men, the *men* are doing the *real* work?"

"Amanda, I didn't mean it like—"

"Stop." She held a finger up to silence the detective. "I know you know the rules. You're here to keep me company and entertain my questions and conversation. And I know you know that I have the power to call off the search at the simple press of a button." She reached into her pocket and pulled out a walkie-talkie, placing it in table. "Do you think their job is more important than yours, right here and now?"

AJ repositioned herself in the chair. "I don't know."

"Well, I do. And I can tell you it's not. *Your* job, right here and now, will yield more information than whatever they think they may find in my house."

AJ's hair tingled again on the back of her neck. The sensation felt like electricity in the air, the ominous crackle and crawl before lightning would strike in a storm.

Amanda's eyes laid fixed on AJ and she could not look away.

"It's time."

—¡—

CHAPTER 48

"SECRETS to ears and wishes to dandelions: both spread in the same fashion."

Gramma told me that once, before she passed.

She told me of the secrets that men try to keep and how they bury them down, down, down into the depths of the ground they walk. But no matter how many feet of earth are above them, secrets—all secrets—beg to be told.

And that's why little birdies and garden ghosts have fed me favor and given me advantage.

Little birdies and garden ghosts have whispered in my ear, spilling long-kept secrets about you. I know you better than you think, little Morning Glory. And I'll keep calling you that because you are a twisted little vine, full of heart-shaped leaves and delicate flowers. I'm doing Conrad one last favor by forcing the sun on you and opening you up from that darkened shade you hide.

And speaking of your Deputy Director, I've known Conrad for a while. I know his wife, Yasmin. I know his two children, Aubreah and Duncan. And I know them better than they think they know themselves. Little birdies and garden ghosts whispered tales of how they came to New Hampshire. You should ask him one day how he wound up here. He's got such a dirty secret he tries to hide from you.

Little birdies and garden ghosts have been whispering secrets to me for decades and I've learned what needed learning to get what I needed got. The Norringtons, Old Man Bates, the police, the town board, customers that walk through my doors—it doesn't matter. All I need to do is gaze into their eyes and watch specters form around them. I watch the words fly from their mouths like flocks of canaries and listen to the songs sung.

Little birdies and garden ghosts showed me you and the secrets you hold, and they told me what to do this week. And on their advice, I hung my paintings up. On their advice, I set in motion certain events that would be delivered to Conrad. On their advice, I've done everything as planned and will continue to do everything as planned until the little birdies stop singing and the garden ghosts fade back into nothing.

Let me be blunt, detective. I know exactly what Conrad and that worthless excuse of a detective-wannabe will or will not find on my property. I know where they'll look, what they'll see. I know better than they do what exactly they're looking for. I know who did what and how. I know everything that goes on within the boundaries of my property. You want answers, don't you?

No need to reply. Of course, you do.

You wonder why I picked you that day at the police station? You wonder why I asked for Conrad, my White-Whiskered Hermit, to run this investigation? Did you think Mayor Giunta, my White-Necked Jacobin beauty, made the call all on his own? Tsk-tsk.

Do you wonder why you, the old maid, are here to babysit me, the haggard crone?

Because little birdies and garden ghosts told me so.

Because this is what was demanded of me and what I demand of you.

You and I—we're a lot more alike than you think. Only, I

don't hide in the comfort of a shell, telling myself a half-truth and pretending to believe it. And I know myself. I know what and who I am. I know why I'm a successful businesswoman and entrepreneur. I know what makes my gardens grow.

It's time to play the ultimate game, here in this barn. It's time for you to learn the truth behind who I am.

Quid pro quo, my flower.

Look up above you, there, and gaze upon my masterpieces. Each painting you see, each blend of brush and acrylic are beautiful specimens with a past. Each hummingbird up there is named after a man who came and went from my life. Each story I tell—some short, some longer—is another puzzle piece to what Conrad and that young vulture will find.

You already know how this started, but don't you want to know how this ends?

Every painting tells a story. And for every story I tell, you must answer a question, fully, in truth. To my satisfaction.

Veritas vos liberabit.

It's time to open you up, little Morning Glory, and learn what makes your garden grow.

—¡—

CHAPTER 49

NATIVE American tapestries hung along the entry walls and in the living room. Woven baskets in desert hues hung from the vaulted ceiling while their green companions snaked towards the southern windows. Ornate pottery propped on carved wooden tables welcomed the detectives to sit on the sofas and chairs next to them. Even the baseboards were adored in all manner of native carvings.

"Ms. Claremont," Maurice said, with his nose propped higher than normal, "is quite fond of the southwest and supports many tribes by purchasing their artwork."

Conrad set his briefcase on the coffee table next to some large Native American books. He opened the briefcase. The plump man and one of the town officers stood at the living room entry. Jack walked around and stared at everything.

"Mr. Kinston."

Jack turned around as Conrad tossed him a pair of latex gloves. "Do we really need to search this room? It just has creepy crap in it."

"Kinston, what's on the walls?"

"Uh, rugs?"

"Potential facades for safes or hidden niches behind. What's on the tables?"

"Pots made from dirt."

"Potential hiding places for knives or other small objects indicative of a crime. What about the couches?"

"I get it. Everything's a potential hiding place." Jack snapped the last glove in place then looked at the lawyer. In a low voice, he asked Conrad, "Do they have to watch us the whole time?"

"Mr. Kinston, my hearing is better than you think," Maurice said.

"Do you have to watch us do our job?"

"I'm here to watch *you*, per Ms. Claremont's instructions. She trusts Mr. McMillan, wholeheartedly. Just not you."

Jack turned his back on the lawyer and made a face. "Where do you want to start?"

"We start in one corner and work our way around, clockwise." He grabbed the digital camera from his briefcase and began snapping pictures of the entire room.

"Why so many photos?"

"Better to have more than not enough."

Conrad worked his way around the room, careful to take photographs at different angles.

"Why clockwise?"

"Superstition."

He scoffed. "*You're* superstitious?"

Conrad ignored the question and walked over to the corner near the fireplace. He clicked on the flashlight and shined it on the floor, then up the wall. "Do you see any grout out of place or feel any breezes along the fireplace?"

Jack ran his fingers around the brick and tested a few of them. He shook his head. "Want me to check the base?"

"Yes. Leave nothing unturned or overlooked."

"What's the flashlight for? What if we just opened the curtains some more?"

"We could do that, but the extra light can pick up on stains or any reflective surfaces." Conrad shined the light into the fireplace and up the flue.

"How many searches have you done in your career?"

"Probably hundreds."

Jack let out a whistle. "You've been in Major Crimes that long?"

Conrad stood back up and shined the light in the upper right corner of the wall, following it down to the floor. "No."

"Oh." Jack sounded disappointed. "How long have you been in Major Crimes, then?"

"Since the second part of 2012." Before Jack could ask another question, Conrad said, "Help me move the couch out of the way. We'll need to check the cushions and frame."

They slid the coffee table away from the couch. The feet hollered against the wooden floor.

"Do be careful with the artifacts in this room, Mr. McMillan," the lawyer said. "Ms. Claremont expects everything to be returned to its original location, condition, and order when you're done."

"It will, Mr. Juniper."

Jack stuck his hands in the crevices of the couch and pulled out a hairband and some coins. "Why'd you come to Major Crimes?"

Conrad slid one corner of the couch away from the wall and shined the flashlight behind it. "Change of scenery."

"Where were you before?"

The Deputy Director ignored the question and kept shining the light on the back of the couch, studying the fabric.

"Where were you before Major Crimes?"

"With the FBI." Conrad propped an arm on the couch. "No more questions, Mr. Kinston."

"Why not? Too personal?"

Conrad glared at his detective.

—¡—

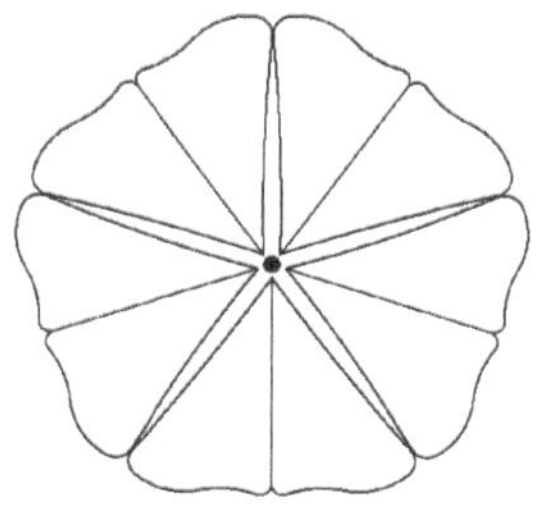

CHAPTER 50

AJ WATCHED the older woman lean back.

"Shall we begin?"

"I don't want to play this game, Amanda."

"This isn't a game." Her ruby lips split open in a smile.

"You can't force me to tell you personal things for your own amusement."

"It's not for my amusement, flower."

AJ rolled her eyes and put her hands on the table. "Stop calling me that. I'm not your flower."

Amanda only smiled more. "Ah, there's the first sign of what I'm looking for. The raw, unleashed emotion you hold back. I want to see and hear more of that."

AJ stood up and walked to the back door. She grabbed the handle to open it. Locked. She shook it once, but the wood did not give. She walked past the table, her eyes fixed on the front door. With a firm grab of the handles and another few shakes, the front doors would not budge either. She tried to press her weight into the doors. They still would not move.

"All locked, my dear."

"Why? Let me out. This isn't funny anymore."

"Shall we begin?"

The question only irritated her more. She walked over to the sides of the building and tested each of the windows, but none would open. Then she saw nails hammered halfway down, locking the frames in place. She slammed her hand against one of the panes. "Dammit!"

"I had the girls lock all the doors and bar the windows."

"Why?!"

"There's no phone reception in here, either. No way to communicate with the outside world except that walkie-talkie on the table." She gestured for the chair again. "Please, have a seat, Ameena."

She glared at the old woman. "If you don't let me out of here, I'll-I'll break the windows and get out!"

"And damage my property? I could have you arrested. You could lose your job for disobeying the Deputy Director."

"You've kidnapped and restrained a government official. *You* would be the one arrested!"

"Have I tied you down? Shackled you?"

"No, but—"

"Of course, I haven't. I've only insured no outside disturbances. The locked doors are to keep others out, not us in."

"But—"

"—and it's your word, a rookie detective who has mental issues, against mine, a respected philanthropist and seasoned businesswoman. You have no proof I've done anything wrong."

"You've lost your goddamned mind!"

"Now you're being rude."

AJ looked around, walked back to the table, and grabbed the chair she had sat in. She carried it over to the window and positioned one of the legs in the center of a pane, preparing to shatter the glass. She arched back.

"Your mother is Jamilla Hassan al-Rashad, an immigrant from Lebanon who met and married Paden Jacob Jardine in 1973 at barely the age of eighteen. They had four children. You're the oldest."

AJ lowered the chair and turned to stare at Amanda.

The older woman stood up and slowly walked towards her. She continued, "You have three younger brothers. Faruq is the oldest of the three, followed by Arif and Nabih. Your mother divorced in the late 1980s and a couple of years later met your stepfather, Ernest Edward Andrewson. Your mother quit her job shortly after your accident in 2012 and she's stayed at home ever since. Your stepfather works at Shaker Regional School District but he's hoping to retire in the next few years." Amanda encroached into AJ's personal space. "Your husband, Michael Anthony Hawthorne, was an F.B.I. agent, always on assignment somewhere away from home. He spent a lot of time away. And you? You used to be a civil engineer at one of the top firms in San Antonio. You left in late 2013 to come up here."

"How do you know all this?" AJ whispered.

"I do great amounts of homework on those who interest me. *You* have interested me a great amount. Since Monday, I've been able to acquire even more information on you than I just revealed."

She turned her back to the detective and started walking to the table. "I have the ability and means to have every single one of your family members fired from their jobs, have their lives ruined, and make you watch as they suffer. I have the connections to have Conrad demoted from his government position and stain his reputation across the eastern seaboard. You don't want to know what I can do to Jack."

Amanda sat back down at the table and smiled. "I can be a vicious cut-throat and bring down the world around you. I don't want to do that. But if you decide you'd rather flee than fight, I can make several calls this afternoon and everyone's Monday will be ruined. OR—" she gestured across the table "—we have a friendly conversation to pass the time. You decide."

The flute music held the tension in the air. AJ felt trapped, unsure of what to do. She looked at the chair and then the window. All she could see were plants at soldiered attention between her and the adjacent greenhouse. The clouds crept by and covered the sun. She looked back at Amanda.

The older woman sat there, inviting her to join. "I don't bite, flower. And I swear, on your children's lives and my daughter's, I would never harm you. I will not harm you. I only want to talk."

AJ white-knuckled the chair. Swallowing her pride, she walked back to the table and sat down.

"What do you want to know?" Her defeated voice was no more than a whisper.

"Let's start with your relationship with men. Have you dated anyone since your husband was murdered?"

"No."

"Not even gone on *one* date?"

AJ shook her head. "No."

"And why not? Do you think you dishonor your dead husband's memory if you started dating so many years after he was murdered in front of you?"

"I don't know." She looked down at her hands. "Why do you keep mentioning he was murdered?"

"I'm forcing the reality to set in because I don't think you've faced it. Have you even kissed another guy since then?"

AJ nodded. "Once. A couple of years ago."

"Tell me about that."

"I quit my engineering job that day and got into a fight with my son. My mom suggested I go for a drive somewhere to clear my head."

"And where did you go?"

"Up the Kanc, in the White Mountains. There was an aurora event happening, and I thought I could grab some pictures of it. I saw it, but never took any photos."

"Why not?"

AJ smiled weakly at her hands. "I was distracted by the guy I kissed."

"What guy?"

"I can't remember his full name. He went by Nick. He was British and had such a wonderful voice."

"And tell me about the kiss."

"It felt amazing. It felt...wrong. Confusing."

"Why confusing?"

AJ looked down at the table and studied her hands. "He was a random stranger, but I'd had such a shit day, it felt right at the time. It felt like I'd known him all my life. But it didn't feel right the next day."

"Why?"

"I'd just met him! You aren't supposed to kiss a stranger within minutes of meeting them!"

"Do you feel that way because you'd just met him or because, in the heat and passion of that singular moment, you managed to forget about your murdered husband?"

AJ shook her head. "That's not a fair question."

"Did you fuck him?"

"No!"

"Fair enough." Amanda leaned back. "That wasn't so bad, was it?"

AJ glared at her. How she wished to break the window and leave.

—¡—

CHAPTER 51

MY, MY, DETECTIVE. I'm impressed. See? The questions are easy to answer. All the questions will be.

Take a look at my paintings. See the first hummer? The one with the colorful beak and white band behind the eyes?

It's a Xantus. They're typically found in southern California and can migrate all the way north to British Columbia. That's a long way to travel.

I named this one **MEKHI**. It means 'he who is like God'.

I see the look on your face. Yes, I named all my paintings. The names are not unique to the birds themselves. They—these paintings—represent some of the men that have come into my life over the last thirty years. Artful and respectful men.

I love art. I love the creative process of making something new from the essence of something old. I taught myself how to recreate the vibrant poses of each bird and focus on every minute detail.

You'll find lots of paint supplies in my greenhouse. That's where I love to paint the most. All kinds of colors, too. I love to watch the paint slip out of its original container and slowly pool or splash down on a new surface. It's invigorating, if you ask me.

I've painted each of these hummers, poured the proper colors over their canvases. I researched each bird, their personalities, and matched them up with the men in my life.

You've wondered why I haven't talked about the men much yet? Simple. You needed to know about the women first. They're the heart of a society, the ones who bleed every month to give life.

Most men aren't important to me. Never really have been. Yes, the laborers are important and the men I employ help make me a success, but most men are insignificant. Except these. The ones I've immortalized into my favorite little birdies.

As I said, this is Mekhi. Came into my life about twenty years or so ago. Before the turn of the century. He'd traveled from Sri Lanka and was on a visitor's visa spending the summer with his family.

He caught my eye one day at the nursery. His sister was picking different fruit trees. They just purchased some land over in Northfield and wanted to develop their gardens.

He had a good, strong back and easily lifted and danced with the large buckets of plants. He did everything for his sister so she didn't have to lift a finger. There was so much respect he held for her.

And I was impressed. Smitten to be exact. Truly smitten by the respect he had for her.

We made eye contact and I smiled. He smiled back.

I don't think we said anything that day, but the next weekend, he and his sister were back at my nursery. This time, she came in asking questions about the soils and how best to grow honeysuckle bushes.

I told her that most properties in the area have wild honeysuckle growing, particularly the yellow ones. I recommended she look for another bush, but she wasn't having it. Her mind was set. She knew what she wanted and what she liked and that fire in her tone was breathtaking.

I respected her. Here was a woman, you'd think would be repressed in her culture, demanding she knew what was best. I like women with sharp edges, those who know what they want, not willing to play games to get ahead.

I smiled and looked at her brother.

He stepped in and it sounded like he was defending me in their language. Not sure what they said, but she kept looking at me. Firm stare at times. Then she nodded to him and grabbed another gallon container of the plant I recommended.

After that, the sister came back a few more times with her brother. Every Saturday for half the summer.

By the beginning of July, Mekhi finally said something to me. In broken English, he said, "I am happy to meet."

I think I replied, "It's nice to meet you, too."

"My name, Mek-hi."

I pointed to myself and said, "Amanda."

He whispered my name and walked off. I found that so odd, but absolutely fascinating. He wasn't being rude, he just walked off to talk to his sister.

Then, I see his sister giving me the same stare she did every weekend. She had one of the best rigid faces I've ever seen, carved from unemotional directness. Couldn't read her. Just saw her dark eyes bore into me and I stared right back.

She finally approached me and said, "Ms. Amanda, my brother has been asking me to talk to you. He wants to know if you are committed to anyone?"

I was a bit confused. "Committed? As in *dating*?"

"Yes. He wants to court you but doesn't want to interfere with your commitment to someone else."

"The only thing I'm committed to is my work. And my gardens."

"I see. Very respectful, Ms. Amanda."

Before she turned to leave, I added, "Would Mekhi like to join me for lunch next week? There's a local restaurant we can meet at."

Without saying a word, she walked over to her brother and

talked to him in her language again. I saw his face light up from across the way. He nodded several times. His sister came back over and said, "Mekhi has agreed."

And that's how we had our first date—family approved and in a public space.

We met at an Egyptian restaurant called Isis. Ever heard of it? Probably not. They renamed it. Stripped the female god's name from the front of the building and called it Osiris. How pathetic is that? All this damned war overseas with the group ISIS and now we can't even have nice restaurants named Isis.

Another female suppressed by controlling men.

I digressed, again. My apologies.

I met Mekhi, there. We enjoyed a good lunch. I remember he ordered a soup with a lot of garlic in it. And I mean a lot. When he would talk about Sri Lanka and his brothers left back there, the odor would punch me in my nose.

I tried to smile the best I could and ignore the foulness. It wasn't that he had bad teeth. His teeth were beautiful, and his smile was warm. No, you could tell he took care of himself. It was that damned garlic he loved so much. I like garlic, don't get me wrong, but the powerful force behind that soup was almost supernatural.

We went on a few more lunch excursions. Same restaurant. He always ordered the same food. The same garlicky soup. That damned garlic soup…

Did you know that olfactory senses can conjure up deep emotions? I learned that a few years ago. When I was painting one of my other hummingbirds up here, I remembered that soup. So, I went to Isis—well, Osiris—and ordered the garlicky mess.

As soon as the bowl was brought in front of me and I leaned in, my eyes watered from a potent and familiar smell and I could hear Mekhi again. It was like his ghost sat next to me as he described his home country again.

I ate every spoonful and now I know why he liked it. It was more delicious than the nose knows. It was potent and profound. It was a fresh memory of my dark-skinned courter. My, but that was a good day.

And, yes, my breath stunk for a while after that. I could smell it in my fingernails and armpits as I sweat. Didn't get too close to my employees back then. And you want to know something, flower?

I had it again and again and again.

Garlicky soup.

I remembered him with each hot sip to my lips. He always reeked each time we were together.

That smell...It's something that sticks with you.

—¡—

CHAPTER 52

EVERY ITEM was set back in its original location while the lawyer and an officer oversaw the search.

"It's not too personal, no. But no more questions. They'll distract you while processing the house."

"I trust you are finding everything to your satisfaction?" Maurice asked.

"Yes, Mr. Juniper," Conrad replied. He continued to jot down his thoughts on his notepad, trying to ignore the smug look on the man's face.

"Where to next?" Jack asked. He wiped his brow with his glove.

"Dining room. And you'll need a new pair of gloves, Mr. Kinston." He tucked the notepad back in his pocket and grabbed the digital camera from his briefcase.

"Why? Are we using new gloves on each room? These aren't even dirty."

"You just wiped your brow with them. They're contaminated."

Jack looked at his gloves. "Oh. Sorry, sir." He pulled each one off and tossed them in the nearest trash can. Grabbing a new pair of gloves, he added, "I wasn't expecting it to be so warm in here."

Conrad walked into the adjacent dining room and started taking photographs of the layout. Stained glass flowers framed each windowpane. Carved wainscoting ran along all the walls, each section decorated with a unique animal. Above the divide, a panoramic mural of dozens of species of hummingbirds adored the walls between painted vines and trees. Each bird sat, sang, flew, guarded, or oversaw an acrylic flower or leaf. In the center of one wall, near the head of the dining table, a large Aztec temple stood out in the background.

"Ms. Claremont painted this herself," Maurice said behind him. "She even did the stained glass and carvings. She's quite a remarkable woman."

"I agree. Quite remarkable." He continued to snap pictures, capturing the detail of each bird and animal.

"She designed the chandelier above the table."

Conrad turned around and looked up at the centerpiece. Eight wooden hummingbirds in full flight spread from the center, each tail arced downward and then up in a spiral, coming together in the center. Beaks pointed up and each wingtip touched the one next to it, making a full octagon, tip to tip. From the birds' feet hung small LED lights.

"She really loves those birds," Jack muttered.

"Yes, Mr. Kinston. Everyone has something they admire."

"I don't."

Conrad snapped another picture and watched as Jack inspected a dining chair. "Be sure to see if the cushion detaches. Look underneath as well."

"Got it." He flipped the chair over, knocking it against the hardwood floor.

"May I remind you," the lawyer started, "that Ms. Claremont is *very* particular with her house and you *are* to return everything to its previous location *and* condition. Please, do be careful with her furniture."

Jack rolled his eyes.

Before the young detective could get another word in, Conrad replied, "Mr. Juniper, trust that we will be considerate in our search. Kinston, help me move the table off the rug."

Both men lifted the thick wooden table and walked it to the living room. They walked back into the dining room and Conrad shined his flashlight across the fabric. Nothing caught his eye. He lifted the end of the antique rug and rolled it to the opposite end, off its original location. The wood underneath was darker, as he expected it to be from an area with no foot traffic.

"Anything?" Jack asked, standing above.

The flashlight made several passes over the wood. Again, nothing caught his eye.

Conrad shook his head and stood up. His lower back ached from bending over. The sciatic nerve rebelled, throbbing deep in his thigh muscle. He could feel his age, something his body occasionally reminded him of when he did something wrong.

"Kinston, roll the carpet back in place." He leaned against the wall to relieve the pressure in his lower back while his subordinate did as instructed. The ache lessened. Without saying a word about his discomfort, he helped Jack return the table back to the same spot on the rug, sitting in the same deep depressions. With little else in the dining room to inspect, they quickly wrapped up and moved to the kitchen.

Less ornate than the dining, the kitchen was a step back in time with yellowed countertops and particle board cabinetry. The Formica tops had deep scratches from decades of wear and tear.

"You'd think it would be more…modern," Jack said.

Conrad ignored the comment. And his back pain. After he finished taking photos, he said, "Open the lower cabinets. Be sure to take photographs before going through everything."

"We have to pull out every pot and pan?"

"Yes." He handed Jack the camera. "Take the lids off, check every part of every surface."

"All this for a knife? Don't you think it's overkill?"

"Absolutely not. It's not just the knife we're looking for, Mr. Kinston. Did you read the search warrant?"

"I read the affidavit, not the warrant." Jack crouched down and looked in the viewfinder. The flash went off on the camera.

"We're looking for any knife or similar object—no matter the size—that could inflict the same wound as Mr. Smith's. Yes, we're specifically looking for a ceremonial knife, but we can't rule out other weapons, including any here in the kitchen."

"Gotcha." Another flash lit up the next cabinet.

Conrad walked back into the living room and grabbed his briefcase. He set it down on the kitchen counter and opened it, pulling out vials and test kits. He reached over and grabbed each of the knives from the wooden block holder and placed them in a row.

"May I ask what you're doing, Mr. McMillan?" Maurice leaned in from one side, examining the contents in front of the detective.

"Testing for human blood, Mr. Juniper. It won't damage any of the cutlery here."

"I hope not. Ms. Claremont..."

He ignored the lawyer's ramblings and swabbed each knife one at a time. Jack continued to *clang!* and *clank!* cast iron skillets and pots from the cabinets on the opposite side of where he stood. The lawyer hovered further away, interest lost on the meticulous and repetitive nature of the tests. None of the knives tested positive for human blood.

Jack searched the upper cabinets, then the drawers. Maurice grew tired and grabbed a barstool to plop down on and oversee the process.

Conrad turned his focus to the appliances, checking all around and behind. He picked up a whiff of herbs from the cabinet next to the stove. Every kitchen nook and cranny offered no support for a violent crime.

"What do we have here?" Jack said, staring into one of the drawers.

Maurice perked up from his stool.

Conrad walked over as Jack dug out a large set of keys from the back of the drawer. There appeared to be a bank deposit key, post office key, a couple of keys to the house. More intriguing, there were several different car keys.

"Honda, two Mazdas, and a Chrysler. Oh, and a Ford!"

The Deputy Director looked at Maurice. "Mr. Juniper, what vehicles does Ms. Claremont own?"

"Well, she owns the Ford Crown Victoria you see in the driveway."

"And?"

"And what?"

"Where are the other vehicles?"

—¡—

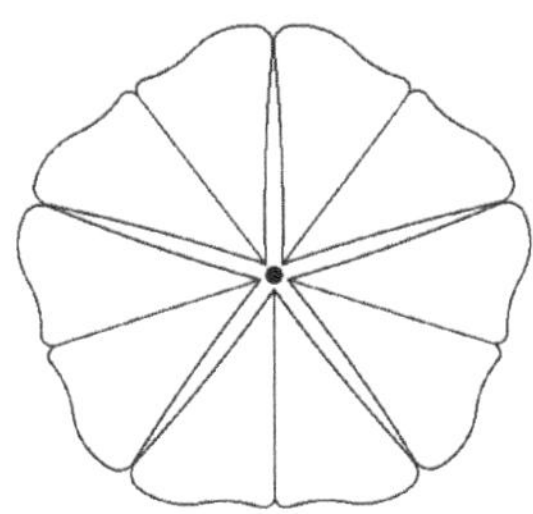

CHAPTER 53

"AND NOW Mekhi is memorialized on my wall, transformed into one of my favorite hummingbirds."

"What happened to him?" AJ asked.

Amanda shrugged. "He just left."

"Just left? Just like that?"

She nodded. "Yes, just like that I never saw him again. I guess he went back to his country after his visa expired."

"But I don't understand. You made him sound more important in your life than just a friend who disappeared after a few dates."

Amanda removed her arm from the back of the chair and sat up straighter. She interlocked her fingers and leaned in towards the table. AJ felt the fierceness behind her stare.

"Why was *he*—a *man,* of all things—so important to me that I'd personify him as my favorite thing?" AJ nodded. "Because he was one of the first males to show me compassion and sincerity after Robert died. He never raised a hand to me. He never said a mean thing about any of the women in his life. And he never made me feel uncomfortable or uneasy. Tell me something, my precious little flower, have you not met a man who did the same?"

"My husband." AJ looked down at the table. She closed her eyes and, in one fleeting memory, saw Michael's brown eyes looking down at her. He grinned as he slid a tiny kitten into her arms.

"Remembering something, flower?"

"Yes."

"Good. Going back to Mekhi. One day, he was no longer around. His sister came by the nursery looking for him. Her usual tough facade had morphed into panic. She asked me if I'd seen him. I told her not for a few days. Last time I saw him was after our last lunch date. He asked for a ride back to my nursery and said he would wait for her."

"The last time you saw him was here, like Angela and Quill?"

Amanda nodded. "Correct. He called his sister—or at least, he called *someone* who spoke the same language as he did. He waited by the front while I continued mixing some potting soil. By the time I was done and checked in parking lot again, he was gone. Seeing his sister in a panic was a new experience for me. She truly did not know where he was. And that concern, that care for her sibling, touched me.

"Some years after he disappeared, I painted him as I saw him. The Xantus. I painted him with seafoam across the neck. And honeysuckle. The painting was not complete without those honeysuckle branches. Mekhi inspired me to start dating again. Never knew what happened to his sister after that. She never bought anything else." She took a large sip of her soda. "Your turn, Morning Glory."

"What do you want to know?"

"You *had* a man in your life. Do you *have* one now?"

"My stepdad."

"Does that really count?"

"Why not? He's been a solid supporter of me and the kids since we moved up here."

"Was there ever a time you resented him?"

"Who, Ernest? Why would I resent him?"

"This is all about the truths you hide, AJ. Was there ever a time you resented your stepfather for his relationship with your mother?"

AJ squeezed her hand shut. "Once. When I first moved up here."

"Why?"

"It was coming up on my daughter's birthday, and—"

"You mean the one-year anniversary of your husband's murder?"

In a soft response, "Yes. That, too. Her birthday was around the corner. My dad came home from work one day and gave my mom flowers. It wasn't a holiday or her birthday or anniversary. Just a random day. Yellow and pink roses."

"And why did you resent that?"

AJ swallowed the guilt back down. "Because they get to grow old together…and Michael and I never will."

"Why else?"

"I don't understand the question."

Amanda sat back and smiled in a way AJ did not like. "What else happened when you first moved here, to New Hampshire, that would make you resent your parents?"

"I resented the fact I had to move back in with my parents and live under my mom's rules. Her rules aren't that bad, but I'm an adult with kids of my own. How do you think that would've made you feel?"

"And?"

"And…and I didn't like the rules. I didn't like the fact my mom forced me to stop sleeping on the couch."

"Why were you sleeping on the—"

AJ slammed a hand down on the table. "Because it was too painful to be in a bed again, alone, and not have my husband there! Beds were a constant reminder that the space next to me used to be occupied and I'd NEVER have that again! I hated the fact I was forced to sleep in a bed because my mom made me do it. I hated the fact I couldn't support myself anymore in San Antonio. I hated having to rely on my parents—again—because my body and soul were broken. There! Does THAT answer your fucking question now?"

Amanda continued to smile in the way AJ did not like. The anger, the hate—it raged inside of her.

"See? Don't you feel the least bit better now that you got that out in the open?"

"No, I don't! I don't like talking about it. I want to put it behind me and move forward."

"The only way the past stays behind you is if you tackle it head-on and put it to rest. But you haven't done that, sweet flower. Your body reeks of anger and resentment and betrayal. Your mind is on fire and you can't bury those feelings and memories away like dirt on hot embers. The fire will still simmer underneath the soil until one day, it will crawl back to the surface and burn everyone around you."

"I don't like that analogy."

"Why? Because it's true?"

The detective nodded. She could not argue with the woman. Everything she said was true.

Amanda kept smiling in the way AJ did not like.

—¡—

CHAPTER 54

OH MY HEAVENLY Blue, we're just starting to peel the layers back and see the bulb of your existence. It's wonderful, really.

See that hummingbird painting next to Mekhi's little Xantus? It's a Plain-Capped Starthroat with a splendidly long beak and narrow flash of color on its throat. I gave this one a splendid coating of gray paint on both sides and complemented him with those beautiful bleeding heart flowers.

That's **ORO**. It's Spanish for 'gold'. Named after a brilliant young man who came into my life some years back.

I like to take winter vacations to the southwest, especially in Arizona and New Mexico. My hummers leave this state every Autumn, around the time the leaves fire up with their spectacular colors. I can go through the holidays without seeing them because I still stay busy with my business, but in the deep wretched stretches of long-lasting winters, when there's no need for a landscaper and visitors dwindle in numbers, I like to make trips south. I begin to miss shimmery flashes of color as they zoom by flowers. I deeply miss my birdies.

So, I travel down south, right before they begin their migrations back up here. I like to take my camera equipment, drive through the states, and stop at unique locations along the way. Ever see the Ozark Mountains in northwest Arkansas or drive through the vast wastelands of southern Arizona? Is it not glorious how diverse the land is? It gives and takes. As do my birdies.

One winter, I traveled down south along Interstate 10 through Las Cruces, New Mexico. Spent the night there and decided I wanted to visit some of the art museums in the area. I wanted to learn everything I could about the Native American history there.

I went to one museum and studied row after row of decorated clay pots on display. I was there for so long, I caught the eye of one of the contractors there, a security guard. We sparked a philosophical conversation and it was like a melody to my ears.

His name was Oro. He was tall, had strong shoulders and dark eyes with the whitest smile I'd seen—even more than Mekhi's handsome face.

We spent about half an hour in the museum discussing some of the history and politics of the area. We parted nicely, and both went about our business and separate ways.

But do you know what happened? The next day, I left Las Cruces and continued on my drive up to Alamogordo. Again, I stopped at another art museum, curious to learn everything I could.

Guess who was working there?

Oro! I couldn't believe it!

He told me his company provided security services for dozens of cities and rotated guards through various museums. It happened to be his rotation that day at that second museum. What were the odds?

He smiled when he saw me, and I couldn't help but smile back. He wore a different security uniform and I caught a glimpse of his toned chest underneath. His black hair was buzzed in the back and his neck pulsed and shone.

We picked up where we left off and drove the conversation

towards fate, luck, and karma. He thought it was divine intervention bringing two random strangers together two days in a row in two different cities.

Was it divine intervention? God's will? Luck?

To this day, I don't know. I'd like to think it was, but I don't believe in conventional religions. I don't like these Abrahamic beasts that dominate the world today. Why should I sit in church and listen to some man's interpretation of some other man's version of the Holy Word? That's exactly what the King James's version is. It's one man's interpretation of what we should believe, all pretending to spread the Golden Rule. Well, here's the Golden Rule for you: he who has the gold—and all kings do—makes the rules.

Haven't you ever wondered why women were snuffed out as equals in these religions? Haven't you wondered why it's the Father and Son and not the Mother and Daughter? Haven't you—

I digressed again.

I must apologize. I have different views than many of my counterparts. That's one religious and proverbial rabbit hole we could dive down and explore, Alice, but not this day.

Let me tell you what I do believe in.

Karma.

I believe in the Big Circle—the Cycle of Life, if you want to call it that. I believe you get out of this world and this life what you put in. There are inputs and outputs. Positive charges and negative charges. A balance of energies and electricity around us.

You want to be happy? Then make others happy.

You want to lie, steal, and cheat? Then your life will be stolen from you in ways you can't comprehend.

Karma comes around and She's the one passing judgement on you, deciding if your life is worthy or if you deserve death. Luck has nothing to do with it. Karma will fuck you if you cross Her.

You get what you deserve.

You are served what you make.

You reap what you sow.

That kind of thing.

And it was that conversation we continued and chatted about at that second museum, Oro and me. It was a fabulous exchange of thoughts and ideas and my soul was thrilled!

Oro must've felt the same way because we exchanged addresses. Not email, mind you. This was before the days of emails. No, we shared physical mail between us.

Don't you just miss those days? Receiving physical mail, a letter from a friend? Instead, we're just inundated with spam and badge notifications on cold devices too smart for our own making. Whatever happened to the smell of dusty paper and metallic ink? Whatever happened to cursive writing and patient correspondence?

Modern technology has made us a nasty lot. We're weak, whiny, and demanding. Almost no one has patience. Everyone has anxiety because they didn't get enough clicks, badges, or likes for something they shared on social media. Malicious information and diseased minds—that's what we have now.

It's exhausting. I'm sick of it. I miss the simpler days of working honest and hard at getting words correct on paper. Whatever happened of those deep friendships you can make and the personality you can read through the words the other has written? You can see the emotion. You can almost feel the emotion in the pressure of ballpoint to paper. You can study the way a T is crossed or a G is looped and know what sort of person you are dealing with.

I digressed again. Heh…typical, I guess.

After a few months of more thoughtful discussions and letters back and forth, I offered Oro a chance to come visit me up here. He made arrangements, and in May the following year, he arrived in New England for the first time. Honestly, I can't remember the date.

He brought all the letters I sent him.

"I wanted to show you all the reasons I fell in love with you," he said.

I was stunned. To see the letters and place them next to the ones he wrote was very touching. But to tell me he loved me? I couldn't say those words back. I can't say them to anyone.

Needless to say, we sat and talked all night, having our debates and discussion of Native American cultures and mythology. Heh. He surprised me with that, the mythology part.

Before he came up to see me, he scoured the museums he worked and asked some of the curators for as much information on hummingbirds as he could find. He thought he could woo me with stories.

There's one story he told me that sticks out, an Apache legend where a young warrior rescued an equally young maiden who'd been attacked by a wolf. The young warrior and maiden married after that and were set to have a beautiful life together.

But the warrior was killed; and a vicious, brutal winter happened after that. It was like the Earth grew cold after his heart stopped beating, saddened his warmth was no more. The elders didn't know what to think about it.

And then, when the young maiden began taking walks by herself, the winter suddenly ended. Fields grew bright with flowers. Crops were healthy again and food was plentiful.

The tribe elders later heard stories that the warrior came back as a hummingbird and would whisper magical things into his wife's ears. When the elders finally caught a glimpse of the bird, they discovered it had the same vibrant colors of the slain warrior. And because the maiden felt peace, and because the land was no longer frozen, the elders thought it must be true.

There were other stories, he told over dinner and wine. There's no lack of interesting tidbits I can share with you. Oro could enchant and talk. He wanted to court me with stories.

It almost worked.

Until one morning he left.

He was just...gone. I never saw him again, never understood what I did wrong, other than not reciprocate those three little words.

I wrote a few letters, but he never replied. I guess he wanted something more, something I wouldn't give him. And when he knew he wouldn't get it from me, he decided to end the correspondence.

Some men do that. When they don't get what they want, they run. They end it abruptly and don't waste any more time or energy on that thing. It's smart, actually. Why waste time with coyness? Why lead a man on if nothing will ever come of it?

I never understood why some women do that. Women can be more cruel and wicked than men, but the wicked and cruel things men do can be far worse.

I think that's what hurt the most—sending letters out and never getting a response back. I thought we had a strong friendship, but I learned that was a lie.

Males of any species flaunt what they have until they attract the right mate. And when their flaunty ways don't hook the little birdie they're after, they move on to another female. They shake and dance and go on the most spectacular and splendid display for the world to see.

The males are the most attractive of the sexes. It's the law of nature.

Honestly, I hate that law…

—¡—

CHAPTER 55

FLUSTERED, Maurice slid off the barstool and held his nose higher in the air.

"Ms. Claremont has owned many vehicles over the years. She has the right to change cars as she sees fit, does she not?"

"Yes, sir," Conrad said. He took out the notepad from his pocket and clicked the pen. "How long has she had the Crown Victoria?"

"Only two or three years, I believe."

"And what did she have before that?"

"If memory recalls, I believe it was a Honda Civic. However, you'd have to ask her about that."

As he wrote down the lawyer's responses, Conrad said, "Kinston, be sure to get some photographs of each of those keys." He glanced at each key and wrote down the vehicle make. As he put the notepad back in his pocket, he saw the light shining on the lawyer's forehead. Sweat beaded across the worry lines. "Mr. Juniper, are you okay?"

Gulping back the obvious nervousness, Maurice said, "I'm fine. It's just stuffy in this space." He walked over to the sliding glass door and cracked it open, letting in cooler air. He sighed relief from the freshness.

"I think I'm done." Jack pulled off his gloves and tossed them in the trash can under the sink. He walked around the bar to the sliding glass door and stood near the lawyer. A sigh of relief came out of the young detective. "Can we open some windows before we continue? I agree, it's stuffy."

"I'll do that right now." The lawyer quickly walked out of the kitchen. Conrad heard latch clicks from the dining and living rooms as Maurice slid random windows open.

"Where to next?" Jack asked.

"The office and study."

"Isn't that room locked?"

Conrad gathered his things and closed the briefcase. They walked out of the kitchen and back around to the living room where Maurice sat, fanning himself with a folder.

"Mr. Juniper, we're ready for the office."

The lawyer stood up, still fanning himself, and motioned for the two detectives to follow him. He led them down a long, barren hallway. The floors creaked under each step. The yellowed walls weeped from neglected years. A door petitioned any entrants, waiting to be unlocked.

Maurice fished for the deadbolt key in his pockets. After several seconds, he found it. The inserted metal and multiple sliding mechanisms echoed in the hallway as the bolt unlatched. He pushed the door open and it creaked with resistance. Taking a step back against the wall, he motioned for the other two to pass him.

"You're not coming in with us?" Jack asked.

"No," Maurice said. "Ms. Claremont's instructions. I'm not to step foot in the office. As this is the case, you will be on your own. And if you need my attention, I'll be waiting in the living room."

Conrad watched the lawyer wobble down the hallway and out of sight.

Jack stepped into the office. He whistled. "And I thought the kitchen looked ancient."

Three walls were covered in faux wood paneling, tuxedo stripes running vertically from ceiling to floor. The fourth wall's beige bamboo wallpaper framed the stone fireplace and mantle. Glitter sparkled across popcorn texture on the nicotine-colored ceiling. Wooden-framed furniture and a metal-framed desk sat under a faded brick red carpet covering most of the floor.

Built-in bookcases with a central display unit lined one entire wall. The glassed cabinet doors were hazy and dull from years of accumulated dust. Books were piled horizontally and vertically, wherever space could be found. Topics varied from psychology to legal systems to anatomy and physiology—a mix-match of assorted references.

An old sound system sat wedged in another built-in nook on the opposite wall. A cassette player and amplifier sat on top of two large speakers. Cassette tapes in yellowed plastic cases climbed the shelving above the equipment. Dozens of decades' old bands waited patiently to be remembered.

A pair of beige and warped Venetian blinds let slits of sunlight into the space. The office tasted of stale tobacco and old dust. It looked like dried, brittle kindling ready to ignite at a moment's notice.

Both men began processing the room in the same manner as the others before. Conrad carefully documented each corner, shelf, and drawer before they began searching through everything. Jack thumbed through the books.

Conrad opened the bottom cabinet doors. The shelves were empty. An office safe sat in one corner. He opened the heavy metal door. Empty. Whatever secrets used to be hidden there were long since gone.

He stood back up and stretched his aching back. He would definitely need to see a chiropractor after this.

And maybe a nutritionist.

Yasmin has been telling me to for a few months now.

He pushed the distracting thoughts away and looked at the upper cabinets in front of him. He opened the glass panel doors, removing each figurine and doll to inspect them.

"What the hell are those things?" Jack asked.

"Kachina dolls."

"Huh?"

"Native American Kachina dolls. Though I'm not sure if these are Hopi or Zuni specimens."

"I don't get it."

"Have you ever traveled to the American Southwest? Ever visited an Indian reservation?"

He shook his head. "Never been outside of New England."

"That's unfortunate. I recommend you travel the States. And the world, if you can. See what's out there. Learn about other cultures, like the ones who created many of the souvenirs and relics in this display case. Do it before you settle down with a family."

"Not sure if marriage is for me, to be honest."

Conrad cracked a slight smile. "When I was young, I had the same thoughts."

"What happened?"

"Love did."

Jack opened his mouth to say something. Instead, he sneezed into the crease of his elbow. Twice.

"Bless you."

"Do you really think there's anything in this old relic? It feels like we walked into a time capsule from my grandparents' past."

"Kinston, anything's possible. We need to search every room. See what we can find."

Jack put the last book back on the bookshelf. "Want me to check the desk now?"

Conrad nodded as he continued to examine the inside of the display cabinet.

From behind, he heard Jack say, "Don't you think it's kind of odd, though, that—" Jack sneezed twice again.

"Bless you."

"Thanks. As I was trying to—" Another sneeze rang out. "Ugh. The dust is getting to me. My eyes are starting to water."

"We'll be done in a bit. You were saying?"

"Yeah. Have you noticed something odd about her office?"

"What, exactly?"

"There's no computer."

—¡—

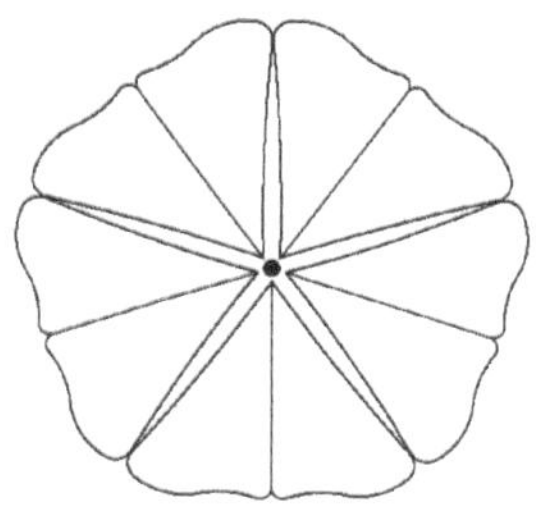

CHAPTER 56

"WHY ARE the males of any species the more attractive ones? They already take what they want, when they want? Why do women have to put on war paint, fit into uncomfortably tight clothes, and be judged if they aren't thin enough, pretty enough?" Amanda flicked a wrist up to dismiss the conversation. "You make it so easy to digress, you know that?"

AJ scrunched her brow. "What do you mean?"

"I'm always going off on some tangent with our conversations this week. Don't you find that odd?"

She shrugged. "I'm not sure. Everyone tells me I'm a good listener. Maybe you're a good talker?"

Amanda chuckled. "Oh, flower, that I am. Years and years of bottled-up conversations begging to come out now with the right audience. And you *are* the correct audience."

Amanda stood up and stretched, then walked behind the front counter. AJ heard the seal of a refrigerator open.

"Would you like a soda?" the older woman asked. "I have some regular and diet ones. Also have some water here."

"Water, please."

A few seconds later, AJ heard the fridge thump shut. Amanda walked back and placed a chilled water bottle in front of her.

The older woman looked up at her paintings and smiled again.

"See these two on the end?" Amanda pointed to the other side of the building where the other half of the paintings hung. "That end one's an Anna's. You can tell from the bright fuchsia neck and face. The one next to it is a Black-Chinned. I can't wait to tell you about those two."

"Why don't you go ahead and tell me now?"

Amanda shook a finger at her as she sat back down across the table. "Nice try. But you're next."

AJ swallowed her water and clenched her jaw. "What do you want to know now?"

"I want to know about the father figures in your life."

"There's only one father figure in my life. My stepdad."

The older woman shook her head. "I'm not buying it. There's more to your story than 'he's my stepdad'." Amanda mocked AJ's voice. "I want to go deeper than that. Tell me about your experience with your stepdad growing up. What was it like? What was your real dad like?"

"I don't have a relationship with my real father."

"Oh, I know. Must be such a story to tell. If you don't want to discuss him, let's start with your stepfather."

"What do you want to know?" AJ's foot tapped under the table.

"Has he ever hit you?"

"No."

"Has he ever hit your kids?"

"No. He'd never do such a thing."

"Has he ever hit your mom?"

"No! Dad's not like that. That's the one thing my mom told him would be an immediate divorce, no questions asked, no going back. She said she could tolerate anything except him laying a hand on her or her kids."

"Have you ever resented him, other than what you already mentioned?"

AJ shook her head and exhaled. "No. Why would I? He loves my mom, he supports me, and he's stepped in to help raise both my kids. Eoghan needs a father-figure in his life, and my dad does that."

"You've *never* resented him, except that your mother's husband lives and yours is rotting away in some grave?"

AJ closed her eyes. She pushed the sickness back down in the pit of her stomach. "I envy their relationship, yes. But I don't resent anything my dad has done for me and my kids."

"Tell me about your envy. Give me a specific example."

She looked at her hands and thought. "My stepdad likes to hold my mom's hand in public. Any time we go out to eat, he grabs her hand and walks with her. She always looks so happy with him. I miss that. I miss being able to hold Michael's hand again."

"What else do you envy?"

"I've never met anyone so…content. My life has been a struggle of ups and downs, too many highs and way too many lows where I've wanted to end it all. But Ernest? His life is mellow and calm. He's always content, always satisfied with how things are going. Even when I've yelled at my kids or had fights with my son, Ernest was the calm voice of reason."

"And that bothers you?"

"Yes and no. He's an anchor in the rough waters, keeping the rest of us afloat. But sometimes, I just want to know what he'd be like if he bottomed out. Just once I'd like to see it, know if the reaction is there."

"You miss the wildness of your real dad?"

"Absolutely not. No. My biological father was a piece of shit and I don't miss anything about him. My real *dad* treats my mom like a queen."

"You keep going back and forth between those words, 'dad' and 'stepdad'."

"Ernest is more of a dad than Paden every will be." She cleared her throat and sat up straighter.

Amanda leaned in. "See that. There's a sharpness to your words when you mention your real dad."

"Amanda, I really don't want to talk about him."

"We do many things in our lives we don't *want* to do. But we always do things we *must*. You haven't dealt with your past on many levels because you don't *want* to. What you don't understand is that you *need* to if you want to ever move forward and stop running away."

"I'm not running away."

"Yes, you are, my dear."

"No, I'm not." AJ grabbed her water bottle and squeezed the lid.

"Tell me about your real father, then."

"No. It's your turn."

"Ah. That punctual dot at the end of your 'no' is all I need to know about that topic."

"He was an abusive alcoholic and a piece of shit. What else do you want me to say?"

"You don't need to say anymore."

"Good. Because I don't want to."

"I do admire your mother's strength in leaving him."

"It was that or wind up back in the hospital," AJ muttered.

"It takes primal courage, or savage fear, to leave domestic violence behind."

She stared at the old woman. "Then why did you stay with Robert as long as you did?"

—¡—

CHAPTER 57

AH. YOUR tongue is as sharp as your sword and you cut to the bone.

Why did I stay with Robert as long as I did?

I have neither primal courage nor savage fear, but I did have primal fear those first couple of years, and it took savage courage to stay many years longer.

Why?

He was a life lesson. He's the reason I'm as solid and successful as I am. He toughened me. He drove me to be the woman I am now.

The man made the woman.

Isn't that ironic, flower?

He made me.

Or so I let other people think. Maybe I was already the rigid and solid specimen you see, and he merely hacked and chiseled away the soft outer coating, sanding down the sweet edges until my glorious hardened core could be seen.

I think it's intriguing what he did. Because behind him came the men who tried to do the opposite. Behind him were the men who tried to pack the sweetness on and cover the sharp and spiny ends.

They all tried.

They all failed.

Even **ETHAN** and **ISAAC**.

Look at that Anna's bird again, the one on the end with the bright colored face next to the red bee balm flower. I named that one Ethan. I dripped his neck in fuchsia and copper. A handsome name for a tall and strong man.

He had a twin brother named Isaac. See that Black-Chinned painting next to Ethan? That's Isaac. The hummingbird itself has a black head with a slice of indigo across its neck. That's what I captured with Isaac. I gave him an indigo slice against all that darkness. Then I complemented him with those bright petunias.

Why not paint identical birds for identical twins? They may have appeared the same, but they were competitive against each other. Their personalities were as complementary as these two birdies and their flowers.

I met Ethan first. This happened right after Robert disappeared. I boarded up my house and took off the following year. I wanted to explore the bright lights and big cities. New York was calling my name back then.

"Come see what we have to offer!" Manhattan said.

"You'll never be the same again!" Brooklyn cried.

So, I left. With nothing more than a suitcase, I took off on the train from Boston down to Penn Station. The autumn leaves were copper and rust. I remember that.

As soon as I got off the train, I was so dumbfounded, I looked like a tourist. My chin was pointed up, gazing at the sheer massiveness of the concrete and steel jungle around me. The lights on Time Square dazzled. I just strolled down the sidewalks gazing in awe at everything. I had every hope of finding an affordable hotel that evening.

But, do you know what happens to someone who's eyes are high? They are at their most vulnerable. Their neck becomes exposed to the predators around them and they fail to see lurking shadows circling around them.

No sooner had I walked a few blocks when I was grabbed from behind by several men. I was shoved in the alley. They grabbed my suitcase, tore at my pockets, ripped my necklace off. They took everything I had on me. Then they tried to take my body.

That's when I heard someone yelling. The men shoved me against the garbage bin and gave me a final punch in the gut before scrambling in all directions. The assault took mere seconds, but I played back those events for hours and hours after that. Funny how a split-second decision can create a life-changing moment and alter time around you.

Another man ran up to me. "Are you okay, miss?"

I was too stunned to answer.

"Miss, are you okay? Are you hurt?"

I think I shook my head. My hands were tucked under my armpits as my arms shielded my chest from an additional assault.

"Do you need a doctor?" he asked. He was so concerned for my well-being.

I remember I shook my head that time. He helped me stand up and took his coat off to wrap around my exposed shoulders. He walked me out of the alley and down the street. Millions of eyes either ignored me or glanced and moved on, but none noticed me. Not until this man.

He took me to a nearby restaurant and sat me down at a corner table. He walked off as I sat there and stared at nothingness, wondering what the hell I did wrong to deserve to be robbed of everything. How much lower could life get? What would happen now?

The man came back and put a bowl of soup in front of me.

"Here," he said, "you look like you could use this."

That's when I finally made eye contact with him. He was tall, European descent. His sandy blonde hair waved 'hello' and his blue eyes said 'hi'. His voice said, "My name's Ethan."

He didn't ask for my name back. Just gave me time to sip my soup before I finally responded with my own.

"I'm sorry that happened to you, Amanda. Have you ever

been to the City?"

I shook my head. "I just got off the train." Then I told him my story. Told him about Robert, about the years of abuse and seclusion, about his death. I told him how that gang of men took everything I had on me, and I didn't know what I was going to do then.

He sat there, respectfully, and listened. In the City That Never Sleeps, in the hustle of New York time standards, this man waited patiently. It felt like he stopped the clock and time ceased to exist around us. Those few seconds of assault were a lifetime ago as I sat in his company and held his attention.

"Why don't you come back to my flat to spend the night? It's a safe place, I promise. You can shower, change clothes. I can give you some money to take the train back home."

"I can't take your money, sir."

His caring smile told me all I needed to know about him. So, I wasn't surprised when he replied, "Let me help you get back on your feet. Not all New Yorkers are assholes."

After I finished my soup, we left and walked a block or so to the subway entrance.

"Don't touch the railing. Germs." Ethan smiled as we stepped down into the City's belly.

Several minutes later, the subway whisked us to our destination. And, several minutes after that, we were standing in front of his apartment building. He led me through doors and narrow hallways until we reached his apartment door.

Ethan was a kind-hearted gentleman, not what I expected. He allowed me to shower and then wear one of his t-shirts and pajama bottoms. When I got out of the shower, I saw he'd changed clothes. He was standing in the kitchen, popping the lid open on a beer can.

"Who the hell are you?" he said.

"Excuse me?" I said, confused at the question.

"How the hell did you get into this apartment, lady? And why the fuck are you wearing my brother's clothes?"

Before I could explain anything, I heard an identical voice

behind me, "Relax, Isaac."

I turned around to see the same face as the one in the kitchen.

"Please forgive my brother," Ethan said. "He's an idiot sometimes."

"Says the person who brought the stray in. How do you know she's not a hooker or will steal your money while you sleep?"

I wanted to yell at Isaac for calling me a whore, but I was so numb, still, that I just walked over to the corner of the living room, as far away from him as I could, and crumbled to the ground. I curled up in a ball and just stared out the balcony door.

Ethan pulled his brother into the bedroom and slammed the door. I could hear their voices raise and lower as Ethan told Isaac what happened. I could hear the whole conversation through the drywall.

I stood up and opened the balcony door. We were several stories above the busy sidewalks, but I stared at the ocean of manmade stars. Car horns cricketed and croaked in the night air.

"Do you want to fly?" I heard from just beyond the balcony edge.

"Helen?" I hadn't thought of her in a forever of moments.

"Do you want to fly?" she asked me again.

I moved closer to the edge of the balcony and looked down. It was further a distance than on that bridge when Helen flew away.

I knew it could be a permanent solution to my temporary problem.

It was inviting, I won't lie.

But I whispered back to the imaginary voice, "No, Helen. Not yet."

"Did you say something?" Ethan asked, standing behind me. Isaac was right next to him.

"No. I'm sorry," I replied. "Thank you for your generosity, but I don't want to be a burden to either of you. If you want me to leave, I can change my clothes and go now. I understand if you don't want me here."

"Ethan told me what happened to you. I'm sorry. I can come

off as a dick sometimes."

"You're not a burden. Stay the night at least."

"Thank you."

The rest of the night was spent sitting in the living room and talking. Both men, polite as ever, threw stories back and forth of their childhood. Both men extended me the courtesy of a clean bed and warm meal. Both men never touched me, nor did they imply or desire anything from me other than the conversation we had sitting around the coffee table.

The next morning, I woke early and washed their dishes, scrubbed their tables and floors, and cleaned their kitchen—all before they woke up. It was the least I could do for them. They were smitten when they walked into the kitchen and sat at the small breakfast nook. I made them both breakfast.

"She should stay longer," Isaac teased. "I could get used to this."

"So could I," Ethan replied.

"It would be nice to stay a little longer. I had hoped to find a job and stay in the City for a bit. At the very least, to recoup what I lost yesterday."

"Why don't you?" Ethan asked.

I saw his brother glance at him, then nod. "I guess it would be okay. But you have to pay your share of rent."

I nodded. "I wouldn't have it any other way."

After discussion back and forth, it was settled. Within a few days, I had a part-time job at a pizza place a few blocks away. I handed over half my paycheck so they could pay the bills. As long as I cleaned and cooked—which I was absolutely fine with doing and enjoyed—I could stay as long as I wanted.

Those are fond memories of New York City. There's never any time to think. You just get swept into the current of moving bodies and you go with the flow.

Ethan and Isaac taught me about platonic relationships, city do's and don'ts, and a subculture I'd never even imagined before. They showed me how to act like a New Yorker and not a target. They taught me to defend myself and hold an intimidating edge to my voice. The music, the movement, the anonymity of it all—I still smile when I think of those two gentlemen.

—¡—

CHAPTER 58

"NO COMPUTER?" Conrad asked.

Jack sniffled and stood back up. "There's no cables or signs of any kind of laptop or computer tower. I don't even see a USB cable or thumb drive. And who keeps an old typewriter anymore?"

Conrad ran his hand along the top shelf of the display cabinet. "It's possible she doesn't own a computer."

"But that's just insane. How can you run a business or survive without the internet these days?" Jack opened another desk drawer and began sorting through the office supplies.

Conrad climbed down the stool and took his gloves off. He jotted down his thoughts on his notepad before grabbing a new pair of gloves. "Good observation, Kinston. We might find a laptop or computer upstairs. Anything in the desk?"

"Just old office supplies. Found some confidentiality agreements."

"Do you recognize any of the names?"

Jack flipped through each. "Yeah. A few of these are the men we already interviewed."

"And the rest?"

"I don't recognize the names."

"Write them down. We can cross-reference them at the office."

Jack sniffled again. "I don't think she's been in this room in forever." He held up a yellow and grey calculator. "Look at this thing. The battery's leaked out. Bet you it doesn't even work anymore."

"Quite possible." Conrad replaced each of the Kachina dolls back in their original positions. No matter how carefully and slowly he handled the figurines, specks of dust trailed off gossamer feathers.

"Have you ever seen anything like this?" Jack pulled out a wooden display case from the drawer and set it on the desk. An antique decorative jar with a dark substance rested in the middle of a circular wooden rack. Several smoking pipes orbited the jar, each standing at attention like a saxophone ready to belt music.

The Deputy Director walked over and studied the contents. "That's a cigar stand. My father used to own one."

"I've never seen anything like this." Jack lifted the lid on the glass container. He peered in and then scrunched his face. "Ugh, that smells awful."

Conrad looked inside and sniffed the contents. "Smells almost like sweet tobacco." He took in a deeper smell to study the aroma. "Apples…and something else. Can't quite place my finger on it."

Jack leaned in again and took another whiff. "Floral, maybe?"

"That's not right." Conrad smelled the contents again. "But, yes, it does smell floral."

"Why's that not right?"

"I'd guess this leaf tobacco was cured many years ago. Most of the time it has a fruity smell, not a floral one."

Conrad spun the wooden pipes around to study each one. The chambers appeared smoky gray; each lip, cracked with discolored wear. Only one pipe out of the eight appeared cleaner than the rest.

On a hunch, Conrad smelled each of them.

"Mr. Kinston, smell each of the pipe bowls and tell me your

initial observations."

Jack did as instructed. "All of them smell musky and like ash except that one." He pointed to the cleanest pipe. "That one smells flowery, like the tobacco."

"Take a few pictures of the tobacco and the pipes, then bag all of it." He took out his notepad again and wrote several items down.

"I don't get it. Why?"

"What makes that display stand out to you?"

"Besides the fact it's ancient?"

"Think beyond age."

Jack stared at the pipes and swiveled the case around on its turnstile. "The one clean pipe."

"What else?"

"I'm not sure?"

"What does Ms. Claremont do for a living?"

"She owns a farm."

"And?"

"And she owns a nursery."

"What does she sell in her nursery?"

"All kinds of plants and flowers." Jack's eyes widened. "Some flowers are poisonous, aren't they?"

"That's correct."

"And you think she mixed some of those poisonous flowers in this tobacco?"

"It's possible. It's suspicious enough to bag it."

"Who do you think she poisoned?"

"I don't know, but we should have it tested anyway."

Jack smiled. "I knew there was something off about her."

"She's a unique personality, but that doesn't mean she's done anything wrong." Conrad put the notepad back in his pocket. "Are you done with the desk?"

"Yeah. I think we're done here."

"Good. Bring the evidence with you and shut the door when you're done."

Jack nodded.

Conrad walked out of the office and down the hallway where Maurice waited.

The lawyer stood up. "I hope you are finding everything satisfactory, Mr. McMillan?"

"Yes, sir. We're ready to move upstairs."

Both men heard a door shut and watched as Jack walked into the living room. He put several bags in a large box.

"What is that?" Maurice asked. His skin paled at the sight of sealed bags.

"Possible evidence, Mr. Juniper." Maurice mouthed incomprehensible words. "Something wrong?"

The lawyer's double chin jiggled with a clop of his jaw. "I'll need to inform Ms. Claremont of this development."

"As you will." Conrad grabbed his flashlight. "Ready to check the upstairs, Mr. Kinston?"

Both detectives walked towards the stairway, Maurice in tow. Conrad clicked the flashlight on and studied each step after Jack shot additional photographs. Every wooden step cracked and groaned as they inched their way to the second floor. The top of the stairs split the hallway in half. Two bedroom doors waited on one end, a third bedroom door and a bathroom waited on the other.

"Ms. Claremont's bedroom is on the left. The other residents share the bedrooms on the right."

Conrad turned to the right, meticulously checking every section of the hallway as they walked towards the bedrooms. He crouched low, checking the baseboards.

"Do you smell that?" Jack asked.

The Deputy Director looked up at his subordinate. The younger man stared inside the first bedroom and took a step in. Conrad stood up and followed him.

The faint aroma of pine cleaner mixed with the potent smell of cleaning product permeated through the doorway.

Jack stood over one of the twin beds. "It's coming from this one." He covered his nose. "Whew! It's strong!"

Conrad nodded.

"Bleach."

—¡—

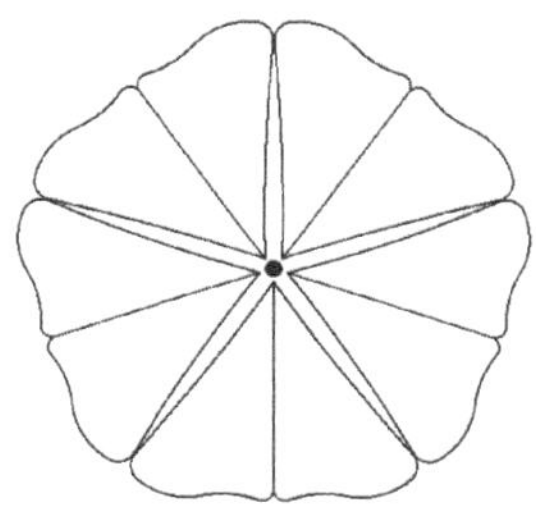

CHAPTER 59

SHE SMILED as she looked up at her paintings. "Ethan and Isaac. They were good men."

"Were?" AJ asked.

"Oh, I haven't talked to them in a couple of decades. I stayed in New York for a few months, got my fill of the Big City life, then came back here. I missed the rural and slower pace of this town."

"Did they ever come up here to visit you?"

"A couple of times. They'd take the train to Boston, then the bus to Concord. I'd pick them up there and bring them to my house. But Isaac didn't like the woods or the bugs or the coyotes at night. Too spooked. Ethan was more up to it, but he went where his brother went. They were damned near inseparable. We eventually went our separate ways, but I do have fond memories of them."

AJ stood up to stretch. Her stomach hurt too much to continue to sit in the same position. She looked at the time on her phone and grimaced.

"What's wrong, flower?"

"How much longer do we have to sit here and talk?"

Amanda smiled. "We can stand, if you prefer."

"I prefer we not keep talking."

"Why? Am *I* not the one doing most of the talking?"

"Well, yeah, but—"

"Then what do you have to lose except a little time today? Huh? This is all worthwhile, I promise."

"How?"

Amanda stood up. She clasped her hands behind her back and walked a lap around, looking up at her paintings. "I'm not just sharing cute stories about ex-boyfriends or fuck-buddies, Ms. Jardine. I'm giving you insight on pieces of the puzzle to fill in with your Deputy Director, when the time comes. And speaking of time, yours is not wasted with me, but I'm beginning to wonder if mine is wasted with you." She looked at AJ as she carefully took steps back towards the table. "Do you want to tell your boss—a man whom you admire more than you think you know, and vice versa—that you were too impatient to sit and listen to a potential suspect's rambling stories instead of providing him crucial pieces to a much bigger part of a much larger narrative?"

"No, ma'am." AJ watched the woman's eyes fixate on their target.

"I don't ask much of anyone. I despise it. Deplore it. All I ask of you is to continue entertaining my feeble mind and old heart." Amanda came within a couple feet of the detective. Her voice dropped. "You are a spectacular garden, Ameena Hawthorne Jardine, and you don't even know it. What fertile grounds we've still to cover." Amanda did a slow lap back across the table, looked up at her hummingbirds, and smiled. "Tell me about your real father."

AJ finished stretching, then sat back down. She pursed her lips and lifted her chin defiantly.

"Not ready yet, flower? Very well. Let's talk about something you *are* ready for. How about your children?"

"What would you like to know?"

"Little Jenna Beth Hawthorne was your miracle baby, was she not?"

"Yes. We're lucky she's alive."

"Agreed. According to the newspaper article I read, she was struck by a bullet while in your womb. Is that correct?"

AJ broke eye contact and stared at the table. "Yes."

"Tell me about her birth."

"I...I can't."

"Because of the trauma and pain of watching your husband die?"

AJ shook her head. "I can't remember most of what happened. I passed out shortly after I was shot."

"What do you remember?"

"Waking up in the hospital days later. I was confused, didn't know where I was. I remember hearing my mom and my brothers in the background, being surrounded by people everywhere and everything hurt."

"When did you find out Jenna was safe?"

"Some doctor told me her condition. She was born premature and the bullet...the bullet grazed her arm. She also suffered from birth asphyxia and was in the hospital longer than I was."

"And you were relieved, weren't you?"

AJ nodded. The younger woman felt her throat constrict and a haze of moisture coated her eyes. The memories always came with the unwanted emotion.

"Do you remember the first time you saw her?"

She nodded again. "Of course."

"Tell me about that."

"It was more than a week after...that day. I could finally sit up and the nurses helped me into a wheelchair. It was uncomfortable."

"Sitting up?"

"Yeah. I could feel every wound and surgical incision shifting. Gravity pulled at some of the stitches."

"What happened next?"

"My mom wheeled me down the hall, to the elevator. I remember the inside of it smelled like freshly ground metal. We went to the NICU and waited for the staff to let us in."

"How long was Jenna in the neonatal unit?"

"A few weeks, I think."

"The staff let you in. Then what?"

"My mom wheeled me down the hallway to a large room. There were all these little clear boxes everywhere with machines attached to them. It looked more like a laboratory on a space station than a hospital ward."

"And your mother wheeled you past each one?"

AJ nodded. "Some were empty, the beds. I remember one of the front wheels on the wheelchair kept rattling against the tile. I remember the beeps and pings of monitors, the smell of diapers and latex."

"What else do you remember?"

"Anxiety. I was scared to see my daughter for the first time, to see how bad she looked."

"And what did you see? What was in that clear-sided bed that looked like a display cabinet for tiny dolls?"

"I saw this small...*thing*. This little baby half the size Eoghan was when he was born. Her chest kept rising and falling so fast. She had monitors and tubes coming out of her, including her foot. I...couldn't see the bullet wound."

"Did that bother you? Did you want to see the same hole put in her that was put in you?"

"Gawd no!" AJ shook her head, then dabbed her eyes. "No! I don't want to think about that."

"How did you feel about seeing the...*thing*...that caused your husband's death and nearly yours?"

AJ whispered, "I love my daughter."

"I know you do, flower, but you didn't answer the question. How did seeing that baby make you feel in that singular moment? What were the first thoughts burning in your mind as you stared up at her from your wheelchair?"

"Why was she alive and not Michael? What did he do to deserve to be gunned down one night?" AJ picked at her finger. "Was it her fault?"

"What do you mean?"

"I looked at her frail body and I wondered if it was *her* fault Michael was dead and in that singular moment I wished I hadn't been pregnant with her because then I wouldn't have had all those awful cravings and we wouldn't have gone to dinner that night and we wouldn't have been walking down that sidewalk because my back ached and she was dancing in my belly." AJ wiped another tear away, then crossed her arms. She looked up at the hummingbird paintings, unwilling to make eye contact with Amanda, unwilling to wipe more tears away.

"You've never admitted this to anyone else before, have you?"

She kept staring at the paintings and the bright gorgets on display. "No."

"You've held that guilt in all these years, haven't you? You resented your daughter's life and wish she never existed, didn't you?" She heard the compassion and softness in Amanda's voice, but that did not make her stomach feel any better.

AJ kept staring up as a tear fell from her cheek onto her chest. She looked at the painting next to the Black-Chinned one. The hummingbird was in mid-flight, looking up. The wings were pulled back and the tail feathers spread forward as if the bird were flying backward. Its neck displayed a vibrant burnt orange that matched the Autumn leaves painted in the background. Yellow, pink, and orange pompoms of flowers decorated the border. In the bottom center, she made out a single word: **MAVERICK**.

Amanda waited patiently for her to respond.

AJ tried not to admit the truth, but she had to say the word. She had to answer that awful question as she stared at the burnt orange neck.

"Yes."

—¡—

CHAPTER 60

EVERYONE believes that a mother will always love their children and never harm them. And the absolute large majority do love and nurture their offspring. The majority will die for them, peel their soul out for them, and do whatever it takes to provide them a better life.

But the majority of the best mothers out there have had, at some instantaneous or brief moment, similar thoughts as yours.

How could they not?

How many sleep-deprived nights have made new moms want to smother their babies? How many times has a mom wished to cover their screaming child's mouth and make the noise stop? How many times has a woman looked down at her stretchmarks and sagging belly and blistered breasts, wishing they'd never been pregnant before, wishing they could have the same knockout body when they were younger? How many selfish thoughts has any one mother had in her lifetime?

Do you think it's not okay to feel that way? Do you honestly believe you deserve to carry that guilt around the rest of your life? Are post-partum depression and severe hormone imbalances evil taboos, punishable for a woman's lifetime?

Don't feel guilty, flower, for resenting little Jenna or wondering what life would be like without her. It doesn't make you less of a mother, but it does make you less human if you think you are. You were vulnerable in more ways than you can comprehend; and vulnerable, exposed, exhausted people have irrational thoughts and make illogical decisions.

It happens.

You can either keep those thoughts to yourself and let them consume you like some aggressive cancer, or you can say the truth once and for all and move on.

You're on a path moving forward—career-wise, parent-wise, spiritually. It doesn't matter. You are <u>always</u> moving forward. Sometimes the path is paved, laid out for miles towards the horizon. Nothing can stop you then. It's a beautiful stretch of asphalt.

But sometimes the road is through a mountain range with potholes, rock slides, and blind curves. You have ups and downs as you slowly ascend a narrow dirt trail. Sometimes you have to stop and move obstacles out of your way, then continue ahead. Always moving onward and upward.

Sometimes you get caught in a rut. Your emotions, your memory, your PTSD—they all make you fall victim to muddy circumstances. You wind up spinning your wheels in certain situations. You want to keep moving forward, but you can't. So, you feel sorry for yourself. Or you sink into a deep depression. The longer your wheels spin, the deeper the rut and the stronger the depression.

If you find yourself in a rut—and we all do, my dearest flower—then have your cry. Yell at the world. Scream your anger. Shed away those negative emotions and expose them to the raw elements.

Get up. Dust yourself off. Crawl, limp, or walk. But keep moving. Keep going. No matter what.

You are not a victim, waiting for someone to come rescue you. You're a warrior and you battle each day against Death. You keep moving forward. You keep going. You get so far ahead of Death that when it finally catches up to you at the end of your days, you can say, "Wasn't that a ride? Wasn't that a great battle I won?"

I was like you are, now, in so many ways. I felt a victim of my circumstances. I felt I'd never amount to much more than some discarded plaything for abusive and evil men. But I'd met Ethan and Isaac who both showed me a different side of what men are capable of being.

And then, a few years later, I met Maverick. I saw you staring at his painting up there. That's an Allen's hummer. I painted his neck that coppery burnt orange, honoring the college town he was from, Austin. Those flowers there? Those are Zinnias. They remind me of Fiesta days in San Antonio.

It was Maverick who taught me to keep moving onward and upward. He not only had such bodily strength from being a former military man, but he had such spiritual resolve it could hit you like a tank and plow right over you.

I met him in Austin, on Sixth Street, the Bourbon Street of Texas for party goers and aspiring musicians. You, being from San Antonio, I'd assume you've been there?

I was on one of my trips in the early years of my business and decided to visit the Texas capital. I wanted to listen to folk music and experience the open atmosphere, but there was a man who kept invading my space. He kept following me around.

After catching him at the third bar I entered, I confronted him. Living in New York taught me a thing a two about deterring creeps. I learned to handle myself—and a few weapons.

My favorite?

Knives. Guns are fine, but they're too loud. People know where you are, what you've done, and how big of a gun you have. It can leave you at a disadvantage.

But a knife? Most people never see it coming. It's silent and never runs out of ammunition. One of my favorite knives was a lipstick weapon I carried in my pocket.

I learned not to carry purses—a brainwashed accessory if there ever was one. I just carry what I need in my front pockets or hidden ones I can easily reach.

I walked up to that tall man, stared up at him with a ferociousness he didn't expect, and demanded, "Who the fuck are you? Why are you following me?" I kept my hand in my pocket, gripping that lipstick container.

He leaned in and spoke close to my ear. "I'm sorry, ma'am, but I haven't been followin' you. I've been followin' the two men stalkin' you." His southern drawl made him forget his 'g's. There was a sincerity in his eyes and a polite charm that grabbed me by surprise.

He wasn't much of a looker, but his protectiveness and chivalry were unmatched with anyone else I met in that state, much less the whole South.

"Which men?" I answered back in his ear.

"Them two in the corner, hidin' their faces." He pointed his chin over to two young men huddled together in secrecy. "My friends are waitin' outside to keep an eye on 'em."

I crossed my arms in front of me and puffed out my shoulders. "How do I know *you* aren't the stalker?"

"Well, ma'am. You don't. But as Jesus is my Savior, I swear on my Mama's grave, I mean you no harm. My name's Maverick, ma'am."

I immediately walked out of the bar and stood just a few feet outside the door. Five other military men, some with their dates, looked at me, then at Maverick as he exited.

"Miss, those are my friends. We met at Lackland Air Force Base in San Antonio." He rattled off each of their names, but I don't remember them anymore.

Everyone was charming and interested in who I was. There was a comfortable level of attention I enjoyed with that crowd. The music swept us down the street from bar to bar as we enjoyed ourselves and the company around us.

The two would-be stalkers never attempted anything. They scurried off shortly after I was introduced to Maverick's friends. Though, I can't say I wouldn't've liked to see them try something. Wouldn't that have been something? The thought of seeing them bleed all over the place was exhilarating. Honestly, I don't know if that's why I stuck with Maverick and his posse all night.

When the bars finally announced last calls, those military men went their separate ways with their dates or women they met that night. My escort was nice enough to walk me to my car where we continued to talk.

I told him about my experience in New York and the struggles I was having with my business. I told him I sometimes felt like giving up.

He leaned against the hood of the Chrysler and said, "Amanda, life ain't a smooth highway to Amarillo and back. It's a dirt road climbin' up an ever expandin' mountain. You can sit in the valley, in the shadows of that mountain, or you can move ever onward and upward."

"I never thought of it like that," I replied.

"Our goals, our dreams are always in front of us. And if we find ourselves in a rut, it's up to us, alone, to get out and keep going. Crawl, walk, or run. But we keep pushin' on. We've a battlefield ahead before Death comes for us."

Such a philosopher, my military Maverick. Such profound and sage advice from a chivalrous soldier.

—¡—

CHAPTER 61

RESTLESS and impatient, Jack fidgeted while Conrad inspected the bedroom and took photographs.

"There's something here, I know it! Why else would the bed smell like bleach?"

"We can't assume anything, Kinston." Conrad took a few more photos, then added, "Go ahead and pull the comforter back."

Jack placed the pillows on one of the other beds then slowly pulled the comforter off. Nothing looked out of the ordinary with the top white sheet. Conrad nodded and Jack peeled it back. The fitted sheet underneath had a couple of large areas with light brown stains.

"Is that blood?"

"Not sure. Cover the windows, please."

Jack proceeded to make the room darker. Conrad grabbed a small spray bottle of Luminol from his briefcase and spritzed the liquid on a section of the stain. He grabbed a handheld UV light and turned it on.

The stain lit up in blue fluorescence.

"Positive!" Jack said, smiling at the discovery.

"Remove the sheet, please."

Jack slid the sheet off the front corners and pulled it off the foot of the bed. The material underneath crinkled. "What the hell is that?"

The lawyer cleared his throat. "Well, of course, you'll find blood here in the girls' rooms. And that's a leak-proof lining," Maurice said from the doorway. "Ms. Claremont had informed me that some of the girls prefer…freebleeding." He murmured the last word, apparently embarrassed to say it too loud.

"'Freebleeding'?"

Conrad sighed. "Mr. Kinston, freebleeding is a way some women observe their menstrual cycles. The positive result is probably from the girls' periods."

Jack quickly dropped the fitted sheet back on the bed and looked at Conrad with disgust.

Maurice cleared his throat again. "Ms. Claremont warned me you might find traces of blood in the girls' rooms and she informed me the uncriminalistic nature of large, and potentially suspicious, stains of blood. Ms. Claremont also informed me that she allows her female employees to take up to three days off per unregulated menstrual cycle and they are welcome to freebleed. That bed is specifically used for such…discrete, personal reasons."

"You mean I touched some girl's used tampon space and vaginal discharge?!"

"It's not vaginal discharge, detective," Conrad corrected his subordinate. "It's the natural process of women shedding the uterine lining."

"I think I'm going to be sick." Jack shivered as he stared at the bed.

"Or single the rest of your life," Maurice quipped.

Conrad almost cracked a slight grin. "Mr. Kinston, however a woman takes care of her monthly cycle is her right. Respect their decisions."

"It's still disgusting. Who wants to sit in their own bodily fluids for days at a time?"

"The…substance and fluid…is collected and Ms. Claremont

adds it to her flower gardens around the two residences."

"That's even worse!"

"Mr. Juniper, what do you mean by 'unregulated menstrual cycle'?"

"Ms. Claremont will not demand if a woman goes on birth control or not. However, women on any birth control or other hormone therapy are not allowed the extra days off. Only those who prefer the natural course of hormones and are willing to freebleed are allowed the extra days off. My client believes any pharmaceutical pill or injection alters the chemical makeup in the uterine lining and, therefore, could alter soil compositions and the way plants could and do grow.

"As you can tell from the smell of bleach, one or more of her employees recently finished their bleed days. As such, the materials are collected, everything is sterilized, and the bed is ready for the next cycle."

"Just the thought of a girl sitting here..." Jack shook his head. "My wife'll be sticking to tampons."

Maurice gave Conrad a knowing look the older men shared.

"Mr. Juniper, did Ms. Claremont tell you anything else about the girls' bedrooms we should be aware of?"

"No, sir. Each bedroom has a designated bed. Sometimes the girls will run concurrent cycles. They either share the same bed or prefer solitude."

"Will you show us the other bed?"

Maurice nodded. "This way."

Both men left the disheveled bed and followed Maurice to the adjacent bedroom. In almost an identical layout as the first bedroom, several beds were waiting for evening occupants. A familiar whiff of bleach led Jack to one particular bed.

"This one," he said.

Conrad took a few photographs and then had Jack peel back each layer of bedding. Similar stains in nearly identical locations echoed the lawyer's claims.

As Conrad studied the bed and the fitted sheet, he finally looked at Maurice. "Thank you, Mr. Juniper."

"Do we still need to process both bedrooms?" Jack asked.

"Yes, Kinston. We do." He walked out of the second bedroom and back into the first, studying the layout again.

Both bedrooms had the same floral wallpaper runner at the tops of the walls. Each wall had a faded antique pink hue with a cream-colored ceiling. Stained and blown glass figurines representing flowers or birds hung in the windows, catching any rays of light they could.

All beds had similar white sheets and pillowcases, though each bed had a unique comforter or quilted top. It appeared the girls were allowed to have a small collection of personal items on accompanying nightstands, but none of the items offered any clues to their backgrounds or to who owned what.

Closets, nightstands, and spaces under beds all revealed the same thing: nothing unusual or out of the ordinary. No items were jammed between mattresses and box springs. No weapons were hiding in coat pockets, tucked in obscure nooks and crannies, or stuffed in socks or between other clothing. He stood back for several minutes and scanned every inch of the room.

"Something wrong, Conrad?" Jack asked.

The Deputy Director hesitated, then said, "No, Kinston. Just making observations."

"Of the décor? Or lack thereof?"

"That, too."

Jack leaned in and whispered, "It almost feels like some sort of cult, doesn't it?"

"What makes you say that?"

"The girls dressed all the same as they work. The closets aren't jam-packed with shoes and dresses, like most women. It's almost too *plain*. What do you think?"

"I'm not sure yet, Jack. I'm just not sure."

—¡—

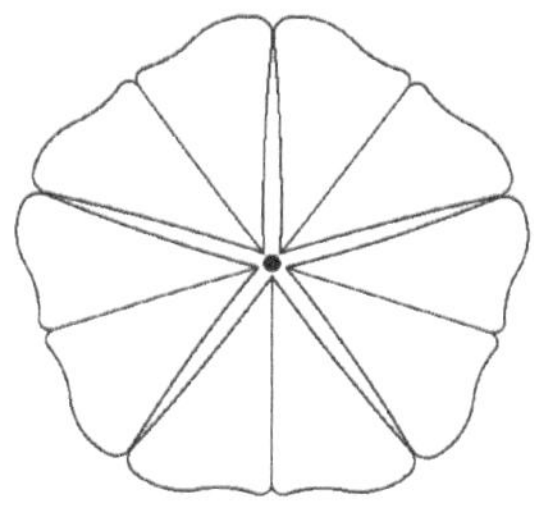

CHAPTER 62

IN THE YEARS since Michael's murder, AJ never wanted to admit the dark thoughts and secrets she carried, the ones she intended to take to her grave. The pain and humiliation of admitting to the resentment of their newborn daughter she and Michael had tried so long to have made her scrape her nails against the table. One thin nail bent backward and shot a resisting nerve up her finger. She welcomed the pain over and over as Amanda talked about her burnt-orange friend.

"Maverick is someone else I lost touch with over the years. I saw him a few more times after that, and he offered some of the most sage and philosophical advice anyone had ever given me. He was a gentleman, through and through." Amanda paused long enough for AJ to finally look up at her. "Were you paying attention, flower?"

"Yeah, I—"

"—or were you too lost in your own humility and guilt from your admission?"

The detective sighed. "That, too."

"Of course, you are. You've a tendency to dwell and over-analyze thoughts, my dear. That little bit of hesitation may one day save your life. Or cause you more harm."

"You would hurt me?"

"No, no, no." Amanda shook her head. "Women like you are safe around women—and men—like me. We are drawn to you, like hummingbirds to flowers. You're a gift to us."

"A gift? How?"

"We can see it in your eyes. We know you listen. You observe. Maybe you're the centerpiece of the garden or what lies at the end of a maze. But you are more special than you'll ever comprehend."

AJ sat back and rolled her eyes. "Special people don't have the thoughts I've had."

Amanda tsked. "Shame on you, detective. Everyone has dark thoughts. Everyone. But not everyone admits them and not everyone acts on them. Those are the sheep who stay herded together and those are the lambs led to slaughter. You, admitting your feelings, makes you the sheep dressed as the wolf after the wolf dressed as the sheep."

AJ scrunched her brow, contemplating the logic of the woman's statement.

With a flick of her wrist, Amanda changed the subject. "Tell me about that resentment you had for your newborn daughter."

"I don't know. I just wished at one point I hadn't been pregnant."

"Oh, so coy, Morning Glory. Try again. Tell me how you felt after that little *thing* was out of the hospital. You were home at that point, correct?"

AJ nodded. "I had to go through several months of physical therapy. The bullets—there were three of them—caused a decent amount of damage."

"One in the chest?"

"Yes. It lodged and cracked one of my ribs. The other two bullets hit my stomach."

"But you survived, and the baby survived, and you were back home in a few weeks. Tell me about what it was like being home again."

"My mom stayed with me for a few months. My dad had to go back to New Hampshire. He couldn't stay too long in San Antonio. My mom, though, she cooked and took care of both kids for me. She drove me to all my appointments and made sure I saw Jenna every day. She said it was important to bond with my baby."

"But did you bond? Or did you reject her like a bitch's runt?"

AJ shook her head and swallowed the distaste of Amanda's words. There were so many thoughts she did not want to admit. "It was hard when she was first home. It was over a month after she was born before she came home. All she did was cry and cry. Nothing made her happy except being held. She cried the most in my bedroom and never seemed to calm down while in there."

"How bad was your postpartum depression?"

"The first few months were horrible. Doctors kept playing around with what medications to give me. I hated them. I hated everyone. At one point, I—" She choked back the words and shook her head several times.

"It's okay to admit the words here."

"At one point, I wanted to end it. I wanted the crying to stop. I thought how easy it would be to just cover her mouth. But, it's not in me to kill. I couldn't do that to my baby! But the thought was there, and I couldn't stop the thoughts from coming. It terrified me!"

"Did you ever think of giving her up for adoption?"

The detective nodded. "A few times. I thought of giving both my kids up. Eoghan's attitude started changing and he, too, resented his sister. No one wanted her. The atmosphere in the house...changed."

"You both resented an innocent baby for something that wasn't her fault. Don't you think the reason she cried in your bedroom is because she could *feel* the negativity? Did you ever think that she could sense the darkness enveloping every single one of you?"

"At the time, when it was happening? No. It never dawned on me that *I* was the one causing her as much pain as she caused me."

"When did you start to realize that?"

"After my mom went back home and I was left alone with both kids."

"Tell me about the first few days, alone, just you and them. How did the atmosphere feel in the house?"

"Heavy. Sad. Angry and negative. Eoghan got into a fight at school with some kid twice as big as him. He came home that afternoon and slammed the door to his room. He refused to come out for a long time. Jenna just constantly cried. My mom told me it would be a good idea to take her for a walk, but I just couldn't do it. I couldn't take my daughter out on that sidewalk and walk past the house where Michael's soul left his body."

"Why not?"

"HOW COULD I?!" AJ slammed her fists into the table. The strength of her outburst shocked even herself. "I...I'm sorry. I shouldn't have yelled."

Amanda watched, calmly as ever before. "Did you ever go to a therapist? Did you ever see a psychiatrist?"

"I had to."

"When?"

"When I went back to work. I tried to act as if everything was normal, but my life was spinning out of control. My mom had gone back home, Eoghan was acting up in school, and my co-workers just whispered rumors behind my back. I finally lost it one day in front of my boss. He said to go to grief counseling, or he'd pull my projects from me."

"And did you?" AJ nodded. "What happened after that?"

"That's when I realized I was fucked up in the head. My whole life was fucked up. My kids were fucked up. The world around me was fucked and I didn't know what to do. I only knew I couldn't keep doing the same thing over and over because it wasn't working."

"Was that when little Jenna's crying stopped?"

AJ sat back and thought. "It might have lessened."

"But when did it stop? When did she stop crying?"

"When we finally left San Antonio and moved up here."

"And when did you finally bond with her?"

"How do you know if I did?"

"You did, flower. You're a protective mother, no different than a warrior defending their tribe or village. You have that instinct about you. That's why I know these feelings you had have long passed. Am I wrong?"

AJ shook her head again. "No."

"You'd travel the world and slay the demons who'd come after your family, would you not?"

"Yes."

"And when did you bond with her? When did the darkness fade with the shadows? When did the light come back?"

"After I sold that house. After I shed my old life and decided to start a new one up here." AJ looked at the table and smiled.

"What are you thinking of?"

"The first night Jenna didn't cry anymore. She was fifteen months old, I think. It was the first night here in New Hampshire. July, I believe. We were on the bed together. Jenna had her bottle tucked under her arm and she snuggled tightly in my arms. The window was open and we could hear the frogs and crickets.

"I just held her, thinking of what Michael was missing. And she just looked up at me and smiled. Her eyes penetrated my soul. I'd spent over a year wishing Michael was still with me, but when I looked at Jenna in that one instant, he was there! He was looking back at me through her. And that was the first night she didn't cry or wake. That was the first night we finally both slept well."

—¡—

CHAPTER 63

ARE YOU surprised that the change in scenery and locale would have that dramatic of an effect on your life and that of your children? You shouldn't be.

For better—sometimes even worse, mind you—a different latitude and longitude makes you see your problems from a new perspective. Sometimes the problems disappear or appear less significant. The world looks bigger or smaller. The sky is bluer or browner, and the sun casts strange shadows across building facades.

Your eyes can be more open, if you let them. Maybe, perhaps, your <u>third</u> eye cracks the lid and sends pulses down your spine—if you believe in that sort of thing.

I do.

I've experienced strange sensations and have seen things science may never be able to explain in my lifetime or yours. In all my travels I never saw it more than I did in the Southwest.

Except in parts of Louisiana.

Hot, sticky nights and cooled low-hanging fog across a bayou is a feeling you never forget. Crickets and frogs, mosquitoes and gnats, they all attack your ears and skin. Your eyes play tricks with moonlit shadows and wraithing mist lit up by the fireflies. You can taste the fluorescent algae and approaching rain.

It's an eerie combination to be bombarded with all your senses at the same time. And, when all your senses are on fire—or when they're deprived—that third eye reveals the ghostly truths around you and through you.

That's where I met **MARK**. At a gas station, of all places. I was driving back from one of my earlier trips in the nineties. He was filling up his truck—some older Chevrolet model—at the pump beside mine.

I watched him carefully check the fishing traps in the bed, then meticulously walk around, examining his tires and a new dent near the back bumper. There was something about his mannerisms that told me he had a strong work ethic and good morals.

He saw me staring at him, then I watched his hazel-brown eyes check out my old Chrysler's back end. He walked over and removed his hat before he spoke. His frizzy, short afro bounced up with the release of the cap. Such a polite gesture, don't you think? A gentleman removing his hat before speaking to someone he considered a lady?

"'Scuse me, cher, you from New Hampshire, up north?" he asked. That thick deep accent of his caught me by surprise, just as much as the combination of his eye and skin color. I'd never heard an inflection like that before, and I'd never seen such a marvel of a man.

"Yes, sir. Heading back home," I said.

"Me, too. I'm in the next parish over. But why you's down here, cher? You a longer way from home den me."

Heh. That accent was something else. I wish I could get it down properly. Very enchanting and gentle, much like a nice, steady spring rain tapping on tree leaves right outside an open bedroom window.

I told him I was only passing through after a business trip. I'd heard quite a bit about New Orleans and wanted to see the town for myself. He told me not to waste my time there. It was a fun city to visit on occasion, but if I wanted to see true Cajun delights, I should head north, deeper into the state.

We chatted for a few more minutes until a car behind mine laid on the horn. The driver motioned for me to move out of the way. Fair enough, to be honest. I told my Louisiana friend I should be back on my way.

"I'm fixin' to eat. Yonna join me?" He cocked a wry smile under that dark skin and all I could do was smile back and cave in. "Name's Mark." There was deep sincerity and curiosity in his eyes that probably matched my own.

"Sure, if you don't mind."

I followed him for several miles to a shack on the side of the roadway. Looked like anything but a restaurant. To my surprise, he unloaded his catch of the day to the restaurant's owner, a *bon ami* of his.

There were a few patrons inside and everyone—the waitress, the cook, the restaurant owner—stared at me from time to time. My likeness as an outsider was a focal point for them, but they were no less inviting and kind. The whole place had an earthy feel that reminded me of my gardens, and, to be quite honest, I felt very much at home.

Mark introduced me to everyone who was there and anyone who walked in. Couldn't tell you their names anymore, just ghostly letters on the tip of my tongue. But, still, he made me feel welcome.

The more we sat there and talked, the more I could understand and pick up on the slang, the accent, the way of their world. I know Ethan and Isaac would've looked down on Mark and his *bon amis*, but they were a distant memory compared to the peace I felt trying jambalaya for the first time.

We were there for what felt like hours. Mark was more of an educated gentleman than he came across as. We touched on Native American cultures and my love of hummingbirds. He told me about summertime on the Yellow Bayou, the differences between hoodoo and voodoo, and how one of his friends swore on his grandpappy's grave that he saw the Rougarou. We talked about my nursery and farm business. Luck had not favored me for a few years, and I mentioned my trip was a way for me to clear my head.

"I'm thinking of selling the farm. Maybe give it to someone else who can have better luck with it."

"No, cher. Dat not de way. Ya heart isn't balanced. Das all you need, bon ami. Balance ya heart again."

I listened to him talk about the Forces of the World and how spirituality was what I needed. His friend chimed in with stories of how he felt the same way about his restaurant, but he found balance again and now he's prospering. Others offered their own anecdotes, all claiming balance was what I needed, that maybe I was taking too much and not giving enough back.

By the time we finished passing stories around—the other patrons were only too happy to have fresh ears listen to their tired tales—it was well into the night.

"Cher, it's not safe *pour vous* out der, dis time a night," Mark said. "De *fifolet* out der, even on de roads."

With talk of mysterious orbs of light and ghosts and everything else under the sun, I knew his concern was genuine. He offered a warm bed at his house a few miles off the highway. He lived with his parents and sister, so he said I'd be safe—protected by their beliefs.

We left my car there at the restaurant and I rode with Mark down to his place. We drove down a winding dirt road to a clearing well off the beaten way.

There were several small shacks around, almost like a very old trailer park. Christmas lights and mason jars were strung about from tree to tree. A few children ran by. An old couple sat in lawn chairs on a rotting deck.

No matter how glum others think the scene is, not a sad or depressed look crossed a single person's face.

I stepped down out of the truck and the minute my feet touched the soft ground, my heart felt joy. My eyes saw the fireflies—or maybe it was the *fifolet*, who knows—but the air danced with a deep magic that surrounded the shacks.

I spent a very pleasant night with his family and slept more peacefully and deeply than I had in years before that.

The next morning, I was treated to a hearty breakfast and more tales of southern Louisiana. We talked more about my business and how I've always felt drawn to the Earth and to gardening. Mark's mom and sister offered me more sage advice than any book I could've found in New Orleans.

They made me a couple of talismans and told me what to do with them. I didn't question it. I knew what I needed to do and how to get my business back on track. When Mark took me back to my car later that morning, I thanked him for all he'd done. I told him I'd come back in a couple of years and bring him up here to visit me. I'd offer to him the same hospitality and love his family did for me.

His generosity would live with me forever.

And that's why I captured my Mark in that Berylline hummingbird you see up there, the one painted that same fluorescent algae green as those backwater bayous. I added Louisiana yellow irises and the *fifolet* in the darkening background.

—¡—

CHAPTER 64

LOGIC DICTATED that the probability of finding any evidence of a crime would go up with each room searched. However, as Conrad examined Amanda's nightstand and Jack searched the large closet, he doubted they would find anything in the master bedroom.

"I'll be in the living room if you need anything," Maurice said, more of an excuse to sit under the fan than anything else.

"What about this?" Jack asked as he stepped out of the closet and held up a worn pair of men's boots. "They're men's steel-toed."

Conrad stood up and stretched his back before he walked over to Jack. He looked at the boots. "They appear quite small. Amanda could wear them if she can't find the size she needs in the women's section. Turn them over."

Jack flipped the shoes over. The tread was worn smooth and appeared slick to the touch.

"Nothing, then?"

"Doubtful."

The younger detective grimaced at the shoes and went back in the closet. From within the space, he called out, "Ya know, this is one of the cleanest and neatest closets I've ever seen. There's hardly any clothes, much less a lot of shoes. I can't even tell if they like to go shopping like normal girls."

"My wife likes to shop from time to time. My daughter? Not in the slightest."

"You have kids?"

"Yes."

"How old's your girl?"

Conrad walked over to the other nightstand and started searching behind it. "Just a handful of years younger than yourself."

"Nice. She's probably the same age as one of my cousins."

Conrad's voice lowered as he pulled a torn piece of paper from behind the nightstand. "Maybe." He flipped the paper over to look at the handwritten words:

in stone
nna Beth
2, 2012

Jack walked over. "Did you find something?"

"Not sure." Conrad handed him the torn piece of paper, then shifted the nightstand over. Nothing else littered the floor except cobwebs and dust. He checked the trash can next to the nightstand but could not find any other torn pieces of paper.

Jack handed the piece of paper back to Conrad. "Should we bag it or toss it?"

The Deputy Director flipped it over a couple of times. A torn-up date and partial name was no coincidence. "Let's bag it. We never know what this could mean."

"I'm done in the closet now. Where to next?"

"Master bath. I'll be there shortly."

Conrad placed the piece of paper in an envelope and labeled it, then joined Jack in the bathroom. He found the young man feeling the tiles in the shower and around the bathtub.

"Have you checked the cabinets and drawers yet?"

"Not yet. I wanted to check the tub first."

Conrad opened the drawer next to the bathroom sink. Yellowed clippers were wrapped in the back. Hairbands, brushes, and combs sat in the front. He ran his fingers across the bottom of the drawer, but nothing stood out. The next drawer offered the same gifts: random makeup bags, an old set of toiletries, and nothing underneath the drawer.

The space under the sink was as much a bust as the drawers. First aid kits—including one for snake bites—were neatly stacked to one side, while toilet paper, cleaning supplies, and sanitary pads were stacked on the other.

Jack stepped out of the shower. "Nothing." He looked at the toilet, then shined his flashlight between the top tank and the wall. "Do you think any of the girls hid or got rid of the evidence?" He lifted the tank cover. It made a heavy *thunk-clank!* noise as he set it down next to the toilet.

"Anything's possible. What are your thoughts?"

"Honestly? The house is too clean for my taste. Where's the clutter? The mess?"

"It's a house full of women. Would there be any?"

"Meh. Guess not. Too bad the warrant doesn't cover the halfway house."

"Judge wouldn't sign off on it," Conrad said as he shined the light under the sink. "Anything around the toilet?"

"Nope."

Another *clank-thunk!* and the tank lid was back in place.

"What about the linen closet?"

"That's my next stop."

He nodded at his subordinate. Other than the random snide comment, Jack appeared, by all means, to enjoy this aspect of the job.

Jack walked behind him. He began searching the top shelf of folded sheets.

Maybe he's not suited for desk work. Could be too soon to tell.

Conrad opened the medicine cabinet. Several prescription bottles with Amanda's name sat on each of the three small shelves. He pulled out his glasses and read a couple of the labels.

"Everolimus. Temozolomide."

"Hunh?" Jack turned around.

"These drugs. It doesn't say what they're for."

Jack took his gloves off and pulled out his phone. Conrad spelled out one of the names.

"Oh shit," he whispered, then showed Conrad the search results:

This medication is used to treat
certain classifications of brain tumors.
Temozolomide works as an alkylating agent,
slowing and/or stopping the growth
of cancer cells in your body.

The Deputy Director turned his gaze back to the medicine cabinet. The opaque bottles stared back. He ignored the surprised look on Jack's face but could not ignore the question asked.

"Amanda Claremont has brain cancer?"

—¡—

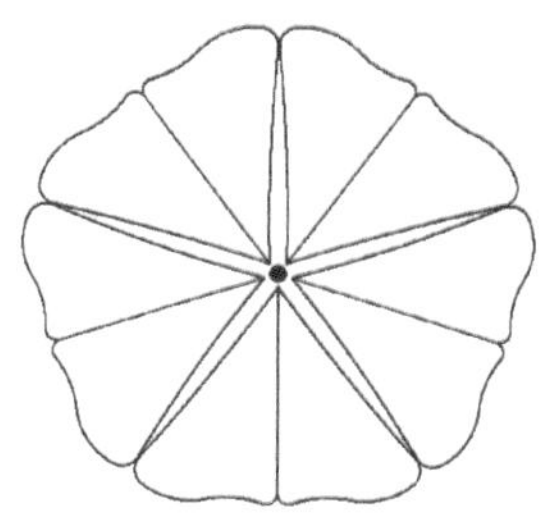

CHAPTER 65

"TELL ME about your son. How did he adjust to the new way of life?"

"Tell me what happened to Mark first."

Amanda shrugged. "Same as the others."

"They just came and went out of your life?"

"Don't many individuals do that? You meet someone. They serve a purpose. And, once that purpose is complete, they move on. You move on. The world keeps turning as it did a thousand years before and as it will a thousand years after."

"Did you ever go back to visit him again? Like you told him you would?"

Amanda stared up at the Berylline hummingbird painting. "He lived out in a very rural part of the state. There were no cell phone towers in the area. I doubt his family even had a landline. This was before smartphones and personal computers were a thing. I did see him one more time, but that was it."

"And you just got in the truck with a random stranger you just met? Do you know how dangerous and dumb that sounds?"

"The world was a little more trusting back then and I've always been a good judge of character. Are you not doing the same thing with me right now? Am I not a stranger to you and you're locked in a large building with me?"

AJ held her tongue. Amanda always seemed to say the right things and her logic was irrefutable. "So, why turn him into a painting?"

"Because he and his family showed me kindness when I least expected it." She spread her arms up at her artwork hanging above. "These were the men who were everything Robert was not. These were the deserving, the good, the kind, the righteous. These were the sort of gentlemen who would spill their blood and sacrifice their souls for the woman they loved or admired. Why not memorialize them?"

"But—"

"Unh unh," Amanda shook her head. "I've said enough about the man in my life. Tell me about the boy becoming one in yours."

"Eoghan?"

"Yes."

"What about him?"

"Tell me another deep-rooted guilt you've sworn never to tell anyone else."

AJ tapped her foot on the floor a couple of times and stared at her fingers. The skin began ripping on the side of her middle finger. The roughness bothered her. She picked at it.

"Eoghan had his own problems after Michael was murdered. He also resented Jenna. I thought it was just the age difference. You know, nearly ten years is a big gap between kids. One day, I heard him tell one of his friends her name was 'Jenna Death' instead of Jenna Beth. How cruel is that?"

"Don't you remember middle school? It's a cruel time for any child."

"Heh. Yeah, I guess." She started picking another finger. "I scolded him for the name he called her. It seemed we were always getting into fights with each other. We'd been close—a momma's boy, I guess you'd call it—until...that day."

"And how are things between you two, now that you're here

in New Hampshire?"

"Ever since I quit my engineering job and switched careers? Things have been much better. He's actually bonding with his sister more."

"And why do you think that is?"

AJ looked up from her hand. "Why do I think what is?"

"Why do you think your relationship with your son is healing now?"

"I switched jobs. I think the stress of my old job was ruining many of my relationships."

"What else?"

"We moved up here and are closer to family."

"What *else*?"

"What do you mean what else?"

"When you looked at little Jenna the first night up here, you saw your dead husband in her eyes. What about your son? What did you see every time you looked at him, right after the murder?"

AJ broke eye contact and looked at the ring on her finger. She twisted the silver round and round several times. "Every time I looked at Eoghan, I saw Michael in every way. His moods. His laughter. His anger."

"How did that make you feel?"

She twisted the ring again. "I resented him. Every time I saw my son, I saw my husband. I couldn't look at him for the longest time."

"So, you ignored your son?"

"No."

"You rejected him, then."

"No! I—"

"You couldn't look at him anymore. Isn't that the same thing as rejecting him?"

"I didn't mea—"

"And don't you think that messed with his mind and was one of the reasons he lashed out, getting in fights? Maybe he thought you loved the girl more than you loved the boy. Maybe he wanted attention from you because you made him feel discarded and useless, a reject."

"I didn't mean to!"

"I know that. But he didn't know that, then. Ask yourself, does he know it now?"

The softness in the older woman's words brought the emotion AJ tried to hide. How the woman could dig so deep into her psyche was a trick she did not know.

She dabbed her eyes again. "I don't know. I hope he does. I hope he knows I love him as equally as I do Jenna. But I'd be lying if I said he's not turning into the likeness of Michael each day and sometimes my heart still aches when the shadows catch him in certain lighting."

"You loved your husband, but your grief for him runs too deep. Do you honestly think he was that much of a saint, that you should memorialize him in all those tears?"

"He was a good man."

"He did good deeds and he may have been a good man, but does that make him a saint? Surely there were things in your marriage that were never quite right."

AJ sat back and crossed her arms. "I'm not saying anything bad about the dead."

Amanda chuckled and mirrored the detective's position. "What do the dead care? They can't hear what you have to say anyway. An asshole is an asshole, living or deceased."

"Michael wasn't an asshole."

"Really?"

Amanda locked eyes with her. There was no denying the older woman's ability to pick up on conversational details and twist words into sharpened objects.

There was no denying she would eventually get her way.

—¡—

CHAPTER 66

KNOW THIS, little flower. We haven't even gotten to the working mechanisms within your heart to see what makes you tick. You're still holding back from me.

No matter. We'll get there before the day's done. Each little chip at your dam brings us closer to you finally cracking and spilling the weight of what you hold back. Each swing back and forth with the pendulum from you to me, to you, then me will both give us the answers we want.

Tick and tock. Tick and tock.
Back and forth, tick and tock.
Have you ever heard a thousand clocks
Cuckoo like rain with ticks and tocks?

It's interesting how your inner workings bring us to my next hummingbird. Look up at that one labeled **MANNY**. Do you see that gorgeous hue of periwinkle blue dripping across his neck? I immortalized him with a Blue-Throated hummingbird and adorned him with trumpet vine. Why the trumpet vine? It reminded me so much of his wooden carved clocks on display.

Allow me to backtrack slightly.

I'd heard that one of my long distant relatives, a maternal cousin of some sort named Beulah, was eager to meet me. She was more curious about me than I was of her, but her mind was being ripped by dementia and she didn't know how much longer she would still be herself. I guess she wanted to make peace with some of the family. Who knows. Her own father passed from a brain tumor and she swore it would skip down to the next generation.

Funny, her thoughts.

She made contact with me in the early 2000s and wanted me to pay her a visit. Said she knew who my father was. She had a home south of Albany by a few miles, off the Taconic State Parkway. It was a pretty little single-story dwelling with iron railing leading up from the driveway to her front door.

I drove over one weekend to visit her for the first time. I was curious to know more about my father and I assumed she could fill in missing pieces of my childhood I'd always wondered about. I was anxious, nervous to the rim, and each step taken towards that front door made my knees quiver.

I took a deep breath and knocked on the door, but Beulah never answered. Another woman—probably around my age, now that I think about it—opened the front door.

"Who the hell are you?" she asked me.

"I'm Amanda, ma'am. Amanda Claremont, Helen's daughter. Beulah invited me."

I watched her mouth tighten, accentuating the smoker's wrinkles on her upper lip. "Yeah, I heard of you. You're not welcome here."

She tried to close the door on me, but I yelled, "Wait! I thought Beulah could tell me about my father. I have so many questions!"

She stopped, then looked me up and down. "We don't allow bastards in our home. And Beulah's dead. The hag died last night." The woman slammed the door.

I felt a hard thump in my chest as my heart skipped several

beats. Imagine that: being offered answers to who I was and yet to have them slammed shut in my face.

Not knowing what to do, I got back in the car and just drove south down Route 9, following the Hudson. I stopped from time to time to peer down to the water's edge. I stood on a bridge and heard Helen's voice again.

"Come join me, darling daughter."

Her calls were enticing. Each time I heard the words, I rushed back into my car and I kept driving further south.

My mind split in half. One part wanted to join Helen. The other wanted to keep running.

"Spread your wings!"

"Get back in the car!"

"You'll never worry about anything again."

"Your flowers need you."

On and on the thoughts tangoed in my brain until my head hurt so bad, I pulled into a parking lot to clear my mind and close my eyes.

I don't know how long I'd been sitting there before a gentleman tapped on my car window. His light brown hair shone in the sunlight. His beard was peppered with a few grays. His eyes, though—they were the coolness you'd expect on a mid-summer's eve.

I apologized and told him I had such a severe headache, I couldn't drive anymore and needed to pull off the roadway. He offered for me to come inside and he'd get me a glass of water and aspirin.

I accepted. As soon as I got out of the car, I realized I was standing in front of an antique store. I didn't even know what city I was in.

I followed the man inside to a water cooler.

"My name's Mandrake, but everyone calls me Manny," he said as he handed me the glass.

"Amanda. Amanda Claremont."

"It's a pleasure. Feel free to take the time you need for the aspirin to kick in."

"Thank you, sir," I replied. "I'm so sorry to bother you."

He shook his head. "Oh, no bother. I own the place. I was taking a stretch break from repairing a clock when a customer said there was a strange car parked in the front. Decided to check it out."

We chatted for several minutes and I finally told him what happened and what caused the splitting headache. The more I told him, the more solemn he became.

"I have to admit," he finally said, "I've never experienced such rudeness from relatives. But when my heart and soul are heavy, I like to just sit in my clock room and listen to it rain. Would you like to hear the rain a thousand clocks can make?"

Oh, but did that intrigue me!

He gently touched my back and led me down a corridor to an adjacent room. I heard tapping and what sounded like loud raindrops falling on elephant-eared leaves. When I stepped through that open door into the clock room, I was whisked into another dimension.

Grandfather clocks, watches on walls, table clocks, cuckoo clocks with pinecone chains—all moving in such sporadic synchronicity it was damned near hypnotic!

And the sound.

Oh, my flower! That magical sound of rain from a thousand ticking tocks and tocking ticks—you'll never hear anything like it. Ever.

There was such a tranquility in that beautiful space, it melted away the remaining headache and removed the tension in my shoulders. I slumped down on the step, sat there, and smiled.

"Incredible, isn't it?" Manny said.

We sat in silence for a lost amount of time until finally I stood up. I thanked him for his generosity.

He walked me back to my car.

"If I'm in the area again, may I come listen to the rain one more time?"

"As often as time allows, you may." He took a short bow, then walked back into the store.

If you only knew how many times I listened to the rain go "tick and tock, tick and tock."

Those antique clocks.

Tick and tock. Tick and tock.

—¡—

CHAPTER 67

IBUPROFEN and acetaminophen bottles stared back at Conrad. He grabbed one, rattled it, and listened to the tone.

"Conrad?"

"Yes, Kinston?"

"Amanda Claremont has brain cancer?"

"It would appear so."

"Did you know this whole time?"

He turned around to look at Jack, then shook his head. "It's not my place to say anything."

"Not your place?" The younger detective scoffed. "She's our prime suspect in a murder case!"

"Mr. Kinston, Amanda is a person of interest. Nothing more at this point." He reached into the corner of the cabinet and pulled out another prescription bottle. "As are any of her girls that live in this house. None are considered suspects."

"You're letting your personal feelings for that woman impair your judgement. Are you even fit to do this search?"

Conrad slammed the bottle on the counter. "That's enough!" He positioned his body directly in front of Jack's and took a step closer.

The younger man backed into the closet door. "I-I'm sorry," he stammered.

The Deputy Director took his gloves off and threw them on the counter, never breaking eye contact. His uncharacteristic anger rose.

*10...9...8...*Conrad forced himself to think before he spoke again. *Never speak in anger.*

He tugged on his suit jacket and straightened his tie, cracking his neck to one side in the process.

"Sir, I—" Jack tried to say. A single finger held up prevented him from continuing.

One deep breath later, the older gentleman spoke in a steady, quiet, and calm tone. "Not. One. Word. If there was even a remote chance that any of my past, present, or future relationships would affect an investigation, I would excuse myself from it. And if you ever question my experience or abilities again, you will be fired on the spot."

Jack nodded. "Yes, sir."

"*That* is how you will always address me. You will *never* call me by my first name again. Understood?" The man nodded again. "Go check the attic. I'll finish here without you."

Kinston bumped into Maurice as he quickly exited the bathroom.

"I heard yelling and came to check on you both," the lawyer said. "Is everything okay?"

"Everything is fine, Mr. Juniper."

"Very well. If I can be of service—"

"Actually, yes. Please see if Mr. Kinston needs any assistance in the attic."

Maurice huffed and opened his mouth, but one glance from Conrad and the lawyer appeared to change his mind.

Once he was alone in the bathroom, he turned his attention back to the medicine cabinet and the pill bottle he slammed on the counter. With new gloves and his bifocals on, he picked up the container and examined it.

Zolpidem? He looked at the information printed on the pharmacy label then opened the bottle to count the contents. *For a week-old prescription, there should be more pills than this.*

On instinct, the Deputy Director bagged the bottle and labeled it. The rest of the medicine cabinet offered no new clues or evidence of any kind, though Conrad's thoughts kept going back to the one prescription and why so many sleeping pills were missing.

With everything finally inspected in the bathroom, he flipped the light off and walked downstairs. He switched out the memory cards on the camera and jotted down more notes in his notepad.

When Jack was still not back from inspecting the attic, the Deputy Director walked around the first floor again and scanned each of the rooms one more time, saving the office for last. Stepping through the threshold of the antiquated space still felt like stepping back in time several decades. The significance of such an abandoned room did not fall on blind eyes.

He ran his fingers across the spines of the shelved books and stopped on a reference book about Mesoamerican cultures. He pulled it out and slowly fanned page after page. Some writing in the margins of one page caught his attention and he flipped back to read it.

On one side of the page, an image showed that of a clawed and decorated Aztec god sitting on the top of a temple. A shaman draped in ceremonial garb stood above a human spread out on a stone altar. The shaman held a bloody knife in one hand and what appeared to be a heart in the other. A curly-looking comma was next to the shaman's mouth. Other figures stood around the altar and prayed to the watchful god as they licked bloody spears.

In the margins were the words "right side-rectus abdominus, pull back", "dome-diaphragm", and "Huitzilopochtli".

"Did you find something, sir?" Conrad turned to see Jack standing in the doorway.

"Did you, Mr. Kinston?"

"Just a few boxes up there, mostly Halloween and Christmas decorations."

"And you searched each box thoroughly?"

Jack nodded. "Even double-checked a few ornaments." He took a couple of steps inside the office and looked around again. "I thought we were done with this room?"

"When you flipped through the books, did anything stand out to you?"

"Not really. There weren't any marked pages or extra papers stuffed between the pages."

"What about any handwritten notes?"

"Meh. A few, but nothing out of the ordinary. Nothing that stood out for any reason."

"Hmm." Conrad closed the book and put it back on the shelf.

"Did you find something I missed?"

"I don't think so." He scanned each of the books on the shelves again, studying the titles.

"Is that a good thing?"

"I don't know, Kinston."

"Would you feel better if we did find the other knife?"

They both walked towards the door. Jack exited first and Conrad put his hand on the light switch, giving the room a final goodbye.

"I'd feel better knowing we haven't missed anything. And knowing that both my detectives are safe at the end of the day."

—¡—

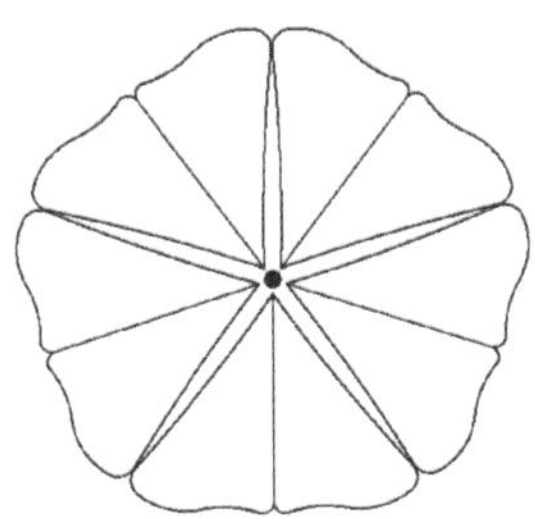

CHAPTER 68

LIGHT AND warmth radiated through the west wall of the main building. It was only a matter of time before rectilinear blocks of sunlight would crawl across the surfaces towards the table.

"Tick tock, detective. Tick tock."

AJ sat back and placed one hand on the table in front of her. Her other hand dangled from her side. She used her fingernail to scrape a loose piece of skin from the side of her thumb and felt her finger throb from the pain.

"What would you like to know now?" she asked.

"I'm surprised, my flower, you didn't ask what happened to this little birdie."

"If I were to guess, I'd say you both kept in touch for a few years and you came to visit him until finally you both lost track of each other."

Amanda nodded once. "You're close. I did visit him several times after that. Each time, we'd just sit and philosophize or just listen to the clocks. The last time I saw him, he invited me to lunch. He told me he'd met a wonderful woman down the street from where he lived and planned to ask her out on a date. I told him I was happy for him. As I didn't want to get in the way of his budding relationship, my visits ceased. I can't recreate that sound in the clock room. But from time to time, I do hear the rain inside this building. I can almost hear it now."

Amanda closed her eyes. AJ thought she saw wrinkled lips quiver once, but it was gone as quickly as it was there. Silence echoed across the concrete floor in between pauses from flute notes. The only other sound was the buzzing, repetitive *swoosh!* of the ceiling fan.

With one deep exhale, the older woman opened her eyes and focused on the detective. "You claimed your husband was no asshole, so tell me about the other assholes in your life."

"Like who?"

"Anyone who's come into your life and made it much more difficult than you ever deserved. Past or present, doesn't matter."

"The latest? I'd say my new coworker."

Amanda chuckled. "Agreed. Though, I do have to admit, I don't see him lasting past this week. He doesn't have what it takes to be successful in that career of yours."

"Yeah, that makes sense."

"Who else? Did you have other asshole coworkers, before you switched careers?"

AJ sat forward and repositioned herself in the chair. "Actually, yes. I think that's one reason why I quit."

"Tell me about the time right before you left. What happened there?"

"I had a boss named Lyle. He was a good guy and always seemed decent with me, but the others on the team would always go bitch to him about the way I did my job. They didn't have the damned decency to talk to me about what I did wrong so that I could improve and not keep making the same mistakes over and over. They just whispered behind my back. There were two girls who were close friends and they would always go quiet when I walked by. The air felt—it's hard to describe it, but it just felt heavy and thick. I felt suffocated there."

"And when did you reach your breaking point? When did Ameena Hawthorne die?"

"When Joseph finally complained too many times."

"Who was Joseph?"

"An engineer like myself. A little bit younger, a lot cockier. Couldn't design a storm drainage system to save his life. He kept messing up on the modeling and calculations, then would blame it on me."

"He's the reason you quit?"

AJ nodded. "One of them. Lyle called me into the office one morning and said it was time for our annual employee evaluations. I thought it would go better than the year before because the previous one was just awful. Everyone told me I was doing too much drafting and not enough design, but no one would train me to do the design because they needed someone who could draft. How's that for shitty conditions?"

"Go on."

"My eval went worse than expected. The same complaints from the same people for the same reasons. Too much drafting, not enough design. Lyle said I'd be put on a probationary period to see if I could improve. He mentioned the last complaint he got was from Joseph, claiming I was the one that cost the client thousands of dollars in extra fees.

"My heart sank. After over two years of trying to prove myself, I finally had to admit I was done. My passion was gone. The joy in learning was gone. So, I did what I thought needed doing. I shook Lyle's hand, looked at him with broken eyes, and said, 'Thank you for this opportunity. Effective immediately, I quit. I won't be a disappointment anymore.'"

"Just like that? You quit?"

AJ nodded. "Just like that."

"When do you think your passion began to decay?"

The younger woman shrugged. "I think it died the day Michael did."

"I believe that's the reason you quit. It was a constant reminder of his death."

AJ rested her elbows on the table and listened intently. "I don't understand what you mean."

"Each day, you'd wake up the same as before and go do the same tasks you did prior to his murder. How uncomfortable was it to sit at a computer desk, hour after hour, and repeat the same commands as you did in your Texas job? How often, in the throws of repetitive clicks, would your mind wander back to your husband?"

"I quit because I worked with assholes who never accepted me."

"You quit because the assholes reminded you of Michael. Now the question is, did they remind you of Michael because of how he died? Or because of how he treated you while he lived? Did the assholes remind you of the asshole?"

AJ slammed her hand down and stood up. "Michael was a decent man! He had his moments, just like the rest of them. He wasn't an asshole because he was born that way. He was MADE that way because of his job!"

She stormed towards the front doors and shook the handles violently, then slapped her palm on the wood.

"We're not done, flower," a calm voice said behind her.

"LET ME OUT!" AJ shook the door some more. The sounds merely echoed within the large space. Her request was never answered. She smacked her forehead against the door. "Let me out. Please. Just let me leave."

"Soon enough, detective. But ask yourself this, too. Do you want to be another disappointment? Do you want to fail your boss by not keeping me company, by not distracting me from what they're doing in my home?"

AJ turned around to face the woman sitting at the table. She leaned her body against the door. "No. I don't want to let him down. I'm just—" she paused for the right words "—suffocating and need to breathe."

"You will, but only after I've plucked all the weeds from your garden."

—¡—

CHAPTER 69

LOVELY little Morning Glory, we're almost done. You'll never have to entertain me again after today, I promise.

Do you know why?

Because we're sharing our deepest, darkest secrets with each other, only you don't fully see mine yet.

Look up at the paintings again. Do you see the Ruby-Throated hummingbird on the end? That one's a special story I won't tell you. Instead, I'll show you when the time's right. And, if you think about it and add up the stories I've told so far, I only have six more adventures to tell of.

I'll even speed things up a bit, but do, please, my gracious and beautiful flower, come sit back down for just a little bit longer.

There…have another sip of water and relax. It's getting quite warm in here and it's important to stay hydrated, don't you agree?

The hummingbird paintings across from each other in the middle—the ones that say **GABRIO** and **ABRAN**—represent two incredible specimens of men who came into my life about ten years ago.

I captured Gabrio as a Magnificent hummingbird and complemented him with an azalea. See that shimmering aqua across the neck? It's a special kind of acrylic that dances in different angles of the light. His forehead is brushed with a royal purple and his chest is adorned with a darker version of the color. One of my favorites.

Across from him, Abran is captured as a Green Violet-Ear hummer. The greens and aquas waltz across the body and neck in such spectacular display! Abran had noticeable ears that stuck out slightly, and as such, I decorated him with violet. All those swords and spikes of lavender are salvia flowers, framing him in a beautiful fashion.

Notice how each pose mirrors the other? Purposeful intent, again. They were sworn best friends and it only seemed fitting that I create a matching pair. I had them hung on opposite walls so they could always see the other.

Gabrio and Abran were a pair of friends with gentle hearts from Mexico who tried to make it in Vegas but wound up somewhere in the middle, down on their luck. Their beautiful brown skin was not nearly as dark as Mark's nor as light as Patrick's—I'll tell you about him soon—but these two had flawless skin and perfect hair that most women envy.

I was headed up to Flagstaff and decided to stop in Phoenix for lunch. I'd just come from Tucson a couple of hours before that. The temperature was well above triple digits. Dry heat or not, it didn't matter. Hot was hot, and this temperature threatened to overheat my Chrysler and anything in it.

I decided to give my car a rest and have lunch in one of the malls. I walked around different shops, then grabbed something in the food court. I sat near two gentlemen and focused on reading the book I'd just purchased when I caught a tail-end of their conversation.

"—hummingbird festival tomorrow."

"Can we make it to Sedona in time?"

"I think so. It's about two hours away."

"What's the bus schedule like?"

At that point, I put my book down and turned to butt into their little chat. "Excuse me, gentlemen. I couldn't help but overhear your conversation. Were you referring to the annual Sedona Hummingbird Festival?"

They looked at each other and then the one with light brown eyes said, "Yes. Have you ever been there?"

"This is my second time to go. I'm heading there tonight and just happened to stop here for lunch and a quick break."

The other one with the darker eyes put his chin on his hand and said, "This'll be our first. I've loved hummingbirds since I was a boy and their vibrancy is right up my alley."

We talked for another hour or so, but I didn't need that long to get to know them. I just knew as soon as I saw their smiles that I'd have company all the way to Sedona and beyond.

Gabrio—the one with the lighter colored eyes—was from Monterrey and Abran was from Monclova. They met in Texas, just across the Mexican border in Laredo. Both had aspiring dreams to make it big and help their families, but the drug wars had other plans. One of the cartels assassinated Abran's family and Gabrio's—those who were left alive—fled to Corpus Christi shortly after. Abran admitted he had an alcohol addiction and Gabrio was trying to keep him sober, though bouncing from city to city and job to job made that near impossible. And, the atmosphere in Vegas just made it worse.

"Why don't you come work for me? I can always use some strong backs in my fields."

"You'd give us jobs?" Gabrio asked.

"And free room and board," I said. "But you have to put the sweat in. And, I've managed to keep many men sober over the years." I cocked an eyebrow at Abran when I said that.

But the dark-eyed friend shook his head. "I'm not suited for manual labor like that. I don't think I'd be of any use to you."

"What talents do you have?" I asked.

Gabrio smiled at Abran and then the latter joked, "I can sew and make a mean carne asada meal."

"Done."

They both looked at each other in shock.

"You'd really hire me to sew and cook?" Abran asked.

"My business runs like a community," I said. "Everyone does their part. If your part is sewing, you can mend coats, hem pants, and make curtains. Not only that, we need vibrant and flamboyant color in our shop. Many of our customers are women and they look for glittery and gilded gifts for their gardens. As far as cooking, we rotate that out with the others."

"Do you mind if we talk about it, between ourselves?" Abran asked.

I understood and appreciated Abran's hesitations. Who wouldn't?

I told them, "Sure. Why don't you think about it over the festival? I'll take care of your hotel for the next two nights, my way of saying thank you for the extraordinary company and laughs you've given this widow. Would you like to meet up later this evening for dinner?"

Both men agreed and we parted temporary ways until later that evening. When we met back up for dinner, I noticed an excitement and energy about them. I knew their answer before they ever said anything.

Both Gabrio and Abran served me well for a few years until the bright lights and warmer climate called for them again. Then, they were gone to serve another purpose somewhere else. But their vitality, charm, color, and vivaciousness enriched me in ways I'll never explain.

—¡—

CHAPTER 70

EVERY CRAWLSPACE, nook, cranny, drawer, and wall were inspected, examined, and scrutinized with both fresh and experienced eyes. Every interior space from the attic to the basement and garage were checked, but no clues offered themselves to the detectives.

They stood on the asphalt driveway looking at the interior of the garage, Jack patiently waiting for Conrad to say something. The forensic technicians sat in the CSI van. The town's officers stood watch. The lawyer fanned himself and finally approached the pair.

"I assume you have searched the residence to your satisfaction, Mr. McMillan?" Maurice's up-turned nose did not hide the double, thick chin or discomfort.

Conrad glanced at him and then back at the home. "The interior, yes, Mr. Juniper. We still need to inspect the outside. Then the greenhouse."

"Very well. I'll wait by the greenhouse for when you're ready." Maurice disappeared around the corner.

"How do you want to inspect the outside…sir?" Jack asked.

"Shoulder to shoulder, at least arm-widths apart. That'll probably be the most efficient. We can cover the ground and home exterior faster that way."

With few words between them, both men kept a slow pace and scanned the grass and landscaping. They zigzagged their way across the front and side yards, then began working on the back.

"What's that humming noise?" Jack asked.

Conrad looked up from the ground. "Humming noise?"

"Almost like an electrical buzz of some sort."

The Deputy Director focused on the sound. Faint, nearly undetectable. He walked closer to the house and inspected a thick pole next to the corner. "It's just the meter running."

Jack had a concerned look. "Then why's it spinning so fast?"

He studied the meter more carefully. The disc spun rapidly around, making at least one full revolution per second. "Good observation, Mr. Kinston. Possibly from the aviary."

"I don't think so. I remember studying something in class about marijuana farms and how high the electric bills are. Thousands of dollars a month. You have to pull some serious juice to get the meter spinning like that."

"Interesting. Maybe she has something set up in her greenhouse."

"That's the next thing on the list, right?"

Conrad nodded.

The pair continued combing the yard and a small flower garden when Jack yelled, "Wait!"

He dropped to one knee near the stone edge of the garden and moved some dirt across the surface.

"Did you find something?"

"Not sure." The young detective held out his hand with what appeared to be a beige stick. "Does this look like a bone to you?"

Conrad gently took the object from Jack's hand and held it away from his face. He twisted it between his fingers to inspect each side. "It does appear to be a bone, but I can't tell if it's human or animal."

"Sir, want me to go grab the techs?"

"Yes, Mr. Kinston. They can dig through the ground here while you and I inspect the greenhouse."

Jack gave a quick smile and ran around the house out of sight.

While Conrad waited, he pulled out his phone and dialed AJ's phone number. It went straight to voicemail.

Must be a dead zone. I'll have Jack check on her shortly.

A few minutes later, Jack walked back with both technicians, Pat Sonnito and Peter Yates. Conrad handed the bone to the senior lead.

She inspected the fragment. "Hmph. It appears quite aged, but I'd guess—from quick inspection—it's a phalanx, human. Could be either of archeological interest or more nefarious origins, hard to tell from just standing here." She turned to the junior technician. "Peter, let's set up a ten-by-ten grid and start with this garden."

"Yes, ma'am." Peter ducked his eyes down to the ground and quickly walked back to the bus.

"McMillan, we'll get set up here and start digging. I'll let you know if we find anything else or if this is just a fluke."

Conrad nodded.

As they approached the greenhouse, Maurice perked up. The lawyer searched through a set of keys and found the one for the lock. A few clinks later, and he pulled the rusty door open.

"As with her other requests, Ms. Claremont has strict instructions that I stay outside her greenhouse. I'll wait for you here."

The detectives stepped inside. The air tasted stale and dusty just like the dried earth on all the gardening tools strewn about. Cinder blocks and plywood waited for surface use or were disassembled and stacked to one side. Buckets, hand-held tools, discarded gloves—all tossed on the tabletops with little care where they landed. Empty planters swung from old ropes or plastic hooks. The skeletal remains of a few plants draped their final acts of life across ceramic edges. Black landscape fabric layered the floor.

One corner of the greenhouse beckoned Conrad to walk over.

A lonely, aged easel coughed out a drawer with a handful of used art brushes. More brushes flowered from rusty cans on an adjacent table. Another rusty can offered colored pencils while more cans tipped their contents onto the table. A couple of blank canvases rested against one wall. Dozens and dozens of crinkled tubes of acrylic paint waited for fingers to squeeze the final contents out.

Jack whistled. "That's a lot of paint!"

"True, but she did say that was her hobby."

Conrad continued to study the space. "What are your thoughts here, Kinston?"

"My first thought? Where are all the plants?"

"Good question."

"It doesn't feel like this place was used in a long time. Doesn't have that thick smell like her other greenhouses at the nursery."

"Agreed. Remember what Ms. Vanderbilt said?"

"Yeah. Amanda comes and goes out of here all the time."

"Mr. Kinston?"

"Yes, sir?" Jack looked in the same location.

Conrad pointed at one section of landscape fabric. "How old do you think this is?"

"It looks pretty new to me."

"And why do you think this old, decrepit structure would have brand new fabric covering the floor?"

"To hide something?" Jack pressed his heel into the ground, then stomped on different locations.

Conrad did the same. Each clop against the floor shot dirt particles in the air. Each pat of rubber sole felt no resistance except earth. Both detectives slowly crossed the length of the greenhouse.

Thung!

They stopped and looked at each other.

Conrad stomped again.

Thung!

Together in unison, they each grabbed a corner of the fabric and peeled it back, exposing the source of the noise.

Jack smiled. "Bingo!"

They both stared down at a rusty hatch.

—¡—

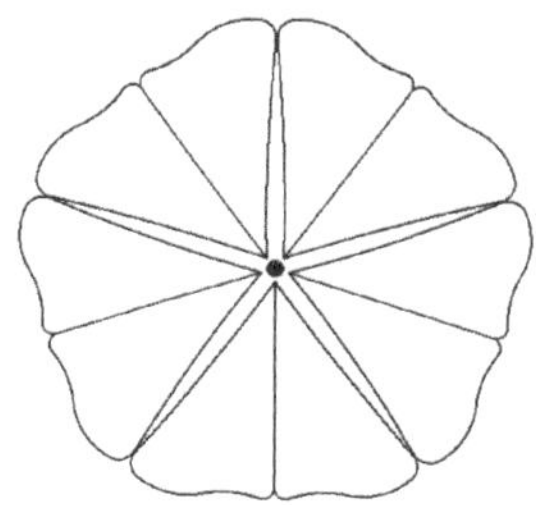

CHAPTER 71

ROBBED of what little dignity she felt she had left, AJ listened impatiently to Amanda's story of Gabrio and Abran. The woman did not hurt or threaten harm, just merely wanted to tell stories—tales, supposedly, vital to Michael Smith's death.

What would your boss say of you if you walked away now? Think, Jardine! Just entertain this woman a little bit longer and you can leave!

"Did you hear anything I just said?" Amanda's glare made the detective shift in her chair.

"They worked with you for a few years."

"Yes. They did."

"And bright lights and warmer weather called them away."

The older woman smiled. "Good. You were paying attention. Perhaps you'll make a better detective than your counterpart shadowing Conrad right now."

"I don't know if I'll make a better detective, but I do know I'll try harder than him."

"I believe you, dear. But tell me, why *did* you become a detective?"

"I needed a career change."

"But it was more than just a career change, wasn't it?"

"What do you mean?"

"There's more driving you than a falling out with your boss or losing your passion to do your job. So, what was it?"

"What was what?"

Amanda sat back and chuckled. "Coy little flower, what was the driving force behind the career change? It wasn't just lost passion or a kiss from a stranger. Why did you truly quit your career—at your age, no less—and go a dramatically different route?"

"What I did in engineering is not too far off from what I'm supposed to do now. And I'm only here because all the Deputy Director's teams are in training in Boston."

The older woman rolled her wrist at the detective. "Go on. Let me hear this."

"I was hired as a forensic geomorphologist. That means I help with searches or finding buried things. I do mapping and imaging of soils and landscapes, as needed. I help analyze aerial photographs and—"

"And you think Conrad just happened to have this job available for you?"

AJ tilted her head. "What do you mean?"

"You think that position existed *before* you applied to the Major Crimes Unit?"

"I guess?"

Amanda slowly shook her head and leaned forward, resting both elbows on the table. "One of these days, you should ask your boss about your position and why he really hired you."

AJ mimicked the woman. "Is there something you want to tell me? Do you know something I don't?"

"I know lots of things. Including that you haven't answered my initial question. Why *did* you become a detective?"

"Why do *you* think I became one?" She stared right back across the table.

"The idea of becoming a forensic specialist—whatever you want to call it with whatever pseudo title given you—may have been planted, but I believe you became a detective to right the wrongs. Maybe you want to find your husband's killers out of guilt for the problems you had in your marriage. Or maybe you wanted to find the men responsible for nearly murdering your unborn child and destroying the life of your other." Amanda leaned in slightly and lowered her voice. "Or, maybe, you want to seek justice for yourself because this wasn't the first time your life was shredded and ripped from your control. Maybe, just maybe, you're seeking justice for an incredible wrong you had or did as a child or was done to you."

The lump of emotion rose up in her throat and AJ tried to swallow it back down. She stuck her chin up. "You want to know about my husband?"

"Of course, Morning Glory."

"Fine. You keep saying Michael was an asshole. He was, to a degree. And you're right. They all are—men, in some fashion or another. Did we have our fair share of problems? Absolutely. That's what happens when you're married to a goddamned undercover FBI agent who's forced to keep secrets from you. That's what happens when you go months without a single word that he's okay and you have no fucking idea where on this planet he is, who he's with, or what he's done with those people. You're left in the darkest parts of his existence and sometimes you forget what it's like to BE married and have a husband.

"He was an asshole because the government made him that way, because the jobs he had to do brought the worst out in him and I was doing my *goddamned* best to keep the family together for the sake of our son. And when I finally became pregnant again—after years of trying and infertility problems—I saw a glimmer of his old self again, before all the fuckery came crashing down around him. We had a chance to start over again. He told them he was getting out. He told them he was done. And he died because of them.

"But regardless of the problems or fights or battles we shared at home, he was STILL nothing like my biological father, nothing like the man who gave his sperm to create me. So, I might not have had control over the man in my life as a child, but I remained in control of the one who was the life of mine."

Amanda closed her eyes and leaned back, inhaling the last words spoken. Her mouth parted to say something, then she stopped and opened her eyes. Her arms extended outward, palms facing the heavens.

"That…that is the earth in which your strength is planted. That is your wielded sword in the battle you intend to fight. That is you telling the Devil and his army, 'not today, not ever'. And speaking of the Devil, it's time I introduced you to someone else."

Amanda stood up and walked behind the register again. She pulled out another two cans of soda, then walked back to AJ, still smiling.

"Stay hydrated, my flower. I don't want you to wilt."

"Thank you, but I'm not thirsty right now."

"Suit yourself."

"You said you wanted to introduce me to someone?"

Amanda sat back down. "Time to show you Lucifer."

—¡—

CHAPTER 72

"WE ARE each our own devil, and we make this world our hell." At least that's what Oscar Wilde once said.

Do you believe that? Do you believe we live in constant Hell, that each of us is doomed to a life of misery and squalor? Do we sledge through muck and shit each day, driving to a hell job or going home to a hell house? Are we the epitome of Satan? Would that make our dreams, hopes, and admirations a saintly God?

I honestly don't know.

But what I do know is this:

When you're in your own handmade hell and you've lost yourself in tangled roadways, only the Devil can give you directions out. That's what my friend, **PATRICK**, told me.

That's why I chose the Lucifer hummingbird—that one, second from the end, next to the Ruby-Throated one—to immortalize him. I decorated his neck and shoulders that vibrant fuchsia-inspired purple and complemented him with the lightest lavender foxgloves I could find. He sits above the stone background, posed like he's ready for battle.

Patrick was a kind soul I met in Chicago one year, sometime back in the early 1990s. He had a raspy voice. Shorter than most guys I knew. His thick curly hair and dark eyes contrasted his pale skin—something I never likened with Hispanics before. But back then, I was ignorant and naïve about so many cultures and the beautiful variety the human body came in.

Have you ever just people watched? Have you ever lost yourself in a thick crowd and paid attention to all the bare skin that graces your eyes?

Try it someday. Just lose yourself in the downtown of a metropolis. Wander in wonder and look at the millions upon millions of busy little bees and ants as they buzz and scurry back and forth, back and forth, each day.

They act as if they have a purpose, but what is that purpose? To pay a bill? To meet a deadline? To piss away a paycheck on pretty petty things?

Those were the questions running through my mind as I sat on a bench in Grant Park, just across from the Congress Plaza Hotel. My time with Ethan and Isaac in New York prepared me for adventures alone in big cities. So, I felt at ease by myself, there on the park bench in the Windy City.

I watched people jog by. Dogs pissed on other dogs' markings. And no matter how peaceful the trees were or how green the park was, the song of cars drowned out the song of birds at every turn. It was frustrating to me. I wanted to sit and ground myself in nature, and I couldn't even do that.

But then, a man sat on the same park bench with me to eat his vendor-made hot dog. He closed his eyes and seemed to savor each onion and mustard bite.

When he opened his eyes, he caught me staring and smiled. He offered his chips, but I declined.

"These dogs're the best, don't you agree?"

"I'm sorry, but I've never had one without sauerkraut."

"Sauerkraut?!" He made a face. "You must be a Yankee from New York, then."

"Or a Chicagoan who doesn't like her dog dragged through

the garden."

He grinned from ear to ear. "I come here every day for lunch and people watch," he said. "I don't think I've seen you here before."

"That's because, until this morning, I've never been here," I replied.

"Oh. Business or pleasure?"

"Business, always."

"Business is when I'm clocked in. Pleasure is when I'm eating this." He pointed to the remainder of his hot dog.

I laughed at his witty remarks.

When he was done with the last bite, he pulled a napkin from his lunch bag and wiped his hands, offering his right to me.

"Name's Patrick."

"Amanda."

"Nice to meet you, Amanda." He pulled out a small thermos and began twisting the lid off. "Do you mind me asking, are you easily offended?"

I leaned away from him and said, "Most of the time, no."

He nodded. "Miss Amanda, I apologize if what I do next offends you. I need a bump before I go back in the office."

I watched him pull out a small plastic baggy from the bottom of his thermos. He crushed the contents inside, then pinched the sides of the bag to his nose. With two quick snorts, he inhaled the substance and wiped the inside of the baggy along his gums. Then he took his napkin, cleaned his face, and put the baggy back in the hidden compartment.

"Beg your forgiveness," he said, clearing each nostril with a quick inhale. "It's my only vice in the world, something the Devil introduced me to."

"No offense taken," I replied. "The Devil introduced me to gardening. Funny how our vices work."

He stood up, then offered his hand again. "It was good to meet you, Amanda. Same time here tomorrow?"

"I'm only here for a couple more days."

"Good. Then I'll see you here tomorrow. Come hungry and I'll treat you to the world's best hot dogs, and I'm not talking New York style."

We parted ways and he quickly walked towards downtown, lost in the midday crowd of people scurrying back and forth.

The following day, I cancelled my plans and decided to go back to the same park and wait for him. Punctual as the day before and true to his word, he brought two hot dogs this time.

"How did you know I'd be here waiting?" I asked him, taking a bite of my bun.

"Because my vice didn't scare you away."

"I don't scare easily."

We talked for the full time his lunch allowed and I walked with him back towards his office when it was ending.

Turned out he did a lot of cocaine. It didn't make him a bad guy. Quite the opposite, I'd say. He used the cocaine to self-medicate and stay focused for his job. He never overdosed, just took small microdoses of white powder for that quick pick-me-up he desired.

I don't condone his behavior. Most coke users have mental or addiction problems. Many will overdose. Most use the drug with others.

Not Patrick. He didn't use other drugs, never smoked anything, and never drank. His only vice was the white line he'd powder his nose with.

I decided to stay a little longer in Chicago and get to know this gentleman a little more.

The next day, we struck up our third conversation and philosophized about people, businesses, jobs, religion—whatever topic flowed between us. He always brought food and manners. And, when I told him I was having trouble with my business, he offered sound advice on how to gain revenue. He remained a gentleman, someone who made time disappear.

From time to time over the years, I'd give him a call and we'd play catch up with our lives. I'd always start with business-related items, and he'd always finish the conversation with pleasure-related topics. We could chat on the phone until first morning light. We could chat about anything, really.

Patrick helped me get this nursery running more efficiently and he did it without an ulterior motive. He always remained a friend over the years and taught me how to beat the Devil back.

—¡—

CHAPTER 73

INCH BY inch, they peeled the landscape fabric all the way to one end of the greenhouse, folding it on top of itself until at least three-quarters of the floor underneath was exposed. Worms, centipedes, and other multi-legged creatures scurried or oozed for cover from the invaders.

Conrad wiped the dirt from the metal door and examined the hatch.

"Where do you think that goes?" Jack asked.

"Not sure, Kinston." He walked back outside and examined the ground around the greenhouse. No indentions, no disturbances in grass, nothing gave away what lay on the other side of the hatch. Decades-old trees provided canopy close by and he doubted the underground contents could be too big.

Conrad walked back into the greenhouse.

"See anything?" the younger man asked.

"Nothing."

"Ready to open this?"

He nodded and grabbed the handle, expecting the hatch to resist, but it pivoted with ease on the hinges. A ladder invited both men down into the darkness.

"Grab the flashlight."

Jack clicked it on, crouched down and pointed the light at the ladder. He followed the rungs down to the bottom, then looked all around.

"Anything?"

"Can't really tell. Looks clear, though." He stood back up and dusted his jeans off. "It just looks like an empty space, but I couldn't see the whole thing from here."

Conrad clicked on his own flashlight, positioned himself on the ladder, and proceeded to climb down. Halfway, he shined the light around him. The ladder appeared to be in the middle of a long tunnel to each side.

His feet made a soft thud on the dirt at the bottom and he waited for Jack to climb down. The damp air felt many degrees cooler, a direct contrast to the bright, warm, and open space above. The tunnel was just wide enough for two people to pass, but still narrow enough to intimidate claustrophobics.

He shined the light down each end of the tunnel, but both ends curved slightly and there was no way of telling what was at either end.

"Right or left?"

"Right."

With both flashlights illuminating the way, Conrad proceeded with slow caution. The tunnel offered no secrets, nor was it rigged in any way to collapse or trap the two men. The sides were reinforced with concrete; the top, with thick rust-colored steel beams holding the dirt at bay. Roots wormed in and out above them. Occasionally, a cold drop of water percolated through and plopped on the ground in front of them.

The tunnel bent to the right. As they approached, a closed door greeted them.

"Where do you think that leads?" Jack whispered.

"Not sure," came a low reply. "Do you see a handle?"

"No, sir."

"Hold my flashlight."

Conrad placed his hands on one side of the door and pushed. It did not give way or open. He placed his hands on the opposite side and pushed again. The door clicked and went forward on a glider. He slid the door to the side as they were blinded by the light within.

Something buzzed by. Both men ducked down as it buzzed by again.

"What the fuck was that?!" Jack yelled.

Chirping and more humming came from inside the lit room. Conrad stepped inside and came face to face with a small tree branch and nest.

"Sir? What is it? What's going on?"

The Deputy Director looked around the familiar space.

"We're back in the hummingbird aviary."

—¡—

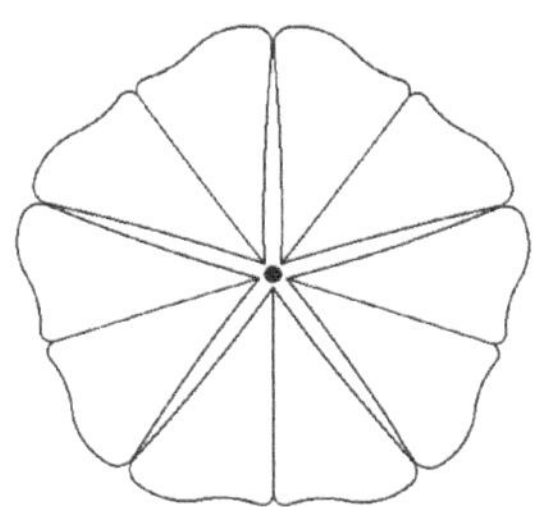

CHAPTER 74

NOT THIRSTY at that moment, AJ declined the drink. She just stared at the aluminum can while Amanda talked about Chicago, hot dogs, and cocaine.

"—and taught me how to beat the Devil back," she finished.

"I don't understand how you can trust someone who took cocaine on a regular basis."

"Flower, just because it's illegal, doesn't make it horrible or any worse than the other addictions out there. How can you trust an alcoholic to do their day job? Or a gambler to pay the bills? What about those addicted to caffeine or sugar, very legal and very real drugs in many food and drink products?"

"You just do."

"Yes, you just do. And you don't judge them for their singular vice."

"What if they're pedophiles or rapists?"

Amanda shook her head. "You can't put the two in the same category, dear. Pedophiles and rapists are a different class and have a different neurological makeup. They get the tortured rewards they deserve and deserve rewards of torture."

AJ looked back at the can of soda. "I don't disagree there."

"Was your father a pedophile?"

She shot a look back at Amanda. "Why would you ask that?"

"Because out of all the men in your life, your father is the one you've tried the hardest not to talk about all week. So, tell me. What did he do to my little flower and her garden?"

"He wasn't a pedophile."

"That's good to know."

"He was a bipolar alcoholic. And a violent one at that."

"A violent bipolar? Or a violent alcoholic?"

"Alcoholic. Both. I don't know."

"What was it like when he drank?"

AJ scoffed. "He beat me and mom. Multiple times. Threatened to kill me more than I can count. He punched holes in the walls, doused the house in gasoline, and pulled a gun on a family member once. The Dr. Jekyll and Mr. Hyde personas made all of us live in fear. Gave one of my brothers nightmares."

"What did he do to you?"

"He found creative ways to abuse me. Child Protective Services was called on him a few times, so he had to get creative then."

"How?"

"Like one time, he made me stand outside in the cold with nothing on but my nightgown. Another time, I had to stand in the corner with my arms straight up and never touch the walls. The second my arms rested against the walls or came down, I had a belt or a wire smacked across my ass. And I'm not talking a few minutes. Oh, that was too easy. He made me stand for an hour or two.

"He once made me chose between eating a spoonful of cayenne pepper or getting ten lashes with the belt across my feet. I chose the pepper because I already knew how bad the pain was on my bare feet. After I told him I chose pepper, he told me I'd get the lashings because he would give me what I did not want the most. There's no lack of bad memories. There's no lack of beatings or torture or abuse, whether they left physical marks or not. But the mental and emotional abuse lasted much longer after that."

"And what was he like when he wasn't drinking?"

"He was *always* drinking."

"Tsk-tsk, detective. Back to playing coy again so soon? We're almost done, I assure you. What was he like when he wasn't drinking?"

AJ inhaled deep and held it for a second before releasing it. Amanda's persistence annoyed the hell out of her, but the sun's descent towards the horizon meant there were fewer and fewer things she had to tell the woman.

"Paden was a decent man."

"Just decent?"

"Yeah. There was laughter. Music always played. He'd entertain my mom's guests. He always had the grill going outside."

"Tell me a good memory."

"He loved the outdoors and working from home. He repaired computers and small farm or gardening equipment. Lawnmowers, tillers, stuff like that."

"Did he enjoy gardening?"

She nodded. "He did when I was growing up. He loved roses and we always had several bushes planted around the house. He planted a few different fruit trees, a pomegranate bush for my mom, and whatever vegetables we wanted. He had patience for that sort of thing."

"Did he like animals?"

"He loved birds."

"And you had a hummingbird feeder at one point, didn't you?"

"How did you know?"

Amanda smiled. "Paden sounds familiar. Gardening, roses, and hummingbirds go together."

AJ thought back and cracked a small smile. "I do have one fond memory. It was when I was a teenager. I saw him watching a hummingbird from the back patio one day. He walked out and stood a few feet from the feeder. A few minutes passed and he took a small step closer. A few more minutes later and he did the same thing again. I think he stood there for over thirty minutes, slowly approaching, slowly getting closer and closer. Finally, he had his hand next to the plastic flower and he waited.

"The bird made another pass and just like that, he caught it! There was such tenderness in his eyes as he held it and called me outside. I was so fascinated and in awe and I'll never forget the pride and happiness in his eyes.

"There aren't many fond memories we shared as father-daughter. But that was one of them. That was definitely one of the few I had."

—¡—

CHAPTER 75

"MEMORIES can either ignite the soul or tear a person apart. There is no between." Mateo told me that.

How appropriate, again, we transition from yours to mine, and especially about the common theme between us: hummingbirds.

Mateo was a kind, but sickly, fellow. His father said he was a "gift of God" and that's why he named his son that. The kid was born with no legs and only one full good arm. I think the birth defect is called Amelia or Ormelia or some such name.

Honestly, my memory is nowhere near what it used to be. Guess that's the price that's asked of me. I'm glad I still have what I have, that way I can tell you all about my birdies.

I met Mateo and his father, Jackson, at the Hoover Dam a few years back. It was right before smartphones made humans dumb.

Look up there, the two near the end. See the one that says **MATEO**? That bird's a Calliope hummer. I gave him a rich pink neck with fingering spines all the way to his shoulders and painted him in a stretching manner, symbolic of his desire to one day have legs and stretch them in a long sprint. I complemented him with a columbine flower, a variety called Blue Dream. It seemed the most appropriate.

The painting next to that one says **JACKSON**. That's a Costa's hummingbird and represents Mateo's father with a darker fingering spine of violet paint accenting his neck and shoulders. He sits on that branch, surrounded by matching catmint, admiring his son in the other painting. That's why those two are positioned the way they are.

Everything's positioned with exact purpose.

I met the father and son at the Hoover Dam. I was coming back from Los Angeles on one trip and, instead of taking my usual southern routes back east, instinct told me to travel through Death Valley and cross Vegas before coming down through Arizona.

So, I did. I came down and took a break at the famed Hoover Dam. They hadn't built that highway bridge downstream yet. The road twisted and swept left to right, right to left to a parking lot. I stopped and walked across the dam, taking dozens of pictures on a small digital camera I recently purchased.

I was on the Nevada side walking to the Arizona side when I saw this father and son pair standing at the state line trying to position themselves to get a good picture. His father looked around for someone to take photos, but no one stopped to help them.

Mateo sat straight in his wheelchair with his head held high. He had a broad chest and strong arm. Had he been born with the rest of his limbs, he would've been an unstoppable athlete. As is, his wheelchair sported bright yellow push rings with a sports-themed backrest.

"I'll take your photo," I said. "I don't mind at all."

"Thank you, ma'am," the father said. "That's very kind of you."

I took several photos, that way they could choose the best ones. They thanked me again before going on their way. Mateo had such an infectious smile about him.

About an hour or so later I was on my way to Flagstaff for the night. It was starting to get dark and I didn't want to drive in that area that late. Too many elk. Too many collisions.

I was almost to Flagstaff when I saw a white van pulled over on the side of the road. A tall older man was putting out flares and a younger one sat in a familiar-looking wheelchair.

It was them!

I pulled over immediately and put my hazards on, hoping to give drivers more warning than just the road flares. When I exited the car, the father smiled.

"You again!"

"Seems like we're destined to meet," I replied. I offered my hand. "Amanda."

"Jackson. That's my son, Mateo."

The young man wheeled himself over and offered his hand. "Nice to see you again."

"Same here," I said. "Can I help in any way? I'm headed to Flagstaff for the night. I don't mind giving you gentlemen a ride somewhere."

"That's nice of you, ma'am, but we're waiting for the tow truck to come get the van."

"Would you at least allow me to pay for dinner, then? I wouldn't be able to live with myself leaving both of you here."

Mateo looked at his father and said, "I can go into town with her and find a hotel for the night."

"Mat, we need to be on the road," Jackson replied.

"Sir, I don't recommend it. If you value your van, you'll spend the night and avoid hitting any elk in this area. I've seen what one can do to an eighteen-wheeler and you won't have a van left if you hit one."

The father finally caved in and allowed Mateo to come with me. We agreed to meet up at a diner we both happened to know of.

Mateo and I sparked a rather fun conversation in the car about everything from basketball teams to national monuments and cities we've both visited.

"My dad's always been a traveler. Ever since Mom died, he's insisted that we go and see as many parks as we can."

"My apologies, Mateo, I didn't know your mom had passed."

"Yeah, I was two or three. Breast cancer. Doctors didn't catch it in time."

"Your father has the right idea. See and do as much as you can while you can."

We were quiet in the car for several minutes. I assumed that bringing up his mother was hard for the college kid. It's hard for anyone.

Finally, he said, "Amanda?"

"Yes, sir?"

"Thank you for treating me like a normal person."

"What do you mean?"

"Everyone looks at me like I'm delicate and frail. There aren't many people who openly talk to me like you have."

"That's because most people are assholes, idiots, or too scared to get to know someone." He laughed at that comment. "Honestly, Mateo, from the first time I saw you at the dam, I saw your heart and the brilliance in your eyes. You're anything <u>but</u> sickly, delicate, or frail."

I saw his chin lift up and confidence beam in his eyes. I was proud of him. I'd only just met him, and I was proud that he was proud. It's a strange thing to describe.

We found a hotel for them and Jackson met us at the diner. The three of us ate and talked the evening away. I told them all about my neck of the woods and everything there is to see and do. We exchanged phone numbers and they agreed to give me a ring in a few months to visit.

And guess what, my little flower? They did! They came to visit, as promised, and in the glory of that New England autumn, they stayed with me and saw everything they could take in.

That's how solid friendships are created. Not on talkative dreams with broken promises, but achievable acts with promises kept.

If only other men were that noble.

—¡—

CHAPTER 76

AFTER MAKING sure no hummingbirds had escaped, Conrad stepped back into the tunnel and slid the door over. He pressed it again and it clicked shut.

"So, the tunnel led to the basement of the house?" Jack asked, turning his flashlight on.

"It appears that way." Conrad clicked his flashlight on and pointed it down the tunnel. They both slowly made their way back to the ladder.

"Where do you think the other end leads?"

"I'm not sure. But we should proceed with a bit of extra caution."

"Why would Amanda have a hidden tunnel leading from the greenhouse to the aviary? Isn't that strange?"

"Well, we were told she's eccentric. Very little would surprise me."

A few minutes later, they stopped at the ladder. Conrad looked up at the opening, then back in the direction of the aviary. He shined the light down the opposite, unventured side.

"Are we going to check that out now, sir?"

Conrad gave a single nod and the pair began to walk down the corridor. Built in the same manner, the tunnel walls felt chilled to the touch and curved to the left, then the right. Water dripped from an exposed root and hit him on the head. The hair on the back of his neck stood up. If he counted correctly, they had taken many more steps than the other side of the ladder.

"It feels like we're going downward a little bit," Jack whispered, shining his light above him.

"I noticed that also."

"I think I see a glow ahead."

Each step brought them closer to a glowing frame, marking the end of their journey. Conrad shined his flashlight across all the corners of the wall in front of him.

"It's another door," Jack said, stating the obvious.

"At least this one has a handle."

Conrad wrapped his hand around the knob and twisted. Unlocked, it squeaked and resisted. He gripped the handle harder and twisted more. The doorknob finally admitted defeat and released the latch. He pulled the door towards him. The hinges moaned in chorus and the tunnel lit up in eerie gloom. He squinted.

"See anything?" Jack asked behind him.

The Deputy Director took a step in. "It's another room."

The younger man grimaced. "Woah. It smells like the morgue down here."

The fluorescent lights flickering above did not startle Conrad as much as the heavy, thick, and much colder air. Or the massive stone and concrete slab in the middle of the room. The slab sloped downward from the back to the front and had a curved notch in the center, several inches lower than the opposing end. A large bucket on wheels sat near the notch's throat.

Chains and shackles hung from the ceiling near the slab's back end and trailed towards a corner crank. Two barred doors stood at attention near opposite ends along the left wall. In between, thick rusted bolts and chains were securely attached at various heights along the wall; iron stains trailed down the wall directly underneath. In front of the detectives, an ominous metal door remained locked and shut, its contents not ready to reveal themselves. The right wall had a larger barred door protecting another enclosure. A recessed area included two folded chairs, a table, and what looked like a tall, narrow bureau.

Conrad looked behind him. A dripping spigot and coiled water hose waited. He noticed rusty drainage outlets in the floor.

He scanned the entire area again. Just like the tunnel, the walls within the room were solid concrete. The only difference: so were the floor and ceiling.

He walked to one of the barred doors to the left and shined his flashlight inside. A small cot with blankets, a couple of pillows, and another bucket were the only contents.

He stopped. A reflection on the ground caught his eye and he bent down to inspect the object. A medicinal needle and discarded tubing lay on the floor, under the cot. Behind him, he got a whiff of stale urine and shined the flashlight on the bucket.

"This looks like a jail cell," Jack said, standing at the entrance. "Smells like one, too."

"And that looks like part of an IV." He focused his light back on the tubing and needle.

"I found something else out here. I think it's an altar of some sort."

Conrad slowly stood back up, relieving his lower back pain, and exited the cell. He followed Jack to the opposite side of the room where the wooden bureau stood.

"What do you make of this?"

A tall, wooden box rested on top of the bureau and against the back of the wall. Several hooks were screwed into the box and items dangled down. A necklace of small shells and beads hung on one hook; a hemp rope with dried claws hung on another.

Conrad pulled out a pair of latex gloves from his pocket. He picked up and studied each miscellaneous item on top of the altar:

a brightly painted elephant carving with the words

MADE IN SRI LANKA on the bottom;
a set of dog tags with the name MAVERICK CHAPMAN and military identification information on it;
a man's antique pocket watch with an elaborate carving of a river and the word HUDSON underneath;
a couple of gay pride bracelets with the names GABRIO and ABRAN;
handwritten letters to Amanda from someone named ORO GARCIA;
a photograph of an older man standing next to a younger one in a wheelchair with the names MATEO and JACKSON handwritten above each;
and a handmade ceramic bowl with the name UMAR stamped in the bottom.

"Are those chicken feet?" Jack asked, pointing to one of the necklaces.

"It appears so."

"What the hell for?"

"Protection, maybe. Some alternative religions use them."

"That's disgusting!"

Conrad opened the narrow drawer underneath the altar. "And *that* appears to be what we're looking for." He focused the flashlight inside the drawer as Jack took a peek. There, in the middle and resting on rabbit fur, was the matching obsidian knife.

"Yes! I KNEW we'd find it!" Jack's excitement echoed off the walls. He reached his hand in.

"Don't touch it yet."

"Why not?"

"We need to document everything first. Go back up to the greenhouse and bring my suitcase. I want to test this area and that slab behind us for blood. Also, bring several evidence bags."

"Are we arresting Amanda now?"

"No. Not yet. She's still only a person of interest, as are the other girls living in her house. There's no hard proof of murder or homicide, and we haven't found any bodies."

"Yet." Jack started to walk back to the tunnel. "Unless she's killed AJ."

"Wait. What makes you say that, detective?"

"Amanda's been spending a lot of time with her. Why would she do that unless AJ's a potential victim?"

The hairs on the back of Conrad's neck stood up again. Jack, for all his arrogant and egocentric comments, made a valid point that he never would have thought of, considering his friendship with Amanda Claremont. Everything in this hidden bunker only led him to the same conclusion as his subordinate.

AJ could be in trouble.

"On second thought, Kinston, go check on Jardine. You have a valid point. Bring her and Ms. Claremont back here and keep an eye on both of them."

"On it."

"If Mr. Juniper gives you any problems, have one of the officers escort him off the property and I'll deal with that situation later. And send Mr. Yates, the young forensic tech, down here with those items I requested."

"Yes, sir."

Conrad dug into his pocket and pulled out his keys. He tossed them across the room to Jack. "Get back as quick as you can without giving away anything."

Jack stepped through the door.

"And, Kinston?" Conrad hollered.

"Yeah?" came a voice in the tunnel.

"Say nothing about what we found just now, not even to Jardine."

"Got it," he heard from the tunnel.

Conrad gazed back inside the drawer and moved the rabbit fur over. The light caught the reflection of another object.

A key.

He scanned the room again. There was only one thing the key

could go to. He grabbed it and walked over to the large vault door in the center of the back wall. He pressed his palm against the metal.

Frigid. What the hell is this?

He studied the door again, then tried the key. A few clicks later, and the lock disengaged. He stuck one end of the flashlight in his mouth and gripped the circular vault handle with both hands.

In a clockwise motion, he twisted.

KATHUNK, CLANK!

The releasing mechanism echoed all around him. As he pulled the door open, cold air rushed out and wrapped around his ankles. And, as soon as the flashlight fell on the contents within, Conrad gasped. The light dropped to the floor and rolled by his feet.

"Oh, God," he whispered.

—¡—

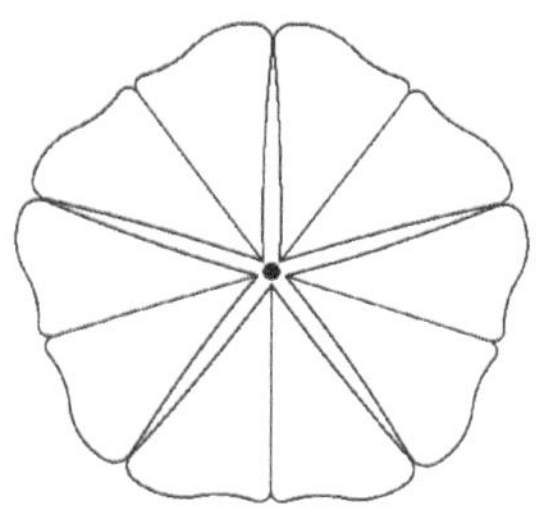

CHAPTER 77

"SOME FATHERS love their children unconditionally and will do everything in their power to save them, protect them. Don't you think that's true?"

AJ nodded. "Not all fathers are pieces of shit like mine was."

"But you have some good memories, it seems. Do you think he's the reason why you love gardening now?"

"Honestly, I don't know. I guess?"

Amanda stood up and walked over to the window, looking towards the lowering sun. She leaned against one edge of the window trim. "You guess? I think the lessons he taught you—however horrible you think they were—are the reason you became a detective. At least, more so than your murdered husband."

AJ also stood up, taking the opportunity to stretch her stomach. She walked over to the older woman. She leaned against the other side of the window trim and looked out the window. The Native American flute music still played in the background. "What makes you say that?"

"Your mother taught you more of who you should become than not. And your father taught you more of who you shouldn't than who you should. Do you agree with that?"

"It makes sense. I refuse to be anything like my father."

"Oh. but you are, little flower. You fight so hard to not become the same violent person he is or was. Yet, that part of him lies dormant within you."

"I'm not a violent person."

"Really?"

"I'm not. And I never will be."

"Let's go back to your childhood then. I have only one more birdie to tell you about before I show you the final one. That means you only have to tell me a few more things and our little talks will be done."

"What do you still want to know?"

"Were you suicidal?"

AJ rolled her eyes. She crossed her arms and walked back to the table, not happy with the woman's question. She knew Amanda already knew the answer to that, but the old woman seemed like she wanted to keep playing games. The detective sat back down in her chair and closed her eyes. She heard Amanda walk around from behind and then move the chair in front of her, taking a seat again.

AJ nodded and opened her eyes.

"What was that, my flower? I didn't hear you say the words."

"Yes. Yes, I was suicidal."

"Why?"

"Because childhood sucked, that's why."

"Please, elaborate for me."

AJ leaned forward and interlaced her fingers on the table. She kept the older woman's gaze. "I was bullied relentlessly in school. We were poor, on food stamps and government aid. My father only cared about his whiskey and beer and the cigarettes he chain-smoked. That's where all the money went. Not for school clothes, not for training bras, not for any sports activities. His own selfish vices and wants. When the schools stepped in, that's when we got things—glasses, lunch boxes, coats. Stuff like that.

"As if that wasn't bad enough, kids picked on me because

of the hand-me-downs I wore, my large coke bottle glasses, my weight, my grades. Anything they wanted to. I hid in the bathroom stalls during lunch in middle school and tucked myself away in a teacher's empty classroom in high school. I couldn't stand eyes looking at me, judging me for every little thing I went through. I hid and shied myself from all my classmates and tried my damnedest to ignore the hate. I tried to ignore the same words said by so many different kids. But you know what happened? I started to believe those words. I grew to believe that I was fat, ugly, useless, and worthless.

"For those students who *were* genuinely nice to me. For every Sally and John who made efforts to spare me the hate and accept me, there were ten Karens and twenty Arthurs. For every kind word said to me, there were a dozen cruel ones. And those were the ones I grew up believing."

AJ wiped the tears from her eyes. She made no attempt this time to hide the pain. "And no matter how awful I felt at school—no matter how much I was tormented or shoved or spit on—it was a thousand times better than the abuse and fear I lived with at home."

She choked back the tears. "Running away wasn't an option. They'd find me eventually and then I'd be beaten to the point I wouldn't be able to move. I knew what would happen. Gawd, did I want to run away!" She wiped her face with her hands. "But I couldn't. By the time I was a Sophomore in high school, suicide felt like it was the only answer."

"And how did you intend to do it?"

"I had a pocketknife. I also had a whetstone and kept it sharp. From time to time, I'd run the blade across my arm and see if I could shave the hair off. Once I knew it was sharp enough, I placed it on my wrist and dug the point in." AJ exposed her wrist upward and made a motion with her other hand. "I dug the point in. Do you know what that felt like?"

"No..."

"It felt the exact same as when my father stuck needles in the back of my hand once. Wanna know why he did that? I stole some change out of a bucket so I could have a snack at school during lunch one day. I stole no more than a dollar's worth of money, and he found out. So, he took a sewing needle and asked me which hand I took the money with. I told him my right hand. He grabbed me and proceeded to stab me several times on the top of my hand. I screamed from the pain and tried to jerk away. But I was small, and he was so much stronger. The more I struggled, the more he stabbed me on the hand. I watched little droplets of blood bead up. He yelled at me as I ran away to bathroom. And when I held the knife to my wrist, seeing that droplet of blood, I panicked. I feared what my father would do to me again if I didn't succeed in killing myself.

"I failed to make friends. I failed to ever get his approval on anything. I failed my mom and my brothers. I failed to even kill myself. In my eyes, at that age, I was the ultimate failure at everything."

Amanda got up from the table and went to the counter. She retrieved several napkins and gave them to AJ.

"Thank you," the detective said, blowing her nose.

"Where was your mom in all this?"

"Working two jobs. Taking care of a toddler and a new baby. Her focus wasn't on me. It was on making ends meet and making sure my brothers were cared for." AJ shook her head. "She didn't know half the things done to me. Not until after the divorce." AJ looked at the napkin in her hand and twisted the end.

"You still have a lot of guilt, don't you?"

AJ nodded. "Yeah." She continued to twist the napkin to a point. "I know I'm not a failure. I know I'm trying to be a good mother and not repeat the past. I know I'm not like my father."

"Then why is there one final secret still left inside you? There's something you've never told anyone, isn't there?"

AJ stopped twisting the napkin and stared in numbness at it. There was one story no one knew.

She nodded.

—¡—

CHAPTER 78

FINALLY, we're reaching the end, my beautiful Heavenly Blue. You should feel the weight being lifted from your body. Everything you've been telling me is only so you can truly move forward.

You don't believe me yet. I understand and respect that. But it takes remarkable strength and unyielding courage to come forward and tell me the things you have.

Look up at the paintings above you. See the one that says **UMAR**? That's the final story to share here.

That's a gorgeous Green-breasted Mango hummingbird. He's in mid-flight, looking up at the fuchsias above him. In order to get those vibrant colors, I smeared different paints across his throat and trailed them down to his groin. I enjoyed painting this one.

Umar was a brilliant blue-eyed masterpiece of human creation. His family originated in Greece and he looked like a chiseled marble statue come to life. He kept his black curly hair pulled back in a ponytail and always dressed nice. His mannerisms, his body, the way he carried himself—perfection!

He was always polite, always helpful. And he was one of my

best customers I've ever had. His family would always send him from Wolfeboro to my shop to get mulch or plants or whatever they were in the mood for. Family was vital to him. He lived to serve his parents, help his brothers, and support his sisters. They'd relocated from Ohio, if I remember correctly.

Umar stopped in at least twice a month. Always knew exactly what he needed. He was prompt, didn't beat around the bush, and paid immediately without question or haggling me down.

One weekend, we had a vicious hailstorm strike our area. This happened just a few years ago. I knew the storm would unleash its anger on my town, so as it approached, I had my girls and the men from the halfway house scramble to bring everything in this building. We had to protect our plants, protect our precious trees and flowers.

We got everything inside as the first few bits of ice slammed against the roof. But we greatly underestimated Mother Nature's fury that day. She threw larger and larger pieces of hail at us until finally one, then two windows shattered, raining glass on us.

My greenhouses were ripped to shreds. The insurance totaled our vehicles—there was no getting those dents out. Our roof began leaking. The Storm, she spared the halfway house and my home. The winery was also left intact.

"Never forget what I can do," the Storm said as she rolled southward and continued to unleash hell on other towns.

The next day, the men cleaned up the mess outside and began repairing the greenhouses. The girls picked up glass and tried to salvage what planters and things they could.

I swept up the mess inside when Umar stopped in for his order. Stunned at the damage, he asked if I was okay.

"No," I said. "The storm took out my feeders and mugs. Most of them were destroyed by the hail after the windows broke."

He walked over and inspected all the broken ceramic and glass pieces. "Ms. Claremont, you have been very kind to me and my family over the years. Let me return the favor."

"How can you do that?" I asked.

"My brothers can help fix your roof. I have a studio and can make more mugs and feeders for you."

"You work with glass?"

"I'm an artisan with my own gift shop and gallery in downtown Wolfeboro."

We talked for a few more minutes as the men loaded up the order in his truck. I told him this order was at no charge. He refused to take the bags of compost and dirt without paying something for them.

"You need this, now, more than I do," he said as he handed me the money. "I'll be back in two weekends with a few gifts for you."

True to every word he said, he came back with several new feeders. "The mugs and ceramic tiles I'm making will take a few more weeks to finish, but you will have those soon, I promise."

I was beside myself when I saw the gorgeous detail and beadwork in the glass. His feeders were as much a work of art as he was.

"I can't thank you enough," I whispered.

"You and your employees are good people. And good people deserve good things."

Each of us bargained the generosity of the other and we finally reached an agreement. He'd showcase his work at my shop. I'd give him whatever his family needed with a steep discounted price. And every two weeks, Umar brought me gifts in exchange for dirt and manure.

There are men, little flower, who will come into your life and show you the absolute best the world can be. If only we had more spectacular Umars to enrich our lives.

—¡—

CHAPTER 79

UNDER A few meters of earth, well below the reach of sun or warmth or living creatures, a buried bunker and hidden container finally revealed long-kept secrets.

Conrad grabbed the flashlight from the ground and pointed it back inside the walk-in freezer. Seven male bodies stood at attention on one side, six mirrored the other side. Each corpse stood nearly naked, with the exception of a modest loincloth and fabric draped across one shoulder. Native-looking armlets and anklets adorned the limbs.

All heads were tilted towards the ceiling, positioned to look at the heavens. Arms were folded across their chests in tomb-like fashion, much like a newly discovered pharaoh from the eighteenth dynasty.

Hands held strange items. He leaned in to study the contents. Every right hand held a small hummingbird, heads and beaks protruding upward to the sky. Each bird's throat glimmered in various colors. Left hands held unique bouquets of flowers.

Ceremonial headdresses and masks covered most of the faces, except for one. The mask lay on the ground, as if it accidentally fell off and exposed the man's face. The eyes and the mouth of that corpse were sewn shut. He assumed each of the other victims would be done in a similar manner.

Conrad blew on his hands to keep them warm. He did not want to be in the icy container any longer than he had to.

The bodies appeared in various delayed stages of decomposition, the older and more shriveled-up were towards the back of the freezer. However, they all had something in common: fresh coats of paint. Each victim had unique markings and color on the necks. The one maskless man had geometric designs fingering across his temple and cheeks. Some of the men had designs trailing across broad shoulders and the chest. One body, possibly the most recent, had vertical markings down the torso and under the loincloth.

Conrad watched as his flashlight cast shadows across each of the necks. The victims all had the same familiar cause of death like Michael Smith's body: a dark and open smile slit from ear to ear.

Most of the men appeared to be young, but there were a couple of older men among the soldiered dead. Many were from different races and ethnicities.

One body was propped on a stool. Conrad shined the light on the arm nub. There were no fresh cut marks, incisions, or scars—just the missing limb. The flowers the victim would be holding in the missing hand were placed on the stool in front of the body. The right hand—the one with the hummingbird—was positioned lower than the other bodies.

That was when Conrad noticed something else. A medium-sized gaping hole in the stomach, just below the rib cage. He tried to shine the light inside the fist-shaped wound but could not see anything. He checked the other bodies; the arms were positioned to cover up similar holes.

The detective heard a noise behind him, then someone knocked close to the tunnel entrance. He stepped out of the freezer and shut the door, keeping as much cold air inside as possible to preserve the evidence.

"Sir?" Peter Yates stood near the entrance. "I brought the things you asked."

Conrad motioned for the technician to come in. "Set it over there in the corner. Where's Sonnito?"

"She's documenting everything she's found so far, sir."

"How bad is it?"

Peter set the box down and ran a hand through his thick dark hair. "It's bad, sir. We've found several bone fragments and a few teeth. She's not sure how many bodies are buried up there, but she thinks it could be more than one or two...dozen."

"Shit!" The Deputy Director tugged his suit coat back into place and walked into the tunnel. "Mr. Yates, tell Sonnito to call in as many CSIs as she can."

"Yes, sir." The forensic technician hustled out of the space and down the tunnel, close behind.

Both men climbed back up the ladder to the greenhouse. Conrad pulled out his phone and tried to dial Jack's phone number.

Dammit! No bars.

He stepped out of the greenhouse just as Pat Sonnito walked up.

"Conrad," she said, "after we found the bone fragments in the first little garden patch, we split up to search the others." She shook her head.

"Pat, what's wrong?"

She pointed to half a dozen clusters of flowers. "Initial findings? There're bone fragments in every one of them."

Conrad felt his chest tighten as he looked around the greenhouse and Amanda's home. Her entire property was littered with small garden islands and clusters. Come to think of it, so was the halfway house and winery. Dozens upon dozens of little landscape clusters.

He hit the redial button and listened to the phone ringing on the other end. He looked over to the horizon to see the sky turning orange.

The call went straight to voicemail.

"Shit!"

"Deputy Director?" A young officer ran up to the Conrad and Pat. He wiped the sweat from his brow.

"Can I help you?"

"Sir, Chief sent me over here."

"Why's the Chief here?"

"You're needed immediately!"

Conrad left the forensic tech and ran down the hill with the young officer. Several police cars were waiting in front of the halfway house. Other officers were positioned behind open vehicle doors, watching the front door of the residence.

"What's going on?" Conrad asked, half out of breath.

"We got a call from one of our guys," the young officer said. "He saw the front door open and knocked. He called for backup immediately."

Police Chief Doug Galvan walked out of the front door with another older officer. "Stand down! It's clear!"

"Chief!" Conrad called out.

"McMillan!" Doug motioned for the Deputy Director to join him on the porch. As soon as Conrad took the steps, Doug said, "Conrad, they're all dead."

"What? Who?"

"All of Amanda's employees. The men are in their beds. Looks like they're just sleeping. But they've been dead since at least this morning. Rigor's set in."

"Oh, God."

"It's worse. The women were found in the basement. Thirteen of them. All in white dresses, all holding flowers like some goddamned cult arrangement. The girls looked like they died in their sleep as well."

Conrad's knees weakened. He grabbed the porch railing.

"You okay, Conrad?"

He grabbed the Police Chief's arm. "Doug, I just found thirteen male bodies in a hidden bunker. We found bone fragments in the flower gardens around the house."

"Where's Amanda right now?"

"At the nursery with Jardine."

"Want me to send backup over there?"

He pulled his phone back out again. "No. Jack's gone to get them. Let me try calling Jardine." He looked up AJ's phone number and dialed. Staring at Doug, he said, "Come on, AJ. Pick up the damned phone."

A few rings later and he heard, "Hello?"

"Jardine, where are you?"

"We're getting in your car, sir."

"Jack's with you?"

"Yes, sir. He said you needed us back at the residence."

"Jardine, listen carefully to me. We found—"

Before he could finish giving his detective the instructions, he heard her scream.

"JACK!"

—¡—

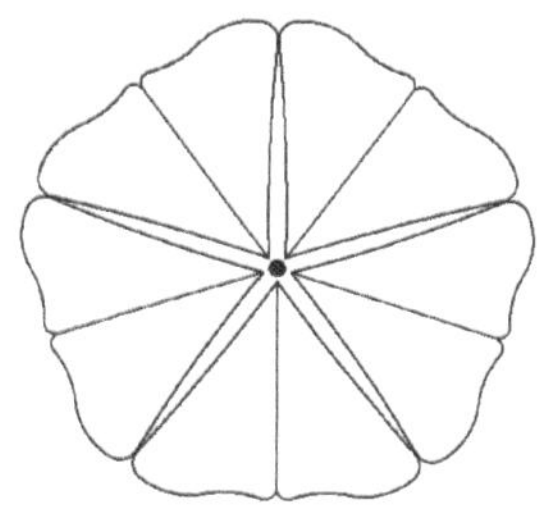

CHAPTER 80

THE LAST hummingbird story came to a close. Amanda stood up. She stretched left, then right, smiling at her artwork hanging above.

AJ also stood up and stretched her arms above her. Her abdomen resisted slightly, but even her body seemed relieved the storytelling was over. She looked behind her, out the window. The clouds melted into oranges and pinks.

"Does this mean I can leave?" the detective asked.

"You could have left at any time, flower."

"But I thought you said—"

"I merely encouraged you to stay and gave you the illusion that you couldn't leave."

Bang! Bang! Bang! Heavy knocks echoed within the nursery.

Both women looked at the door and walked over. Amanda took her keys from her pocket and unlocked the door.

Jack stood on the other side. His eyes darted back and forth between the women.

AJ knew immediately something was wrong. "Jack?"

"AJ, um, the Deputy Director needs us back at the residence.

Like, right now."

"Everything okay?"

He opened his mouth but was cut off.

"Good timing, little bird," Amanda said. "We just wrapped up our storytime. Well, *I* finished. I'm still owed a debt of one more story by your colleague here."

Jack's eyes darted over to the older woman. "Conrad wants you to join him at your house. He has some questions for you."

Amanda chuckled. "Oh, I bet he does. I need to use the restroom first before we go. Too much soda. I'll be right back." She walked to the opposite end of the building and disappeared behind the bathroom door.

AJ leaned in and whispered, "Jack, what's going on?"

He whispered back, "I can't tell you yet. But it's bad."

"What is it?"

Jack continued to whisper. "We found a hatch in the greenhouse that lead underground to a tunnel. One end of the tunnel led to some bird sanctuary."

"The hummingbird aviary?"

"Yeah, that!"

"We didn't see any hidden doors when we were down there."

"That's what Conrad said."

"Where did it open up?"

"One of the cages, I think. The door was like a panel that popped forward and slid sideways when you pressed it. Like a secret entrance of some sort."

"Where did the other end go?"

"Led to this hidden room with a big concrete slab and some sort of altar."

"An altar?"

"Yeah. We found a bunch of different items on top of this bureau. But check this out. The other ceremonial knife? It was in the drawer under the altar!"

"Oh, shit!"

"Yeah. There was some underground vault, but I don't know what's in it."

Amanda opened the bathroom door and walked over to the register area again. AJ heard the refrigerator door again. "Anyone else need to go before I lock up here?"

The detectives shook their heads.

"Anyone want a drink for the road?"

Again, they both shook their heads.

"Very well."

The older woman walked towards them and they exited the building. Amanda secured the door and all three walked to Conrad's SUV waiting in the parking lot. She got in on the driver's side behind Jack.

AJ climbed in the front passenger seat. As soon as she closed the door, her phone rang.

"Hello?"

"Jardine, where are you?"

"We're getting in your car, sir."

"Jack's with you?"

She looked over to see Jack checking his phone. "Yes, sir. He said you needed us back at the residence."

"Jardine..."

AJ never heard the rest of Conrad's sentences. The sound of his voice disappeared as Amanda sprung forward and wrapped one arm around Jack's forehead, jerking his head back against the headrest.

She never saw the knife in the older woman's hand. She only felt the warm arterial squirts hitting her chest and face. The phone fell from her hands as she screamed her coworker's name. Her hands flew forward to plug the gaping slit across her colleague's neck, but Amanda had other plans.

The woman, even in her sixties, was much stronger than AJ ever thought. She pinned the detective's head against the headrest in a similar manner and held the same knife to AJ's throat. The younger woman tried to reach for her gun, but Amanda yanked her hair back and pressed the knife hand harder against her jugular.

"Stop. Think carefully, my little flower," she said in a slow and calm manner, "Think of your children. You want to live for them, don't you?"

"Y-yes!"

"Slowly extend one hand up and retrieve your gun with the other hand. Don't try anything or you'll have a matching red smile like Jack's."

AJ looked at her partner and watched the man struggle to hold his neck as blood oozed between his fingers and down his chest. She saw the terror in his eyes as he tried to stop the inevitable. She grabbed her gun and handed it over to Amanda.

The older woman released her head and sat back.

"Jack!" AJ flung herself forward and pressed her hands into his neck. She was oblivious to the gun trained on her. All she could do was press hard against the young man's wound.

His eyes locked with hers, dilated from fear. He gripped his phone in one hand and grabbed AJ with the other, pressing harder.

She watched the color slowly drain from his face. "Stay with me, Jack!" She turned to the woman in the back seat, "Let me save him, please!"

The gun remained pointed at the detective's chest. "He's already gone, flower, he just doesn't know it yet. Now, push him out of the vehicle and crawl over to the driver's side. Again, if you try anything, you won't leave this parking lot alive."

AJ whispered to her colleague over and over, "I'm so sorry, Jack. I'm so sorry!" Her hands trembled as she did what the woman said.

He fell with a sick *plop!* just outside the door.

Amanda exited from behind, shutting both car doors.

AJ watched as Amanda, with the gun still pointing at her, crouched down to say something to Jack. She could not make out the words. For a split second, the detective thought about starting the car and ramming the woman or jumping out of the passenger door and running as far away as she could.

She'll gun you down first, you idiot! You can't outrun a bullet! THINK! Stay alive for Eoghan and Jenna!

Amanda stood up, gun still trained on AJ, and walked to the passenger side. She opened the vehicle door. "Hand me the phone. Slide over to the driver's side and keep your hands on the steering wheel."

Her hands clammed up. She watched Jack's blood drip onto her lap. She wiped her hands on her thighs and tried to get rid of the blood the best she could. Her stomach tightened. "Amanda? I think I might pass out."

"Take a deep breath, flower. I truly don't want to hurt you. Just think of your little Jenna and Eoghan at home. And how strong you need to be for them. Put your hands where I can see them."

Amanda shut the passenger door and locked the car. She took the phone and tapped the 'Speaker' button. "Conrad?"

"Amanda! Where's AJ?!"

"Our little morning glory is here in the car with me. She's safe, as long as she keeps a level head and doesn't do anything rash."

"What have you done to Jack?!"

—¡—

CHAPTER 81

UNLESS you want him to die, Conrad, I suggest you get over here as soon as you can. Jack's had…an accident. He's bleeding out and I honestly don't know how much time he has left.

What have you done?!

Tick tock, Deputy Director. I left the kid with a parting gift and told him where I'm taking our precious flower.

Amanda!

Do hurry. Maybe Jack can do at least one courageous act in this world before he dies. Goodbye, my White-Whiskered Hermit. Give Tony, my wonderful White-Necked Jacobin, my regards.

AMANDA!

Now, my Heavenly Blue. Drive.

Take a right and head towards downtown.

I think that conversation went as expected. What do you think? Nevermind, I don't care what you think right now.

Slow the car, no need to speed. Roll my window down, please. You won't be needing this phone anymore. I do hate the distractions of modern technology, but it served me well just now. Maybe you and Jack would've been able to stop me from slicing his neck had you both not been distracted by your phones.

Oh, my Morning Glory, please don't cry. I truly don't like plucking my flowers if I can avoid it. And you haven't even fully blossomed yet. That would be such a shame right now.

Remember I told you that I'd show you the Ruby-Throated hummingbird? That's where we're going now. That's where I want to take you.

You owe me a final story.

I owe you the last hummingbird.

Now, where's my walkie-talkie? Ah.

Are you there?

...Yes...I'm here...

It's time to finish our last play in this game.

...Yes, mother...

Light the altars, my little foxglove. Send my birdies home.

—¡—

CHAPTER 82

ROCKED by Amanda's words, he yelled her name again.

"Now, my Heavenly Blue. Drive."

She hung up.

"Conrad, what's going on?" Doug asked.

"Get me to the nursery NOW! Send a bus over there ASAP!" He ran down the porch steps.

The Police Chief rushed behind him.

They jumped in his squad car and Doug peeled out of the parking area. The car bounced down the driveway. Sirens and lights went on as he fishtailed onto Coatlicue Road and sped the short distance to the nursery building. Another cruiser's lights flashed on behind them.

He pressed the communicator near his collar. "Shut down this road and get a bus over to Claremont's!"

The Police Chief fishtailed again coming off the road and into the nursery's parking lot. Conrad braced himself for the sudden turn and the abrupt halt. Headlights caught the sight of someone on the ground across from one of the greenhouses.

"Kinston!" Conrad yelled, jumping out of the vehicle before

it stopped. He rushed over to the man and pressed his hands to Jack's open neck. "Jack! Jack, stay with me! The ambulance is on the way! Do you hear me?"

Kinston looked at Conrad, then stared straight up at the sky. A gurgle of blood spurted from his mouth and a convulsion jerked his whole body. Jack slowly went limp in his arms. The detective's phone fell from his hand and bounced on the asphalt.

"Jack!" Conrad placed him down on the ground and tilted his head to the side to clear the liquid in his throat. He began performing CPR.

"Conrad, he's gone," Doug said. "Look at the blood pool around him."

"I. Have. To try," he said with each chest compression.

Doug bent down to grab his friend by the shoulders. "Deputy Director, he's deceased. There's nothing you can do to save him."

After a few more compressions, Conrad stopped and sat down on the ground. He swallowed the emotion back. Hating to admit defeat, he knew his friend was right.

Jack was gone.

"It's my fault! I sent him over here. *I* should've been the one to get Amanda!"

Doug helped him back to his feet and stared him in the eyes. "This isn't your fault. Understand? None of us saw this coming. Not from her."

Conrad looked at the dead detective then the noticed the light illuminating from Jack's phone. He grabbed the device and wiped the blood off. Kinston was in the process of typing a text message to him:

OPSIDDE FAWN BRRR

Before he could ask the Police Chief what it meant, a loud explosion went off nearby.

The ground rumbled underneath and the sky glowed orange behind the nursery building. They ran over to the side of the building and looked beyond the front fields. Grayish smoke billowed from above the halfway house. The glow became brighter as flames rose to the sky.

A few seconds later, another explosion rocked the ground, this time to the left of the halfway house.

"That's Amanda's house!"

A series of loud synchronized pops swept the cornfield as the wooden canopies on top of all six stone temples erupted in flames. Fire exploded in different directions, igniting the dead corn stalks. The altars began to glow. More synchronized sounds came from the front field as flames cast strange shadows on the totem poles. Each pole exploded closer and closer to the two men, shooting sparks in every direction. A larger explosion went off to the immediate left. Glass shattered. Debris and tiny shards went flying everywhere as the winery building went up in flames. Another explosion went off even closer, this time at the barn that housed all the farm equipment.

"Get down!" Doug yelled just as the shockwave whooshed through the potted trees and shoved the men away. "We need to get out of here!"

They both covered their heads and watched as fire towered above them. They scrambled to their feet. Doug ran towards the cruiser. Conrad went back to the body on the ground.

"We need to leave!" Doug yelled over the rising noise around them.

"We need to get Jack!"

Doug ran over and grabbed Conrad by the arm. "There's no time! Let's go! NOW!"

An orange glow went up around the men. Flames licked the polymer lining as the greenhouses raged in fury. There was only one more building left and he knew what was coming next.

"GO GO GO!"

They ran to the cruiser. Doug threw it in reverse before the doors shut. He slammed the gas pedal down and peeled out into the roadway as the final explosion shot wood straight up in the air. The car shook violently from the aftershock of the red barn's obliteration. The Police Chief whipped the car into the adjacent

Ag-Equip lot before he slammed on the brakes. Ash fell like soft snow. Debris pinged and bounced off the hood and windshield. Thick hazy smoke engulfed the area, extinguishing first responder lights. A few smaller explosions occurred.

The air turned orange. The ground turned grey.

All Conrad could do was stare in shock.

"Why didn't I see this coming?" he whispered.

—¡—

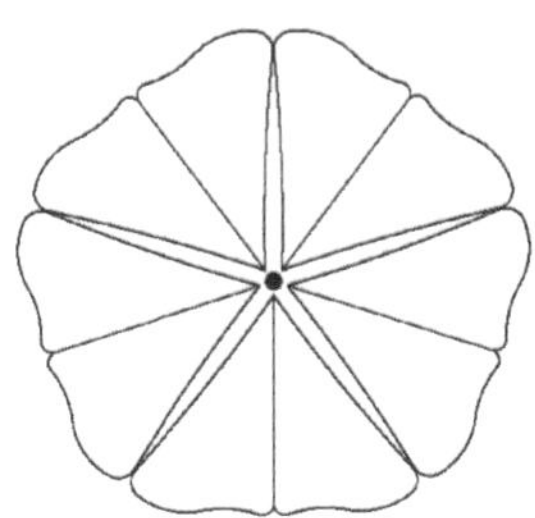

CHAPTER 83

EVERY MUSCLE in her body tensed and fired commands to fight or flee. Her brain struggled to stay calm even as her body shook from the fear.

Amanda kept the gun pointed at her, even as they waited for the light to turn green again on Central Street. The police station was just a few blocks away.

AJ fantasized about crashing the vehicle in front of the station and having several officers rush over to apprehend the woman. If only she could get her hand on the door lock and open it before the old woman pulled the trigger.

"Take a right on School Street all the way to the end."

Amanda's voice startled AJ back into reality, one where they would avoid the police station. She continued to keep her hands on the wheel and did as the woman instructed.

Her thoughts went to Eoghan and Jenna. She wanted desperately to hug them and never let them go again.

Maybe I can ram into a parked car or something? Knock her unconscious?

"Prospect Street is just ahead. Take a left."

Another jolt back to reality. She turned on Prospect and coasted downhill to the intersection. They were back on Central Street just to the left of Trestle View Park.

Just pull out into traffic. Let the car get t-boned on her side. Problem solved.

"Pull into that parking area in front of us and park the car."

Each thought was countered with a fear of failure. And a bigger fear of never seeing her kids again.

"Turn the car off and give me the keys."

Again, the detective did as instructed. "Wha-what are you going to do?"

"It's not what *I* will do." Without breaking eye contact, Amanda grabbed the bottle of water she brought with her and handed it to AJ. "Open it."

She took the bottle and twisted the cap off. The seal was already broken.

"Drink."

Her stomach tightened. "It's poisoned, isn't it?"

"I'm not going to harm you. But I do need you to drink this, dear."

"You poisoned it! Amanda, I have two little ones at home who need their mother. You know they already lost their father!"

"You're not a lamb being led to slaughter, if that's what you believe."

The detective shook her head. "I don't want to drink this! I want to see my children!"

Amanda sighed and her face went rigid. "My precious flower, I can shoot you right now, killing you. Or you can take a chance that I'm telling the truth and drink that water. One action sends you to your murdered husband. The other, to your children. You decide."

AJ stared at the plastic bottle and the deceptively clear liquid.

She stopped thinking and drank, quickly finishing the bottle.

With a smile, Amanda motioned at the door. "Time to go for a walk."

They both exited and the older woman wrapped one arm

around AJ's and tucked the gun in her side. She leaned in and whispered, "Do I need to remind you not to try anything?"

AJ shook her head.

"Good. Let's go."

They walked across Central Street to the Winnipesaukee River Trail entrance. Water raged to the left of them and drowned out most other sounds. They walked around the bright orange guard and proceeded up the trail. A woman jogged towards them with her dog and passed by quickly, not giving them any attention. Even if AJ screamed for help, the river rapids would drown them out.

There was still plenty of daylight, even though it was well into the evening and the sun was setting. They walked up the steep incline until her calves burned. They walked until the path leveled uphill. Amanda made her stop to catch her breath before they kept going.

Last autumn's leaves hugged the asphalt trail on both sides. Vegetation hesitated to grow too soon. Few flowers pocketed the path. The only deciduous growth were light brushings of yellow and pale green on the tree tips above them. Mostly, everything looked dead right before Spring's eruption.

A young man on a motorized skateboard zoomed by them, not giving the two women a single glance. AJ's heart sank further the farther they walked.

The river continued to rage and all she could do was keep walking. She wanted to jump down the steep embankment and wade into the water, but she knew the current would take her away. She knew survival would be slim.

To the right, residential houses towered several stories up the steep hillside. She doubted anyone would see them or call the police. The pair just looked like a mother and daughter walking in the park.

Up ahead, she caught a glimpse of a bridge just as her step wavered. The asphalt path ended where a dirt and gravel one began. AJ looked at the dried footprint impressions sprinkled in all directions.

The water raged even more. Instead of wanting to go down the embankment, the mother of two only thought to stay away.

"Just a short distance and we're almost there, my flower."

Skeletal remains of dead brush stood at attention and welcomed them as they approached a fork in the road. The main trail curved to the right and a smaller path led to the left, to the bridge.

A man appeared from around the bend and slowly walked past them. His smiled faded as he looked at AJ and her clothes. AJ looked down. She forgot about all the blood on her arms and pants.

"Miss, are you okay?"

"She's fine," Amanda said.

"I wasn't talking to you." He took a step closer, then froze in fear.

The older woman pointed the gun at him. "I said she's fine, didn't I?" He nodded quickly. "Run along now, like a good little bird, before I change my mind."

The man bolted down the path and was out of sight within seconds.

She wrapped her arm around the detective and pulled her to the left onto the small trail. "Hmph. Looks like we may have company sooner than I wanted."

Seeds spiraled down from the trees above them. The cooler air hugged her skin. AJ's legs started to feel heavy from the quarter-mile trek. She wanted to sit down, but her counterpart had a good grip on her arm.

"Watch your step," Amanda said. "The rails stick out higher than you think."

AJ took careful steps between the iron rails and wooden planks. She could hear the thunderous sound of the rapids getting louder and louder. The planks opened up and exposed the vertical drop under her feet. Her knees shook, but Amanda held firm.

"Keep walking."

"How much further?"

"Just a few more yards, flower. Then you can rest."

AJ stumbled a couple of times but held onto the woman. The height of the bridge and the gun in her side did not scare her as much as the thought of falling into the angry rage below. The water held hatred she had never seen before.

"Right here. Sit."

AJ practically fell into a sitting position. She was glad to be off her feet. Her legs felt extra heavy. She looked out at the water and the curvature of the spills went in and out of focus. She tried to concentrate on them, but Amanda's voice called her back.

—¡—

CHAPTER 84

"THIS IS my Father's world,
And to my listening ears,
All nature sings, and round me rings,
The music of the spheres."

Helen sang that the morning she died. Did I mention that in my story? I can't remember. I wish I had more time to tell you all my stories, my precious flower, but I don't.

That man I let live? He's already called the police. I guess I only have a few minutes before they get here.

That's a bit unfortunate. I do enjoy my time with you. You've been a refreshing fragrance in the air, a sweet rose disguised as a delectable morning glory.

Unlike that weed of a coworker you had.

Do you know why I killed Jack? He wasn't worthy of being a detective. He'd never make a good one, but you knew that. I did you and Conrad a favor by getting rid of him. There's enough shit in this world, we don't need more. There are dozens more like him I took care of.

I'm sure that's why Jack came to get us. Conrad sent him because they finally found my hummingbirds and all the fragile bones of birdies whose wings I clipped over the years.

Oh, I'm not referring to the aviary, my dear.

If Jack had seen my little birdies—the same ones I painted and told you about—then his reaction to us would've been much different. I think Conrad saved that honor for himself.

What do you think?

In fact, I wonder what your boss thought when he saw my works of art, my magnificent hummingbird warriors? Guess I'll never know because I won't have the opportunity to ask him.

Do you understand how truly destructive weeds work? You can clip them from above, but the worst ones must be dug out all the way. And if you don't dig the root out, the nasty weed will never go away. You can bury it and rebury it over the years, but the thing just creates deeper and deeper roots. It keeps growing. It will eventually—and always—resurface.

And, if you keep doing the same thing you've always done, you'll keep getting the same results: a weed with roots so deep, you'll never rid yourself of that monstrosity.

Let's dig all the way down, now that you're in a passive state, and let's see how deep we can go. It's time to rid your garden of the weed you keep feeding.

So, tell me, Heavenly Blue, that singular secret you had as a child, the one you've never mentioned to anyone else before.

—¡—

CHAPTER 85

BETWEEN the shock of ceremonial corpses and the death of one of his own, all he could do was stare in silence for several minutes and attempt to process the rapid sequence of events as everything unraveled in front of them.

"Conrad?"

He turned to Doug in the driver's seat. "I..."

"You don't have to say anything."

"I can't believe...*this*."

"I don't think any of us can."

Sirens wailed by as a caravan of fire trucks and more first responders surged to the scene. Chatter buzzed everywhere on the radio. Smoke continued to mushroom towards the sky. He could smell the charring remains of burning buildings through the air vent of the cruiser.

Conrad looked at Jack's phone again and the message the detective tried to type:

OPSIDDE FAWN BRRR

"What's that you're looking at?" Doug asked.

Conrad showed him the message. "I don't know. Something Jack was trying to type as he lost blood. Any clue where this is?"

Doug shook his head. "Amanda said she told Jack where I can find them. This has gotta be what Kinston was trying to tell me."

The radio dispatcher called in. "Chief, you there?"

"Yeah, Marge," he buzzed back.

"We just got a frantic 9-1-1 call from downtown. A man said he was held at gunpoint by two women."

The men looked at each other.

"Where?"

"Winnie River Trail, Chief. Over by the Sulphite Bridge."

Conrad grabbed Doug's arm. "That's where she's taking my detective!" He shook the phone. "Jack was trying to say Upside Down Bridge!"

Without another word to the dispatcher, Doug threw the car in drive and peeled out of the Ag-Equip parking lot. Claremont Farms was in the rearview. Sirens and flashing lights sped past them in the opposite direction.

Within minutes they were on Central Street in front of the Trestle Bridge Park. Doug hopped the curb and stopped just in front of the bright orange gate. Both men jumped out of the car and looked at the gate.

"Locked!" Doug yelled over the rapids. "We'll have to go on foot."

"What? I can barely hear you!" Conrad strained to understand what his friend said.

Doug motioned for him. "GO! I'll call for backup!"

The Deputy Director began running up the inclined path, but his body started to resist the sudden spurt uphill. He stopped, out of breath. Shedding his coat and vest, he walked as quickly as his heart allowed.

The Winnipesaukee River raged next to him. The water heaved and bellowed across the boulders and shore. He could no longer hear the sirens behind him nor anything ahead of him.

The asphalt ended. He knew he was close to the bridge, making it out just beyond the thin tree canopy. The cooler air calmed his mind as he pulled his gun out and took the safety off.

How many times had he brought his wife and kids here during the summer and biked down this trail? How many times had Yasmin climbed down under the Sulphite Bridge to the water's edge and tried to take photographs of its charred underbelly? How did he miss the connection between Amanda's mother and the City of Franklin's tarnished gem?

He could almost make out the bodies on top of the bridge through the dead brush. He quickened his steps and cut across the fork in the road to the bridge's small trail.

Ahead of him, in between the railings and close to the center of the bridge span, he saw AJ laying on her side. She appeared unresponsive. A split-second vision of Aubreah in danger made him tighten up.

The older woman knelt beside her.

"AMANDA!" he yelled, but she never responded or turned to look at him. The water ranted and raged too loudly.

Conrad straightened his arm out, gripping the butt of the gun with his other hand. He tried to line the gun's sights with the older woman's center mass, but he couldn't get a clean shot.

Another few steps closer.

He kneeled.

"AMANDA!"

This time she heard him and glanced over at him. She turned her attention back to the younger woman and planted a kiss on her cheek.

Then she stood up and smiled.

—¡—

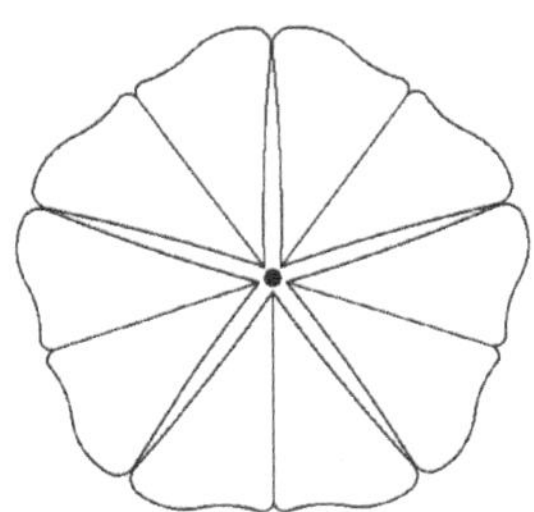

CHAPTER 86

ONCE SHE stopped focusing on the water and looked at Amanda, her mind relaxed. She felt unusually calm and centered. The cool river air and oxygen-rich forest intoxicated her.

"Amanda?"

"Yes, flower?"

"What was in the water I drank?"

"Something to make you a little more cooperative. And a bit sleepy. Now, tell me your deepest secret, my dear. Tell me what's behind the drive in your eyes. What is your root fear you don't wish the world to know?"

"My secret?" She shrugged. "I never understood what I did until years and years later. It scares me, now, thinking about it."

AJ looked at the rapids again. The water rose and fell, over and over, hypnotizing her. All thoughts went away, except those of a pigtailed little girl, feet planted on the ground, butt in a tree swing rocking back and forth. Back and forth.

"I think I was six or seven. It was before my first brother was born, I remember that much. My parents got me this small kitten.

It stayed outdoors. My father—my biological father—didn't allow animals in the house."

"This was years before the divorce, wasn't it?"

She nodded. "Yeah. Before the divorce."

"What kind of kitten did you have?"

"A Siamese. Blue eyes. Dark tips for ears and cream-colored fur." Her eyes went to her hands and the torn cuticles, but she no longer picked at the skin.

"What are you remembering?"

"Sitting on the swing, rocking. Back and forth, back and forth."

"What did you do?"

"Every day I'd get home off the school bus. I'd put my things in the house, then look for the kitten. I wanted to play with it. While I sat on the swing." AJ stopped and closed her eyes.

"What happened to the kitten?"

"Honestly, I don't know. One day I was playing with it—gawd, I can't even remember if it was a girl or boy, just IT. I don't remember when I started doing *that* either. I just did it over and over and over."

"What did you do?"

"Every day, after school, I'd pick up this Siamese kitten. I'd cuddle it in my arms and go sit on my swing. I remember the wooden board. It had chains bolted on each side. I'd sit and rock back and forth on this swing. I'd take—" She choked back the words and stared at Amanda. "I'd take a small handheld shovel and hold this kitten down. I'd hit it repeatedly over the head until it cried and wailed. I'd hit it until it cried. Then I'd put the shovel down and pet the kitten until it purred again. Until it knew it was safe with me again.

"Day after day, I'd beat this kitten on the head with the shovel. Then I'd pet it until it started purring again. And I did this until one day there wasn't a kitten anymore. It was just gone."

"Keep going, dear."

"I thought it was a normal thing to do. I thought that's what I was supposed to do to show the kitten I loved it. But then the kitten was gone. My parents said it ran away, but I think—" she choked back the words again "—I think I killed it! I killed the only living creature I loved back then!"

Amanda got down on her knees and hugged her.

AJ never resisted. She forgot about the gun. Forgot about the horror that just happened. She grabbed Amanda's shirt and held it, sniffling at the memory.

"It wasn't until years later, after my parents divorced, that I realized the violence I did against this innocent creature. I had done to that cat what my father did to me, and I thought it was the normal thing to do! How am I supposed to deal with that, knowing I might have taken an innocent life from this world?!"

"How were you supposed to understand that hideous evil when you were such an innocent yourself, my flower?"

Her arms weighed heavy against Amanda's chest as the older woman rocked her gently. She closed her eyes. The image of an eight-week-old bundle of fur rocked her mind.

"I can still hear that kitten's cries. It sounded so much like my kids when they were born. My children sounded exactly like that kitten! And every time I heard my babies cry, especially Jenna, I was afraid I'd take a shovel to their heads. I was petrified I'd kill them! And I've lived with this fucked up fear every day since my son was born. I've lived with this fear that I'd do the same thing to my babies as I did to that cat! I'm not a monster!"

"My little flower, you're capable of many things, but hurt your children? You'll never do that. You protect and nurture."

"Amanda?" AJ leaned her head back. She tried to focus on the woman's eyes, but the drug in her system worked fast to prevent her. "How do you know I won't abuse my kids? How can you be so certain I'm not like my father? How do you know I won't kill?"

"Because, Ameena Jardine, you're driven by an absolute fear of failure. You failed to save your husband, you failed at your engineering career, you failed to survive on your own. You're petrified of becoming a failed parent. But you know something? What you haven't seen, my precious Heavenly Blue, is that your fear of failure is why you will always succeed and win. It's why you won't ever harm your children and those you love. You will protect them, whatever the cost. Even if you have to kill."

"I'm tired, Amanda."

"I know. So am I."

"Are you going to kill me now? Now that you know my horrible secret?"

Amanda tucked some of AJ's hair behind her ear. "I've killed dozens upon dozens of men, but never women if I can afford it. Never the daughters I always wanted."

AJ's eyes drooped. "You...killed?"

"Yes, dear. I did the world a favor. Robert, Quill, Michael—dozens of them. Men such as them didn't deserve to continue living. So, I killed and sacrificed. I've cared and nurtured. I took and I gave. That's the way of the world."

"But...the men...you told me about? Wha..."

"Shhh. Rest your head."

Amanda gently lowered AJ's head down on the wooden plank. She felt the woman plant a motherly kiss on her cheek, then reach her hand in her pocket. She pulled out a tube and applied it to her lips. Deep red lipstick. The older woman smiled down and caressed the detective's forehead.

AJ closed her eyes.

—¡—

CHAPTER 87

OH, MY SWEET Heavenly Blue, you have no idea how happy you've made me this week. From the moment I saw you, I knew you were special to me. Much like I knew each of those men in my life were also special. There are things I've always known and never questioned.

You're so much the daughter I wish I'd known and been able to mother. All my other flowers are special to me, but you radiate above them all and I've enjoyed so much of my time with you.

Those stories I told you, they weren't trivial or without reason. Those men I spoke of, the birdies in my paintings, those are my hummingbird warriors who'll see me on the other side of this life. They're of excellence and purity bound for only Heaven and I painted them, bled them, sent them into a state of torpor.

Do you understand that? They're in a sleep state waiting for me to wake them, waiting for us to arise to the Thirteen Heavens, just as the Aztecs did over a thousand years ago.

I cared for all my birds. I let them probe my flower and drink my nectar. I fed, bathed, tended their needs and desires—took care of them in the best way I could, and they provided me with the substance that made my crops rich and my business prosperous. Every few weeks, they gave me a bit of their life so I could add it to my land and enrich the Earth in my fields. Year after year, I did this.

When the Earth whispered, "Give me the hearts of these righteous men so I may give you success and prosperity and life," I bled them dry. I dressed them in ceremonial garb and painted them as brilliantly as any warrior should be. I placed them in torpor and misted my gardens with their Essence. These men gave me their hearts and I gave them to the gods. I gave them everything and, in return, they gave me more.

They were my Warriors.

I was their Feeder.

I've been guarding my warriors while they sleep, while their spirits metamorphosize into hummingbirds and make my gardens grow.

That's what Conrad found. He found their sleeping chamber. He saw decades of secrets and uncovered the truth of my success. But I had to light my altars before he saw anything else.

I have so many secrets because my warriors are only a small part of this entire narrative.

I'm sure, after tonight, the truth will be unearthed one layer at a time, and I'll be the talk of the town for decades to come. Isn't that a wonderful thing? I'll never be forgotten. That's the legacy I leave. I've purified the world of some of the evil men do and captivated the goodness of a few chosen souls.

Don't forget, there are a few decent men left in this world. Conrad, my White-Whiskered Hermit. Tony, our wonderful mayor and my White-Necked Jacobin. They would've made excellent warriors.

Your son, too. I just know he's a lot like Conrad. If he's anything like his mother, he'll be the good we so desperately need to fix the fuckery left behind.

I know the memories of that kitten and what you did still haunt you, but you'll never be like your father. You'll never do that again because you know the difference between good and evil. Your son will never be like him either.

I hope you can still hear my words and remember that.

Yes, you're capable of vicious acts against innocent creatures, but that's not your nature. That's not who you've grown to be.

And sometimes violence does not beget more violence because two polar opposites can cancel themselves out.

Violence is sometimes necessary to end violence.

Ah, I just heard Conrad call my name. I wish I could ignore him, but I can't.

He looks at you like he does his daughter. He knows things about you, flower, and he's more protective of you than he lets on. Look to him as the father figure and mentor you need in this world. Maybe he's your own hummingbird warrior you want in your life.

No, I don't doubt you'll make an excellent detective, Ameena. You'll help make the world better.

Grow your seedlings strong.

Make the gardeners proud.

He's calling my name again.

It's time.

I hope you'll always remember my Ruby-Throated sacrifice I give you.

I'll always be your hummingbird warrior.

And, you? You'll always be my feeder, precious flower.

Please, do me this favor, if you can still hear me.

Tell my story, Morning Glory.

Make my birdies famous.

—¡—

CHAPTER 88

KNEELING on the first plank, Conrad took aim at the older woman.

"AMANDA!"

She glanced up at him, then he watched her caress AJ's head. She gave the younger woman a kiss on the forehead and stood up.

With two steps backward, she smiled, then shouted, "Please, do me this favor, if you can still hear me. Tell my story, Morning Glory. Make my birdies famous."

Conrad saw her tilt her head to the sky and flash her arm across her neck. A sparkle of light reflected off a shiny surface. Something fell and bounced on the planks. Amanda's throat and chest turned ruby red, contrasting the white and beige clothing she wore.

She fell backwards.

"AMANDA!"

Conrad ran across the planks as her body dropped into the river and disappeared. The only thing he saw in the rushing current below was a light pink trail wisping downstream.

"AJ!" He grabbed his detective's head and lifted it. "Ameena!"

She remained unresponsive.

—¡—

"Has she woken up yet?" Yasmin asked.

Conrad shook his head. "I don't know." He leaned back in the waiting room chair and held his wife's hand.

"Did you ever tell her?"

He shook his head again and squeezed her hand. He had tried, on more than one occasion. "Not yet."

"Do you still want to?"

"I don't know." He blinked the emotion from his eyes. "What if I lost her? What if she doesn't want to come back on Monday?"

"Well, baby, then you were wrong about her and you'll be down two detectives." She leaned in and whispered, "But you're not wrong. Be there for her, no matter what it takes. Even if it means losing your job again."

They saw an older woman walk into the waiting room. Conrad stood up when he recognized AJ's mother. "Mrs. Andrewson?"

"Yes?" Jamilla came over.

"I'm Deputy Director Conrad McMillan, Ameena's boss."

Without warning, the woman wrapped her arms around his neck and hugged him. "I'm indebted to you, sir! *Inshallah*, God willing, my family will make this up to you!"

"How's she doing?"

"Good. They ran a bunch of tests. She was only given a sleep drug. No other injuries or anything, but she doesn't want to talk to me. She's too embarrassed. Too upset at whatever happened." Her eyes pinkened.

"May I see her?"

"Yes. Maybe she will be more willing to talk to you."

He introduced his wife, then left Jamilla and Yasmin in the waiting room. Down the hallway, his steps echoed against the walls until he reached his detective's hospital room. A nurse walked out.

He peeked through the door and saw AJ wipe her eyes. With a gentle knock, he walked in.

The young woman sat up and tried to wipe her face again. "Sir, I wasn't expecting you."

"How are you feeling, Jardine?"

She smacked her hands on her thighs. "I feel like shit, sir. More than a total failure right now." She shook her head. "I'm so sorry, sir. I'm a bit emotional and a little fucked up in the head right now." She whirled a finger next to her ear.

"I think we're all a little fucked up in the head at the moment."

"I keep replaying the events over and over. I couldn't save Jack. I couldn't save him! I should've rammed the car into traffic or something—anything to stop her! Maybe she'd still be alive, too!" She shoved the palms of her hands across her eyes and wiped more emotion way.

Conrad sat on the bed next to her and touched the top of her hand. "You did the right thing, the *only* thing that kept you safe and alive. Kinston's death is not your fault. Neither is Amanda's."

"She locked me in that building with her. She made me tell secrets about myself I've *never* told anyone else. I sat there and listened to her stupid stories and—"

"Jardine, don't beat yourself up."

"But I can't remember ANYTHING after I was drugged! How can I even do this job anymore?!"

He squeezed her hand. "Detective, you did what I asked of you. You followed orders. And those are not stupid stories. Those are murder and missing persons' cases we now need to investigate. You did your job and now other families will be able to have some closure."

She sniffled. "I didn't think of it like that."

"We have dozens of cold cases we can now go through and I'll need your help for that."

"You still want my help? Look at me, Conrad! I'm a fucking wreck." She covered her mouth. "Sir, I shouldn't have used your first name."

"But saying 'fucking wreck' is fine?"

"I—" She noted a glimmer in his eyes. "Are you joking with me, sir?"

He cleared his throat and stood up. "You're the detective. You tell me."

"I think so, sir."

He gave her a gentle smile. "Get your rest. We'll talk more Monday morning." He turned his back to her and walked to the door.

"Sir? You want me back?"

The sound in her voice made him stop.

How much you sound like Aubreah right now…

He turned his head. "Ameena, I want you to take the weekend to think about what you want. I won't force you to come back, but I'd be lying if I said I wouldn't be disappointed if you didn't show up to work on Monday."

"Yes, sir."

"Now, get your rest."

"Yes, sir."

He closed the door behind him. And made sure no one saw the stray tear he wiped away.

—¡—

Monday, May 14, 2018

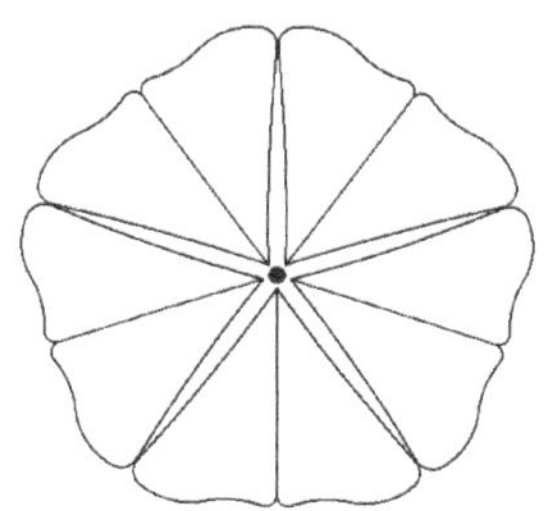

CHAPTER 89

"SIR?" AJ knocked on the door frame. "You had a message to come see you."

"Come in and shut the door, Jardine."

"Yes, sir."

She sat down across from him, as she had done the week prior. Her eyes immediately went to the scratch on the desktop. Her stomach sank at the Desk Scar.

"Stop looking at that."

"Yes, sir."

"Do you know why I called you in?"

"Not really, sir. You want to know my decision?"

"I don't have a resignation letter, so I think I know."

"Actually, my mom made me come in."

"And not your sense of duty?"

She watched his mannerisms.

Stoic as Day One.

"I'm more afraid of my mom than you." She cleared her throat and changed the subject. "The doctor released me Saturday morning. I stayed in bed until late Sunday night. Mom came in and said I needed to get ready for work the following day. I told her I didn't know if I wanted to go back. She said—and I quote—'The resting dog does not chase the chipmunk.'" AJ mimicked her mom's Middle Eastern accent.

"And what did she mean by that?"

"Something like 'Get your ass to work and stop feeling sorry for yourself.'"

"Do you feel sorry for yourself?"

AJ glanced down at the Desk Scar. "I feel sorry for the people I let down, especially Jack."

"He was an unfortunate casualty. That's the nature of this business. Do you think that's why I called you in here, detective?"

"Yes, sir."

"That's not why. And no, you haven't. If you quit, then you only let yourself down. I can hire any number of people to take your place."

She grabbed her fingers. "Oh."

"Dust your britches off, throw your tail in a sling, and keep marching onward, Jardine. This might've been the first case you've lost, but it won't be your last."

She nodded.

"There's another reason I called you in. Saturday morning, I received a call from Washington. We had to turn jurisdiction over to federal."

"What? The F.B.I. is taking over our case? Why?!"

"Based on the information you provided over the weekend, this crossed multiple state lines. It doesn't belong to the state anymore."

"Are they taking everything over, sir? What about the missing cases here in New Hampshire?"

"We're allowed to handle our own missing persons, but we aren't allowed anywhere near the Claremont property. Not yet, anyway. And, whatever we do uncover, we have to copy D.C. on. That includes any missing persons cases we solve that could be related to this nightmare."

"Yes, sir."

"Also, you're not allowed to bring up or discuss this case with anyone. Not family, not coworkers, and not the media."

"Wait. Why? Do they want us to pretend this never happened and it gets swept under the rug?"

"Sometimes that happens, Jardine."

She crossed her arms. "That's not fair! We worked on this all week! We're the only ones who really know what happened. I'm the only one who knows all of Amanda's stories, even if I can't remember what happened on that bridge."

"And you can expect to be called sometime in the future to be debriefed, detective. We're not done with this case. We just aren't running the show anymore."

"Can I at least talk to *you* about it? Because I still have questions."

"You can always talk to me, AJ. Don't ever forget that."

"The news didn't say much about what happened. Are they covering that up, too? Did they find her body at least?"

"Feds put a gag order on the whole thing. They need to wrap their heads around the carnage left behind. Sonnito discovered multiple bone fragments in all the gardens around the house, then more around the halfway house. Seems every little landscape island was also a burial site of some sort and we're looking at dozens of victims.

"Not only that, she lied to us about her aviary. It's not registered in the federal database. We couldn't find any info on state or local permits."

"Wow."

"You didn't hear that from me, though."

"If she lied about that, what else did she lie about?"

"I don't know. What I can tell you is that the Franklin PD, Amanda's lawyer, us—we're all told to keep quiet. D.C. told the media a gas main exploded across the property, killing everyone in all the buildings. No one's the wiser."

She swallowed the lump back down in her throat. "And what about Amanda?"

"They found her body the next day about a mile or so downstream, over by the dam. You saw the news reports yourself. They claimed she was so distraught from losing everything that she jumped off the bridge and committed suicide."

"That's not what happened!"

"I know that. You know that."

"What about the house and the evidence? What about that secret bunker? The aviary? Her hummingbird paintings? The mysterious foxglove? The—"

"At ease, detective. It's not our jurisdiction anymore. Officially, not our problem. Unofficially, they're trying to recover as much evidence as they can. Not everything was lost in the fires, luckily. Right now, none of us know exactly how many bodies or parts of bodies will be found on the Claremont property. We don't know how many she killed. Other than a lot."

"But, sir, aren't you curious to know what happens next?"

Conrad set his elbows on his desk and interlaced his fingers. He stared at AJ for a few seconds. "Jardine?"

"Yes, sir?"

"Does your passion for asking so many questions means you're staying on the job?"

"Maybe." He raised an eyebrow at her. "Yes, sir. Regardless of what happened, I still want to try this."

"Good. If other detectives had even a pinky toe of what you bring to the table, we'd never see another cold case again."

"Sir, you want me working cold cases?"

"Between your primary job description and training, yes. I think you'll have a knack for it."

"But what about last week? Don't we need to process any of the pictures taken? What about the evidence we collected? What about—"

"Jardine?" Conrad sighed.

"Yes, sir?"

"Go finish orientation."

"Yes, sir." She stood up and walked to the door.

Conrad put his reading glasses back on and turned his attention to his computer monitor. "You'll make a great detective, Ameena, even if you annoy the piss out of me sometimes."

"Thank you, sir?" It was more of a confused question than a reply as she opened the door.

"And AJ?"

"Yes, sir?"

"Stop calling me 'sir'."

She nodded as she made eye contact one more time. There was an odd twinkle in his eyes.

"Get out of my office."

She saw him crack a narrow smile in approval as she shut his office door.

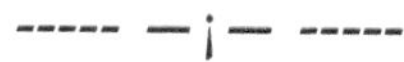

THE HUMMINGBIRD FEEDER

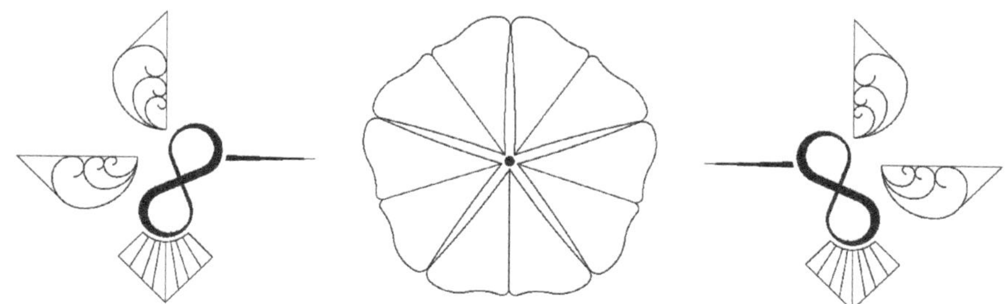

APPENDICES

A—Helpful Information
B—List of Characters
C—The Hummingbird Warriors
D—Arabic Phrases & Pronunciations
E—Maps
F—Sulphite Bridge
G—The Hummingbird Narratives
H—The Fibonacci Series

A – HELPFUL INFORMATION

MISSING PERSONS.

To report and identify missing persons, please go to the Department of Justice website here:

https://www.justice.gov/actioncenter/report-and-identify-missing-persons

For missing children, it is important to ACT IMMEDIATELY and contact your local law enforcement first, then call the National Center for Missing & Exploited Children:

1 (800) 843-5678

For missing adults, visit the National Missing and Unidentified Persons System (NamUs):

https://www.namus.gov/

DOMESTIC VIOLENCE.

If you are in a situation and afraid to use your computer due to domestic violence and your internet usage being monitored, call the National Domestic Violence Hotline:

1 (800) 799-7233

Or reach out to their website here:

https://www.thehotline.org/

POSTPARTUM DEPRESSION.

There is always help available if you are suffering from postpartum depression. Please reach out to your friends, family, or a professional. You are not alone. Call the Substance Abuse and Mental Health Services Administration (SAMHSA) hotline:

1 (800) 662-HELP (4357)

Or reach out to their website here:

https://www.samhsa.gov/find-help/national-helpline

B – LIST OF CHARACTERS

(In alphabetic order by first name)

Abbott. Labrador retriever mix. The Andrewson's goofy and clumsy dog. Companion to Costello.

Abby. Amanda's employee.

Abran. One of Amanda's hummingbirds.

Amanda Marie Claremont. Businesswoman and owner of Claremont Farms and Nursery.

Ameena "AJ" Jardine. [Uh-meen-uh Jar-deen] AKA Ameena Hawthorne. Detective for the I.S.B., former civil engineer. (Ameena means 'trustworthy'. Jardine means 'garden' or 'orchard'.) Daughter of Paden Jardine and Jamilla Andrewson. Widow of Michael Hawthorne, mother of Eoghan and Jenna Hawthorne.

Angela Briggs. Employee of Amanda's. 17. Senior in high school when she disappeared. Last seen July 16, 2010.

Arif Jardine. AJ's brother.

Aubreah McMillan. Conrad's daughter. Senior in high school.

Audrey. Amanda's great-grandmother.

Becky. Human Resources supervisor.

Beulah. Amanda's maternal relative.

Cassandra "Cassie" Owen. Assistant Deputy Medical Examiner and coroner.

Chris Galvan. Police Chief Galvan's son.

Clara Galvan. Police Chief Galvan's daughter.

Conrad McMillan. I.S.B. Deputy Director and AJ's boss.

Costello. Labrador retriever mix. The Andrewson's goofy and clumsy dog.

Daniel Leopald Norrington. Owner of Norrington Meat Farms, Amanda's next-door neighbor.

David. One of the men workers on Amanda's farm.

Debra Norrington. Amanda's next-door neighbor.

Duncan McMillan. Conrad's son. In middle school.

Ellie. I.S.B. receptionist.

Emily Vanderbilt. Amanda's employee.

Eoghan Hawthorne. [Ee-un] Son of Michael Hawthorne and Ameena Jardine. Older brother to Jenna.
Ernest. Amanda's great-grandfather.
Ernest Edward Andrewson. AJ's stepfather.
Ethan. One of Amanda's hummingbirds.
Faruq. AJ's brother.
Gabrio. One of Amanda's hummingbirds.
Geneve Cumberson. Conrad's neighbor.
Greg Montgomery. Another detective at I.S.B.
Helen. Amanda's mother, daughter of Victoria.
Isaac. One of Amanda's hummingbirds.
Jack Kinston. New detective-in-training hired at the same time as AJ.
Jackson. One of Amanda's hummingbirds.
Jamilla Hassan al-Rashad Andrewson. [Jah-mee-lah] AJ's mother. Current wife to Ernest Andrewson. Ex-wife of Paden Jardine.
Jean. William's second wife, step-mother to Audrey.
Jenna Beth Hawthorne. AJ's daughter.
Joe. One of Amanda's employees.
Jordan Cumberson. Conrad's neighbor.
Joseph. Civil engineer from AJ's old firm.
Kaylee Jenkins. Amanda's employee.
Lyle. AJ's old boss from the civil engineering firm she worked at.
Manny (Mandrake). One of Amanda's hummingbirds.
Maria Ellanogek. Amanda's employee and roommate.
Marge. Radio dispatcher.
Mark. One of Amanda's hummingbirds.
Mark Graves. One of the field workers, Amanda's employee. Only worked there 6 weeks.
Mateo. One of Amanda's hummingbirds.
Maurice Juniper. One of Amanda's attorneys.
Maverick Chapman. One of Amanda's hummingbirds.
Mekhi. One of Amanda's hummingbirds.
Michael Anthony Hawthorne. AJ's husband. Former F.B.I. undercover agent. Father of Eoghan and Jenna Hawthorne.
Michael Smith. One of Amanda's workers.

Nabih. AJ's brother.
Officer Matthews. The other officer who interviewed Amanda when her husband went missing.
Old Man Bates. Owned property adjacent to Amanda. She bought it from him.
Oro Garcia. One of Amanda's hummingbirds.
Paden Jacob Jardine. AJ's biological father.
Pat (Patricia) Sonnito. Senior forensic technician, set to retire in a couple of years.
Patrick. One of Amanda's hummingbirds.
Patrolman A. Kennedy. Police officer who responded to May 11th incident and took the Norringtons' statement.
Peter Yates. Forensic lab technician.
Police Chief Doug Galvan. City of Franklin Police Chief. Friend of Conrad.
Quillard "Quill" Shaw. One of Amanda's workers.
Richie Morgan. One of Amanda's workers.
Robert Daniel Claremont. Amanda's husband who died in the 1980s.
Sadie. Norrington's Border Collie.
Sargent David Brady. Franklin PD officer who interviewed Amanda in 1985.
Tiffany Devry. I.S.B. employee.
Tony Giunta. As himself, mayor of the City of Franklin, and a White-Necked Jacobin. (almost one of Amanda's hummingbirds).
Umar. One of Amanda's hummingbirds.
Vanessa. One of Amanda's employees.
Victoria. Amanda's grandmother, born in 1900.
William. Amanda's great-great-grandfather, father to Audrey.
Yasmin McMillan. Conrad's wife.

C – THE HUMMINGBIRD WARRIORS

1. **MEKHI**: means "he who is like God".
Hummingbird: Xantus
Paint colors: Seafoam across the neck, colorful beak and white band behind the eyes
Flowers: Honeysuckle branches

2. **ORO**: Spanish for "gold"
Hummingbird: Plain-Capped Starthroat
Paint colors: Gray paint on both sides, narrow flash of color
Flowers: Bleeding hearts

3. **ETHAN**: means "strong and long-lived"
Hummingbird: Anna's
Paint colors: Fuchsia and copper on the neck and face
Flowers: Red bee balm

4. **ISAAC**: means "he laughs"
Hummingbird: Black-Chinned
Paint colors: Black head and a slice of indigo across the neck
Flowers: Bright petunias

5. **MAVERICK**: means "independent"
Hummingbird: Allen's, in mid-flight looking up, wings pulled back, tail feathers spread forward
Paint colors: Burnt orange, vibrant neck
Flowers: Yellow, pink, and orange Zinnias with Autumn leaves in the background

6. **MARK**: means "god of War"
Hummingbird: Berylline
Paint colors: Fluorescent algae green neck
Flowers: Louisiana yellow irises with a fifolet in a darkening background

7. **MANNY**: means "god is with us"
Hummingbird: Blue-Throated
Paint colors: Periwinkle paint dripping across the neck
Flowers: Trumpet vine

8. **GABRIO**: means "god is my strength"
Hummingbird: Magnificent
Paint colors: Aqua paint across the neck, flash of royal purple on the forehead, chest has a darker color
Flowers: Azalea

9. **ABRAN**: means "exalted father"
Hummingbird: Green Violet-Ear
Paint colors: Mix of aquas and greens across the neck and body with violet trails from nose, eyes, to ears.
Flowers: Salvia and lavender

10. **PATRICK**: means "nobleman"
Hummingbird: Lucifer, posed ready to fight, sitting against a stone background
Paint colors: Bright purple across the neck, neck and shoulders a vibrant fuscia-inspired purple
Flowers: Pale lavender foxglove

11. **MATEO**: means "gift of God"
Hummingbird: Calliope, stretching
Paint colors: Rich pink streaks on the neck with fingering spines to the shoulders
Flowers: Blue Dream columbine

12. **JACKSON**: means "God has been gracious"
Hummingbird: Costa's, sitting on a branch
Paint colors: Violet and silver with darker fingering spines of violet accenting the neck and shoulders
Flowers: Catmint

13. **UMAR**: means "tiger of god"
Hummingbird: Green-breasted Mango, mid-flight looking up at flowers
Paint colors: Dark green, purple and bright aqua straight down the torse, trailing from the mouth and nose, down to groin, with white on both sides
Flowers: Fuschia

D—ARABIC PHRASES & PRONUNCIATIONS

Habibti. [ha-beeb-tee] Dear, sweetheart, loved one—when spoken to a female

Inshallah. [een-sha-lah] If Allah (God) wills it, God willing

Lah. [la-ah] No

Shukran. [shoe-krahn] Thank you

Shway shway. Slow down, easy does it

E – MAPS

The following pages include Google images of central New Hampshire, the City of Franklin, and the location of the Sulphite Bridge.

For an extensive map and layout of the Claremont Farms and Nursery, along with her adjacent neighbors, please check the author's website.

Central New Hampshire

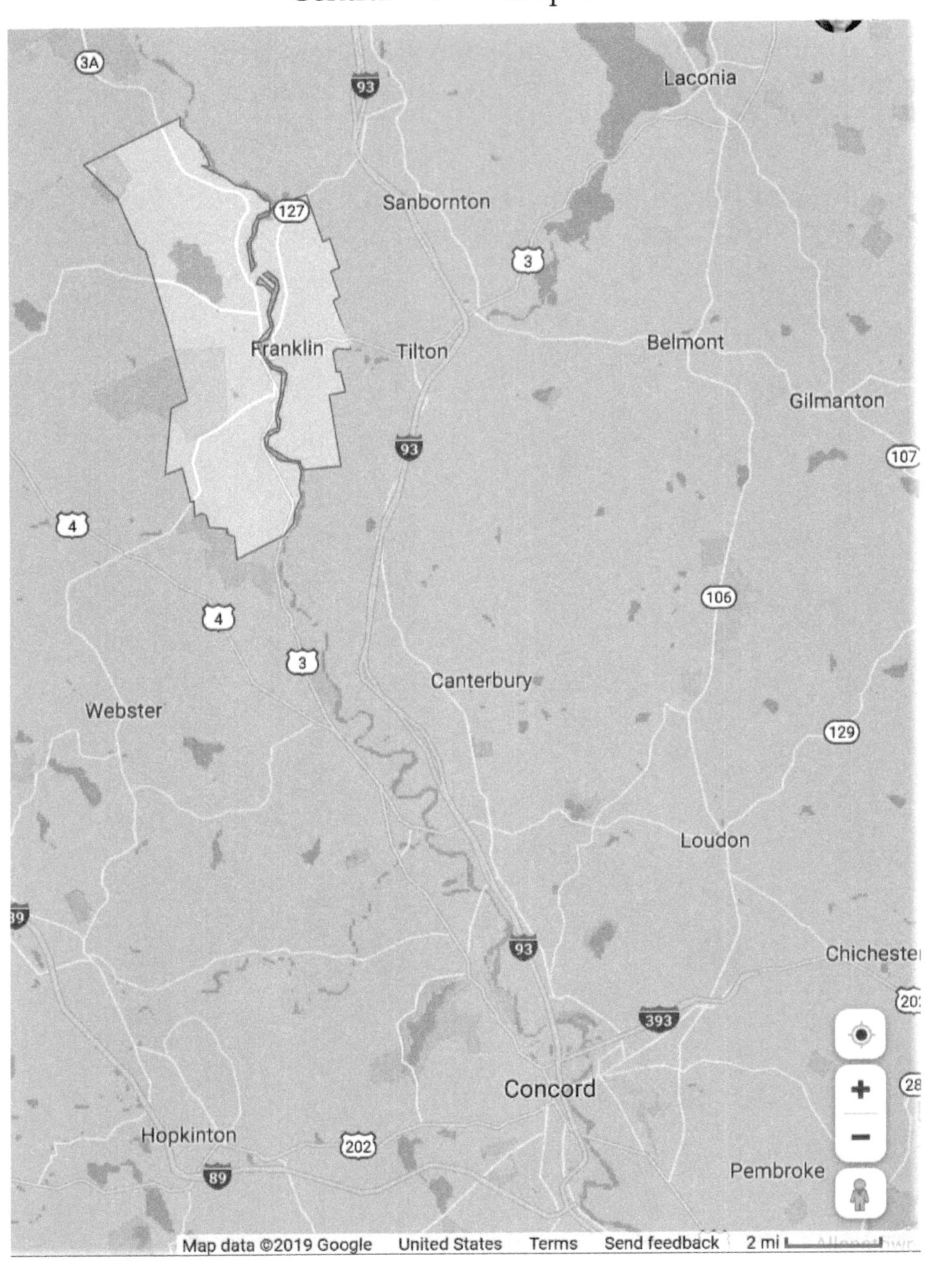

City of Franklin, New Hampshire

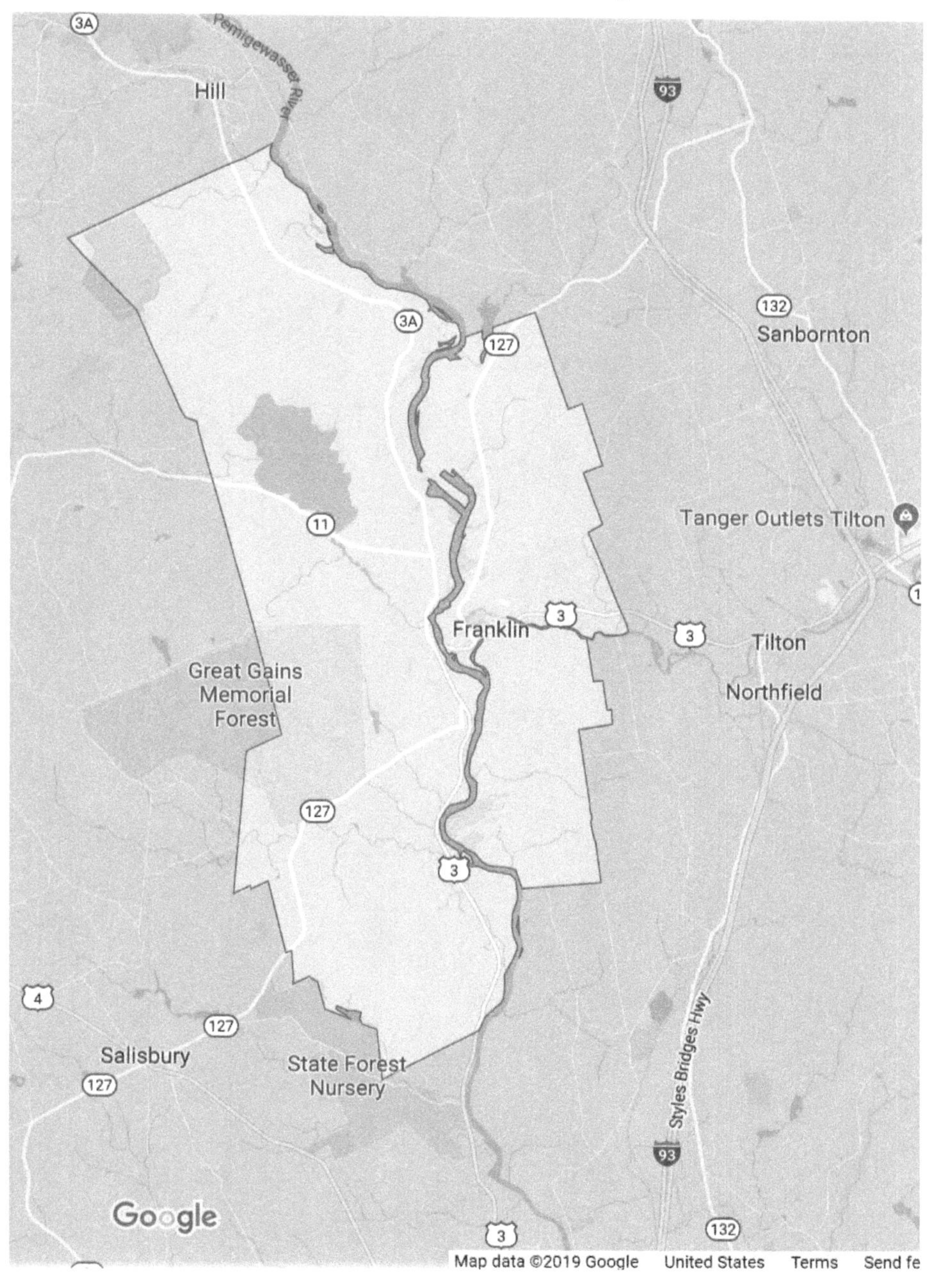

Downtown Franklin and the Sulphite Bridge

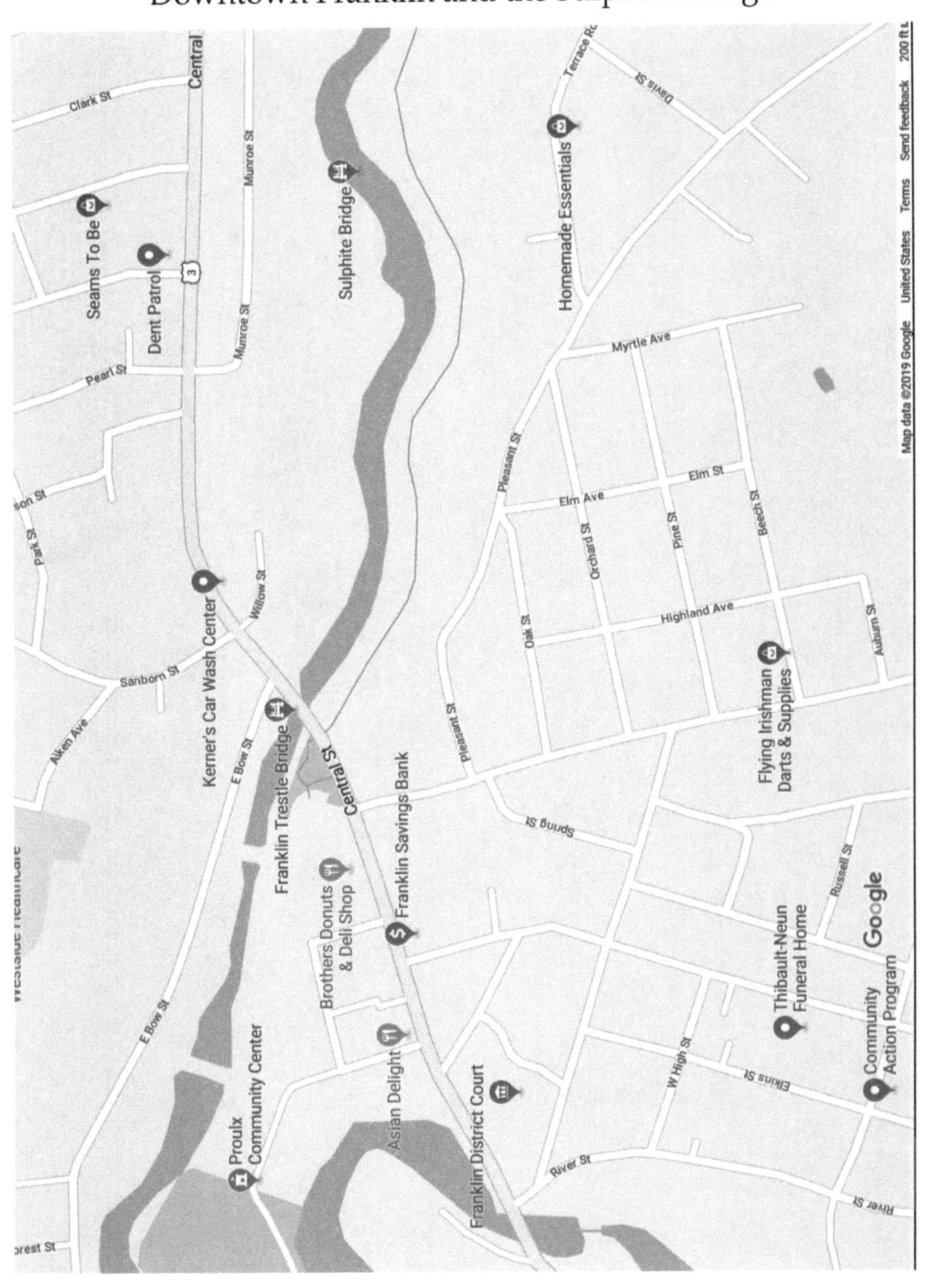

F – SULPHITE BRIDGE

In 1896, the Sulphite Bridge, also known as the Upside-Down Bridge, was built by Jonathan Parker Snow and Robert Fletcher for the Boston and Maine Railroad. This uniquely structured bridge replaced a truss bridge that had been built a few years prior by the Franklin and Tilton Railroad.

The bridge had been used for decades to transport supplies to the pulp and paper mills along the Winnipesaukee River, including sulfur, an essential ingredient in papermaking. Thus, the bridge was called the Sulphite Bridge.

The railroad served as a primary transportation until 1973 when it was later abandoned. On October 17, 1980, the bridge caught fire, burning the interior walkway underneath the railroad. Arson was suspected, but no one was ever arrested for the incident.

The Sulphite Bridge is the only "upside-down" railroad bridge remaining in the United States and is listed on the National Register of Historic Places.

It can be visited and seen along the Winnipesaukee River Trail in the City of Franklin, just east of Trestle View Park.

The following pictures of the Sulphite Bridge were taken by the author.

G—THE HUMMINGBIRD NARRATIVES

THE HUMMINGBIRD FEEDER is the first of (potentially) several books in a series revolving around Amanda Claremont. Collectively, these short stories and novels will be called THE HUMMINGBIRD NARRATIVES.

Future books being considered include the following:

THE HUMMINGBIRD WARRIORS
THE HUMMINGBIRD FLOWERS
THE HUMMINGBIRD AVIARY
—with potentially more after this

There are also award-winning short stories, corn maze designs, and extensive maps, puzzles, and clues which will be revealed in the future.

Amanda has so much to offer readers!

H – THE FIBONACCI SERIES

While THE HUMMINGBIRD NARRATIVES will have more of Amanda Claremont to offer readers in the future, Detective Ameena "AJ" Jardine and Deputy Director Conrad McMillan are part of a larger storyline called THE FIBONACCI SERIES, a 26-book series in the making. This series chronicles several unlikely heroes waging a vigilante war against a deadly drug cartel.

Books 1, 2, and 3 of the series are called THE JARDINE TRILOGY and have already been released. Combined, they tell AJ's story from her limited, third-person perspective. MODI IND0RUM (Book 1), ABBAC1 (Book 2), and ZEPH1RUM (Book 3) were Karma's debut novels and introduce a complex world of mystery, suspense, murder, romance, and revenge.

For Book 1, MODI IND0RUM, Part 1 of THE JARDINE TRILOGY, go here: https://www.amazon.com/MODI-IND0RUM-JARDINE-TRILOGY-FIBONACCI-ebook/dp/B07BKTX6R4/

For Book 2, ABBAC1, Part 2 of THE JARDINE TRILOGY, go here: https://www.amazon.com/ABBAC1-Part-JARDINE-TRILOGY-FIBONACCI-ebook/dp/B07BKNTJL3/

For Book 3, ZEPH1RUM, the conclusion of THE JARDINE TRILOGY, go here: https://www.amazon.com/ZEPH1RUM-Three-JARDINE-TRILOGY-FIBONACCI-ebook/dp/B07BKT4WDP/

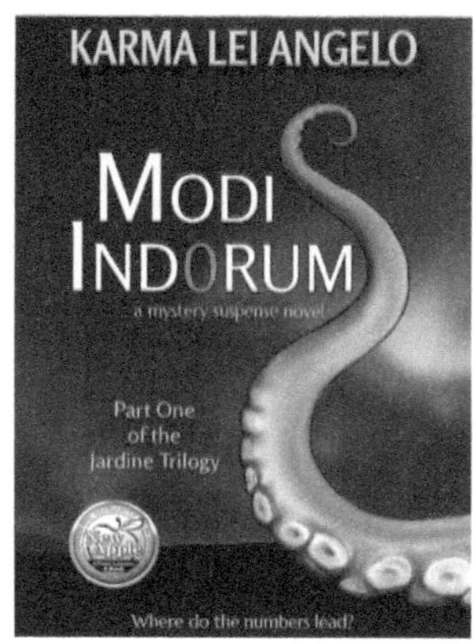

ABOUT THE AUTHOR

Karma Lei Angelo is a former civil engineer-turned-writer and entrepreneur living in central New Hampshire. She is owned by three cats and multiple dogs too adorable for words. She's also obsessed with hummingbirds, gardening, designing, and unusual things.

www.ingramcontent.com/pod-product-compliance
Lightning Source LLC
Chambersburg PA
CBHW020603310726
48979CB00008B/1325/J